D0056997

ONLY ASHES REMAIN

ONLY ASHES REMAIN

REBECCA SCHAEFFER

HOUGHTON MIFFLIN HARCOURT
Boston New York

hmhbooks.com

The text was set in ITC Legacy Serif Std.

Library of Congress Cataloging-in-Publication Data
Names: Schaeffer, Rebecca, author.
Title: Only ashes remain / Rebecca Schaeffer.
Description: Boston ; New York : Houghton Mifflin Harcourt, [2019] |
Summary: With her self-healing ability widely known, Nita's only chance
for survival is to become too feared to be targeted again,
starting with killing her betrayer, Fabricio.
Identifiers: LCCN 2018057416 (print) | LCCN 2018060028 (ebook) |
ISBN 9781328863607 (ebook) | ISBN 9781328863553 (hardcover)
Subjects: | CYAC: Revenge—Fiction. | Supernatural—Fiction. |
Monsters—Fiction. | Dissection—Fiction. | Black market—Fiction. |
Horror stories.
Classification: LCC PZ7.1.S33557 (ebook) | LCC PZ7.1.S33557
Onl 2019 (print) | DDC [Fic]—dc23
LC record available at https://lccn.loc.gov/2018057416

Printed in the United States of America
DOC 10 9 8 7 6 5 4 3 2 1
4500766247

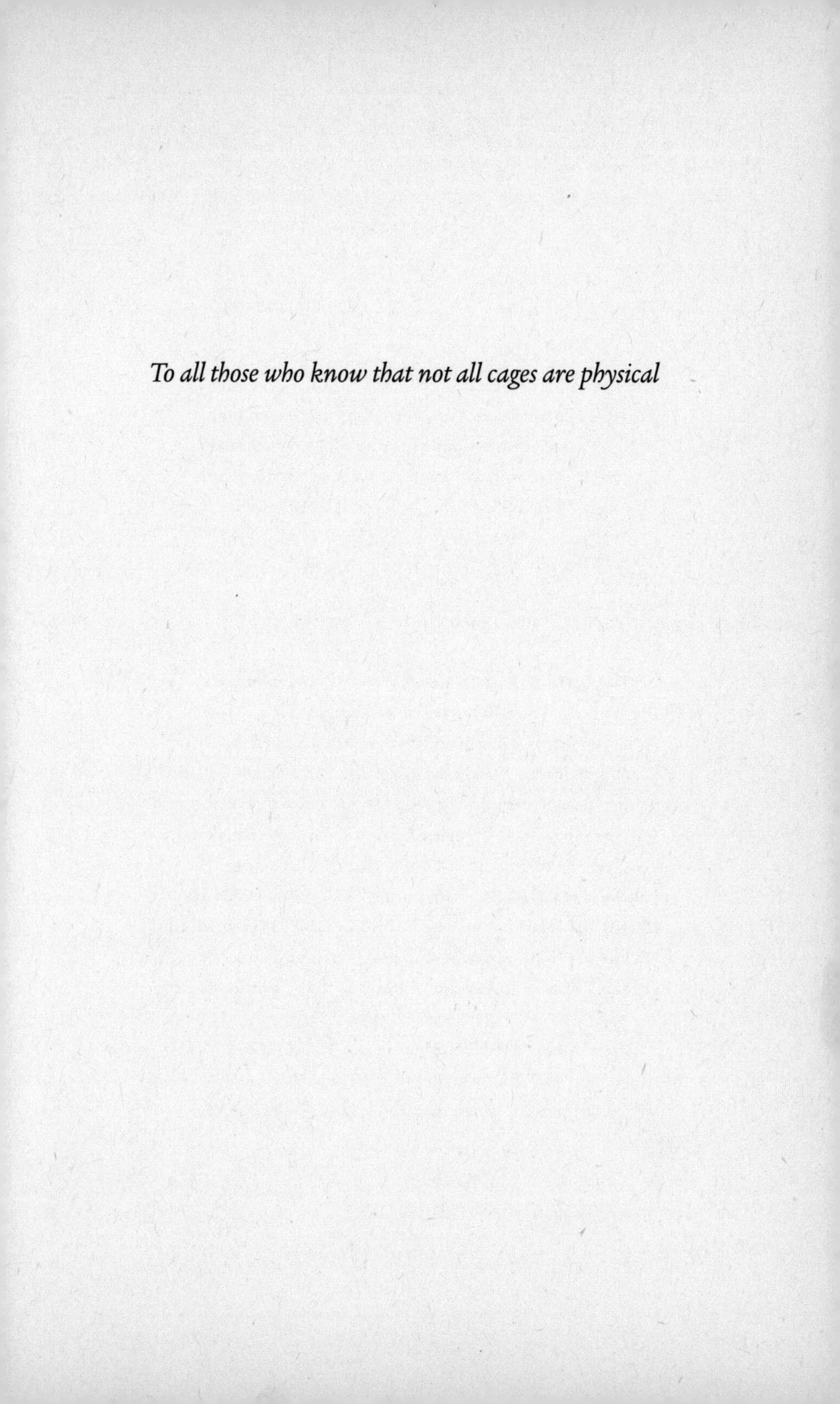

To all those who know that not all cages are physical

ONE

Nita, meet Fabricio."

The fluorescent lights of the INHUP refugee center made the white walls glow like a hospital, and Nita wondered for a brief moment if she was in some sort of hallucination. After all, the set of circumstances that had brought her to the International Non-Human Police had the quality of a nightmare—complete with kidnapping, torture, and Nita burning all her enemies alive at the end.

All but one.

He stood in front of her now. A few inches taller than her, his pale face was framed by slightly mussed dark brown hair, and his huge blue-gray eyes stared at her with shock she knew was mirrored in her own gaze.

Fabricio. The boy she'd saved.

The boy who'd betrayed her. Who'd thanked her for helping him escape, taken the money and bus ticket she'd offered him, then turned around and used the phone she'd given him to sell her to the black market. Who'd left her to be kidnapped, cut up, and sold piece by piece.

Rage boiled in Nita's veins, heating her body from the inside out. Her jaw clenched tighter and tighter, until she forced it to loosen to avoid breaking a tooth.

"Nita?" Agent Quispe, the INHUP agent in charge of Nita's case, stepped forward, the lines of her buzzcut black hair sharp in the bright light. Her Spanish was slow and calm, with a distinct flavor that reminded Nita of her time living in Peru. "Are you all right?"

Nita blinked and forced herself to nod. "Of course. Sorry, I must have spaced out. What were you saying?"

Quispe frowned slightly and squinted, an expression Nita had come to associate with the agent trying to parse Nita's Spanish. Her father was Chilean, but she'd lived in Madrid until she was six, and the blend of accents was often hard for people to understand.

"I was saying that I've noticed you keeping to yourself a lot. And since we just received another refugee your age, I thought you two might want to meet."

Quispe waved Fabricio forward. His eyebrows pulled together before smoothing out. A tentative smile crossed his face.

Nita glared. What the hell was he smiling about?

Then she realized: he didn't know she'd discovered he was the one who sold her to the black market. Fabricio was still playing a part, resuming the role of the scared victim.

Nita stepped forward, fist clenched, wanting nothing more than to smash his skull into the floor and dissect him while he lay dying, the way she should have done when her mother caught him the first time.

She took a deep breath. She was in the middle of the INHUP headquarters in Bogotá. There was an agent standing right beside her. This was not the time to commit murder.

No matter how much she wanted to.

Nita swallowed and forced a grimace onto her face. She needed to play it cool for now, and not give any indication they'd met before. And hope Fabricio didn't give her away.

If INHUP found out how they knew each other, Nita's connection to her murderous mother would be exposed, and Nita's crimes would be laid bare. And she had a lot of crimes under her belt. You didn't grow up with parents in the business of dissecting unnaturals and selling their body parts online without committing a few felonies.

Nita couldn't force herself to extend her hand to him. In a clipped voice, she said, "It's nice to meet you."

He blinked and hesitated, then smiled softly, his voice gentle and whispery. "You too."

Quispe looked between them, as if she could sense the tension. "Fabricio will be staying here for the next little while. I thought you two would have a lot to talk about, since you've both spent time in the black market."

Nita could almost hear her unspoken comparison. Both of them had body parts hacked off. Both of them had those parts sold and eaten.

Nita shifted her foot, trying not to think about the gaping absence where her toe had once been, and she kept her eyes firmly away from Fabricio's missing ear. It wasn't too hard, since the evidence was covered by hair.

Nita turned to Quispe. "Yes. It was a good thought. Thank you. I'd like to get to know my new floormate."

Nita swallowed after the words came out of her mouth. Stilted. Fake. Why couldn't she be better at this kind of thing?

But if Quispe noticed Nita's failing communication skills, she didn't comment. "Of course."

She turned and left them alone. After she was gone, the silence was overpowering. Fabricio opened and closed his mouth like he wanted to say something. Nita pursed her lips and looked around.

She didn't like being inside an INHUP building. INHUP was a means to an end for her, and she didn't trust them. Supposedly they both prosecuted and protected unnaturals—or "non-humans." Honestly, Nita thought calling people like her "non-human" was just as offensive as calling her "unnatural." It probably traced back to INHUP's monster-hunting roots, before they started advocating for unnatural rights as well as policing them.

Nita was using INHUP for their protection, but she knew corruption had burrowed into the soul of the organization. She was concerned about building surveillance, and the conversation she wanted to have was not one that should be overheard. By INHUP or whoever INHUP might be selling the information to.

"There's a garden outside," Nita announced. "Let's talk down there."

Fabricio nodded once, slowly, and followed her.

They made their way through the office. Pristine white walls and white tiled floors caged them in, like a futuristic prison. Other unnatural refugees wandered the halls of the protective housing. Some Nita could've passed on the street and never known they were different.

Others were part octopus. Nita's eyes examined a tired-looking man in a hall, her eyes sliding down to the eight purple tentacles he had instead of legs. *Ningyo.* Japanese mermaid. She would have bet money on it.

People said that if you ate their flesh, you'd gain immortality.

People said the same thing about eating Nita.

She tried to pull her mind away from the thought. The memory of Boulder cutting off her toe, popping it in his mouth, and swallowing it whole. His promise to come back the next day and the next, each day taking a different part of her and consuming it until there was nothing left of Nita but bones and teeth.

It didn't happen. You escaped. He's dead. It's over, a soft voice whispered in her head.

But it didn't feel over. Not when she was hiding in INHUP. Not with Fabricio walking next to her. Not with her face and her ability circling the black market forums. People were willing to pay a lot for a girl who could manipulate her own body – they thought eating her would grant them the same power. Who knew, maybe it would.

Nita didn't intend to find out.

Her hand twitched at her side, reaching for a scalpel that didn't exist. What she wouldn't give to be in her dissection room right now, all her problems vanishing in the simple, clear peace of a dissection. Taking a body apart piece by piece, the world reduced to the organs in her hand and in the jar on her desk.

But the image was spoiled by the memory of Fabricio, trapped and screaming in a cage, disturbing the perfect solitude of the room.

As they turned a corner, Nita tilted her head to get a look at the side of Fabricio's face, but his hair hid the bandages well. She could hardly believe it had been less than two weeks since she'd first seen him in that cage.

He caught her staring and flinched. Then he looked away, his hand hovering protectively over where his ear had been. He swallowed and lowered his hand.

"It's better," he replied, answering her unspoken question as they walked. His accent softened the edges of his words, *y* sounds whispering into *sh* sounds. "I'm getting the stitches out tomorrow."

Nita didn't respond.

She wished her mother had killed him. She wished she'd dissected him. None of this would have happened then. Nita wouldn't be missing a toe—even though she'd used her ability to meld the skin over where it once was, there was an absence, as though her nerves hadn't quite realized they ended in a new place now and still reached out, expecting a toe to be there.

She also wouldn't have spent the past week watching people die in the black market. Wouldn't have had to murder them herself.

She could still remember the moment she read the text exchange on her captor's phone and realized that the person who'd sold her to the black market was Fabricio all along. The moment of sheer disbelief, followed by the sudden rush of rage, hot and vicious.

Now her anger simmered, a steady glow in the pit of her stomach. If she let it loose, she'd only end up with more problems. She wasn't sure she cared. She wanted to let it all out, no matter what the repercussions.

Be rational, Nita. You can't murder him with all these surveillance cameras around.

Nita hated when her brain made sense.

On the first floor, near the back of the building, thick metal double doors opened into a small garden. A high brick wall surrounded it, covered in vines and ivy, and several people sat on benches and under trees. The sun was steady and hot, and sweat quickly dripped down Nita's back.

Nita led Fabricio to a secluded part of the garden, near a floripondio tree. The bell-shaped flowers hung from the branches like unlit pink lanterns, beautiful and gentle. Also, one of the most poisonous plants in the world. Nita plucked one of the flowers and twirled it in her hand. So deadly. Hidden in such a pretty shell that no one ever guessed until it was too late.

Finally, Nita turned to face Fabricio. He shifted awkwardly under her gaze. He wore blue jeans and a plain gray T-shirt, a twin to Nita's own INHUP-issued clothes.

"I'm glad you decided to run away," he finally said.

Nita opened her mouth to tell him he very well knew that she didn't run away. But she stopped. She could accuse him all she wanted, but he'd just deny it. Even if he admitted it, what point was there in tipping him off that she knew what he'd done? She couldn't kill him in front of all these people, and if he knew she knew, he'd be on his guard.

And he should be. Because there was no way Nita was going to let him get away with what he'd done to her.

So instead, she said quietly, pretending she believed his ignorance, "I didn't run away. I was sold on the market."

He winced, and his face twisted in sympathy. "I'm so sorry. I know how awful that can be."

He ran a hand through his hair, exposing the hint of stitches creeping down one side of his head. Nita turned away and tried not to remember his screams as her mother tortured him while Nita stood by and watched. And did nothing.

Maybe that was why he sold her. Because she did nothing until the last possible moment.

"Was it your mother?" he asked, voice soft. "Was it punishment for helping me?"

He seemed so genuine in his concern, and Nita felt a sliver of doubt creep in. Could those messages have been sent by someone else? But then she remembered how easily he'd played her before, stared at her with huge eyes, manipulated her into thinking he was completely innocent so she'd free him. Her eyes narrowed. She wasn't going to be played again.

"No."

His hands hovered, then lowered. "I'm sorry. I didn't mean to pry. If it's all too fresh."

He gave her a gentle smile, and Nita wanted to punch it off his face. Manipulative little sneak.

He hesitated, then asked, "Your captor . . . she didn't hurt you, did she?"

"Well, she was working with a zannie, so why don't you take a guess?"

His face went gray. "A zannie?"

Zannies ate people's pain, which made them expert torturers. Nita could see Fabricio's imagination filling in all the blanks of her time in the market with all the horrific things zannies did.

"Yes." Nita's voice was cold. "Sometimes, when I close my eyes, I can still hear the screaming."

Fabricio flinched as though she'd hit him. His eyes widened, and something passed across his face, something that looked like it might be guilt or regret. But it was gone in a blink.

Nita carefully didn't mention she'd ended up making an ally of the zannie in her escape. She wanted Fabricio to feel as shitty about what he'd done as possible.

Also, she wasn't sure what the fact that she'd befriended a monster like Kovit said about her. Nothing good, likely.

"God, I'm so, so sorry," Fabricio whispered, and the horror on his face seemed so genuine, if Nita didn't have evidence against him she'd really think he meant it. "I can't believe she hired a zannie."

Nita opened her mouth to make another caustic remark, but stopped. Fabricio had specifically said "she" when referring to Nita's captor. Multiple times.

Nita hadn't mentioned her captor was female.

Nita played back the conversation, checking to see if she'd

used any feminine descriptors, pronouns, any cue in her Spanish that could have indicated gender. Nothing.

More proof. As if she needed it. She already had the messages between him and her captor, Reyes, hammering out the details of the deal.

But perhaps some small part of her had wondered if someone had stolen the phone from him, or if maybe a corrupt INHUP agent had confiscated it or . . . something.

Nita crushed the flower in her hand. All doubts were extinguished.

"We'll have to be cautious where we talk," he said, eyeing a passing agent. His eyes roved around at the walled-off garden, lingering on all the security cameras and INHUP agents. "You might get in trouble if they knew who your mother was."

Ah. There it was. The veiled threat. The reminder that he knew exactly who she was, and if he wanted to, he could destroy her chances of getting a plane ticket home from INHUP.

Well, two could play at that game.

"Yes." Nita loosened her grip and twirled the crushed flower. "And we'll have to be careful about mentioning your father too."

He stiffened, whole body going rigid, eyes widening. Like a poorly oiled puppet, his head jerked to face her, and he whispered, "Pardon?"

"Your father." Nita tilted her head to one side as her fingers played along the petals. "Quite the bigwig, I hear. Knows all the monsters."

Fabricio swallowed and replied carefully, "Where did you hear about my father?"

"The market I was sold in, of course." Nita spoke in the mild tone of someone innocently commenting on the weather. "I hear he runs one of the biggest law firms in the world. They specialize in shell corporations, tax evasion, and all sorts of other things for rich people. Especially rich black market people."

His hands clenched. "And? You of all people should know better than to judge someone based on their parents."

Nita flinched as if he'd slapped her. She looked away.

"Tell me, Nita, if we're judging people by the sins of their parents, who is in more trouble?" Fabricio's voice was tight. "Me? My father helps monsters save their money. Or you? Your mother kidnaps, murders, dissects, and sells innocent people."

"I'm not my mother." But after the events in the market, she wasn't quite sure anymore. She'd killed a lot of people to escape, guilty and innocent alike. "I helped you."

"You did." His shoulders slumped. "And I'm not my father."

No, you're much worse.

Nita didn't reply, just looked at the flower. Fabricio was the same. Beautiful and gentle on the outside, hiding a toxic inside.

Fabricio's jaw was tight and his gaze angry. "Is this why you've been so cold to me? You think I'm just another money-grubbing asshole like my father?"

She shrugged, playing it nonchalant. "I don't know. I don't know you."

"I'm not. I'm nothing like him." His voice was bitter. "And I never want to be. I don't want anything to do with him or his business. All it's ever brought me is pain."

"And money. I hear someone of your standing lives quite well."

"I'd rather have my ear back."

Nita raised an eyebrow. "What does your ear have to do with your father?"

"You didn't really think your mother kidnapped the child of one of the most notorious men on the black market to sell his body on the internet, did you?"

Nita's stomach dropped. "What?"

His lips pressed together into a thin line. "Your mother was sending me back to my father, piece by piece, every time he refused a demand."

Nita swallowed. Fabricio could be lying, but it made sense in a way. Why would her mother kidnap the child of someone so important just to make a few bucks online? No, blackmail was far more her mother's style.

"Are you even an unnatural?"

He sighed. "I'm exactly what she said I was. Pieces of me would make money."

Nita nodded slowly. "But?"

"But . . ." He looked away. "I'm more afraid of *who* I am than *what* I am. No one would go to all the trouble she did to kidnap me just to sell me. But to blackmail my father? The sky is the limit."

Uneasiness coiled in Nita's stomach. She'd wanted power

to protect herself—to make Fabricio's reality hers. Everyone wanted her for *what* she was, and in order to avoid looking over her shoulder her whole life, she wanted to make them afraid of *who* she was.

Now she wondered if that was such a great idea.

"Why?"

He blinked. "Why what?"

"Why was my mother blackmailing your father in the first place? I mean, there are far easier targets if it was simply about money."

He shook his head. "I don't know."

No, this didn't make sense anymore. Something in this picture wasn't right.

"One good thing that's come out of all this." A half smile flitted across his face. "Now I can be a nameless refugee that INHUP will protect. I gave them a fake last name. No one needs to know who I am. I can start over." He looked at her. "I suppose I should thank you and your mother for that. If no one here knows who I am, no one can leak that information or try and use me for my father's connections."

Nita gave him an incredulous look. He was one of those every-cloud-has-a-silver-lining people. She supposed if he were in her shoes, he'd say that her experience in Mercado de la Muerte—"Death Market"—had given her much-needed industry perspective.

Ugh. She hated people like that.

A warm wind slunk through the garden, and Nita realized her nose had started to burn under the hot noon sun, and she healed it before it could progress. She'd been so distracted she hadn't noticed. She wiped her forehead and jerked her head to Fabricio.

"Let's go back inside."

He smiled tentatively. "It's hot out here. They need air-conditioning for outside."

Nita didn't smile back.

As they approached the building, Nita stopped and turned to Fabricio. "Let me make one thing clear."

He paused, smile falling. "Yes?"

"If you in any way reveal who my mother is, or our connection, I will tell INHUP about your father. You'll be sent home, and your little escape plan will be ruined."

His eyes narrowed, flint and steel, and Nita finally caught her first glimpse of the real person beneath the friendly facade. "If you say anything to compromise my protection and put me in danger, I'll tell them about your mother. And your complicity."

Nita pursed her lips. "Then we'll both have to stay quiet, won't we?"

They held each other's gaze for a long moment and then, as one, turned and reentered the building in silence.

Nita shoved the floripondio flower in her pocket as she went, a poisonous promise to herself.

TWO

NITA RETREATED TO HER ROOM. More white walls, white pillows, white sheets. The only spots of color were the blue blanket and the gray foldout chair in front of a white desk.

She locked the door and looked down at her hands. She'd managed to cut her finger on the stem of the floripondio flower at some point.

Nita concentrated, increasing blood clotting factor, accelerating cell growth. The veins repaired, and the cut closed over. She wiped away a small speck of blood, all evidence of an injury gone.

She flopped down on the bed, which sagged in the middle, and closed her eyes, turning over Fabricio's words in her mind. She replayed the scene, stalling on the part where he claimed her mother was blackmailing his father. It felt like the truth, but not the right piece of the truth.

No, Fabricio was a master of mixing truth and lies to make himself the most sympathetic person possible. He'd known exactly how to manipulate her into letting him out of her mother's cage, despite Nita's sense of self-preservation. He'd let her believe her mother's lies, because she might have hesitated freeing him if she'd had any inkling he'd been involved in the black market.

And Nita would have hesitated. Any potential stain on his character, and her mind would have supplied her with a million justifications for why it was okay to kill him, take him apart piece by piece like her mother wanted.

So he'd been very careful to act the perfect, tragic innocent.

Fool me once, shame on you, fool me twice, shame on me.

Nita carefully pulled the crumpled flower from her pocket and turned it around in her hands.

Small and deadly. She could end him in a moment.

But a part of her wasn't sure that was the best course of action. Wasn't sure that killing Fabricio would solve more problems than it created.

She tried to put herself in Fabricio's shoes, figure out why he'd sold her. He didn't need the money, his father was rich. He was already on a bus to INHUP, so it wasn't like he needed money to escape either, if he couldn't access his father's money.

For a brief moment, Nita wondered if Fabricio had sold her because she'd told him her father was Chilean and Fabricio was Argentinian. The relationship between the two countries had been strained for a long time. It got worse in the eighties, after the Falklands War between Argentina and the United Kingdom, when Chile was the only South American country to side with Britain.

But the more she thought about it, the more unbelievable it sounded. Selling a person on the black market because of events in a war that happened before they were born, especially after that person had saved him, was just absurd.

Not that his reasoning mattered. There was no excuse that could justify what he'd done.

A knock interrupted her musings.

Nita hurriedly tucked the flower away and opened the door.

Agent Quispe stood in the entranceway, her smile friendly and professional. "Nita, I hope I didn't catch you at a bad time."

Nita shook her head. "No."

"Good. I just wanted to let you know that your new passport came." Quispe held it out to her. "We're booked on a flight to Toronto in two days. We can't fly you straight to the US for legal reasons, so you'll go through some processing in Canada, and then we can fly you home."

Nita swallowed and nodded, even though her heart sank. After Toronto processing, she was supposed to go home, to that suburban house in Chicago. The house she hadn't seen since she left when she was twelve, dragged around the world by her mother, hunting unnaturals to sell.

To her father, who she hadn't seen in person since she was twelve.

She'd imagined a grand reunion, running into his arms. If she closed her eyes, she could still feel the warmth of his embrace, the way he'd stroke her hair, the gentle timbre of his voice.

But her father wasn't there anymore. There would be no tearful reunion, no warm hug, no sinking into his arms and letting herself believe that somehow, someday, everything would be okay.

Her father was dead.

Her eyes began to water at the thought, and she shoved the rising tide of emotion away ruthlessly. Now was not the time.

Quispe seemed to realize what was happening. As she should, she'd been the one to tell Nita about her father's murder a few days ago. And to show her the picture of her father's murderer, a vampire on the hunt for her mother.

Quispe's eyes softened. "Have you contacted any other family members yet?"

Nita shook her head. "I'll email some people. I'll let you know more tomorrow."

Quispe hesitated a moment. "I'm sorry about your father."

Nita's face almost cracked, everything leaking out and onto the floor, the grief like a demon trapped in her skin, just waiting for Nita to lose her strength so it could break free and leave only tatters of her skin shell behind.

She shrugged and looked away, trying to hide her face from Quispe. "It's fine."

"If you want to talk—"

"I don't."

There was a short pause, and Quispe sighed. "All right. If you need anything else, let me know."

"I will."

Nita slowly closed the door, hesitant at first, in case Quispe had something else to say, then quickly when she realized it really was the end of the conversation and slowly closing the door looked super awkward.

Nita ended up slamming the door in the INHUP agent's face, which was, of course, more awkward.

Her body shook slightly, and she leaned against the door. She swallowed and looked down at the stiff material of her American passport. She thumbed through the pages, each covered in washed-out images of national monuments. She flipped to the picture page, and looked down at her photo, taken by INHUP. Her frizzy brown curls were pulled back, and their slight orange tint was even more pronounced in the passport material's shine. The freckles across her nose and cheeks looked like blood spatter in the harsh light, and her brown skin looked grayish with exhaustion. She stared into the camera with too-intense eyes, like she was challenging the photographer.

Her first passport she didn't remember, but her second she'd gotten when she was ten. Her father took her to get the pictures, and he'd made funny faces at her from behind the photographer that made her laugh and ruined every take. When the photographer turned around, her father stood there, stoic and stern, one eyebrow raised as though to ask the photographer if there was a problem.

It had taken nearly half an hour to get a decent shot, and afterward they'd gone for ice cream. She'd gotten a waffle cone with sprinkles around the edge, and sat there giggling at her father's ice cream mustache as he did impersonations of the teachers in school she didn't like.

Grief swamped Nita, crashing through her like a tidal wave, all the stronger for those few moments she'd managed to hold it off while Quispe was there. It smashed against her ribs, rattling them, before retreating and pooling in her empty chest cavity, like a lake of tears waiting to be shed.

Her father was dead.

No more goofy faces. No more ice cream.

Nita leaned against the wall, then slowly slid down to the floor, fingers clenched around her new passport, her eyes tightly closed, trying to stop the tears before they started. Because once they started, they took ages to stop.

Nita had been walking down the hall yesterday and seen someone with the same pair of glasses as her father. That had been enough to set her off, crying into flower bushes and hiding in her room for the rest of the afternoon.

Part of her just wanted the pain to go away. She wanted to stop feeling awful all the time. She wanted to skip to the part where she was over it, where the grief was nothing but a distant memory.

Even as she thought that, it felt disloyal to her father. He deserved to be cried over. He was the only good person in her life, he had always been her friend and ally when her mother took things too far. How dare she try to avoid thinking about him to avoid pain?

She didn't know if it was selfish to not want to face the pain, or if it was like an open wound, where she had to wait for it to scab over before she could poke at it without making it bleed again.

Nita curled on the floor for a few minutes, trying to get control of her tears. When she finally rose, she went into the bathroom and blew her nose. She splashed her face with cold water and let out a short huff of breath.

Her reflection stared back at her, haunted and angry. She

tightened her jaw until her reflection didn't look sad anymore, just determined.

She nodded to herself. She was in control.

She flopped onto her bed and closed her eyes. The tears had given her a pounding headache, and all she wanted to do was fall asleep and forget for a while.

Reluctantly, she opened her eyes and pulled out her phone. Quispe had reminded her of the one thing she had to do before bed.

Quispe had only returned Nita's phone right before they met Fabricio. Nita hadn't had a chance to see if it still worked after taking a dunk in the Amazon River. Soaking it in rice was supposed to fix it, but who knew.

She ran her finger over the screen, thinking of her captor, Reyes, the first owner of this phone. Nita could still see her cold eyes. How she'd worn the same expression talking about money that she'd worn ordering people tortured. Blank. Empty.

Nita shivered and pushed the image from her mind. Reyes was dead. Nita had killed her. And that was one death she'd never regret.

Huffing, Nita unlocked the phone and logged into her "safe" email, hands trembling, not sure if she wanted to see what awaited her or if she wanted to be ignorant forever.

Her heart raced, and her fingers trembled slightly as she checked her messages.

There was one new email from her mother. She clicked it open.

Nita, answer your phone.

That was it. It was dated the same day Nita had been kidnapped. Her mother couldn't have known Fabricio had her phone.

Nita clicked reply, but hesitated, not sure what to say. If her mother was alive, why hadn't she come to rescue Nita? Nita's picture and location were all over the darknet—there was no way her mother hadn't seen. But she hadn't come.

Unease coiled in Nita's stomach. What if she was dead?

What if she *wasn't*? What if she just hadn't cared enough to save Nita?

Finally, annoyed with her whirling thoughts, she answered, *I'm with INHUP. They're flying me to Toronto for processing.*

She sent the message and was about to log out of email when she paused.

Kovit.

Her heart skipped a beat, and before her thoughts caught up with her fingers, she'd typed the email address he'd given her into a new message.

She hesitated. What could she say?

Hey, how's your bullet wound? Tortured anyone lately?

She sighed. Why was she even entertaining this? Kovit was a monster. He literally tortured people for food—and he *liked* it. A lot.

But he was also her friend, strange as that sounded. Nita had never imagined herself having friends, but if she had, they wouldn't have been psychopaths who worked as mafia torturers.

But he might be the only one in the world she could truly trust.

She closed her eyes and pictured his smile, dark with promises of pain on their enemies, and something in her chest tightened. She missed him.

Before she could second-guess herself, she wrote *How are you?* And sent it.

She watched her email for a long time, waiting for a reply, before clicking the phone off and curling up in bed, listening to the hum of the air conditioner until sleep overtook her.

Nita stood in a dissection room. Everything was white and sterile and wonderful, and she was taking a body apart. She had a scalpel in one hand, and in her other, she held a still-beating heart. It thumped in her latex-gloved palm, and in the way of dreams, this seemed completely normal.

The heart was blackened, and as she watched, it grew blacker, inky tendrils of disease spreading through it. The ink spread to her hand and she ripped her gloves off to dislodge the black threads, dropping the heart. It shattered on the floor like glass, and suddenly Nita was back in Death Market.

The glass from the heart had transformed into the glass from when she and Kovit had broken out of the cage.

In the background, someone was screaming.

Mirella.

Mirella, Nita's fellow captive, had been tortured by Kovit as punishment for fighting against their captor. Trapped in her cell, Nita had listened to those screams until they burned into her memory.

They were burning now. Each scream sent a streak of flames down the corridor, and Nita found herself running toward the sounds until she encountered a closed door.

She threw it open. Death Market was on fire.

All of the buildings around her had been engulfed in flames. People screamed as fire charred their bodies, and someone ran down the street, toward the river, clothes and skin alight. She almost caught the memory of a scent, but it was gone before it was formed.

She turned around, refusing to look at the scene, and stood face-to-face with Kovit. His hair, black and silky, was brushed out of his face, and his dark eyes regarded her. A small smile twitched at the corner of his mouth, and an answering smile spread across her face.

He took a step forward, until they were nose to nose, and suddenly they weren't in the market anymore, they were on the dock in Tabatinga, Brazil, where they'd parted ways and he'd leaned forward to whisper his email address in her ear.

Except this time, instead of telling her his email, he whispered, "I'm going to make you scream."

Then he kissed her.

Nita bolted upright with a shriek, and her phone fell off her bed and clattered to the ground. Her face was sticky with sweat and her heart beat a staccato rhythm in her chest. Her body felt flushed with heat, almost feverish, and her skin was clammy. She swallowed, her throat dry, and put her hands to her lips where the dream Kovit had kissed her. Her mouth tingled at the touch.

What.

The.

Fuck.

Eventually, Nita lay back down, but it took a long time for her to fall asleep again.

THREE

THE NEXT MORNING, Nita woke slowly, lying in her bed for several minutes, drifting in and out of dreams before she decided it was time to start the body modifications she'd been planning.

When Nita had arrived at INHUP, she'd decided she was going to be proactive instead of reactive when it came to the black market. They wanted to kidnap and cut her up because she had the ability to manipulate her own body.

So she had decided she was going to use that same power to prevent them from ever capturing her again.

Her whole life, she'd been cautious with her ability. She'd had a series of bad hospital experiences because she'd screwed around with things better left alone and didn't know how to fix them. Since then, she'd taken things slow, made copious observations, and hadn't done anything too drastic.

The time for caution was over. She needed to use all the tools available to her if she was going to survive.

She'd been weak from overusing her power when she first

arrived, so she hadn't done much complicated stuff. But now that she was recovered, the sky was the limit.

First, she completely stopped the production of myostatin in her body, a chemical that inhibited muscle growth. Next, she began modifying herself from the skeleton out. Bones, then muscles, ligaments, and tendons. She wasn't changing her skin, because she hadn't yet figured out how to toughen it without creating saggy joint jowls, like a rhinoceros.

She'd sink like a stone in water, but that was a small price to pay for the benefits of tougher bones and stronger muscles.

It was a long, laborious process, and she turned off her pain receptors for it. Nita decided to start from the bottom and go up, worried if she started at the top and reinforced her skull, her head would be too heavy for her neck.

She got up to her hips before she decided she was too tired to continue. She couldn't shake the sensation that her legs were wearing huge, heavy boots, even though she had the muscles to cope.

She rolled over, picked up her phone, and checked her messages.

Sure enough, there was one from her mother.

I'll pick you up in Toronto—T.

That was it.

Nita's chest felt hollow, like she was a dissected cadaver, her organs long since ripped out and sold.

It's not safe to send information over the internet. Especially with you in INHUP, she told herself, but that didn't make her feel any better. Her mother hadn't even said something simple like "I'm so glad you're okay" or "I missed you."

Nita lowered her eyes. If her mother wasn't hurt, dead, kidnapped, or otherwise restricted—if she could answer emails overnight and meet Nita in Toronto—why hadn't she rescued Nita from Death Market?

Nita let out a breath and got out of bed. There was no use speculating now. She'd have to ask her mother when she saw her.

As she dressed, the floripondio flower fell from her pocket onto the tiled floor. Nita knelt down to pick it up. She twirled in in her hands. Consuming a few petals of this would be enough to kill someone.

Someone like Fabricio.

She hesitated, looking at the flower. Did she really want to do that? Did she really want to kill him?

Nita had done terrible things. She'd murdered her captor, she'd burned a market full of people alive.

She'd do it again.

If she were back in the market, back in her cage, if she had a chance to do everything over, she didn't think she'd do anything differently. She would still kill her captor. She would still ask Kovit to torture a man to steal his money. She would still burn everyone in the market alive. She wouldn't enjoy it, but she'd do it. She would do anything and everything necessary to protect herself and stay alive.

So did she want to kill Fabricio? The boy who'd betrayed her and left her to that horror?

Yes. She did.

But did it make *sense* to kill him? His death would raise suspicions. She could be caught.

Yet leaving him alive was a far more dangerous prospect. He knew who she was, who her mother was. If he ratted her out, Nita could be arrested. And once she was in prison, well, anything could happen. She was money waiting to be made for the right murderer. Even the guards would be tempted by the amount of money the black market would offer for her body parts.

If she ratted on Fabricio . . . what? He was the son of a powerful man running a legal firm. Sure, everyone knew his father was neck deep in the black market, but they couldn't *prove* it. And they certainly couldn't prove anything about Fabricio. And even though he'd sold Nita, her evidence would never be enough to convict him.

The only danger to Fabricio was if a corrupt INHUP agent tried to use him for blackmail like her mother had. Or, if Fabricio was to be believed, being shipped home. She didn't know why he was so afraid of returning, or what terrible secrets he was hiding, but whatever they were, she couldn't trust they were enough to keep his mouth shut.

No, Nita needed to eliminate this threat before he changed his mind and betrayed her again.

She took a Kleenex and laid it flat on the counter. She crumpled the flower petals, shredding them into thin strips, holding them over the air conditioner until they dried out, then crumbled them into a fine powder. They looked a little like pink tea mix.

She carefully wrapped the flower dust in her Kleenex and tucked it in her pocket.

Giving herself a firm nod in the mirror, she left her room and went to see Quispe.

Outside of the refugee wing, the INHUP building was bustling. Men and women in button-up white shirts and slacks strode with purpose, briefcases in hand. Nita waited with a group of other people at the elevator. When it came, it was already overcrowded, and the idea of being crushed against so many bodies made her cringe. She imagined the stench of body odor from dozens of people, the press of skin against skin, someone's hand caught in an uncomfortable position that they'd say was accidental but was probably on purpose.

She took the stairs.

On the third floor, she clanged out of the stairwell and into a hallway with gray tiles and beige-yellow walls. Cubicle style desks were scattered around the room just like a regular office building.

Framed photos of famous INHUP agents covered the walls. There was Nadezhda Novikova, founder of INHUP and killer of the Russian vampire Bessanov. Bessanov had supposedly wiped out entire military platoons single-handedly, but in the end he'd been taken down by a sixteen-year-old girl out for vengeance.

Nita may not have liked INHUP, but she'd always been impressed by its founder.

The pictures continued along the wall, starting out black-and-white and eventually gaining color. Smiling and stern men and women of the past stared out at her. Some of the labels had explanations of who they were: head of the first INHUP office in South America, in Montevideo, Uruguay; the agent who foiled a major unnatural trafficking ring and saved nearly ten thousand unnatural children; the investigator who captured a famous serial killer hunting in northern Brazil.

Nita actually had heard of that one. Everyone had thought the killer was an unnatural because the faces of the victims had been eaten, so INHUP got involved, but it turned out he was a human after all.

Most people forgot that last part.

Nita stopped in front of Quispe's small office, tucked in the corner away from the cubicles.

When Nita first arrived, she'd checked for Quispe's name on the list of corrupt INHUP agents she'd stolen from Reyes. She hadn't found it. It didn't mean Quispe wasn't corrupt, but it made Nita relax all the same.

Quispe looked up when Nita entered. "Yes?"

Nita cleared her throat. "I got an email from my aunt. She's going to pick me up from the office in Toronto."

Nita and her mother had a signal system. The *T* at the end of her message stood for Theresa—Nita's nonexistent aunt Theresa. Nita had an entire backstory for her fake aunt memorized, and her mother had the forged documents to back it up. It was one of their many aliases.

Quispe lowered her laptop screen so it dimmed. "That's great."

Nita swallowed the lump of fear in her chest. "Yeah."

"Are you sure you wouldn't like to avail yourself of some of INHUP's protective services? That video of you . . ."

That fucking video.

Reyes took a video of Nita demonstrating her healing abilities and posted it to all the wrong circles online. It meant everyone who wanted to hunt Nita knew her face. And unlike the rest of her body, that wasn't something she knew how to permanently modify.

It destroyed all Nita's chances of living her life without looking over her shoulder every five minutes.

Nita shook her head and lied, "I'll be fine."

"All right." Quispe didn't sound like she believed Nita, but she let it go. "The flight leaves tomorrow. Be ready to leave for the airport at three a.m."

"Three a.m.?" Nita's eyes bugged out.

"The flight is at six." Quispe sighed. "I know. We can sleep on the flight."

"We?"

"I'll be escorting you to Toronto and handing you off to the agents there."

"I see." No unsupervised time, then.

"Make sure you go to bed early tonight." Quispe rubbed the bridge of her nose. "It's going to be a long day tomorrow."

Quispe went back to work and Nita smiled. "Of course."

She left the office and made her way back to the stairwell. Several floors down, her phone buzzed.

She had a message from Kovit.

Her fingers swiped across the screen, fast and sure.

I'm okay.

Nita closed her eyes, and let herself sink in the stairwell with relief. She hadn't realized how worried she'd been about his bullet wound. The risk of infection was so high, given the dirt and river water that had gotten in it, and the hours of dehydration rowing their tiny boat back to civilization.

I'm in Detroit, visiting a friend.

Nita frowned at that. She wasn't sure if he meant an actual friend, a former colleague that he couldn't talk about because he was worried their communication was being monitored, or someone else entirely.

Then she realized: Detroit was only a few hours' drive from Toronto, wasn't it?

Something squiggly wriggled in her stomach. She wasn't sure how to feel about that.

How are you?

How was Nita? A mess. Her father was dead, she wasn't sure she even wanted to see her mother, and the video of her was still all over the internet, making her more recognizable to all the wrong people by the minute.

She closed her eyes and remembered that moment on the river, both of them covered in blood, where Kovit had asked her to come with him. But she'd gone to INHUP because she wanted a ticket to North America, she wanted to see her father. She didn't want the anonymity Kovit did.

And she didn't want to spend her life pretending the screams of the people he tortured didn't bother her. Because she was frightened that she wouldn't need to pretend for long. It was already almost truth.

Even though she'd made the right decision at the time—Kovit didn't have enough money to fly both of them away and get medical help—a part of her regretted it.

Before she could stop herself, she responded, *I'm okay. Flying to Toronto tomorrow. Maybe I'll see you soon?*

She pressed Send and shoved the phone in her pocket before she could regret anything.

She let out a long breath, then felt for the Kleenex-wrapped poison in her pocket.

If her plane was tomorrow morning, she had work to do.

Because she wasn't leaving INHUP without killing Fabricio.

FOUR

THE SMALL DINING ROOM had been mostly empty the three days Nita had been in INHUP, despite the fact that there were at least a dozen other refugees here. There were a table and chairs and a small kitchen including a fridge stocked with prepared meals. But tonight was different. Fabricio sat at the table, eating a piece of toast with manjar on it. An empty frozen dinner tray sat beside him.

He looked up when she came in, and his shoulders tensed. "Buenas noches."

"Buenas." Nita replied. She should have given him a smile, or asked a pointless question like "did you have a good day?" or "are you enjoying your toast?" but she wasn't a good actor, and it just seemed like a waste of energy.

He gave her a soft smile. "How did you sleep?"

A short smile did curl her mouth then. Pointless question, check.

"Good, thanks." Nita walked past him to get a frozen dinner. She unboxed it and shoved it in the microwave.

Nita programmed the timer, and the microwave hummed to life. She watched the food heat. Her father once told her not to stare at the microwave while it heated things, but Nita figured she could just heal her eyes if anything went wrong. Her heart tightened a little at the memory.

"I hear you're leaving soon." Fabricio's voice was soft. "Are you going into the UPP?"

"The what?" Nita turned around to look at him.

His blue-gray eyes were steady. "The Unnatural Protection Program."

Nita shuddered. "No."

His eyebrows tugged together. "Why not? They can give you a whole new life."

"I'm good. I can take care of myself." And they'd probably disapprove of her penchant for dissecting dead bodies. Nita's fingers tingled, aching for a scalpel.

"Then why are you here?"

Nita shrugged. "They're flying me home, aren't they?"

"I guess."

The timer dinged, and Nita took her dinner out and put it on the table across from Fabricio. "I'm getting a drink, you want something while I'm up?"

He considered. "Can you grab me an orange juice?"

"Sure."

Nita retrieved the bottles from the fridge. She took them to the counter and cracked the lids on both of them.

"Where will you go now?" asked Nita, turning to look at Fabricio and hiding her arm from him as it dipped into her pocket for the poison. "Will you join the UPP?"

Fabricio shook his head. "They're going to get me a new identity, and I'll just . . . start a new life somewhere."

"Where?"

"I don't know."

"Argentina?"

"No." Something haunted passed across his features. "Not Argentina."

Behind Fabricio, the door to the kitchen opened and someone walked in. He turned around to look, and Nita seized her chance, sprinkling the powdered flower into his orange juice, twisting her body to block the security camera's view.

She stared at the poisoned juice for a moment, watching the small powdered petals float into it and mix with the pulp. The bright orange hid any trace of the pink flowers.

She swallowed, throat dry. Was she really sure she wanted to do this?

Heart slamming in her chest, Nita turned to face him, holding a bottle in each hand. The bottles were slippery in her sweaty palms. How easy it would be to drop one, letting the poison spill out and away across the floor.

Her fingers loosened slightly, and the bottle slid.

Then Fabricio was there, taking it from her before it could fall to the ground. For a moment, their fingers almost touched and Nita could feel the warmth of his body. The life of it.

She thought of how Mirella's blood had spilled across the docks when she was shot, her pink hair spread around her, mixing with the blood. She thought of her own bloody handprints on the glass of her cage, watching as the same man who shot Mirella ate Nita's toe.

She wiggled her foot. The toe still felt like it was there sometimes, a phantom feeling. But it was gone forever, just like her trust in Fabricio. Her hesitation was just as phantom as the feeling of the toe—it was a remnant of the girl who saved a boy she didn't know from monsters, not realizing the boy himself was a monster who'd turn on her at the first opportunity.

She knew what she had to do.

Her jaw tightened, her rage at Fabricio's betrayal rekindling, and she let him take the bottle.

He took a sip and frowned, licking his lips.

Nita had forgotten it might taste funny. She cleared her throat and tried to distract him. "So why don't you want to go back to Argentina?"

Fabricio shrugged and looked away. "Just not interested in following the family business."

Then he took a long, deep drink of his juice.

Nita's smile widened. *Gotcha.*

"There's more to Argentina than just your family business." Nita smiled, trying to make him as uncomfortable as possible. "As far as I know, they only have an office in Buenos Aires, no? Argentina is more than just one city."

He took another awkward sip, clearly trying to avoid having to answer. "I just don't want to go back."

He continued awkwardly drinking to avoid conversation while Nita ate. His eyes were on something in his memory, far away, as he drank. Whatever it was he was thinking about, it was clearly something he didn't like.

When she finished her meal, she rose and stretched. "I'm going back to my room now."

He blinked at her and held his head. The empty bottle slid from his fingers and clattered on the table. "Yeah, I think I will too. I feel tired."

He rose, slightly wobbly, and accompanied her down the hall. Nita snuck glances at him as they walked. His pupils began to dilate, and his breathing changed rhythm.

They reached his room, one white door in a hallway of many. He leaned against the wall, blinking rapidly. "I don't feel so good."

Nita opened his door. "Let me help you to bed."

She took his arm and dragged him inside. He stumbled, nearly bringing them both to the ground, but Nita kept an iron grip on his arm as she pulled him along.

She let him go when they reached the bed, and he keeled over into it, groaning.

"I think something's wrong." His words slurred slightly. "I need to go to the doctor."

Nita examined his room for cameras, and once she was satisfied of where they were likely to be, she leaned over Fabricio and put her hand to his forehead. It was clammy with sweat.

He stared up at her, gaze unfocused. "Nita, can you call someone?"

"No, I think I won't," Nita whispered.

He frowned. "What?"

She took her hand from his forehead and leaned in close to whisper, "I know what you did, Fabricio."

His mouth opened and closed. "What are you talking about?"

"I know you're the one who sold me out to the black market."

He shook his head, eyes widening. He really was a great actor.

"I didn't!" he hissed. "I couldn't have! I was on a bus to INHUP."

"Yeah. And during your trip you texted your contacts on the black market. You sent them my pictures."

"I don't have contacts on the black market!"

Nita rolled her eyes. "Sure you don't, Fabricio *Tácunan*."

He winced and looked away. Nita crossed her arms.

"Okay, yes, I have contacts. But I wouldn't have sold you to them. You *saved my life*. Why on earth would I do that to you?"

"That's what I wanted to ask you."

"I didn't do it, Nita." He shook his head. "Why do you think I did?"

"Can we cut the crap, Fabricio? I have the messages you sent Reyes. I can show them to you." Nita held up her phone. She tilted her head and examined his increasingly unfocused gaze and trembling hands. "But it's a waste of time. And you don't have much of that."

"I don't have . . ." He tried to get up, and Nita took a step back. He wasn't even able to turn over. "What have you done?"

"What I should have let my mother do." Nita's voice scraped against her throat, trying to block out the memories of his screams when her mother cut off his ear. "Saving you was the one good thing I did in my life, and I've paid for that kindness in blood and screams. I learned my lesson well. I won't make the same mistake again."

Fabricio jerked forward, trying to reach for her. "Nita, please, I'm sorry for everything you went through, believe me when I say I understand."

"Oh, I know you do. That's what makes it all the worse."

"Nita, it's not what you think, I swear!" Tears streamed down his face.

"Oh? Then what is it? Tell me."

He just shook his head mutely, his body trembling, whether from poison, fear, or something else, Nita didn't know.

"You're a liar, Fabricio. The best I've ever met." Nita turned and walked away. "But you betrayed the wrong person this time."

Fabricio cried out as Nita walked away, and there was a thump as he fell off the bed and tried to crawl toward her with jittering limbs.

"Nita, wait. Please. I can explain everything."

Nita stood at the entrance to his room, and looked back at him once. He gasped each breath, lungs heaving, and his brown hair was a tangled mess. He reached out as though to grab her ankle, but he was too far away.

"I saved your life. It seems only fitting I take it away," she said, flicking off the light.

"Nita!" he gasped into the darkness.

"Goodbye, Fabricio."

She left the room and closed the door behind her.

FIVE

SEVERAL HOURS LATER, Nita dragged herself out of bed to catch her flight. She hadn't actually slept. She'd lain on her bed, staring at the ceiling, imagining Fabricio slowly dying in his room, sobbing softly as the hallucinogenic properties of the plant made him lose his mind even as the organs in his body slowly shut down one by one.

Murderer, her mind hissed to her in the darkness. *You killed to survive in the market, but this is just petty vengeance.*

No, she whispered back. *It's preemptive self-defense. Fabricio sold me out once. He could do it again.*

But her mind wouldn't rest. At one point she even rose to go to Fabricio. To see if he was dead, to call for help for him, she didn't know. But the knowledge that if he survived he'd tell INHUP what she'd done kept her from leaving the room.

What was done was done. There was no backing away now.

At three in the morning, she rose for her flight. Quispe was waiting in the back seat of a black sedan with two cups of coffee. Nita took one and sipped it as she climbed in. She wondered if she'd taste if it were poisoned or if she'd just slowly collapse like Fabricio. Not that she thought the INHUP agent would poison her. Mostly.

Dark circles hid under Quispe's eyes. It didn't look like she'd slept much.

Once they were buckled in, Quispe turned to Nita, folding her hands in her lap and taking a deep breath before she spoke. "Nita, I have something to tell you."

Nita stiffened at Quispe's tone. They couldn't have possibly discovered Nita had poisoned Fabricio, could they? "What is it?"

"It's Fabricio."

Nita's voice was a bit too high. "What about him?"

"He missed his appointment with his doctor to get the stitches in his ear out yesterday evening." She rubbed her temples. "We found him unconscious in his room late last night. He's been taken to the hospital."

Unconscious. Not dead.

Nita's shoulders relaxed, and she hated that a small part of her was relieved. That a little piece of her hadn't wanted to be the kind of person that could kill a boy in cold blood, when her life wasn't on the line that instant.

That part of her was going to get her killed someday if she didn't learn to quash it better.

Quispe was expecting a response, so Nita covered her mouth and said, "How terrible."

Quispe's voice was gentle. "I know you two were getting close. I'm so sorry."

Nita shook her head. "Will he be okay?"

"We don't know." But Quispe's tone made the answer sound a lot more like *no.*

Good, Nita thought, banishing the traitorous guilt in her chest. *He'll never betray anyone again.*

Beneath her hand, she smiled.

When they finally arrived at the airport, their flight was delayed for an hour.

Quispe took a seat in the departures area, black pleather airport seat squeaking, and gestured for Nita to join her. Quispe observed Nita as she sat, and Nita tried not to sweat. Had she done something to give herself away?

"Is something wrong?" Nita finally asked. "You're staring."

"I'm sorry." Quispe sighed, her perfect poise slipping for a moment. "I was just thinking about your father."

Nita swallowed down the hurt that bloomed in her chest. "What about him?"

She was silent for a moment. "Did you know I lost my father when I was a year older than you?"

Of course Nita didn't. How could she? But all she said was a soft "No."

Quispe nodded, face tight. "A car accident on his way to work."

"Oh."

Quispe looked at her, and Nita wondered if she was supposed to have said something more. Was she supposed to express her sympathy? She didn't really care about the INHUP agent's dead father. But she forced herself to play along. "I'm sorry for your loss."

Quispe sighed and leaned in close to Nita. "It was an awful time. My mother couldn't support all of us, even with the rest of the family's help. I decided to get a job after school to help out. It was my first job with INHUP, at the La Paz office, translating Quechua legends into Spanish."

Nita was intrigued, despite herself. "What kind of legends?"

Quispe smiled. "Local folktales of monsters and heroes. You know the type. Tales about pishtacos hunting the mountains, searching for human fat to eat. Creation myths about Pachamama—Mother Earth—and her children. The kind of things INHUP likes to comb through for pieces of information on local undocumented unnatural species."

Nita leaned forward. "Tell me about them."

Quispe shook her head and gave Nita a gentle smile. "We've gotten off topic." She placed her hand on Nita's shoulder. "Look, Nita, I just wanted to say, I know how hard the loss of a parent can be. I know how life altering it is. It can make you change all your plans, and it can hurt more than anything. And if you want to talk about it or you need help figuring things out, I wanted you to know you can talk to me."

Nita quietly took Quispe's hand from her shoulder. "Thank you for the offer. But what would really help right now is if you just stopped bringing it up."

Then Nita got up and walked away.

She couldn't go far, it wasn't a massive terminal, but it was big enough for her to walk far enough away that she couldn't see Quispe.

Nita rubbed her shoulder where the INHUP agent had touched her, shuddering. Why did the woman have to go poking into Nita's business? Nita had lost her father. She didn't need an INHUP agent trying to butt in and act like a surrogate parent. Nita didn't need to "talk about it" or "figure it out." She just needed to be left alone and not have it brought up every five minutes.

Nita wandered the halls, looking for a distraction, something to take her mind off things before she ended up wallowing in her own grief again.

A family sat at the small coffee shop, all of them chattering together, a dozen people with luggage, from old grandparents to small children. Nita's heart tightened at the sight. A part of her wished she had that, wished she had more people in her life than just her parents, more connection with her father's culture than just pieces of a language and knowledge of which soccer teams to root for.

Intellectually, she knew she didn't want a big family. Too many people, too many forced interactions, too much nosiness. But she wanted something, some more connection to her roots. Especially now that her father was gone.

No. She wasn't going to think of that. She needed a distraction, she refused to start crying in the airport.

She found a combination magazine stand/breakfast shop and browsed the selection. Most of it was pop culture, some politics, local news. One paper blared a headline about men disappearing in one of the logging camps in the Amazon, blaming "las patasolas," a type of unnatural Nita was unfamiliar with. But there were no details afterward, so she put the paper down and searched for something more interesting.

She paused her flipping on a page of a newspaper condemning INHUP for not adding kelpies to the list of dangerous unnaturals.

The Dangerous Unnaturals List was composed of types of unnaturals it was okay to shoot on sight, since killing them was considered preemptive self-defense. It had creatures like kappa, which ate human organs, and unicorns, men who consumed the souls of virgins.

It also contained zannies. Like Kovit.

If anyone in the world knew what he was, they would be within their rights to murder him on sight. And if anyone ever found out Nita knew what he was and didn't report him, she could be arrested.

It was easily the least of her crimes.

She rubbed her temples, resisting the urge to check her phone for more messages from Kovit. It wasn't even six in the morning yet. He wasn't going to answer.

She succumbed and checked anyway. Of course, there was nothing.

She rolled her eyes at herself and looked back down to the paper. She had some time to kill, so she let her eyes wander through the article. It was an opinion piece, condemning INHUP for not adding kelpies to the list despite never having found a kelpie that hadn't murdered someone.

Nita tapped her finger on the paper. So far, the Dangerous

Unnaturals List consisted of unnaturals that were, fundamentally, human on the outside. They could interbreed with humans and looked mostly human inside and out.

Kelpies were none of those things. Outside and inside, they were as non-human as unnaturals came.

Though they could look human if they chose.

Originally from the Scottish Highlands, they were semiaquatic, like crocodiles. Some researchers speculated that kelpies were related to crocodiles, but Nita thought this was clearly wrong, because reptiles needed warm water to thrive, and kelpies needed cold. That's why these days they were only found in Scotland and on the east coast of Canada and the States. They'd come over with the waves of immigrants hundreds of years ago as conditions in the Highlands became more perilous, and they'd never left.

In legends, kelpies would appear as beautiful horses by the side of the water. If you got on the horse, it would ride into the nearest lake, drown you, and feast on your rotting body.

But kelpies could also look human and lure their victims to the water that way.

Whether they could physically shape-shift, it was some sort of illusion, or something else entirely, no one knew. A body had never been dissected or studied, so no one even knew what their real form looked like.

They were also very rare these days. Because they couldn't reproduce with humans, their species was dying. Between laws, hunters, and technology making it more difficult for them to run from their crimes, kelpies were slowly going extinct.

Nita let her eyes wander over the rest of the article. It was talking about species that had been famously exempted from the list, despite eating humans, like ghouls. Ghouls were one of the oldest recorded species, originating in the Middle East and appearing as far back as ancient Sumerian texts as "gallu." The article talked about several famous cases of ghouls living off people in crematoriums, and how the species as a whole couldn't be condemned as evil.

Nita sighed and put the paper down. She didn't know what she thought of the Dangerous Unnaturals List anymore. She'd been a staunch fan for so long – in theory, killing monsters was good. But things got more complicated after she'd befriended one of those monsters.

She shook her head at herself and wandered back over to Quispe. Their plane had started boarding, but Quispe remained seated, her phone pressed against her ear. She was nodding, forehead creased, and listening intently to whoever was on the other end of the line.

Nita hesitated a few steps away; Quispe looked up and saw Nita and the boarding line for the plane.

"Thanks, keep me updated." She hung up and gave Nita a smile. "Good news!"

"What?"

"Fabricio's going to be okay." Quispe's whole face lit up. "The doctors say he's going to pull through."

Nita stared, mouth slightly open. A tiny bit of relief bloomed in her chest. The last little remnant of the girl who'd felt so good for saving him, who'd been so proud for doing a good deed. The girl who wanted too much to pretend she wasn't bad.

But Nita wasn't that girl anymore. It was a phantom guilt she felt in the same way she felt her severed toe, and she pushed it away and let anger fill the place where it had once been.

She tried to imagine what would happen now. Fabricio would wake up. If he hadn't been planning to tell on her before, he would now. Her shoulders tightened, and her fingers curled into fists at her side.

Fabricio was like a goddam cockroach.

She forced a smile onto her face. "That's great! Do they know what happened to him?"

Quispe shook her head. "They think he ingested something. They pumped his stomach, and have been treating him for severe toxic shock. He's still not conscious yet, but they're hopeful for later today."

Nita gritted her teeth. She couldn't have Fabricio ratting her out before she got to Toronto. She'd be arrested before she could leave INHUP custody. She needed to do damage control.

"Can you send him a message for me?" Nita asked.

"Of course!"

Quispe handed Nita her phone, and Nita frowned at the blank email screen. How to threaten Fabricio not to talk without giving away she was threatening him?

I'm so happy to hear you're doing better after being sick. I'm glad INHUP is there to take care of you. It's too bad they can't contact your parents to let them know how you're doing.

I've enjoyed our chats, and am eager to continue them another time, when we're both out of INHUP. Until then, enjoy INHUP's hospitality for as long as it lasts.

Nita stared down at her message. Clunky, but she thought it got the point across.

If he told them what she'd done, she'd tell them what he'd done. She'd reveal who his father was and ruin all Fabricio's plans.

When he got out of INHUP's custody and back into the real world – it was on.

Nita didn't know how or when she'd do it, but she would find a way to destroy Fabricio once and for all.

SIX

THE FIRST HOUR of the flight to Toronto was awful.

Nita tried reading, but couldn't focus. Ditto with movies. All she could think about was her upcoming reunion with her mother. She couldn't stop playing out imaginary conversations in her head.

In some of them, Nita screamed at her mother for everything that had gone wrong, threw broken dishes at her, and told her she never wanted to see her again. Obviously, that was nothing more than a fantasy.

In other scenarios, her mother told Nita it was her own fault for breaking the rules, for not following her mother's instructions precisely. For not toeing the line. And Nita was forced back into the dissection room, trapped with nothing but dead bodies and tools for company, never to see the outside world again.

She shivered softly at the thought, because it was so horrible and so believable. She'd replace the glass cage of the market for one of her mother's making.

Nita couldn't let that happen again. She couldn't go back

to the cage, even if it was one made to protect her. Even the idea of a small room with no way out made her skin crawl.

After a while, Nita decided her thoughts were going nowhere but in circles, so she ramped up melatonin production, leaned the seat back, pressed her cheek against the window, and forced herself into sleep. She would see her mother soon enough. They could lay it all on the table then.

They had a lot to talk about.

She woke when they were landing with a crick in her neck. A line of drool ran down the window, and droplets of it spattered her shirt. She massaged the muscles around her neck and popped her spine back into alignment.

The plane hummed, and the speaker buzzed with some announcement. Nita had missed the English, and they were on the French now: ". . . votre sécurité est notre priorité . . ."

Below her, the city spread out as far as she could see. It was a metropolis of almost seven million people, and had surpassed New York as most diverse city in the world, according to Google. Towers spread in clumps here and there, tall and silver, like giant palace complexes surveying the peasantry below. Suburbia sprawled around them, a sea of houses intermingled with large swaths of green. Aside from the patches of skyscrapers, most of the buildings looked red, and Nita wondered if brick was popular.

It took nearly an hour for them to go through customs and get to the baggage claim. The walls of the airport were papered with posters with a waving Canadian flag in the background and curly, handwritten-style type reading BIENVENUE AU CANADA! WELCOME TO CANADA!

Quispe fixed her clothes as they waited for her baggage. She'd kept her sleeves unbuttoned and her jacket only partially done up in Bogotá, but not here. She smoothed the front of her jacket, fingers pressing into the fabric and ensuring everything looked perfectly arranged and professional.

"What are you doing?" asked Nita.

Quispe smiled at her, tight and formal, as she pulled her small piece of luggage from the rack. "Making a good impression."

"Have you met anyone at this branch before?"

"A few people." Quispe gestured for Nita to follow as she rolled her luggage toward the exit.

Nita watched the INHUP agent's face with interest. "You don't like them."

"I respect the work they do, and I've never had anything but positive interactions with them."

"But?"

"But they're people." Quispe shook her head ruefully. "And most people judge you the instant they meet you, if not before. I want to make sure they judge me the way I want them to."

Nita thought about that as she walked. About how even Quispe tailored herself to change how people new perceived her. That perception was based on first impressions, and that Nita's first impression on the black market was as a victim.

And how if she wanted to be left alone, she'd need to change that impression.

Exiting the terminal through a large set of automatic doors, Quispe stretched her neck, searching. Nita took in the crowds with wide eyes. Metal bars prevented anyone from approaching those exiting the terminal, and people had swarmed up against them, shouting, pressing close, and waving hands. There were so many Nita wondered if there was some celebrity coming through, but although many people held WELCOME signs, they didn't seem to be welcoming the same people.

Too many people. Nita balled her hands. She wanted out. Away from this crowd of strangers. Her eyes flicked around, trying to watch everyone, and she kept close to Quispe. Someone brushed by her, and she flinched.

She hated people.

She tried to keep an image of her dissection table in her mind's eye, the smooth metal surface and the calming glass jars. In her hand, she held a scalpel, and it was silent and empty, just her and the dead body on the table.

She really wanted a dissection. The sooner she was away from INHUP, the sooner she could find something—or someone—to take apart.

"Agent Quispe!" A tall woman in a navy suit approached them. She had dark red hair verging on purple and cool-toned white skin.

"Ah, Agent Bronte. Good to see you again." The two of them shook hands. Quispe turned to Nita, and said in faintly accented English, "Nita, this is Agent Rachel Bronte."

"Lovely to meet you." Bronte extended her hand.

Nita didn't take it. She turned to Quispe and asked in Spanish, "Are we going now?"

Quispe blinked. Then responded in English, "Agent Bronte will escort you—"

"You're not coming?" Nita interrupted, sticking to Spanish.

Quispe gave in, switching back to Spanish. "Yes, I'm coming, don't worry. I didn't fly all this way to turn around now."

"Good." Nita didn't like the idea of getting into an INHUP car without at least one person she knew.

Quispe smiled at them both. "I'll be back in five minutes. I'm just going to make a quick call."

She disappeared into the airport before Nita could protest, and Nita was left with Bronte. The other INHUP agent quirked an eyebrow as Nita hunched away from the crowds.

"You get along well with Agent Quispe?"

"Not really."

Bronte's perfectly drawn eyebrows drew together, but she tried to smile. "You have a lovely accent. It sounds almost British. Were you raised in the UK?"

Nita sighed. "No."

This wasn't the first time this had happened. So many years away from the US, and her accent had flattened out a bit, taking on aspects of the English that surrounded her in other countries. In Germany and Vietnam, when she'd heard English, it was mostly British. She hadn't realized she'd absorbed enough to get an accent. It would probably go away if she stayed in North America long enough.

She could have explained all this to Bronte, but she didn't want to, so she ignored the INHUP agent and pulled out her phone to make a show of looking busy while waiting for Quispe to return.

Nita connected to the free airport wireless, letting herself disappear into her phone so she could block out the rest of the world.

There was a new message from Kovit.

So, things didn't work out in Detroit. I might be in Toronto later this afternoon.

Nita's heart leapt. Kovit was coming.

Then it sank again. Because her mother was coming too.

And if her mother ever found out what Kovit was, she would murder him. And it wouldn't even be a crime.

Though Nita was pretty sure her mother could be arrested for selling Kovit's body parts online.

The thought made her nauseous. The idea of her mother, smiling while she tore Kovit apart like she'd tried to do to Fabricio, like she'd done to so many other people. She could imagine her mother even demanding Nita perform the dissection.

No.

No matter what, Nita could never, ever let the two of them meet.

It wasn't five, but closer to fifteen minutes later when Quispe returned. She smiled when she arrived, and looked between Nita and Bronte. She spoke in English. "Did the two of you have a nice chat?"

Nita remained silent, and Bronte sighed. "Come on, the car is this way."

The three of them made their way outside to the arrival section parking. The air was crisp with spring chill, and Nita almost groaned in pleasure to finally be away from the heat and humidity of Bogotá. She couldn't remember the last time she'd felt cool in a natural, non-air-conditioner-induced way.

The crowds were just as dense here, and Nita dodged around a group of old white men in long black robes and tall black hats who took up half the sidewalk, only to nearly bump into a young couple chatting in a blend of English and Chinese.

Nita edged as far away as she could from the people in her path, but there were just too many. When Bronte and Quispe stopped in front of a black SUV, Nita dove for the door.

Inside, it was blissfully, blessedly silent, like she'd entered a different world. No more crowds. No more strangers.

The beige vinyl slid under her fingers as Quispe slipped in beside her. In the front, a short white man in black sunglasses looked at them in the rearview mirror. With his black suit and no-nonsense expression, he looked like he belonged in a Men in Black movie.

Nita found that strangely comforting. It was the way she'd always expected an INHUP agent to look, and there was something deeply calming about seeing her stereotype made flesh.

The man turned his head, and for a moment his square jaw and cleft chin gave him the same silhouette as Boulder, the man who'd stolen Mirella's eye and cut off Nita's toe and eaten them.

She shivered, feeling the lack of sensation where her toe had once been.

"Should I turn the AC down?" asked the driver, noting Nita's shiver.

She nodded. "Yeah, it's a bit cold."

They pulled away from the airport. A long stretch of highway blurred into a different highway, this one weaving high above the ground in between towering glass condos and businesses. The condos were so close to the highway she wondered if she could reach out the window and touch them. Inside, she could see people walking around. Ugh. She couldn't imagine living somewhere so public. Why didn't they close the blinds?

They turned off the highway, and the sun vanished, the world going dark. Buildings towered high above, blocking all natural light and creating an artificial twilight in the center of the city.

Traffic was slower here, and they crawled through downtown for at least half an hour before finally stopping in front of a tall glass and steel building, indistinguishable from every other building around them.

Outside of the building, a metal sign as tall as Nita proclaimed this was the Canadian headquarters for INHUP. Which really just meant it was a bureaucratic building where all the paperwork was done, and all the actual facilities and investigative teams were in some unmarked compound in the suburbs.

In front of the building, a group of protesters squatted, waving illegible signs. Nita angled her head to get a better view.

Quispe raised her eyebrows as she took in the scene. "So, are these protesters angry about giving monsters civil rights, or angry that the Dangerous Unnaturals List sets a bad legal precedent for human rights?"

Bronte snorted. "Neither. These ones are here about a specific case."

A small brown woman in jeans and a Blue Jays jersey walked by, holding up a sign that read DON'T SEND CHILDREN TO MONSTER PRISON. She was joined by her friend, a tall white woman with neon pink and blue hair carrying a sign that read BANNIKS AREN'T EVIL.

Nita leaned back in her seat. She knew there were specialized prisons for certain types of unnaturals who were harder or more dangerous to incarcerate, but she had to agree with the protesters here—banniks shouldn't be in them.

Banniks were no more dangerous than any human. Eastern European, and traditionally called bathhouse spirits because they loved all things warm, people liked to say they could predict the future. The truth was that they were simply keen observers, and they never forgot anything. Perfect memory and a talent for seeing patterns. If a man isn't coming home at night, it doesn't take a seer to figure out that there's trouble in a marriage.

"What happened?" Nita asked as they passed the protesters and turned down a sloping ramp toward a parking garage.

"A pair of kids robbed a convenience store at gunpoint, they both got sentenced to a year. The human one went off to juvie, but now there's a kerfuffle over which prison the bannik should go to."

Nita frowned. "What's the argument for sending the bannik to an unnatural prison?"

"The claws."

The only external way to tell a bannik from a human was their fingernails, which grew curved and pointed. Most kept them trimmed short and painted them to hide their blackish color, and they could pass.

Nita was silent, shuddering. She imagined what would happen if she were ever captured and charged. In a human prison, she'd soon be murdered and eaten by people who wanted to see if eating her really did grant them immortality.

In an unnatural prison, she'd probably just be killed by one of the monsters they contained.

Nita swallowed, rubbing her sweaty palms on her pants. She did not want to end up in either prison. It would be a death sentence.

Bronte scanned her card and the parking garage doors opened, metal shutters rattling upward. They parked the car and made their way to the elevator in silence. Nita's sneakers scuffed the concrete floor, and she shivered at the sound, trying to put the idea of prison out of her mind.

The elevator barely fit four people, and Nita wedged herself as deeply into the corner as she could to avoid touching anyone. There was a soft ding every floor they passed, and Nita's heart began to race, as her meeting with her mother changed from a threat in the future into the very real present.

The doors opened to reveal polished white marble floor, high ceilings, and far too many mirrored surfaces.

A woman waited in front of the reception desk, just below the massive blue and white arrow of the INHUP logo that adorned the back wall. Her figure was slim and curvy, and her black hair was tied back severely, but not quite well enough that Nita couldn't pick out the hint of red dye on the tips tucked into the bun.

Nita stopped.

Her mother turned around to face her, a wide smile spreading shark-like across her pale face. "Hello, Nita."

SEVEN

NITA'S MOTHER APPROACHED, smile stretching. Her lipstick was such a dark red it was nearly black, making her look like a combination of Snow White and the Evil Queen.

"Darling." Her voice was sticky and syrupy sweet.

Nita hunched her shoulders out of instinct. That was never a good voice. She cleared her throat. "Aunt Theresa."

Her mother's sharp eyes took in the two INHUP agents, and then she walked up to Nita and enfolded her in a hug.

Nita stiffened, her whole body going rigid like she'd seen Medusa. Her hands were fisted at her sides, and her heart beat a panicked pace in her chest.

Nita's mom was hugging her.

Nita's mom never hugged her.

That was something her father did. Her father took her in his arms and rested her head against his chest, warm and steady. Her father brushed the tears from her eyes and placed a gentle hand on her back. Her father loved her unconditionally.

Her father was gone now.

This hug wasn't warm or gentle. It was sharp and angular and awkward, and Nita just wanted to crawl away from it. Her mother's fingers curled into her back, nails digging in painfully. If Nita were anyone else, they'd have left bruises.

Finally, mercifully, her mother pulled away and smiled at the INHUP agents, her teeth so white they looked bleached. "Thank you so much for bringing her back."

Both INHUP agents looked uncomfortable under her mother's smile. Nita could see it in the way Quispe's hand twitched at her side, and Bronte turned away, eyebrows drawn together ever so slightly.

Bronte cleared her throat and glanced between them. "You're her aunt? I thought Nita mentioned you being her mother's sister."

"That's right."

"But you're . . ."

Bronte waved her hand vaguely, and Nita sighed.

"I take after my father," Nita answered, not even having to ask what Bronte was referring to. It was always the same thing.

Back in North America only a few hours and this already. She'd forgotten how tedious it was. Her skin wasn't particularly dark, but it was noticeably darker than her mother's, and in the years she'd spent living in the US when she was younger, half-formed statements like Bronte's had been a common feature. They never got less annoying.

Bronte smiled wide, clearly hoping it would cover the sudden awkwardness. It didn't. "Oh, of course."

Beside her, Quispe might have rolled her eyes.

"Well," Bronte said, clapping her hands together. "Let's get the paperwork started, shall we?"

The paperwork, as it turned out, took nearly half an hour and required multiple pieces of ID (all fake) from her mother, signatures on at least three forms from both of them, and her mother showing a picture of the two of them together when Nita was younger. Nita hadn't even known there *were* pictures of her and her mother together. She wondered if it was Photoshopped.

Nita was also required to give contact information independent of her mother, so she gave one of her many extra email addresses. One she rarely logged into but she could still check if she was so inclined.

When everything was done, Quispe and Bronte each handed Nita a card with their contact information. Nita pocketed them with a smile, though she doubted she'd ever use either.

They also gave her the new passport, but her mother plucked it out of the air and pocketed it before Nita could even raise a hand. Typical.

Then it was over, and the two of them were walking out of the Toronto INHUP office.

Her mother grabbed Nita's arm the instant they were outside and tugged her to the curb. The street was four lanes , but felt oppressively narrow with the towering buildings on either side and the press of traffic, cars, pedestrians, and cyclists.

Her mother flagged down a taxi and dragged Nita into it. Nita twisted out of her grip as they got in, and her mother gave her a sharp glance.

"Where to, ma'am?" asked the driver, a middle-aged white woman with owlish glasses. No less than six air fresheners hung from her rearview mirror, all of them shaped like books.

Her mother waved her hand. "Just drive straight for a while."

They moved through traffic faster than Nita expected, but still not quickly. Shifting in her seat, she looked over at her mother. There were so many things she wanted to ask, but she didn't even know how to start, and she didn't think she could with the taxi driver listening in anyway.

Her mother unclipped her hair, and it tumbled down to her shoulders in slinky black and red strands, framing a heart-shaped face, like Nita's. Same jawline, same nose, same lips.

Same power.

"Do you have a phone?" her mother asked suddenly.

Nita hesitated. "Yes."

"Give it here." Her mother held out her hand.

Nita crossed her arms and shifted away, pressing her body against the door. "Why?"

"I'm going to throw it out the window."

Nita's eyes widened. "*Why?*"

"It could be bugged."

"I'll turn it off, then." Nita pulled it out, careful to turn away so her body shielded her phone. She didn't want her mother reaching out and stealing it.

"There are hacks that can fake that."

"Fine. I'll turn it off, put it on the floor. Wait until we get out. If it's warm, it's still on and bugged. If it's cold, it's fine."

Her mother pursed her lips, then nodded. "Fine."

Nita powered the phone off and placed it on the carpeted floor of the taxi, then used her foot to shield it and prevent it from sliding her mother's way.

They continued riding in silence for the next few minutes. Her mother's fingers drummed a steady rhythm against the car door, and Nita's fingernails dug into the fabric of her sweat-pants.

When the taxi approached an intersection, her mother opened the door without warning, and the taxi driver cried out.

"We're getting out here." Her mother pulled money out of her pocket. Purple money, and plasticky, like it was from a board game.

"It's the middle of the road!" the driver yelped, but she took the money.

Her mother jerked her head, and Nita picked up her phone from the ground and followed. The surface of the phone was cool to the touch.

Nita mentally let out a sigh of relief as she pocketed it. Not bugged.

Her mother raised an eyebrow at the phone. She pursed her lips but said nothing, just wove between the honking cars until she hit sidewalk. Nita followed.

They were out of the downtown core, and the sun was once again visible. The buildings on the street seemed to be two or three stories, mostly made of faded red brick. Quirky signs advertised boutique shops, and restaurants with lavishly painted entrances invited people to come in for dinner.

The streets were crowded with people, long queues of chatty

teens and university students gathering in front of the bubble tea shops, many restaurants full to bursting. The crowds on the street itself were heavy, and they flowed like water, pushing people along at the same pace. A small Asian girl stopped in front of a storefront with a squeal of glee, grabbing her hijabi friend and tugging her toward the store, and the people continued to flow around them, never stopping or slowing, just adapting.

Behind the cheery street, rows and rows of towering white and gray condo buildings clawed their way toward the clouds and, beyond them, the not-so-distant monolith towers of downtown.

A streetcar trundled by, or Nita assumed it was a streetcar. It went along rails set into the road, and it was red and black, but it was smooth and streamlined like a high-speed train.

Nita's mother snapped her fingers, and Nita spun to her and glared. She hated when her mother did that.

"Come, Nita." Her mother's frown vanished into a thin, sharkish smile. "Are you hungry? Why don't we get lunch?"

Nita's stomach rumbled before she could respond, and her mother's smile stretched. No, not sharkish. Snake-like.

Her mother merged seamlessly into the crowd and Nita stumbled in behind. They passed dozens of restaurants, but her mother didn't look at them. There was even an outlet store called "The Black Market," and for a moment Nita wondered if that was where they were going, but her mother strode past it without a glance.

When they finally stopped, it was in front of a restaurant that advertised authentic Venezuelan food. It was the first restaurant they'd seen without a line out the door, and Nita had to admit waiting in line in these kinds of crowds held no appeal.

The inside was small and dark. A large round table was occupied by a group of laughing college students, and a series of smaller square tables lined the wall. The whole place echoed with the noise of dozens of people all trying to talk over each other, covering the faint music in the background. The counter looked more like a coffee shop than a restaurant, with a till and a row of glass containers with muffins and cookies. There was a coconut cream cake in a display case that looked particularly good.

Nita's mother chose a sheltered table for two. The waiter appeared in an instant with the menus. Her mother didn't even look at them as she ordered a cocktail and an arepa. Nita blinked down at the menu and ordered the first thing she saw, the special of the day. She liked ceviche and was too ravenous to wait for the waiter to come back later. She hadn't eaten since Bogotá.

Once the waiter was gone, Nita shifted in her seat. Across from her, her mother was still, a faint smile on her face as she examined Nita.

Nita cleared her throat. "I—"

Nita was interrupted when the waiter returned with her mother's midafternoon cocktail.

Her mother swirled the drink and took a sip. "I've heard you've had quite the adventure."

That was one way of putting it. "Yes."

Her mother smiled. "I'm very impressed, Nita."

"About what?"

"You." Her mother put the drink down. "You managed to not only break out, but eliminate the culprits. I'd expect nothing less of my child."

Nita felt a buzz of pride at the praise, and she sat up straighter. Compliments were few and far between when it came to her mother.

Just as soon as the buzz came, though, it was gone, replaced by an oily, heavy sludge in her chest. "Why didn't you come?"

"Hmm?" Her mother sipped her drink casually.

"Why didn't you come help me?" Nita's voice broke a little. "You knew where I was. You had to know."

"I did." Her mother looked down at her hands. "I knew."

"Then *why?*"

Her mother sighed. "I'm sorry, Nita. I confess, I thought you'd run off after our little tiff over the prisoner. I didn't realize until I saw the online video that you'd been abducted."

Nita clenched her jaw. If she'd truly wanted to run from her mother, she'd have done it when she was freeing Fabricio.

"Fine. But then why didn't you come when you saw the video and had confirmation I'd been kidnapped?" Nita pressed. "I was there a long time after it was uploaded."

Her mother leaned back and pursed her lips. "I tried, Nita."

"You *tried?*" Nita's voice went high and sharp. What kind of lame excuse was that?

Her mother's jaw tightened further, and she snapped, "I have a lot of enemies, and going to Mercado de la Muerte is difficult at the best of times. I flew into Tabatinga to hire a boat and encountered some . . . problems."

Nita raised an eyebrow in disbelief. "You were run out of Tabatinga? *You.*"

Her mother ground her teeth. "I'm not a god, Anita. I'm not all-powerful."

Nita had never expected to hear her mother admit anything like that. She was too proud. Nita swallowed, trying to fathom what could have stopped someone like her mom. "What happened?"

"An old enemy of mine made it . . . difficult for me to stay in Tabatinga. It's not important." Her mother brushed it aside. "I survived."

Nita crossed her arms, "And then what, you gave up?"

"No, I was in the process of hiring someone else to pick you up for me when I heard the market had been destroyed."

Nita looked away, her anger melting.

Her mother had tried to come for her. Just knowing that set something tight and painful loose inside. The childish, relieved part of her wanted to cry, but the rest of her knew that her mother would only get angry if Nita started weeping on her.

Her mother took another sip. "Have you heard about your father?"

The sludge in Nita's chest rose back up, threatening to choke and overwhelm her. Her eyes burned, but she refused to wipe them in front of her mother. "Yes."

Her mother nodded and suddenly she looked tired. Nita could see the shadows of grief under her eyes, and the new lines carved around her mouth.

Then it was gone, in one sharp motion, and her mother was

her mother again, cold and cruel. "Well, good. I don't have to explain, then."

Nita pressed her lips together. "I want to know who the vampire is."

Her mother tilted her head. "Vampire?"

"My father's killer."

Her mother's gaze sharpened, and her casual demeanor was gone. "Explain. Now."

Nita turned away. "A vampire came to see me while I was in the market. He wanted to know how to find you. He was between one and three hundred years old, I'd say. Hair was brown and white striped like a zebra."

Vampires were Eastern European, fast and strong and long-lived. But the older they got, the more white their hair had. And the whiter their hair, the weaker they were, meaning the young were wildly strong and the old were weaker than kittens, but with centuries of knowledge to draw on. Usually around seven hundred years was as long as they could last before dropping dead.

"And how do you know this was your father's killer?"

"When I went to INHUP, I tried to get them to call Dad." Nita tried to push down the pain, the memories, and the oozing wound in her soul. She would not show weakness in front of her mother. "They had security footage of Zebra-stripes in the area when Dad died."

Her mother's fingers drummed on the table. "I see."

Nita pressed her fists into her legs, trying not to tremble in rage. "INHUP told me he was a hit man for hire."

"Yes." Her mother nodded absently. "I know him."

"Mom," Nita snapped. "What is going on?"

Her mother waved it away. "Nothing."

"My father is dead. It's hardly nothing."

"Nothing I'm willing to talk about." Her mother's mouth thinned. "It's personal."

"Personal." Nita's voice was deadpan. "Would this have anything to do with Fabricio Tácunan's father? You know, the boy you kidnapped."

Her mother mildly scolded, "I told you not to talk to him."

"Yes, so I wouldn't find out you were using him as *black-mail.*"

Her mother *tsk*ed. "If you knew half the things he'd done, you wouldn't be so quick to judge."

"Fabricio?" She already knew plenty he deserved to die for.

"No, his father." There was an unspoken "obviously" in her tone.

Nita ground her teeth. "So you kidnapped his kid."

"Nita, enough."

Nita pressed her hands into the table and leaned forward. What the hell was her mother involved in? Vampire hit men. Kidnapping powerful people's children. Something bigger was going on here.

She narrowed her eyes. "Does Fabricio's kidnapping have something to do with Dad's death?"

"You think Alberto Tácunan hired the vampire to kill your father?"

Nita hadn't actually thought of it in those specific terms, but it made sense, now that she thought about it. "As retaliation."

"I suppose it's possible," her mother admitted.

Nita couldn't believe how calm her mother was. She'd basically started a turf war that had led to Nita's father dying and Nita sold on the black market. And she didn't even sound apologetic.

"Are you kidding me?" Nita rose. "Are you fucking kidding me?"

"Nita, sit down."

"No." Nita took a step away, shaking her head. "I'm done. I'm done with this."

"Don't be ridiculous." Her mother took another sip of her drink. "Sit down and we can continue discussing this like normal people."

"I've heard plenty."

"Fine." Her mother shrugged. "Once you're done sulking outside, you can come back here."

"I won't be back."

Nita was shocked when the words came out of her mouth. She'd never defied her mother to her face before. Always sneaking around behind her back, hiding her betrayals. Releasing prisoners in the dead of night, stashing college money under her mattress.

Not this time.

Her mother just raised an eyebrow. "You're being ridiculous. Of course you'll be back. You need me."

"I don't."

"In case you've forgotten," her mother hissed, finally rising, "your face is all over the internet, and all the wrong people know what you can do. You have a giant target painted on your back. You need me because those people will never stop looking for you. I can protect you. I can keep you hidden."

"I don't want to hide." Nita's voice was cold, and her spine straight. "I have plans for my life, and they don't involve being hidden. I'm going to go to college. I'm going to become an expert in unnatural biology and present at conferences."

"Oh, not this again." Her mother rolled her eyes exaggeratedly. "You'll be kidnapped and murdered and eaten before that ever happens."

There was truth to that. Nita knew it would be dangerous. She knew people would attack her.

So she was going to make sure everyone was so afraid of her that no amount of money would tempt them to attack her.

Nita let out a breath and turned to leave.

Her mother snapped her hand around Nita's wrist. Blood-red nails dug into Nita's skin.

"Who will give you bodies to dissect?" her mother hissed.

"I'll find them myself."

"And money?" Her mother's lips curled up. "You do know you need money to live."

"I know." Nita didn't have a cent to her name. "I'll find a way."

Her mother's eyes narrowed. They stood, silent, staring at each other for long moments. Sweat beaded down Nita's back, but she refused to lose this staring contest.

"If you leave, you will be annihilated." Her mother's voice was a whisper. "And I won't lift a finger to help you."

Nita suppressed a shiver. There was a cadence of prophecy to those words.

She clenched her jaw and twisted her wrist from her mother's grasp. "I don't need you."

Then she left, her mother's gaze burning a hole in her. But Nita didn't turn back.

EIGHT

THE COOL SPRING AIR was bracing as Nita strode down the street, freezing her lungs until they burned. The crush of people had thinned, allowing her to walk faster, nearly jogging away from the restaurant. Her heart raced, and her whole body hummed with adrenaline. She felt like she'd chugged an energy drink—buzzed and nauseous at the same time.

She didn't know where she was going, but she needed to keep moving. After a block, she looked back, half convinced her mother was following three steps behind her, shark smile on her face, ready to tear Nita apart for her defiance.

There was no one. Just a few other pedestrians and a panhandler with a flute trilling a slightly off-key song.

Nita kept walking, wanting to gain distance from her mother.

She still couldn't believe it.

Nita had defied her mother. To her *face.*

It was impossible.

This wasn't the first time Nita had gone against her mother. There was the dact incident when she was twelve. Nita still occasionally woke up with nightmares about the dead dact bodies her mother had left in Nita's bed. But that had been a secret. She had skulked out in the middle of the night, never confronting her mother.

Nita had only confronted her mother to her face once.

Nita had been fourteen. She and her mother had been living in Germany for two years, and her mother was talking about relocating them to Vietnam so she could find new unnaturals to hunt. Nita had been delighted at the idea of not having to dissect so many unicorn bodies. The first one was interesting—the four hundredth was not.

She'd decided that, given that things were already changing, it was a good time to call a family meeting to ask for a few other changes. She'd wanted to tell both her parents she'd decided to go to college and ask them to let her take the test for her GED. She'd already found several places to study and could take the test in Hanoi, so actually getting her parents onboard was the final hurdle.

Her father was on Skype, his face taking up the whole laptop screen. There in spirit, but not there in flesh to protect her if things went wrong.

And oh, how wrong they'd gone.

First, her mother had laughed, like it was some sort of joke. When Nita insisted she was serious, her mother's smile had died and she'd said no. Nita, angry, young, and stupid, had jutted out her chin and arrogantly asked, "Why?"

Before Nita could blink, her mother had grabbed her wrist, yanked her so close their faces were inches apart, and hissed, "Because I said so."

Nita didn't remember her mother letting her go, though she must have. She didn't remember going to her room to cry and hold a GED study prep book close to her chest. Her mind skipped all that, to the next memory, of her mother slowly tearing out the pages of the study guide one at a time until the book was nothing but a hard shell and a pile of paper.

Then her mother had whispered, "If you have time to waste on this, then you have time to run more errands."

Nita hadn't objected. She'd spent the next month going with her mother on her hunts. Nita would wait in the car or outside the building until the hard part was over, and only come in to help her mother load the body. It was messy and bloody, and her hands were always painted with red.

She'd taken to wearing her dissection gloves at all times. She never knew when she'd be called on to cut a body up to fit in a small suitcase.

After a month of this, her mother had casually asked, "Are you still thinking of college?"

Nita had tensed, sensing a trap. "No. Of course not."

"Why not?"

She'd looked away. "Because you said so."

And her mother had smiled, long and thin, and things went back to the way they were before. No more trips with her mother. No more trips anywhere, really. Just Nita and her dissection room, peace and silence.

Nita had learned a lesson, though not the one her mother wanted her to. She didn't stop wanting to go to college, she just kept it a secret. She'd stolen money, hoping to save enough to take her GED and apply for college. If her mother didn't know, then she couldn't punish Nita.

But Nita had never defied her mother to her face like she had today. This was more defiant than she'd been in the college discussion, more than the dact war, more even than freeing Fabricio.

Her hands were still shaking.

She wondered what her punishment would be.

Squeezing her eyes shut, Nita swallowed back the terror oozing up her throat like acid, and instead focused on praising herself. She'd done a good thing. She'd stood up for herself. She hadn't let her mother trample her dreams.

Nita looked up at the bright sun and let the warmth suffuse her body. She leaned against the side of a brick building and the rough surface scraped her clothes. She took another breath of cold air, and her lungs felt like they expanded wider than she'd ever thought. People walked down the street, ignoring her, and the cool air was bracing. Almost cleansing.

It was strange. She felt terribly vulnerable, but also wonderfully light, almost giddy. She was frightened of the uncertainty, of the depth of how much she had to do and how little she had. But she was also full of helium, like the sun, and she just wanted to smile.

It was like she'd shed a great burden when she'd left her mother. She'd been carrying a planet on her shoulders, and now that it was gone, she could see the vastness of the universe and how small she and the planet she'd been holding were. It was daunting, but it was also breathtakingly beautiful.

She was alone. And that was okay.

A blast of cool air made her shiver.

She was alone—which meant she was completely unprotected, and the entire black market wanted her in a cage to take apart and sell.

But they didn't know where she was. She had time to formulate a plan.

She thought about her end goal—to become a researcher in unnatural science, to present papers at university conferences, to research and dissect various unnaturals with the blessing of universities and governments around the world.

She thought about the black market that stood in her way. And how she could get rid of it.

She needed the market to respect her, to fear attacking her so much they left her alone. But how could she ever give herself that kind of reputation? Especially now, alone, with no money, in yet another foreign country?

She stilled. She didn't have to do this alone.

She pulled out her cell phone and connected to the Starbucks Wi-Fi across the street.

Swallowing, she sent an email to Kovit. *Hey. Are you in Toronto now? Can we meet?*

The response came a moment later.

I'd love to. Where are you now?

Nita smiled and began setting up a rendezvous.

NINE

NITA STOOD IN FRONT of a small café, a wooden sign with black letters burned into it hanging above the door. It had a jungle theme that made Nita shift from foot to foot, reluctant to step in. It felt like stepping into the past, returning to the market along the Amazon River. If she opened the door, Boulder or Reyes might be waiting for her, tranquilizer guns and chains in hand.

Her missing toe tingled, and she bit her lip, trying to banish the memories of Mirella screaming from her mind. She could hardly believe only a week had passed.

Nita's fingers curled around an invisible scalpel. She focused on all the wonderful dissections she'd do when she had a moment to herself, trying to soothe her nerves.

Inside, the café was full of cushy faux-leather chairs that wasted far too much space and small, too-short tables. The walls were patterned with more trees and plants. A painted monkey stared out at her with huge blue eyes and a wide, toothy smile. In the corner, a jaguar hung on a tree, almost completely obscured by a real, leafy plant in the corner. Even the ceiling was painted green with leaves meant to emulate the claustrophobic sense of being trapped beneath the canopy. The room was lit with lanterns that gave the café a dim, almost romantic atmosphere.

It looked nothing like the actual Amazon, but that didn't make it any less surreal to step inside. It was fuller than Nita expected, and the noise assaulted her ears, voices chattering and echoing in the small space. She ran her eyes across the seating, searching for a familiar figure.

There.

Kovit lounged in a cushy chair, staring pensively at a picture on the wall of a group of grinning bleached-blond girls holding a giant snake. His eyes were dark and fathomless, and thick dark eyebrows were arced in a question. He was smiling slightly, and there was something undeniably *wrong* with the smile.

Nita's heart did a familiar fear flip when she saw him, and she flexed her sweaty palms.

She swallowed, watching him for a moment. He looked so innocuous in a dark green sweater and jeans, so . . . normal. Like he belonged here. At the same time, there was an indefinable sense of danger from him. People who walked by gave his seat a wide berth. They didn't seem to even be doing it consciously—they just walked all the way around another table to avoid him, and sat at the table next to him despite how crowded it was.

It was like their subconscious could sense the danger and avoided him, even though their conscious couldn't identify why.

Nita had always heard that girls liked "bad boys," but none of the girls were giving Kovit appreciative glances or approaching him, despite the fact that he was definitely attractive. He'd eaten pain recently, and his face glowed with health, his hair as shiny as a shampoo commercial. His eyes were dark and thickly lashed, and his skin was warm brown.

She wondered if the girls-like-bad-boys stereotype was a lie, or if Kovit was so far from bad boy and so deep into straight-up monster that he didn't count anymore.

When she was in the jungle, it had been easy to justify allying with Kovit to herself. He was a monster, no question, but they had the same goals, and working together was the fastest way to get out. But out here, in the real world, it was different.

She knew that he hurt people. She knew he enjoyed it. He'd never made a secret of the fact that he could get his pain without torture, by sitting in emergency rooms or going to a war zone. But he chose not to.

He chose to make his own pain. He chose to be the monster people painted him as.

Her mind knew this, but her feet carried her over to him. Her heart rate spiked, and Nita's ability let her sense every red blood cell rushing through each vein and capillary.

She stopped in front of him, and he turned his gaze on her. His mouth stretched into a warped grin, crooked and slightly off, though she was hard-pressed to say how.

She grinned back, and she wondered if her smile was as broken and twisted as his was.

He laughed and rose. "Nita."

"Kovit."

She waited for him to take the lead, because she had no idea what to do now. Shake hands? That felt weird and formal. Hug? Equally weird and too intimate.

Social situations were confusing.

Nita sat down quickly, before he could do anything or the distance between them could stretch.

"Hungry?" he asked, still standing.

Her stomach growled, and she remembered she hadn't eaten anything with her mother. She'd left before the food came. It was already nearly dinnertime.

"Very," she admitted. Then she hesitated. "I have no money."

He waved it away. "This one's on me."

She sagged in relief, and he flashed her a grin and went to the counter. His walk was a little slow, and one hand hovered over his side before falling again. Over the bullet wound he'd gotten trying to save her from being cut up.

Nita shoved away the memory, but the sound of the gunshot and the feel of the knife against her skin lingered in her mind.

Kovit approached the cashier with a smile Nita guessed was meant to be friendly but wasn't. The cashier, a pretty black girl with cornrows, flinched, glasses slipping down her nose and catching on her nose ring. She pushed them back up, and punched his order in with trembling hands.

He returned a moment later, leaving the girl at the till still shaking.

"Did you really need to terrify the cashier?" Nita sighed.

Kovit let out a breath and ran a hand through his hair. "It wasn't intentional. I'm not used to people."

Nita understood. He hadn't had to interact with normal people much in his life. She didn't know how restrictive the mafia family he'd worked for had been, but she'd repeatedly got the sense that the creepy smile and constant fear was something he'd worked to inspire as a survival mechanism. And she didn't think he'd ever been in a situation where he needed to turn it off.

Nita never had to interact with people much either, but for her, it was more a lack of skills than using the wrong skills in a situation.

A moment later the girl came over, two plates of curry balanced on her hands. Her eyes kept nervously flicking to Kovit as she handed them over, and she walked quickly away once freed of her burden.

Nita attacked the food, shoveling food into her mouth like she hadn't eaten in a week.

Kovit laughed and leaned back in his seat. "Did INHUP not feed you?"

Nita rolled her eyes and swallowed a bite of chickpeas. They were a bit salty. She'd forgotten how much North America liked salt. "Not since this morning."

He raised an eyebrow. "I see you enjoyed your time there."

Nita nearly choked. "Hardly."

"I'm all ears." He put down his curry and propped his chin in his hand.

Nita sighed. "It was just uncomfortable."

He raised his other eyebrow. He wasn't going to let it go.

She sighed, and leaned closer and lowered her voice so no one else would overhear. "I had to murder someone without getting caught, and it didn't go right."

"Well, you clearly did the not-getting-caught part right, or you wouldn't be here." He grinned, lowering his voice to match hers.

Nita couldn't help but grin back. "For now."

"So, who were you trying to murder?"

Nita gave him a quick rundown of what happened with Fabricio.

"Well," Kovit said when she finished. "At least when you're both out of INHUP's clutches it'll be easier to murder him."

"Agreed. And I won't have to use poison." Nita clenched her jaw. "I want to make him scream for what he's done."

Kovit's eyes darkened, and he licked his lips. "I can help with that."

A small thrill sizzled through her body. "I might take you up on that offer."

"Anytime."

She shivered at his voice, full of dark promises.

Someone walked by, and both of them went silent. Kovit leaned back, the darkness in his face vanishing.

"How goes your search for your sister?" Nita asked to fill the sudden silence.

Kovit's sister wasn't a zannie, like him, just a regular human. She'd missed that little genetic gift. Kovit had told Nita that he hadn't seen his sister since he was ten years old, when she'd hidden him from INHUP agents storming their house to murder their mother. INHUP agents Kovit himself had called after his mother tortured his classmate.

Shortly after, Kovit had been scooped up by an American criminal organization and taken away from Thailand. When he and Nita had parted in Brazil, he'd said now that he was free, he wanted to find his sister.

Kovit sighed. "I don't know."

"You don't know how the search is going?"

He clarified. "I'm second-guessing if it's such a good idea."

"Why wouldn't it be?"

"What if she doesn't speak English?"

Nita blinked. "So? Don't you speak Thai?"

"I did." He looked away. "I mean, I do. But I haven't spoken it since I left Thailand when I was ten. There was no one to talk to. So I don't know. What if I've forgotten how to speak?"

Nita leaned forward. "You'll relearn. Or maybe she speaks English. You won't know if you don't try and find her."

"I did. Try. No hits online."

"Yet."

"Yet," he agreed.

She raised her eyebrows. "It sounds to me like you're making excuses. Did something happen to make you doubt if you should look for her?"

"No," he said, but he looked away, and changed the subject. "We need to find somewhere to stay tonight."

Nita let the topic lie. "Yeah. A hotel?"

"Hotels are expensive. Hostels are cheaper."

"One of those, then."

"All right." He hesitated. "Do you have ID?"

Nita shook her head.

"You need to show ID. It's the law in Canada." He shrugged at her look. "I Googled."

She sighed, thinking of her brand-new passport in her mother's hands. She wasn't getting that back anytime soon. "Maybe you can book a hostel and just check in yourself, and then sneak me in the window?"

Kovit tipped his head back. "Not a bad idea. But I think the only way we could do it would be in a hotel."

She frowned. "Do you have the money for that?"

"Nope." He mused. "I could mug someone?"

"Let's hold off on that as long as we can." Nita's answer was a bit too fast, and she took a breath before she explained, "I want to maintain a low profile."

"All right. Do you have a better idea to get money?"

"No." Nita snorted, yanking her hair back from her face and tying it back. "I feel like all we ever do is try and figure out how to get money when we run out."

"Money makes the world go round." Kovit's voice was singsong.

She grinned. "That it does."

They were quiet for a time, before Nita finally offered, "We could sleep in the park?"

Kovit made a small sound of distaste. "No."

"I don't know what else to do."

She could contact her mother. But after her dramatic exit, she'd rather sleep on a bench than go back to her mother.

Kovit hesitated. "There is one other option."

"What?"

He ran a hand through his hair, and wouldn't meet her eyes. "I was in Toronto before, three years ago, with my friend Matt and the Family."

"Who's Matt?"

Kovit blinked and looked away. "He was my friend in the Family. He screwed up, and I was supposed to torture him as punishment, but—"

"But you helped him escape. And as punishment you got shipped off to South America." Nita nodded. "I remember."

Kovit cleared his throat. "Well, anyways, a few years ago when we were in Toronto, Matt had an . . . incident."

"What kind of incident?"

"The kind that the Family couldn't find out about." He shivered.

Nita raised an eyebrow. "What happened?"

"It, uh, it involved a body to clean up."

"Matt murdered someone?"

Kovit shrugged. "I mean, you didn't think he was some saint, did you? He worked for the Family. He was friends with *me*."

Nita snorted. "*I'm* friends with you."

"Yes, and you've got a bigger body count than me and him combined."

Nita opened her mouth to deny it. She wasn't like Kovit. She didn't thrive on others' pain, she did what needed to be done to survive. But she closed her mouth without saying anything. Because in terms of sheer numbers, he might be right.

She'd burned a whole market full of people alive.

A strange emptiness opened inside her when she realized

that. It wasn't that she hadn't known that she'd done something awful, but she'd always just assumed she wasn't as evil as Kovit, that she had the moral high ground on him.

She wasn't so sure anymore. And that thought made her stomach lurch, made her wonder how skewed her perception of her own misdeeds was becoming that she hadn't even realized when she'd crossed that line.

Nita forced a breath out, and tried to draw them both back into the story. "All right, so, you needed to get rid of the body."

"Yeah. Matt knew someone who ran a cleanup service for incidents like that."

"Meaning this wasn't the first time Matt had needed a cleanup." Nita's voice was deadpan.

Kovit shrugged and wouldn't look at her. "I doubt it."

Nita shivered, something in the back of her mind deeply uneasy at the thought. Kovit wouldn't look her in the eye when he talked about the body. If she didn't know better, she'd think he was ashamed.

Any crime that made Kovit feel guilty was *serious*.

She cleared her throat before imagination let her take that thought too far. "So you think this person who covered up for Matt will put us up? Seems risky, and we already have a money problem."

"He takes payment in information too." Kovit still wouldn't look at her.

Nita considered what she had to offer. A list of corrupt INHUP officials. Knowledge about her mother, the fate of Mercado de la Muerte. "That might work."

Kovit took out his phone, but hesitated. "There's something else you should know about this guy."

"What?"

Kovit sighed and leaned back. "He's a kelpie."

A kelpie.

Well, fuck.

"You want to trust a kelpie?" Nita was incredulous.

"You're trusting me, and I'm a zannie," he snapped.

Nita flinched. She swallowed and went to tell him that was different, but stopped, because it wasn't, not really.

Nita sighed. "Fine. So you trust this kelpie?"

"Not at all."

She glared. "Then why are we even considering this?"

"Because we're out of options." He raised an eyebrow. "Unless you have another idea?"

She didn't.

"Fine." She frowned. "But do we have any assurance he won't drag us under the water and eat our rotting corpses?"

Kovit shook his head. "None."

TEN

KOVIT CALLED THE KELPIE and set things up. After he hung up, he placed his phone on the table.

Her eyes snagged on Kovit's phone. A *smartphone.* Last she'd seen, he'd had a dinosaur-age flip phone, and it had been shattered across the floor of their prison in the market.

"Nice phone," she said casually. "Where'd you get it?"

"Detroit." He flashed her a grin. "I needed a phone so I mugged someone before I left."

Nita found herself unsurprised. She didn't ask if his victim had survived the mugging. She didn't want to know.

"Can't they track it?" she asked.

"Nah. I factory reset it and tossed the SIM card." Kovit clicked his phone off. "You can also thank that Detroit man for your dinner."

Nita snorted. "Speaking of Detroit . . ."

The smile fell from his face, and his shoulders slumped. He opened his mouth, then hesitated and looked around at the crowded shop. "I don't really want to talk about it here."

Nita raised her eyebrows. He was willing to talk about

mugging someone in the café, but not whatever happened there. She wondered if he'd killed someone. If so, she hoped he'd dealt with the body before he left. She didn't want the police on his tail.

She shivered at the thought. Even without them knowing he was a zannie, Kovit would be in danger from the police. They were in North America now, and law enforcement wasn't kind to brown boys. Or brown girls, for that matter. They would have to be on their guard.

She reconsidered. She wasn't actually sure what Canada was like. She knew about the States; it seemed like every day there was a splashy tale of police brutality on the news. But Canada was a mystery. Better safe than sorry, though. They needed to stay as far away from the authorities as possible.

"Well," Nita said, "you can tell me on the way to this kelpie."

Kovit hesitated a moment, then nodded. "All right."

They rose and left the restaurant. The sky had darkened while they had dinner, and now the street was lit by glowing restaurant windows and bright condos, squares of light stacked on top of each other like a ladder to the moon.

The temperature had dropped, and the wind had a bit of a bite. Nita almost wished she had a jacket. This morning she'd been sweating in Bogotá, and now she was shivering in Toronto. It wasn't even that cold, but it had been years since she'd been anywhere that could be considered cold, and she wasn't used to it. She wondered if it would be weird if she stepped a little closer to absorb Kovit's body heat.

You're being ridiculous. You have complete control of your body. Use it.

Nita blinked. She immediately enacted measures to reduce heat loss, closing her pores, increasing circulation, and upping her internal body heat the slightest bit.

There. Much better.

They walked away, Kovit leading them with Google Maps. He hesitated every few steps, until Nita took the phone from him, glanced at it, and pointed them in the opposite direction.

"Thanks," he said.

"No worries." Nita had lived in five different countries in her life, and traveled to more on her parents' hunts, and she'd gotten lost enough that she'd learned over the years how to orient herself quickly and get herself found again.

The crowded streets dropped away into the darkness of less populated side streets, and suddenly it felt less like a crowded city of flashing lights and too many people and more like wandering the market at night. Dark and full of monsters she couldn't quite see.

She shivered softly. She was out of the market. She needed to stop seeing it in every shadow that looked a little strange.

Nita forced her mind away from the memories that tried to boil up, and gave Kovit a sideways glance as they walked. "So, are you going to tell me what happened in Detroit?"

Kovit's face fell, eyebrows scrunching in and mouth turning down. The flickering shadows from the streetlights along the road made his face shift and change with each step they took. "I haven't really talked about my time with the Family, have I?"

Nita shook her head, mute.

"They took care of me when no one else would. When I was

alone in the world." He looked down at his curled hands. "They were good to me. My handler, Henry, treated me like a son. He made me feel accepted. It was good. Mostly. But—" He tilted his head to the side. "I was isolated. I wasn't allowed to speak Thai. I wasn't allowed to go out."

"It sounds lonely." Nita thought of her own childhood, locked in her parents' house with only books and dead bodies for company.

"I suppose. I didn't really think so at the time, but I did feel trapped. I know why they did it, they didn't want me to develop empathy. Mostly, I was just bored." His eyes were distant. "They eventually let me play games on the internet. I became obsessed with *Pet Crossing*."

Nita gave him a blank look.

"It was a computer game." Kovit clarified. "You took care of magical pets. You could customize their looks. There were games to win clothing and accessories for your pets."

"Oh." Nita had never played video games. Seeing the dreamy smile on Kovit's face, she wondered if she'd missed out.

"Anyway," he continued, "I started looking up online forums to try and find cheats for the game. I made some forum friends. We eventually grew out of *Pet Crossing*, but we'd been in this forum together so long. There were six of us, all around the same age, and we created our own group chat." They stopped at a red light, but he didn't seem to want to stop moving, and he shifted from foot to foot. "Obviously I couldn't talk about my family. So I made up one based off what I thought American families were like."

Nita smiled softly. "I imagine it looked terribly realistic."

He laughed. "In hindsight, it looks so fake. I'm sure everyone knew I was lying."

The light turned green, and they crossed in silence. Kovit stared off into the distance, and Nita gently prompted, "So, Detroit?"

"Detroit." He swallowed. "I thought, after I left you, I could meet some of them. In real life. I'd never been free to before. And I just . . ."

"You wanted to see them." Nita tried to imagine having a friend she'd never met, someone she only knew over the keyboard and the glowing screen, but even the thought seemed absurd. How would she know they were real, that the person on the screen was the same as the one in real life?

But then again, it was just as easy to lie in real life.

The more she thought about it, though, the more she understood. The computer was one more line of defense. She could edit and clarify her sentences before she sent them. She could be silent or lie and say someone had called her away. She could log off when she tired of people, and if she decided she didn't want to be social, she could ignore the messages.

She could see the appeal.

"Yeah. We agreed to do a meet up. Four of us found a time we could all be in the same city. Only May and Vince couldn't make it."

"It didn't go well?"

He hesitated. "It did, at first, I guess. I don't know. May was the one I talked to most. She always got it without me having to explain, you know?" A small, sad smile flitted across his face. “But she wasn’t there. And Vince was usually the person who smoothed things over when stuff got awkward. If he’d been there, it might have been better. But those of us who were there were still—I mean, we were still friends. But over time, I could just see . . .”

“See what?”

“I disturb people.” A thin, creepy smile crossed his face. “And I don’t mind that. It’s worked well in the past.”

“But you didn’t want to scare them.”

He nodded. “And it got worse. It turned out that Anna had severe fibromyalgia.”

Oh. Oh no.

“That comes with considerable pain, doesn’t it?” Nita had a bad feeling about where this was going.

“Yes.” He dragged the *s* sound out into a hiss. “Oh, it can be quite considerable.”

She closed her eyes, not wanting to hear the rest, but unable to quell her curiosity. “What happened?”

“I was me. You’ve seen me with pain. It’s not like I can shut off if I absorb it or not. And I was”—he swallowed—“deeply affected. I couldn’t even function normally. It was so obvious.”

“They found out you’re a zannie?” Fear laced her voice.

“I told them it was seizures,” he admitted. “I don’t know if they believed me. I wouldn’t have believed me.”

Nita wouldn’t either. Seizures usually weren’t enjoyable, and Kovit getting high on pain made him look like he was lost in ecstasy. Though both involved spasming muscles, that was where the similarities ended.

"I didn't want to have to kill them if they learned what I was. I was already disturbed by the fact that I was eating the pain of a friend. It felt so wrong."

"So you left." Nita finished.

He nodded, and his hands curled into claws by his side. He stopped and Nita looked up. They'd reached the subway station.

Hesitating, Nita took a step closer to him, so she was standing beside him, their arms brushing. "Do you regret going to see them?"

"I don't know," he whispered. "I never knew that Anna had fibromyalgia. She never mentioned it. She even tried to hide it when we met up, but, well." His smile was twisted and self-deprecating. "There's no hiding pain from me."

"No, I imagine not."

"We were all keeping so many secrets." His voice was quiet. "Was it ever a real friendship, without any of us seeing the real faces of each other? How many secrets does it take before it's all a lie?"

Nita tilted her head to the side. "I don't know. Do you really need to know every detail about someone to be their friend?"

He looked at her, gaze frank and open. "I don't know."

"You started with shared interests. But you don't really have those anymore."

"No."

"So, what connected you?"

"I don't know." He shook his head, fingers running through his hair and mussing it up. "Things. It never really mattered to me what we talked about. They were just . . . an escape. A way for me to not lose touch with the real world."

He looked down. "When I was feeling awful, I could go online, and they were there. They had no idea what was wrong, but they'd say nice things. They said things I needed to hear. They made me feel like I was more than my life. They gave me perspective."

Nita shrugged. "Maybe that's what friends are, then. People who say the things you need to hear."

He laughed, his smile crooked. "And what do I need to hear?"

She looked at his hand, curled into a fist, and put her own over it.

His skin was warm, and her hand tingled, like mild electricity.

"I'm here, Kovit. I've already seen your monster." She met his eyes. "And I'm not leaving."

He stared at her, eyes dark and brows drawn together. Then he raised his arms and enfolded her in a hug. His arms were gentle as he pulled her close, and their cheeks brushed. Nita's heart raced, and her palms were sweaty where they wrapped around his back.

"I did need to hear that," he whispered. "Thank you."

Her arms tightened around him. "Always."

But she wasn't sure if she was telling the truth.

ELEVEN

THEY WALKED DOWN the stairs to the subway platform in silence. It was crowded near the stairs, so they strolled to the very end of the platform where it was emptier. Thick, towering pillars were scattered along the pathway, holding up the ceiling. Nita wondered if the weight of Toronto above would crush them without the pillars.

A couple of students were sitting on the only set of metal chairs, bulky backpacks in their laps. Kovit met their eyes and smiled at them. It was not a nice smile.

Both of the students stared at Kovit for a moment, then the petite redhead pulled her heavily muscled Asian friend to his feet and tugged him away, heading for the other side of the platform. Their eyes never left Kovit.

It was always fascinating to see bulky, tough-looking people cower in front of Kovit, who was lean and wiry and on the short side.

"You really need to tone down the serial killer look in public," Nita sighed, watching until the two students had completely vanished from view.

He snorted. "It's not that far from the truth."

Nita just raised an eyebrow. "Are you trying to scare me or something?"

He grinned at her, smile wide and crooked. "Are you scared?"

He was smiling, but there was something in his eyes that made Nita pause before she answered.

"No," she lied, even though the screams of the girl he'd tortured still haunted her nightmares. Then she told the truth. "I know you won't hurt me."

But just because she wasn't afraid for herself didn't mean she wasn't afraid at all.

Kovit walked a few steps away to check the timetable, and Nita shuffled her feet before taking a seat on a metal mesh chair. Kovit had scared away its previous occupant for her, it would be rude of her not to use it.

She leaned back and looked up at the cement ceiling and the bright fluorescents jammed into it. There was a noise behind her, but she ignored it, pretending the other passenger wasn't there.

Until a garrote pulled tight across her throat, cutting into her flesh.

Nita tried to gasp, to scream, to make any kind of sound, but the garrote dug into her throat and choked off her voice so only gurgles of blood escaped.

Her fingers shot up, clawing at the garrote, but it was embedded too deep already, she couldn't pull it out. She reached around, grabbing for her attacker. But her hand scrabbled against a smooth jacket, and the garrote sliced into her fingers when she slid them under the wire to block it from her throat.

Time slowed down as her neurons frantically connected the dots. If the garrote severed her artery and she couldn't remove it, it wouldn't matter that she could heal because she would continue to be cut.

She needed to get the garrote out first and focus on healing damage later.

Snarling, she stopped her instinctive repairing of blood vessels that were only getting damaged again, planted her feet on the ground, and shoved backwards.

The back of the metal chair dug into her spine, but Nita ignored the pain.

The human body was capable of incredible feats when scared. Mothers lifted cars off children or broke through walls.

Nita cared more about her life than about any child. And she wasn't going to die here.

Nita prepped her sympathetic nervous system, adrenal glands dumping cortisol and adrenaline into her bloodstream. She restricted her carotid arteries and rerouted her blood directly to her muscles.

Nita jerked backwards, a fast, sudden move using all her strength. Bolts popped from the ground as the chair was ripped from its mooring.

Nita and chair shot back, into her attacker. For a split second when she hit, the pressure from the garrote released, and her hands snapped up and grabbed it, ripping it out of her assailant's hands, even as the wire sliced deep into her fingers.

Nita and her attacker tumbled to the ground, and her

slippery fingers peeled the metal from the tender flesh of her throat. She immediately began repairing the damage to her body, sealing blood vessels and patching skin back together, while her too red handprints left marks on the floor.

A man in a long beige trench coat kicked the chair off of himself, his black army boots clanging against the metal. Nita bared her bloody teeth, pulled herself onto her knees, and grabbed the chair. She swung it at his legs as he attempted to rise. It hit with a crunch, and the man fell back to the ground with an oomph as the air left his lungs.

Then Kovit appeared from behind her attacker, switchblade in hand. Before Nita could blink, he'd pinned the man with a knee and pressed a knife against his throat.

Nita knelt on the floor, gasping for breath, and realized the entire interaction had only taken seconds. She swallowed, throat dry, and heaved a shaky breath.

Voices echoed elsewhere on the platform, and Kovit's eyes flicked to the chair. Nita rose and quietly put it back. She scuffed at the bloody handprints on the gray floor with her sneaker, but they weren't going anywhere. She looked up at Kovit as the voices got louder and indicated a pillar at the end of the platform with a jerk of her head.

The man in the trench coat resisted when Kovit tried to pull him toward the isolated corner. Kovit casually slid his knife under the skin of the man's cheek, the blade sliding in flat and thin, so she could see the shape of it bulging out from under the skin. He pressed his other hand against the man's throat to prevent his scream.

"Resist, and I'll skin your face," Kovit hissed. His body

shivered slightly as the man's pain flowed through him, ecstasy making his eyes half lidded and a twisted smile pulling the corner of his lips. But his hand stayed steady on the knife. Controlled.

The man's eyes bulged, tears collecting at the corners, his mouth open and gurgling as he tried to scream but couldn't. He winced at every expression that crossed his face, the muscles of each gasp and gurgle pulling at the skin being cut by the knife.

Kovit pressed the knife deeper, and the man tried again to make a sound against the pressure of Kovit's hand on his throat, but nothing came out. Finally, he went limp as Kovit and Nita guided him behind the pillar and out of view.

Kovit shoved the man against the far side of the pillar, pinning his arms between their bodies with one arm, while the other one kept the knife in the man's face. The man was in his late twenties, white, with blue eyes, a cleft chin, and a quivering lip. She didn't recognize him.

Nita wiped her bloody hands on her shirt. "Who are you?"

The man's eyes flicked to her, then he swallowed and looked to Kovit. Kovit dug the blade in and whispered, "Answer her."

"Allen. Allen Burns."

He gasped as he spoke, the movement of his mouth tugging against Kovit's knife, and blood trickled down the side of his face, coating it red.

Kovit looked to Nita, and she shrugged.

"Why did you attack me?"

He hesitated, and Kovit's knife dug into his face. Allen

whimpered, snuffling and snotting as the tears choked him. Kovit shuddered, a soft moan escaping his lips.

Allen tried to turn his face away, but it only made the knife cut deeper, and he stopped, voice nothing more than a whimper. "The money. Please."

"What money?" Nita pressed.

"I saw the video of you on the internet." His watery eyes flicked down to the dried blood on her now-healed neck. "People will pay a lot of money for you."

Nita frowned. So this was some random attack? But what were the chances?

Something was missing here.

Kovit sensed it too. He tilted his head to the side. "Where are you from?"

"Buffalo."

"Buffalo. New York." Kovit made a face and said in distaste, "You're one of that bounty hunter gang. The Pompasaurus?"

"The Pomadors." His voice was mildly strangled with offense, and Nita rolled her eyes. Why did people always pick such stupid names for their groups?

"That." Kovit's eyes narrowed. "And why were you in Toronto?"

Allen stared at them, brows furrowed, lip quivering. "I told you. She's all over the internet."

A chill slid down Nita's spine that had nothing to do with the air conditioning. "Are you saying you came specifically to Toronto to hunt me?"

"Well, yeah." He swallowed again, and the fine dusting of stubble across his face scraped against Kovit's knife.

Nita frowned. "How did you know where I was?"

He hesitated, and Kovit slid the knife in deeper. Allen tried to scream, but Kovit cut off his airways so it turned into a desperate choke.

"Answer her," Kovit hissed.

"I bought the information," he gasped, once Kovit had eased up on his airways. "Online."

"And it included that I would be on this subway at this specific time?" Nita's voice was dry.

Allen hesitated, and Nita frowned. Then her eyes widened.

She yanked her phone out of her pocket. It was warm. Too warm.

She stared at it. She'd been so careful. So certain.

Idiot.

She should have copied the information and ditched the phone. Let her mother toss it out the window.

She yanked the back of the phone off and popped the battery out. She pocketed each part of the phone separately.

"We need to go," Nita murmured to Kovit. "We need to go now, before more people show up."

Kovit nodded, then turned to the man. "Did you bring any friends today?"

"I thought one person would be plenty to take on a little girl." Allen's eyes narrowed. "But my associates will learn from my mistake. They'll come in force next time."

Great. Just what Nita needed. Black market hunters out for both money *and* vengeance.

Allen's eyes flicked to Kovit. "Though I would have thought

twice about coming alone if I'd known you'd hired a zannie for protection."

Kovit's jaw clenched. "What makes you think she hired me?"

Allen stared at him. "Zannies only have employers and victims."

Kovit's eyes narrowed, fingers tightening on his knife.

"He's my friend." Nita's voice was quiet.

Allen gave her a pitying look. "Zannies don't have friends, they're not capable. You're a fool if you think differently."

Nita caught the look of hurt that crossed Kovit's face before it transformed into rage.

"No, you're the fool." Nita whispered, as Kovit's knife dug in and peeled the skin of his cheek off in one neat slice. The piece of flesh hung on the blade a moment before Kovit flicked it off.

Allen opened his mouth to scream, but before he'd filled his lungs, Kovit leaned forward and shoved his switchblade in the back of his neck.

"You don't know me." Kovit's voice was cold.

It was an excellent strike. Very little blood, instant death from the spinal cord severing. Neat. Tidy. The kind of death Nita liked. Kovit really was good at what he did.

Allen's body slumped against the pillar, and Kovit sighed softly, his eyes dark and heavy-lidded as the last trickle of pain slid through him. He examined the crumpled form with regret. "I would have liked to play awhile."

Nita shivered and looked away from the hungry expression

on his face. She could see his imagination in the curl of his smile and the flash of his teeth. It made her body want to huddle in a corner and hide.

Voices echoed through the platform, becoming louder as a group of shadows headed their way. Their shoes clicked on the cement floor, and Nita's eyes narrowed.

The train pulled into the platform with a whoosh of air. Kovit took her still-bloody hand, and she stepped over the dead body and followed him. Her shoe made a small bloody half footprint to match the scuffed handprints.

Nita glanced back at the crumpled form against the pillar. He looked small and fragile, as though he'd just slumped against the pillar to rest from a long day of work and fallen asleep, sliding down to curl at the base.

The train doors slid shut, and they were rolling away, body disappearing from sight.

TWELVE

YOU HAVE BLOOD all over your shirt." Kovit said, his voice soft.

Nita looked down, and sure enough, her entire gray INHUP shirt was dark red with streaks of blood. It formed a strange almost Rorschach pattern. It looked kind of like a man falling, unraveling as he went.

Nita edged closer to Kovit, glancing surreptitiously around the car. There were only a few people, and no one had noticed them yet.

Kovit unzipped his sweater and handed it to her. She put it on without hesitation, zipping it up to hide the gore. It was still warm, and it pressed the cooling blood on the shirt against her skin, making her shiver.

More people got on at the next stop, and Nita shifted closer to Kovit, away from the press of strange bodies. She kept her neck tucked into the sweater and shoved her bloody hands into the pockets. Her eyes stayed trained on the red stripes on the gray floor, slightly raised.

Kovit pulled her toward two seats facing backwards. The seats were strangely laid out, facing every possible direction so they looked haphazardly thrown in the car.

The two of them sat in tense silence. Nita wondered what would happen when the body was discovered. Were there security cameras? Had they left fingerprints? Were their fingerprints on file?

She'd been in Toronto less than a day and with Kovit less than an hour before she'd been involved in a murder.

And she hadn't even had a chance to dissect the body.

No, we aren't supposed to think like that.

Why not? He was evil. We didn't know him. Why shouldn't we want to dissect him?

Because . . . well, actually, yeah.

She closed her eyes and tried to pretend she didn't feel the eyes of the people in the train car on her. In her pocket, her hand twitched for a scalpel. What she would have given for a chance to take that body apart. She just wanted a few hours of peace. Of straight lines and clear glass jars. Of labels and weights.

Nita pulled her phone from her pocket, and carefully examined each piece for physical bugs. Pulling the battery meant that the phone couldn't be tracked by any spyware on the device, but it wouldn't help if someone had just stuck a physical tracking device on there.

There was nothing.

She looked down at the two pieces of the phone and thought of leaving it on the subway. It wasn't like she could ever use it again.

But then she had a better idea.

She pocketed it as the subway doors opened, and Kovit tugged her sleeve.

"Come on," he whispered. "The blood is seeping through your clothes."

Nita looked down and saw he was right. She hunched over herself, trying to hide the stains. They left the train and ascended the stairs. They were in a transfer station, and Kovit snagged a touristy T-shirt on a newsstand and bought it.

They found a handicapped washroom, and Nita took the new T-shirt from him and went inside.

The room was grimy, and there were stray pieces of toilet paper on the floor. But it was empty and she was alone.

Nita locked the door.

She leaned against the wall and just breathed, taking huge gulps of air and trying to steady her nerves, calm the adrenaline rush.

Finally, she stripped off Kovit's sweater and the grimy T-shirt and used paper towels and the bathroom sink to start washing the half-dried blood covering her body.

The water was warm, and it melted the dried blood from her skin and soaked her body in a faint red sheen as the blood trickled down the sink drain. Nita ran her hands over her throat, where the garrote had dug into her flesh. She swallowed, the memory of pressure choking her air out and digging into her skin.

She shook as the enormity of her situation came crashing down around her.

Her location was up on the internet.

There were potentially hundreds of bounty hunters after her, and she didn't even know what her enemies looked like.

But they all knew what she looked like.

She pressed her forehead into the mirror and gripped the sides of the sink, bracing herself, as water trickled down her bare chest, washing all the evidence away.

It had been necessary to kill the man. She knew it, she accepted it. But still, she waited for the guilt to hit, the sludgy feeling she got whenever she thought of eyes darkening and bodies falling, life leaching out of people.

There was nothing.

Nita took deep breaths and waited, telling herself it was okay to feel emotion now that it was all over. But still nothing came. She tried to remember the last time she'd cried over a murder. Had it been Reyes, her first kill?

Yes. It had. But even though the screams from the people she'd murdered in the market had haunted her dreams, she hadn't really cried for them. She'd felt something—guilt perhaps, though she wasn't really sure if that was an accurate word for the strange mix of revulsion and satisfaction that came when she thought of her escape.

But for this man, Allen, there was nothing. Just . . . emptiness.

And that scared her more than feeling guilt ever could.

She'd been hesitant and jittery over murdering Fabricio, but in a way that felt comforting. She wasn't completely a bad person if she was conflicted about murder, right? In a way, her guilt made her feel human, made her feel more justified in her killing. After all, if she felt guilt, then surely that meant she was still good enough to recognize right from wrong.

But this nothingness was different. The man in the subway was like Boulder's guards, dead at her hand, nothing more than blurry memories of blood. Unimportant. Not worthy of the emotional capacity it would take to care.

It was scary how desensitized to murder she was becoming.

Nita tried to think of her future, imagine who she'd be when all of this was over, but all she could see were the blurry out-of-focus faces of a million dead black market hunters.

She let out a long sigh. When would it end? Probably not until the whole black market was as scared of the sight of her as that receptionist was of Kovit.

She wiped blood off her face. Now, there was a thought.

She felt a smile curling up her lips, cracked and broken, twisted in a way that was slightly wrong. It was the kind of smile Kovit would appreciate.

This was a disaster.

But it was also an opportunity.

She knew there was a group hunting her. She knew how they found her.

This was the perfect chance for her to show everyone: Nita was not someone you should mess with.

THIRTEEN

IT TOOK ANOTHER FIFTEEN MINUTES for Nita to ensure all the blood was gone and put on the new T-shirt. The fabric was soft and deliciously clean. She still felt a bit grimy—washing blood off in the train station washroom wasn't quite the same as a shower—but she was confident at least most of the blood was gone. She shoved her gory T-shirt into the waste bin on the way out.

They boarded the streetcar and headed off to see the kelpie. As they rose from the underground and went along the shoreline, Nita looked out the window uneasily, not liking how close they were to the cold waters of Lake Ontario. Her mind supplied her with all sorts of stories of kelpies drowning people.

There were a lot.

She shuddered, wondering how many bones of his victims sat on the bottom of the lake.

They got off at Bathurst and walked up the dark street, away from the water. Nita wasn't comforted.

"Whatever happens, if he tries to lure us into water, we run," she told Kovit.

He snorted, and turned down a long street of brick buildings advertising artsy stores, antique shops, boutique clothing, and used book stores. Despite how close they were to downtown—the lights of the CN Tower weren't that far off—the whole area looked a bit grungy.

"I feel like there's no way he could lure us to the water without being extremely overt about it."

"He's a kelpie. They're semiaquatic." Nita frowned. "His place will have water somewhere. I bet it has a pool or something in the basement that connects to the lake."

Kovit frowned. "Maybe."

"If he lures us into the basement, we leave."

"All right."

Nita didn't know how Kovit could be so calm about this. Maybe it was simply that he'd met the kelpie before, or maybe he had less fear of dangerous unnaturals because he was one. Either way, Nita intended to keep her guard up.

They ended up in front of a small shop. The sign out front was peeling, white paint coming off and making the sign striped. It read ANTIQUE SHOP, but Nita knew a pawnshop when she saw one. The door was a dark green that looked brown in the evening light. The glass windows displayed old furniture, Victorian chaises with faded upholstery, curio cabinets full of ceramic dancing girls, all haphazardly crammed together so that you could only look at them from a distance, not actually get to them.

The sign in the window read CLOSED, but the lights were on. Kovit knocked on the door, dislodging a sign on the door that said SELL YOUR SOULS HERE! WE PAY BETTER

THAN THE DEVIL AND HAVE A FASTER PAYMENT PLAN THAN GOD.

"Interesting sense of humor." Nita commented.

Kovit looked at the sign and snorted. "You have no idea."

The door swung open suddenly, and a voice said, "It's not a joke. Sometimes people want to sell souls to unicorns."

Nita looked up at the kelpie. He looked perfectly human. Maybe Kovit's age, with skin so white it looked almost ghostly. His black hair had a slight wave to it, and his eyes were that murky hazel that seemed almost yellow.

"I can't tell if you're pulling my leg or not," Nita admitted.

He grinned. His smile flickered like a hologram, just for a second, and another smile appeared beneath it. This one wasn't human shaped at all. Rows and rows of needle-thin teeth, slightly yellowed, each about the length of Nita's finger, all pressed together so tight they seemed to overlap each other, a forest of impossibly long teeth on a jaw not even remotely related to human biology.

Then the human smile was back, like the other one had never been. Normal, flat teeth, a little too white, like they'd been bleached.

Nita snuck a glance at Kovit, but he seemed perfectly calm. If he'd seen the glitch in the kelpie's smile, he was hiding it very well.

"Well, don't stand there, come in." The kelpie stepped aside and waved them in. Kovit entered easily, but Nita hesitated, eyes flicking over the kelpie's face, now perfectly human. He raised his eyebrows at her, and she stepped inside.

It was, if possible, even more cramped than it looked, and they wove their way through piles of curiosities. She bumped into a bust-high marble pillar holding a statue of a screaming horse head with a lightbulb on top and a tasseled lampshade. Nita wondered who in the world would buy—or even make—something that hideous.

The kelpie paused at the counter and turned to grin at them. "So, shall we go discuss things down in the basement?"

Nita stared at him, then slowly turned to Kovit. This was their cue to run, though she hadn't thought it would happen quite so fast. But Kovit just stood there, a slightly startled expression on his face.

Nita repeated, "The basement."

"Yes." The kelpie smiled. "I have a lovely underground pool there."

Nita stared at him, her mind not sure what the hell was happening, and if this was some sort of farce because that was the same as declaring, *Come to my underground murder chamber,* until the kelpie doubled over in laughter.

Nita scowled in understanding. The twat was playing a joke on them.

"Oh, God, Kovit, I knew you wouldn't warn her. The look on her face."

"I thought your sense of humor had improved." Kovit's voice was dry.

"Ever the optimist."

Nita turned to Kovit. "He did this to you, and you didn't warn me?"

"No, he invited us to chat over dinner, picked a beachside restaurant, and suggested we all go swimming together." Kovit's voice was deadpan. "It wasn't funny then, either."

The kelpie continued laughing. "Oh, it was priceless. I still remember that moment of horror on your face. Your life flashing before your eyes. It was beautiful."

Nita scowled. "It's not funny."

He grinned at her. "Yes it was. You looked like all your worst nightmares had come true, and you couldn't believe they would be so blunt about it."

Nita's scowl deepened.

"I can't resist. Every time they come in, they always think the same damn thing. Kelpie, water, basement murder chamber." The kelpie grinned at her, eyes dancing with mischief. "Really, if they'd stop stereotyping, then the pranks wouldn't work."

Nita raised an eyebrow. "So you don't have a pool in the basement where you murder people?"

"I never said that." He winked and gestured toward a table. "We can talk there."

The kelpie made his way over to the table, and Nita followed. It had a three-thousand-dollar price tag and was covered in bags of marbles, fifty-year-old Barbies, and a bronze helmet, among other things. He gestured for them to sit.

Nita sat gingerly, the old wicker chair groaning beneath her, and Kovit followed suit.

"Kovit." The kelpie grinned again. Nita waited for his smile to change back to something else with more teeth, but it stayed firm. “It’s so nice to see you. And you’ve brought a friend. Be polite, introduce us.”

“Nita, this is Adair. Adair, this is Nita.”

“A pleasure.” Adair grinned at her and gave a half bow while sitting. He didn’t extend his hand, and neither did Nita.

“Yes, I’ve heard a lot about you,” Nita responded.

“Oh, has Kovit been talking?” Adair grinned. “It’s been what, three, four years?”

Kovit shifted uncomfortably. “Around that.”

Adair nodded sagely, closing his eyes slightly to give himself an aura of thought. “Yes, and such circumstances last time! Why, your friend had made himself quite a mess. I eat people, and even I didn’t know that three bodies could have so much blood in them.”

Nita turned to Kovit slowly, but he was avoiding both of their gazes. “Yeah,” he muttered. “Me neither. You always discover new things when Matt’s temper is involved.”

Nita mentally readjusted her image of Kovit’s friend. Again. She never wanted to meet him.

“But I hear there was some trouble in the Family. That temper get away with him again?” Adair asked, expression sly.

Kovit shrugged. “Something like that.”

Adair’s lips curled, and his eyes shone. For a moment, Nita thought they flickered too, no longer the round human shape, but tilted and elongated, like a cat’s eyes had been stretched too long and thin in Photoshop. They were also yellow and slitted, like a crocodile’s.

But then they were back to normal and Nita was once again left wondering if she’d seen it at all.

"You're staring," Adair said.

Nita blinked, and swallowed. "Sorry."

"Do you not like this face?" he asked. "I can change it."

Before Nita could protest, his skin began to ripple, like waves on the water, like someone had thrown a pebble in the chest of a hologram, and the changes spiraled out. For a moment, his skin was clear, almost translucent, and caught the low light and sent rainbow patterns spinning around the room.

And then Nita was staring at a completely different person.

A middle-aged man with a too-large nose, sallow skin, and bushy eyebrows looked back at her with the same smile as before.

"Is this better?" he asked. It was disconcerting, because it was still the same voice coming from a totally different face.

Nita wanted nothing more than to reach over and touch his skin and see if the illusion held, or if he skin would feel like water, or scales, or something else entirely.

Then he rippled again, and he was a pretty girl, around Nita's age, with long blond hair and blue eyes. Piercings ran up one ear. Her face was pale, with rosy cheeks and plump lips, but her expression was all sly Adair-ness.

Kovit flinched away, and Nita wondered if this was a face he knew. "Change it back, please."

Adair pouted. "Why?"

"You know why." Kovit raised his eyebrows. "Besides, if you keep changing features, I'll never recognize you."

Adair laughed and changed back to the elderly man. "This the one you wanted?"

"You know it's not." Kovit rolled his eyes. "And besides, you look *old* now."

Adair grinned and whispered, "How do you know I'm not old?"

Nita thought about that. He could look any age he wanted, and no one would ever know the truth. He could be anyone. But then she remembered that it had still been the same voice, young and masculine, coming from each of the bodies. It was nothing more than a surface illusion of some kind.

She'd love to figure out how he did it.

Kovit sighed. "Who cares how old you are?"

Nita nodded. "Your age has no impact on whether you can help us or not."

He turned to her. "Of course I *can*. The more important question is, *will* I?"

His skin rippled again, and Nita paid close attention this time, increasing the concentration of rods and cones in her eyes as much as possible to try and see beneath the watery surface. She thought she caught a glimpse of something black and multi-jointed, covered in leathery hide, but she couldn't be sure.

Then the Adair of before was sitting in front of them, wavy black hair in exactly the same style as before, not even tousled.

"So, Nita, will I?" He tilted his head. "Kovit says the two of you need a place to stay incognito for a few days while you figure out how to get out of town. Is that right?"

Nita nodded, and Kovit said, "Yes."

"Good!" Adair stretched like a lazy cat before a nap, eyes half lidded as he watched them. "So, what do you have to offer?"

Kovit leaned forward. "Information."

"What kind?" Adair steepled his fingers on the table.

"I can tell you about my break from the family," Kovit offered.

"Boo." Adair made the whistling sound of a bomb falling and crashing to the ground. "I know *allllllllll* about that already." He looked at Kovit with something like sympathy. "Sorry about Matt, by the way. I know you were close."

Kovit looked away. "It's fine. I'll see him again one day, when the heat's cooled off and it's safe to reach out."

"Mmm." Adair eyed Kovit. "That sounds nice. But you still don't have any information for me."

Nita sighed. "I have a list of corrupt INHUP agents."

That got Adair's interest. "Oh?"

"One name a day for as long as we stay." Nita crossed her arms.

He shook his head. "Names alone are no good. For all I know, you're making them up."

"I'm not. The list was stolen from Reyes. Also known as the Queen of Parts, a player in—"

"El Mercado de la Muerte, yes, I know who she is. Was." He considered, then shook his head. "Again, it's just names I can't verify."

Nita hesitated again, then took out the two pieces of Reyes' phone. "This phone had conversations and text chats between Reyes and some of the people on the list. But I can't put it back together without setting off the GPS locator on it and bringing black market hunters down on us."

Adair took the phone from her and turned it over in his

hands. It took Nita a moment to realize he was doing what she'd done, looking for physical bugs.

Satisfied, he put it down, then tapped a finger on the table. "I have someone. She might be able to retrieve the information without setting off the tracking. I'll bring her in tomorrow."

Nita leaned forward. "Does that mean you accept my deal?"

Adair drummed his fingers on the table and nodded. "If we can get the information off the phone as well, I accept."

"No. You can't kick us out if your hacker turns out not to be good enough."

Adair traced a finger over the phone and looked over at the two of them. Then he nodded. "Fine. You can stay here." He leaned forward, and hissed. "But if you bring the black market hunters to my shop, I swear to God I will hunt you down wherever you run, drown you in Lake Ontario, and eat your rotting corpses."

He leaned back, and his perfect smile returned. "Deal?"

Nita swallowed. "Deal."

FOURTEEN

ADAIR LED THEM to the back of the pawnshop, into the "staff only" area, which consisted of a stairwell up and a stairwell down.

He led them up.

Nita looked back at the dark stairwell down and wondered if there really was a murder lake in the basement. Not that she planned to go look.

The stairs were cramped and rickety, and led them to the second floor of the pawnshop. It was a pretty barebones room, slightly warmer than the pawnshop but still a bit too heavily air conditioned to be comfortable. A mini fridge sat in one corner, a fold-out couch bed perched against a wall facing a closed door she assumed led to the bathroom, and everything else was just creaky bare wood floor and peeling lime green walls.

Nita looked around at the room. "You get people staying here often?"

Adair shook his head. "No. I used to store business files up here, the ones I used for taxes."

"You mean the ones that made this not look like a money-laundering scheme," Nita clarified.

Adair grinned and touched his nose. "Yes, that."

"So why the change?"

"I had an unexpected guest for a while. I needed somewhere for her to live, so I set this up. She's since moved out, and I haven't changed it back yet."

Moved out, or been eaten? Nita wondered, but she didn't say anything.

"Now," he said, turning to Nita. "My first name from your list."

Nita didn't pull the list out. She'd memorized it by now. "Agatha Washpenny."

He clicked his tongue. "Knew that one already."

Nita shrugged. "Not my problem. One name a day. That was the deal."

"So it was." Adair tossed a key onto the mini fridge. "This will get you into the shop when it's closed. Which is most of the time." He paused. "Also, don't eat anything in that fridge." He considered. "I mean, you could. But I *reallllly* don't think you want to."

Nita made a face. "Anything else we need to know?"

"I don't live here, so you'll have a ten-minute head start if you blow my shop up. Make the most of it." He smiled, and this time when it flickered to that impossibly long, thousands-of-*Alien*-style-teeth image, she was reasonably sure he did it on purpose, because beside her, Kovit flinched.

Adair turned to leave but paused, "Oh, and you know the

story of Bluebeard? Marries a lovely young lady, invites her into his home, says don't open the basement door, she ignores him and finds a bunch of skeletons of his ex-wives?"

"Yeah."

"Well, I'm Bluebeard, and I'm telling you upfront the basement is full of rotting skeletons so please don't go down there unless you want to join them. In which case, you're more than welcome! If you're going to kill yourself anyways, best to donate your body to my food stores."

He laughed, and Nita wasn't entirely sure how much of what he said was true, how much was him mocking her and Kovit.

"Understood?" Adair asked.

"Yes." Nita pursed her lips. "What time should we expect your hacker tomorrow?"

"In the morning. I'll call her tonight." He nodded at them. "And if that's all, I'll be off."

Without waiting for a response, he turned around and tromped away down the stairs, whistling softly.

Nita stared after him when he was gone. The stairs creaked as he descended, and after a few moments, the front door slammed. Nita walked to the small window that looked over the street, just catching a glimpse of Adair walking away, toward Lake Ontario.

Nita shook her head and sat down on the bed with a sigh. They had a place to stay. They were safe, for now. Adair probably wouldn't betray them until he could see if his hacker could crack the phone.

So, they had until morning at least.

Nita flopped onto the bed, suddenly exhausted as the day caught up with her. Kovit lay down beside her. His hair tumbled into his eyes and Nita resisted the bizarre urge to brush it away.

She turned away and cleared her throat. "Can I borrow your phone? I want to check something."

Kovit frowned. "You're not downloading a browser for the dark web are you? I don't know how secure the Wi-Fi is."

Nita shook her head. Accessing the dark web required a specific browser so that your actions were untraceable. But if you set it up wrong, you could end up compromising your computer or phone. Nita wasn't willing to risk it, since they only had the one phone left.

"No, there's no point. I have no reason to think that man was lying. My phone's GPS coordinates are probably for sale online." Nita pulled up a regular browser. "But the bigger question is, who put them up there?"

Because Nita had a suspicion. And she wanted to confirm it.

She logged into the email she'd given INHUP, and there was a message from Quispe waiting for her.

Nita, I hope you and your aunt are having a good time. Shortly after you left, I learned Fabricio had regained consciousness. He's going to be fine. And he was touched by your message, and sent one of his own, below.

Nita scrolled down to Fabricio's message.

Nita, I was deeply impacted by your words about INHUP and safety. It's so nice that you're thinking of me.

I've been thinking of you too.

And while I can't see you in person right now, I know you'll make many new friends everywhere you go—friendships just like ours. I'd bet money you'll meet lots of new ones in Toronto.

That. Little. Shit-weasel.

He'd just all but confessed to sending all those people after her. Friendships like ours? And that line about money at the end—he was profiting off it. He was the one selling her location online.

Nita nearly threw Kovit's phone into the wall, but resisted at the last moment. They only had the one phone.

Fucking Fabricio. Not only was he alive and getting other people to try and kill Nita, he was getting *them* to pay *him* for doing it.

If only she'd added more poison. She remembered that moment when she'd heard he wasn't dead, where part of her had sagged, relief slipping through her, a traitorous sliver in her soul. It was gone now. There was only regret that he wasn't dead left.

"I'm going to fucking murder you, Fabricio," Nita hissed.

And this time, she wouldn't fail.

Kovit leaned over to read the message over her shoulder. "Translation?"

She translated it for him. He'd only been living in South America for a month when they met, and it hadn't been enough time for him to pick up much Spanish.

He rested his chin on his hands. "That is a very passive-aggressive friendship message."

Nita glared at him.

Kovit sat up. "So what're you going to do?"

Nita closed the phone and tossed it back to him. "I'm not sure yet. But I'm going to send Fabricio a message he won't soon forget."

He raised his eyebrows, but didn't question her further.

Nita looked down at the phone. She had the start of a plan. But it wasn't ready yet.

"So, Adair's quite a character," Nita commented. "You have interesting friends."

"I wouldn't really call him a friend," Kovit replied, rubbing the back of his neck.

Nita raised an eyebrow. "How do you know I wasn't referring to Matt?"

Kovit winced.

Nita raised her other eyebrow. "Are you interested in telling me what happened there?"

Kovit sighed. "We were supposed to be up here on a business thing. My . . . services were being loaned out to another group."

Nita raised an eyebrow. "Just another day at the office?"

"Welcome to my childhood. Matt came because he was"—Kovit's smile was tight—"good at dramatics."

Kovit looked away, and Nita remembered Adair's comment about bodies and blood.

"And what went wrong?" she asked.

"Matt got a little . . ." Kovit made a face. "Into things. He killed an important person in the Family. He said it was an accident."

Nita kept her expression neutral. "And do you believe that?"

"No."

Nita raised an eyebrow.

"The man was an evil shit." Kovit elaborated. "He was the nephew of the head of the Family, and when you're related to the head of the Family, there's nothing you can't do. When I was eleven, he asked me to torture a girl who called him ugly."

Nita was tempted to ask if Kovit had done it, but she wasn't sure she wanted to hear the answer.

Kovit was lost in memory. "The whole Family—they're all really fucked up. The head of the Family's daughter has a grudge against unnaturals, thinks they're all monsters. Which, given the type of unnaturals the Family hires, isn't too unbelievable. She once tricked a vampire we hired for an assassination into the sunlight and then lit her cigarette on his body as he burned alive. And the head got famous for murdering families of police officers investigating him." Kovit looked away. "Mostly children. He always went for the most vulnerable."

"Sounds like a great group of people." Nita snorted. "So, you think Matt killed this guy on purpose?"

"Probably. This wasn't the first time they'd worked together, and there was no love lost between them." Kovit shrugged. "Anyway, this guy died. So we called Adair and asked him to make it look like the man disappeared, ran off with some money and left us hanging."

"It seems it worked."

"Yeah. Adair's good at what he does. He somehow managed to even fudge security camera footage at the airport to make it look like this guy got on a plane to the Caribbean."

"Impressive." Nita considered. "Did you guys get in trouble?"

"For not 'stopping' him from running away?" Kovit shook his head. "No. One good thing about the Family is that they don't have a tendency to blame you for other people's actions. Not like some of the other criminal organizations I know of." A bitter smile crossed Kovit's face. "I was too valuable to punish, anyway, and it would've been pointless to punish Matt. He got away scot-free."

"That time."

Kovit's mouth thinned. "Yeah."

There was a crisp finality to the word, and Nita decided not to press for more details on the incident that had led to Matt's punishment. She didn't think Kovit was ready to answer yet.

"Why didn't you leave?" she asked instead. "You'd killed your supervisor. You were paying Adair, he probably could have faked your deaths. You could have started a new life."

"I considered it," Kovit whispered. He lay back and looked up at the ceiling, his eyes far distant. "I wasn't really happy. But it was a comfortable sort of unhappy."

"Comfortable?"

"Yeah. I knew how to act and what to do and who to be to stay alive and be myself. I had my online friends when it became too much. And I had Matt for the day-to-day. They fed me. I never had to worry about being arrested for my . . . dietary requirements."

Nita shivered.

He ran both hands up his face and pushed his hair from his forehead. "And I just didn't know what I'd do outside of it. I didn't want to join another criminal organization—that was just exchanging one life for more of the same, except without all the good parts. And I couldn't fathom what else I would do."

Nita blinked. "You could have gone to university?"

"And paid with what money? To study what?" He shook his head. "I don't even have a proper education." He shrugged. "And even if I did, what's the point? I'll just end up outed as a zannie at some point and killed. Any job I get, if there's people, there's pain, and someone will connect the dots eventually."

"Not necessarily," she protested, but it sounded false even to her own ears. His words rattled around in her head, both fatalistic and undeniably true. What was the point of planning a future if any path you chose ended with you murdered?

It was the same thing Nita struggled with now—she couldn't pursue her own dreams without risking kidnapping and murder. For Kovit, he'd have to literally change INHUP's laws.

They both walked along a high wire, and any false step could send them plummeting to their deaths.

He closed his eyes. "I think, more than anything, I was just young. And I didn't want to deal with the real world. It was simpler to stay where I was. Easy."

"You have to deal with that now, though," Nita whispered.

"I know." His hands fell to his sides, and he stared at the ceiling. "But I feel like nothing's changed. I still don't know who I am when I'm not part of the Family." He hesitated. "And I don't know what kind of person I want to be."

She opened her mouth. She wanted to say something profound, something that was wise, that would make him feel better, that would help him discover himself.

But no words came.

So she just lay down beside him, curling close to his body, and rested her head on his chest. He was warm, and her body tingled softly against the heat. His arm wrapped around her shoulders, pulling her close, and the rise and fall of his chest was slightly erratic. She placed her hand over his heart to still it.

Slowly, his breathing evened out. Nita let her eyes drift closed, and eventually, they fell asleep.

FIFTEEN

THE NEXT MORNING, Nita woke up with bleary eyes and a soft moan. She pressed her hands over her eyes as shattered pieces of sunlight broke into the room and scattered across the floor like a spreading disease.

The sound of the shower water drumming against the tiles echoed even through the closed bathroom door, and Nita rolled over sleepily. She reached for her phone before remembering it was compromised and she couldn't use it.

She bit her lip. She really wanted to take Kovit's phone and download a browser that could connect her to the darknet. She needed to know what kind of chatter was happening.

The internet was not anonymous. Oh, sure, for the average person it was. But to the government, it most assuredly wasn't. Nor to hackers. Or internet providers. There were a lot of people who had the capability to know what you were doing.

That was how the dark web was formed. Initially, Nita had heard it was designed for journalists to communicate with sources without being traced. She'd even heard that it was designed by the FBI for anonymity. But it wasn't long before pedophiles, black market dealers, and everyone else who didn't want the police looking too closely had joined in the fun.

Estimates about how big the dark web was varied wildly – some said less than ten percent, some said more than ninety. Whichever it was, it was true that only a portion of the internet was accessible with Chrome or Safari.

On the dark web, money couldn't be traced. Bitcoin and other cryptocurrencies were used, and with them, you could buy anything your heart desired. Including Nita's location.

She looked around for Kovit's phone and found it charging in a corner. Nita couldn't look at the darknet without downloading the correct browser, but she tried a few Google searches. As she suspected, nothing useful without darknet connections.

She checked her safe email and found one new message. It was from her mother.

Nita, your location has been compromised. You need to come home so I can protect you.

That was it. No explanation, no other relevant information. The way she always did. Keeping Nita ignorant to stay the powerful one in the relationship.

She deleted the message.

Then she looked at the message from Quispe containing Fabricio's veiled threats, and smiled. She decided to compose her own.

I'm so happy to hear Fabricio is doing well. Can you pass this response on to him?

Then Nita paused, fingers lingering above the keyboard.

Thank you for your kind words about friendship. Indeed, I have met some friends here, and I'm enjoying my time with them as much as I enjoyed my time with you. This afternoon will be my first step toward my new life, and I'm sure you'll hear all about it soon. Please look forward to it.

Then she smiled and pressed Send.

She plugged Kovit's phone back in just as Kovit came out of the shower, hair damp, still wearing yesterday's clothes. He shivered as he walked.

"Cold?" Nita asked, looking for the thermostat.

He sat down on the bed and shook his head. "No. It's fine. Someone in the building next door fell down the stairs while I was in the shower and twisted their ankle."

"Oh." Nita wasn't sure how to respond to that. "I guess it's free food."

He snorted. "I wish. It's just annoying."

Nita tilted her head in a question.

He sighed. "Cities are hard. They're full of small pains. Thousands at any time. I can't eat that, but I can feel it. It's like I'm always being rained on, each tiny pain a small drop that hits me. In an area with a small population, it's just a sprinkle, easily ignored. But cities are a downpour, I'm constantly soaked with pain."

"But you can't eat it?"

He shook his head. "It's not enough. I don't know how to explain." He frowned, eyes searching the room until they settled on one of the tall wooden beams in the wall. "It's like my hunger is a giant tree. If I want to sate it, I need to chop the tree down. Small, insignificant pains are pins. You can stick hundreds of thousands of pins in a tree and cover it like a pincushion, but it won't do anything to chop the tree down." He licked his lips. "If you want to cut it down, you need a chainsaw. And not just for a few seconds, that tree is large, it'll take you all afternoon to cut something like that down, even with the chainsaw."

Kovit ran a hand through his hair and gave her a self-deprecating smile. "I'm not sure that even made sense."

"It did." Nita had already known that zannies couldn't survive without severe pain, the kind only found in torture, but she hadn't really thought about the mechanics of it that way before. "How often do you need to eat like that?"

He shrugged. "Whenever I get hungry."

She let him have his evasive answer. He was pulling away, toweling off his hair, and she got the sense this line of questions was making him uncomfortable. She let it drop.

He pulled a bottle of pills from his pocket and popped one.

"Antibiotics?" Nita asked.

He nodded. "Four more days of them."

"How's your wound?"

"All right." His hand hovered over his side. "I got lucky. Really lucky."

"Painful?"

"Not so bad. I've been eating frequently, so my pain levels are pretty low."

Nita knew he wasn't talking about eating pizza. The more pain he ate, the less he felt himself. The longer he went without eating, the stronger he felt his own pain. If he went too long without eating pain, he'd die. He would begin to feel the phantom pain of the person he'd last consumed, stronger and stronger, worse than any actual pain he'd inflicted, until his heart failed from the shock.

So Kovit ate frequently. She didn't blame him, but she also didn't ask who he'd hurt to get his pain, or if they survived. Nita accepted what he was, but that didn't mean she wanted to hear the gory details.

A clatter downstairs distracted her. Both she and Kovit sat up.

A woman's voice trailed up the stairwell. "That hurt! Adair, you put that chair there on purpose to trip me!"

"Would I do something like that?" Adair's voice was faux-innocent.

"Yes."

Adair's laugh trickled up toward them, and the woman kept crashing into things as she maneuvered through the shop.

Kovit raised his eyebrows. "I suppose that will be the hacker."

The clatter stopped, and Nita could hear them in the stairwell.

"I'm keeping them in the basement—"

"I lived here for three months, Adair, I know where the guest room is. And it's not in your sketchy murder basement."

Well, at least Nita had her answer about their room's previous occupant. Alive and grumpy.

"How do you know it's a sketchy murder basement? Perhaps you'd like to come down and see for yourself?"

"Dammit, Adair, it wasn't funny the first ten times, it's not going to be funny now!"

"It's always funny."

"Murder jokes are never funny."

"Who says it was a joke?"

The door to the room burst open, and a flustered woman —girl—entered. She was probably around Nita's age, maybe even a year younger, with long dark brown hair pulled into a ponytail, and light brown skin. She wore ratty jeans with holes in the knee, and black T-shirt pulled over a long sleeved purple turtleneck.

Adair entered behind her, grinning. Now that Nita was rested, she felt like she could see even more clearly, and his smile kept switching back and forth between the long, thin million teeth and the normal human ones. The more she stared at it, the more of a headache it gave her, so she tried not to focus on it, and let the illusion do its work.

"Ah, Nita, Kovit." Adair swept into the room and stood to the side, arm raised like he was welcoming a red carpet celebrity. "I'd like you to meet my hacker, Diana."

Diana rolled her eyes, but she was also trying and failing to suppress a smile. Nita would have cringed from the spectacle of that entrance, but Diana seemed accustomed to his behavior.

She gave Nita and Kovit a tentative smile. "Nice to meet you."

Nita didn't respond, because she was staring at Diana's teeth.

They were fake.

A white retainer, like people used to sleep at night to prevent TMJ. But there was only one reason someone would be wearing something like that during the day—to hide their real teeth.

And there was only one species Nita knew of that looked completely human on the outside except for their teeth.

Nita blinked at her. "You're a ghoul."

Diana stiffened and turned to Adair. "What did you tell them?"

He held his hands up, palms out. "Nothing!"

"It's your mouth guard," Nita clarified.

"Oh." Diana's hand went up to her mouth and lowered. "I've been meaning to get a new one."

"I think it looks fine, Diana. They look like real teeth," Adair chimed in.

Diana sighed. "Then why could she tell they were fake at first glance?"

They continued bickering like an old married couple, but Nita just stared. How did she keep getting herself in these situations? She was with the two species of unnaturals that actually *had* to eat human flesh to survive, and here she was, one of the most coveted pieces of flesh around.

Her mind flashed back to Boulder popping her toe in his mouth and swallowing it, and Nita pushed the image away. She was out of the cage. No more pieces of her would be cut off and eaten.

Kovit leaned against the wall, his creepy smile back in place, wielded like a defensive weapon. "Well, I see how you two came to connect. Did you bond over a murder victim you were both eating?"

Adair laughed, but Diana stiffened. "I'm not a killer."

Kovit raised his eyebrows. "That meat comes from somewhere."

"It comes from Adair."

"Ah, I see, so Adair murders them so you don't have to."

Diana flinched. "Adair doesn't murder anyone for me."

But she didn't sound certain.

Adair smiled gently, in a way that made Nita quite certain he had murdered people to feed Diana and he was simply indulging her strange dislike of murder. "Of course, Diana. But let's not talk about that. Let's talk about the phone."

Nita took the pieces out of her pocket and handed them over to Diana. Her fingers were warm, warmer than a human's would be. It wasn't by much, but Nita could feel the heat radiating off the girl's skin. She wondered, if she touched it, would she burn?

Diana examined the phone the same way Nita and Adair had, turning all the parts over, looking for physical tampering.

After a long moment, she said, "There's no physical bug."

"Yes, we know that." Adair's voice was crisp. "Can you get the information off it or not?"

"Without triggering the GPS beacon?" Diana chewed on her lip with her fake teeth. "I'm not sure. It's a software bug, but I don't know what kind." She looked up to Nita. "Do you know anything about it?"

Nita shook her head. "No. I thought I was careful."

Diana frowned. "How long have you had the phone?"

"A few days."

"It was probably bugged before you got it, then. Someone just activated the tracking on it."

Nita shook her head. "I checked it right after I left INHUP. I'm pretty sure there were no background programs running."

"Did you connect to Wi-Fi at all after that?"

Nita nodded. "I used the Starbucks Wi-Fi."

"It's possible it was activated then. It's hard to say." Diana chewed her lip with her fake teeth. "Sorry, phone bugs aren't my specialty."

Nita waved it away, frowning. "So it's possible INHUP might not have bugged me. Someone else might have bugged the phone months ago."

"Possibly," Diana said, still turning over the phone and frowning.

"All of this is lovely," Adair said in an impatient voice. "But can you get the information off?"

Diana bit her lip. "Maybe."

She pulled a laptop out of her bag and sat on the dusty wooden floor. It groaned as she shifted position, and she ignored it. Her converse shoes were black with little red strings of DNA stitched all over them. Nita looked down at her own formerly white, now mud-colored INHUP-issued sneakers and wondered where she could get a pair like Diana's.

"I can't turn it on or risk the bug sending out our location." Diana's eyes were glued to her computer as she typed something in. "But I might be able to retrieve data without actually turning it on."

She plugged it in, and Adair leaned closer. Nita stayed where she was, and Kovit leaned against the wall, watching everything with a tight, cold gaze.

Diana pulled it up with a grunt. "There's some files, but they're encrypted."

"Can you decrypt them?" Adair asked.

She sucked on her fake teeth. "Maybe. In time."

She unplugged the phone after the files had downloaded and handed the pieces back to Nita. Nita shoved the pieces in her pocket.

Adair sat down beside Diana while she typed. She turned to him. "You hovering won't make it go faster."

Adair smiled. "It won't make it go slower, either."

Diana rolled her eyes.

Nita turned to Kovit and nodded to the door. She picked up the keys from on top of the mini fridge on her way out.

"We'll be back later," she called.

Adair raised a hand and waved goodbye. His smile flickered softly, back and forth, back and forth, between human and monster.

Nita turned away and didn't look back.

She made her way down the narrow stairwell and through the cluttered shop, Kovit not far behind. She tripped on a table leg and crashed into a cardboard cutout of a life-size clown.

From above them, Adair called, "You break it, you buy it! I know where you live!"

Nita's scowl deepened as she pulled herself off the cardboard clown, which was no worse for wear. "He's insufferable."

Kovit grinned and held out his hand. "I actually thought that one was kinda funny."

Nita sighed, accepting his hand and letting him pull her to her feet.

Once they were out of the shop, they headed back toward the station. In the light of the day, the area wasn't nearly as ominous as it had seemed at night. The street was wide and the sidewalks well paved. A pair of college students walked past speaking Polish.

As they approached the streetcar station, Kovit took her arm and pulled her aside, into a narrow alley. "Nita, wait, where are we going?"

Nita raised her eyebrows and gave him a small, wicked smile. "We're going to show those black market dealers I'm not someone to be messed with."

SIXTEEN

NITA RAN HER HANDS over the polished fake marble countertop in the show apartment she stood in. The kitchen was pristine and empty, never touched by food. The only things in it were meant to model the possibilities for whoever moved in—a single small jar of salt on the spice rack, a plate in the dish rack, and a cheese grater and potato masher in a series of small wooden cubby holes along one wall.

It hadn't taken too long to find a building that suited Nita's needs. This one was completely empty—most of the apartments had been purchased ages ago, but construction had only just finished, and move-in dates weren't until next month.

From the outside, of course, the building looked like nothing more than a normal condo complex. No way to know you weren't supposed to be in there. No way to know that if you screamed, no one would come for you.

Nita planned for a lot of screaming.

Her phone buzzed—not Reyes' phone, she wasn't foolish enough to try using it again. She'd snagged an old, slow smartphone on the way out of Adair's pawnshop and then gone to the store and bought an overpriced data plan for it with the last of Kovit's cash. Reyes' phone was safely tucked away in pieces in her bag.

She checked the notification. Payment had gone through, and the game was on.

Nita had officially sold her own location on the black market.

First—and most pressing—problem solved. Now she had some loose cash. Well, cryptocurrency, which she could convert to cash.

More importantly though, it meant that soon the black market associates of the man who'd attacked her on the subway would be on their way to the empty apartment condo she was sitting in.

She swallowed, wiping her sweaty palms on her jeggings. This was her plan. There was no need to be worried. Everything was under control.

"Nita?" Kovit came around the corner from the other room, pausing behind the cream sofa, the only furniture in what Nita assumed was supposed to be the living room.

"Yes?"

"Did they take the bait?"

She nodded. "They're on their way here now."

Kovit watched her, his dark eyes unreadable. He had a crease between his eyebrows, and he hesitated a moment before asking, "Are you sure this is a good idea?"

She looked away. "Of course."

He raised his eyebrows. "You don't sound very sure."

She sighed. He was right. She wasn't sure it was a good idea. But she didn't know what else to do.

She'd initially considered turning on Reyes' phone again and luring every dealer in Toronto into the building and then blowing it to kingdom come. Down they'd all go in one fell swoop. Along with some innocent passersby and Toronto's air quality.

But she'd decided that blowing up would be too risky. It would be hard to control all those people going in and out, getting the timing for the explosion right would be impossible, and what if the different groups started fighting with each other before she was ready and the police were called? It wasn't contained, like the market in Peru had been. There was too much uncertainty, too many ways for it to go wrong.

And even if it did go exactly according to plan, a lot of people would die. It was a bit much, even for her. Which, she thought, was practically a good deed. All those people she might have killed but wasn't going to.

That was how good deeds worked, right?

Yeah, not even you believe that, Nita.

Shut up.

She forced her thoughts away from that. "I'm open to other options."

Though it would have been nice if he'd mentioned his other ideas before she'd set everything up with this black market group. But she still had time to ditch the building, take the money, and run if he had a different plan.

"How about leaving?" He leaned forward. "Look, we have a safe place to hide. We could lie low for a bit, get out of town, and just forget this. Leave the black market behind. Use the money you just got selling your location online and buy a ticket somewhere."

"Kovit . . ."

He could hear the rejection in her voice, and his became a little more desperate. "We can live anonymously. Disappear with me," he pressed, leaning forward, close enough that Nita could feel the heat radiating from his body. "We can vanish. They'll never find us."

She shook her head slowly. "They will. The world is too small to hide from the internet." Nita's voice was firm. "The black market will still be hunting for me. I can't just play the victim. I have to do *something.* Waiting around to be found and killed or hiding for my whole life isn't an option."

"I get it. I do." He sighed and ran his hand through his hair. "But this feels very . . . not you, Nita. Luring people places to murder them?" His mouth curled in a tight smile. "I thought I was the one people were supposed to be afraid of being locked in a room with."

Nita snort-laughed, even though she knew she shouldn't, knew exactly how horrifying Kovit could be. Then she cleared her throat and said, "Well, they *are* coming here to kill me."

"But you set the bait and the trap." He frowned, humor vanishing from his face, and something solemn taking its place. "It's different. It's not like in the market, where there was only escape or death. Everything there felt like self-defense. This is an attack."

"I like to think of it as preemptive self-defense," she said with a grin, trying to lighten the mood.

Kovit glared. "You know the only place that uses that term is the Dangerous Unnaturals List, right?"

Her smile fell. "Sorry. I didn't mean—"

"I know." He leaned against the back of the couch, fingers digging into the top of the cushions, and tipped his head up. He was silent for a long moment before he asked, "Did you ever think about making rules? Like I mentioned in the Amazon?"

She hesitated, then looked away and nodded. "Yes."

He tilted his head and raised his eyebrows. "Did you make any?"

"Yes."

He watched her, waiting for her to elaborate. But she remained silent, eyes turned away. She didn't want to tell him her rule.

Because if she told him, he'd realize she'd based it off him. Not based it off the rules he'd made—based it on not *becoming him*.

Nita was willing to do whatever it took to protect herself, to keep herself safe now and in the future. But she wasn't willing to become like Kovit, like her mother, hurting others simply for the pleasure of it.

That was the line she'd decided she wouldn't let herself cross.

She turned away from him, almost afraid he could see that truth in her eyes. More than anything, she never wanted him to see this truth, because she knew it would cut him deep. "I made my lines."

"And this doesn't cross them?"

She met his eyes square on. "No."

His eyes were dark and worried. He didn't say anything, but she could feel the doubt radiating off him as surely as if he'd spoken.

She tilted her head back and let the fluorescents blind her for a moment. "I need to prove to the market once and for all that I'm not someone they should take lightly."

Kovit was silent, but his chin tilted down, casting shadows across his face.

Nita swallowed and pressed on. "I need them to understand that anyone who messes with me will regret it. I want them to fear me so much they won't dare hunt me."

Then, and only then, would they leave her in peace.

Kovit's hair fell in front of his face, and she willed him to understand. Wasn't that what he'd done to survive in the mafia? Become so much the monster, played up every one of his misdeeds so that people whispered in terror about him?

"This group is already hunting me, and they're probably angry I killed one of their own. I need to get rid of them. If I kill them, I can use it as a building block for my reputation," Nita continued, her sweaty palms slippery on the too-shiny kitchen counter. "El Mercado de la Muerte's destruction was one block. This will be another." She swallowed and forced her voice to sound determined, as if making herself sound sure on the outside would make up for all the doubts she had inside. "And I will make as many bricks as necessary to build a wall to protect me."

Kovit's face was still as he examined her, and Nita had the disconcerting feeling he was wondering what he had gotten himself into. If he had traded working with one monster for another.

Both of them had always been surrounded by monsters. Perhaps there was no one else they could empathize with, no one else who would empathize with them. Like calls to like, and Nita was beginning to wonder day by day if she wasn't just as much of a monster as Kovit, but in a different way.

He was silent a long time before turning away. He looked out the window, down at the entranceway below, and whispered softly, "They're here."

SEVENTEEN

THEY TOOK THEIR POSITIONS in practiced movements. Kovit went to stand in the small closet by the door, shielded from view of those entering, and Nita crouched behind the kitchen counter.

The seconds ticked by. Nita's breathing was fast and sharp, anticipation making her leg shake and her hands tremble.

Was Kovit right? Was this a bad idea?

Well, it was too late now.

The door didn't crash open, but whispered, as though the people were hoping to surprise her. She slipped silently forward, knife ready.

She peered around the corner, and there they were. Three of them, two men and a woman, spreading out across the apartment. One was still by the door, one was approaching the kitchen, and the third had gone to the window.

Nita let her eyes wander over them. Her research had indicated that this group was actually pretty infamous. With the dead man on the subway, that made four people. Too few, she suspected, to wipe out the group entirely, though maybe enough to wipe out everyone who'd come to Toronto. But that wasn't really the point of this, though it would have been convenient.

She watched them walk, trying to figure out who of the group was in charge.

Nita's eyes narrowed as the tall man by the window gestured at the woman by the door, waving her toward the bedrooms.

A smile curved Nita's lips. *Found you.*

In the closet, she could see movement in the shadows, and she nodded at it.

Now.

She was moving, lunging for the man on the other side of the kitchen counter, knife raised. He never had a chance. Nita's blade took him in the back, right in his upper spine, instantly paralyzing him. Spinal fluid blended with blood and oozed from the wound as the man crashed to the floor, screaming.

Nita didn't care if he made noise. It was more important that he didn't feel the pain. The last thing she needed was to incapacitate her partner.

While Nita had been pouncing, Kovit had come from behind, and slit the throat of the woman near the door. Her body lay in a growing pool of blood, and by the time Nita looked up, Kovit already had the third man, the leader, kneeling on the ground, arm twisted behind his back and knife at his throat.

Nita pulled the kitchen knife from her victim with a squelch and stepped over his dying body to help Kovit.

The man on the ground turned his head, even as Kovit

twisted his arm tighter. The man gasped, and his eyes fell on the two dead bodies of his comrades. For a moment, his face was transformed by grief—his mouth turning down, eyebrows falling, lip trembling—before it hardened as he gasped in air, as though steeling himself for what was to come.

The man shook, and he met her eyes with his own watery brown ones. "Look, I'm sure we can come to some kind of arrangement."

Kovit snorted. "That's how you know a black market businessman. Always trying to make a deal."

The man's eyes flicked up to Kovit. "I think anyone would try to make a deal in these circumstances."

Nita couldn't fault him for that.

"I have money—"

"Hush, now." Nita put a bloody finger to her lips and smiled.

He blanched, and immediately went silent. Nita got a little thrill, enjoying how fast fear silenced him. Fear of her. He couldn't see the nerves churning underneath, just the front she presented. And that front scared him enough to obey.

Energy buzzed through Nita. Kovit was wrong. This was exactly the right plan. She could already see it working. If she could just make the whole world see her like that . . .

There was a gun at his belt he'd never had time to draw, and Nita casually pulled it out and shoved it in the waistband of her pants, like she saw in the movies. It was a lot less comfortable than it looked, the metal digging into her skin.

She ignored it and patted the man down. He tried to move, but Kovit twisted his arm tighter and dug the blade into his throat hard enough that a fine trickle of blood dripped down and spattered the floor.

Nita found a wallet and cell phone, which she pocketed, and another gun, which she shoved in Kovit's waistband. He gave her a look like, *Why are you shoving guns down my pants?* And she just shrugged like, *Well, where else do I put it?*

He looked meaningfully at the counter, and she rolled her eyes and took the gun back and put it on the counter.

Kovit never moved his knife from the man's throat. Their captive's brown eyes followed every movement Nita made, and his eyebrows pulled together. He licked his lips, and his eyes kept flicking to the dead bodies of his friends. Probably thinking of what he could bargain with.

But this wasn't a negotiation.

Nita turned away and took her phone out. She padded over to the other two dead bodies. The one Kovit had killed lay by the door, her face resting beside a sign asking people to take their shoes off before entering the apartment. Her eyes were large and glassy, and she smelled awful already.

Nita snapped a photo.

She went to the next one, the one she had killed. She felt a strange hesitation to approach, but she wasn't sure why. He was dead. It didn't matter. She'd killed before.

She shook her head. She was being foolish. She knelt down, took a picture of his face, then turned away sharply, back to the kitchen.

Kovit had taken the time to bind the man with duct tape to one of the kitchen chairs.

Nita frowned. "What are you doing?"

Kovit blinked, and gave her an innocent look. "We're going to kill him, right?"

She nodded, once.

He grinned, cruel and crooked and violent as he plucked the cheese grater from the shelf. "Then I want to have fun first."

The man turned his eyes upward, saw the cheese grater, and began to scream. Clearly, a threat of impending torture was scarier than Nita and her bloody request to keep quiet.

"Please," he begged, eyes flicking between Nita and Kovit. "Anything you want."

Nita swallowed, trying to look anywhere but the cheese grater.

Kovit was still smiling, and he leaned over the man and whispered softly in his ear. "Sadly, you have nothing we want except your death. And I'm hungry."

The man's eyes got huger, and in horror he whispered, "Zannie." His eyes flicked to Nita. "Please. Please don't let it hurt me."

Kovit's smile didn't waver, but his fingers clenched tighter on the grater.

The man was shaking, his eyes on the cheese grater, as though he was imagining exactly what kinds of things could be done with it. Nita was too, but she didn't let that show.

"Well," she said, taking the man's wallet from the counter and pulling out his credit cards. "A PIN number for these would be a nice start."

He gave it immediately, his breaths coming in soft sobs. Kovit pulled out his phone and typed them down.

The man swallowed, gaze focused on Kovit like he was

afraid he was one of the weeping angels from *Doctor Who*, always moving closer the moment you looked away from them. His eyes turned to the cheese grater, slowly, like he was turning his head to see the monster behind him.

Finally, he closed his eyes and clenched his jaw.

Kovit jerked suddenly and spun to the man, swearing, even as the man emitted a moan that sounded more like a suppressed scream. Kovit grabbed the man's jaw and tried to pry it open while Nita stood there staring.

"What's happening?" she asked.

The man's body jerked and spasmed and his eyes rolled toward Kovit, red-rimmed and scared. Blood bubbled from between his lips.

Kovit finally managed to open the man's mouth and a torrent of blood streamed out, a wash of red covering the bound man and spattering across Kovit. So much blood.

"He bit his tongue off." Kovit's voice was inflectionless. "He's drowning in his own blood."

Nita stepped forward, but there was nothing to be done. The tongue had an artery, and if you bit through it, it could kill you, albeit more slowly than if you cut the artery at your throat or your groin. Which was probably why the man had decided breathing in the blood and drowning himself in it was the better way to go.

Kovit was pounding on the man's back, trying to get him to cough up the blood, but he'd closed his mouth again and continued to inhale blood to prevent himself from coughing it out, even as his chest spasmed, choke reflex trying to save him.

Nita stood still. It was pointless to stop him from drowning when the blood loss would kill him soon anyway. Besides even if she could help him, she wouldn't. She was going to kill him anyway. If he wanted to spare himself from whatever Kovit planned, she couldn't really blame him.

Kovit shivered softly as the pain flowed through him, and the man choked on his own blood, gasping and retching. This continued for seconds, minutes, a horrifying tableau that Nita was frozen in.

Finally, the man died.

Kovit let out a small soft sigh when it happened and looked mournfully from the cheese grater to the man.

Nita held back any signs of relief. She hadn't wanted to see the results of Kovit's experiments with the cheese grater. She let out a short breath and took a picture of the dead man's face. She needed to finish the plan.

She turned on data and opened the browser that would allow her access to the darknet. Her whole body relaxed and a gentle smile crossed her face when she saw the pale, stylized onion in the corner. It was familiar, a relic of her childhood. She'd been working on this internet for as long as she could remember. This was her world.

She made herself a new account in the major black market forums. Her fingers hovered over the username box until she finally typed in *SCALPEL*.

Kovit looked over her shoulder as she wrote. "Your username is Scalpel?"

Nita blinked and looked up. "Yes. And?"

"It sounds like a supervillain name," he commented.

Nita rolled her eyes. "Well, no black market dealer uses

their real name. Going by Scalpel is better than a picture of my face."

"True, that."

Nita posted a review of the GPS link selling her phone's location.

You hunt me and I hunt you, in Peru or Canada. I will burn you down.

She uploaded the pictures of the murdered people, with a screenshot of her online exchange with them selling her information to lure them in. When she finished, she closed the phone and took a deep breath.

She'd killed people hunting her.

Her stomach tightened, and she straightened her back. She felt strong. She felt powerful, like she could do anything.

She kind of liked it.

And that, more than Kovit and his talk of rules, more than anything else, finally scared her. She liked feeling powerful. She liked feeling like she'd won.

Luring those men in and killing them made her feel powerful, in a twisted sort of way. In control. She wondered if this was how Kovit felt when he hurt people, this feeling of control in a world where they were almost always helpless and tied to other people's whims. She wondered if that was why he made his own pain rather than take what already existed. She wondered if that was why she dissected.

She swallowed, and her chest tightened.

Something was really wrong with her.

"Nita?"

She shook her head. She was being silly. Why shouldn't she

feel triumphant? Why shouldn't she be proud? She'd killed bad people. She'd sent a message.

She straightened her back. This was exactly what she wanted. She should feel proud.

"Yes?" she asked.

He opened his mouth, but she never heard what he was going to say.

Because the front door blew off its hinges.

EIGHTEEN

NITA AND KOVIT dove in different directions as the door flew inward, followed by a rain of bullets. Kovit rolled behind the couch, and Nita ducked behind the kitchen counter.

Two figures stepped through the door, guns blazing like they were trying to make fireworks inside the deserted apartment.

Nita lay flat on the floor behind the counter, trying not to be seen. She wished she could see Kovit by the couch, because she was worried the flimsy couch fabric would afford little protection from the bullets.

She peered around the corner tentatively.

There were two people, both of them with scarves over their mouths like a Wild West film, presumably to protect them from the security cameras they thought were operational. They weren't, Nita had checked.

One was a man, mid-twenties, white, medium-brown hair. The other was a girl, maybe Nita's age or a little older. Also white, with dirty blond hair that was short and pressed against her head like it was painted on. A series of stud earrings and small hoops ran up one pale ear, while the other only had a single stud. There was something familiar about her, but it was hard to tell because most of her face was covered in the scarf.

The girl smiled, sharp and cruel. "Come out, come out, wherever you are."

She hefted her gun, and narrowed her eyes as she swung it around.

How the hell had the black market found them here?

Nita tried to recall if she'd posted anything specific when she taunted the market. Were there clues to the address in the background of the pictures? But even so, they were here so fast.

Or maybe, she realized, eyes widening, they'd been tailing the group that Nita had lured here. Hunting the hunters when they realized they'd caught the scent of prey. They had probably been lurking outside the building, and waiting until the other group had caught Nita, then planning on bursting in and stealing her.

Dammit.

The girl and the man began walking forward, and Nita tensed. If they went much farther, they'd see Kovit behind the couch. And they'd have a clear shot.

She knew she was the target, but she didn't want to find out if they'd shoot anyone with her.

Taking a deep breath, she dove out from behind the counter.

The two black market dealers spun toward her, guns

blazing, but Nita was already moving, ducking around them and into the hallway outside the apartment.

They fired at her as she ran, and Nita scrambled down the hall and around the corner, toward the elevator banks.

There was no time to wait for the elevator, so she kept going, shag carpet squishing under her feet and white walls blurring past.

She pumped her body with adrenaline and cortisol, her recently enhanced muscles pushing her faster than she'd ever run before. She pounded down the hall and ducked into a stairwell. She nearly tripped and tumbled down the steps but caught herself.

Behind her, the stairwell door smashed open, and another rattle of gunfire ricocheted off the green cement walls.

Nita ducked into another floor.

She bolted down the hall, another row of doors and winding halls that looked more like a hotel than an apartment complex.

One of the doors opened.

Nita's eyes widened as a women in a white coat came out, clipboard in hand, purse slung over her shoulder. Probably a building inspector or a real estate agent.

She blinked when she saw Nita. "Hey, you can't be in here—"

Nita shoved her out of the way and ducked toward the open door.

Behind her, someone fired a gun.

Nita flinched.

The woman screamed as she went down, blood staining her white coat, her purse tumbling from her arm and the contents spilling across the no-longer-beige carpet. A tube of lipstick smacked into Nita's shoe.

Nita didn't stop.

She went through the apartment the woman had been in and straight to the window. She ripped the latch down and it swung open. She dove through, down one story and onto the pavement below.

Then she was off running again.

Surely they wouldn't dare chase her when she was outside? There were more witnesses and potential casualties.

Her mind flashed back to the woman who'd taken a bullet meant for Nita, and she suddenly wasn't so sure.

She needed to stop running before more people got hurt. That meant either killing her pursuers or hiding.

Killing them seemed risky, since it was two on one. Instead, she found a manhole and yanked the cover up and lowered herself down. She clung to the ladder as she went deeper into the sewer. The lid was heavy as she dragged it back over her.

She tried to breathe through her mouth because the sewer reeked, but that just meant she could taste the sewer, not just smell it. The darkness was complete—there was no light to see by, so there was no point in altering her rods and cones for better vision. Her hands were slippery on the cold metal ladder, and now that she'd stopped, she was aware of how slick with sweat she was, how loud her heartbeat was in her ears, how fast the blood was being pumped through her body.

Swallowing, she clung tighter to the ladder.

Above her, the telltale crunch of footsteps approached.

"Which way?" asked the man.

Nita narrowed her eyes. She'd assumed the man was in charge because he was older, but that clearly wasn't the case.

"Gold, which way?" the man repeated.

"Shut up, Daniel."

Feet scuffed against pavement. A rustle of fabric.

Light bombarded Nita from above.

"Found you." Gold's bandana stretched from the smile hidden beneath it.

The man grabbed Nita by the hair and yanked her out of the sewer.

Nita screamed as her scalp stretched. The human body wasn't meant to be held by the hair, and her skin tore, blood trickling down her face and between her eyes.

Nita reached for the hands holding her, even as she shed clumps of hair, trying to loosen their grip, but another set of hands grabbed hers and yanked them behind her back.

Her knees scraped against the pavement, and suddenly the pressure on her hair was gone and her hands were firmly bound. Nita looked up into Gold's face.

Gold smashed the butt of her gun across Nita's cheek.

Pain, sharp and wild and sizzling, scorched through Nita's veins and ricocheted through her skull. She opened her mouth, and blood trickled out.

"Hello, there, healing girl." Gold tapped a foot on the ground. "You've led us on a merry chase."

In the distance, police sirens roared. Nita wondered if someone nearby had called for help after hearing all the gunshots.

The apartment building she'd picked was empty—or supposed to be—but all the buildings around it weren't. And gunshots were loud.

Gold's eyes were cold. "You've made this unnecessarily messy."

Nita's eyes narrowed. "Why? Because *you* shot a civilian?"

Gold snorted. "Like you care."

"What's that supposed to mean?" Nita snapped.

"You unnaturals are all the same. Monsters through and through. Even the ones that don't have to kill people."

The way she said the word *unnatural*, so full of derision and hate, made Nita startle. She knew there were people out there who hated unnaturals. She'd grown up hearing horror stories about the Unnatural Extermination Agenda, a huge, far-too-popular hate group, and she'd seen plenty of people on TV talk about eugenics and eliminating unnaturals from genetic pools. But knowing the hate was there, seeing it on the TV, that was different than having it thrown in her face.

While Nita wasn't going to deny the fact that she was becoming a monster, or maybe always had been, she was also very sure it had nothing to do with being an unnatural and everything to do with the life she'd lived.

"Well, I wonder what that makes you?" Nita spat. "Killing just because you can."

"Nah, not because I can. I have orders." Gold gave her a smile, sharp and angry. "Fabricio says you die, then you die."

Fabricio.

Again.

That horrid little shit-weasel.

She should have added more poison to his drink.

"Whatever he's paying you, I can double it," Nita lied.

Gold snorted. "Nothing you could pay me would be worth getting on the bad side of Tácunan Law."

Tácunan Law. Fabricio's father's firm. The one he claimed he "didn't want to be involved with."

Not that she'd ever believed him.

Gold cocked her gun. "We've got a pretty close relationship with them that's mutually beneficial, and we're not planning on disappointing."

The pressure on her hands, bound behind her back, increased, and Nita bared her teeth. Gold had made a grave error if she thought she could take on Nita.

Nita might be bound, but there were things she could do. She toughened the flesh of her throat and numbed her mouth.

Then she spat stomach acid on Gold.

Gold screamed and fell back, fingers reaching up to claw her cheek and neck as the acid ate through the flimsy scarf protecting her face.

Nita ignored her and snapped her head backwards. It hit cartilage and bone as the man holding her hands screamed, nose cracking.

He released her, and Nita was stumbling to her feet and running, hands still bound behind her back.

She didn't look back to see if they'd survived, didn't pause as the sirens roared ever closer. Her mouth tasted like vomit, and her throat was scorched and burned from the concentrated acid. She healed it as she went, but it tingled with something in between pain and pins and needles.

Thoughts tumbled through her head in a scattered, convoluted mess as her feet pounded a panicked rhythm down one street, then another, never stopping, never faltering.

Fabricio hadn't just put her location up online. He'd also personally hired a group of thugs to murder her. Overkill much?

Or not. Since Nita was still alive.

Nita finally ripped her hands from her bindings and made herself a promise.

Fabricio Tácunan was going to die. All hesitation, all guilt, all regret was gone. She would kill him. Even if she had to fly all the way back to Bogotá to do it.

NINETEEN

NITA'S STEPS EVENTUALLY SLOWED as she rejoined the crowds on the street. Police sirens roared in the distance, and Nita knew that the shots in the apartment building had definitely been called in. The distinctive white and red of an ambulance roof was visible in the distance.

Maybe the woman who Gold had shot had survived. Maybe she'd used her cell phone to call for help, and that was why the ambulance was coming.

Nita swallowed, remembering the way she'd fallen, the spatter of blood on the carpet. The small scream and the silence.

She didn't think the woman had survived.

Nita pushed through the crowd, cringing as other people pressed against her, a crushing wall of humanity. She'd somehow got onto a main thoroughfare, and it was awful.

She kept her head down as she walked, hoping to avoid notice. There was blood in her hair that had dried and streaked it a sticky black. She got a few strange looks, but there was nothing she could do.

The pavement was hard under her feet, and towering gray

monoliths gave way to warm brick buildings. Time seemed to lose meaning in the crowd, and she wasn't certain how long she was crushed in the masses before she escaped.

She cut down a side street, stepping in a shallow puddle that soaked through her shoe. Her breathing was still harsh, and her heart still pounded a frenetic beat as she took the stairs down to the subway. She'd pumped so many stress chemicals through her body, and now she needed to calm them. But she didn't quite want to yet, just in case the trouble wasn't over.

She wondered if she could live her whole life hyped up on adrenaline and cortisol. Probably not. She needed to sleep sometime.

The station was packed, and Nita had to walk to the very end of the platform to find somewhere less crowded. She leaned against a pillar and sighed. It had all been going so perfectly. Her trap had been flawless, and yes, it had been a little gorier than anticipated, though not as much as it could have been, if Kovit had been able to play with the cheese grater. But the plan had worked.

Until Gold showed up.

Nita thought of the dead woman. Her huge black eyes, wide and frightened as the bullet took her down. The image of blood soaking through her clothes and spattering the beige carpet slithered through Nita's thoughts.

Her fists clenched at her sides, and she wished she had her scalpel in hand. She tried to imagine her dissection room, that calm, slow peace of taking a human apart, but she couldn't seem to focus, and the images shattered before they even fully formed.

She leaned against the car door as the subway sped away from the scene.

What a mess. And this was only the beginning. There were going to be a lot more casualties before this was all over.

A thin line of worry gnawed its way through her heart. What if more people from the black market had showed up at the condo after Nita fled? Had Kovit made it out okay?

She pulled her cell phone out of her pocket and texted Kovit.

I'm fine. Heading back to Adair's place now. Did you get out okay?

A small red circle beside the text told her it was undelivered, probably because there was no service underground. She shifted, hoping he was all right.

She transferred at Union to the weird underground streetcar again.

The girl beside her on the train was clearly getting reception, and the news crackled tinnily through her earphones.

"Four are confirmed dead in an apartment building near Yonge and Eglinton. Eyewitnesses at the scene heard gunshots and called the police, who arrived on scene to find several dead. One witness caught a cell phone video of a teenage girl fleeing the scene, pursued by two masked, armed assailants. While police are still refraining from comment, one spokeswoman says that they can't rule out gang-related violence."

Cell phone video. Nita rubbed the little spot between the bridge of her nose and the base of her eyebrow that was always sore. She tried to think if she'd done anything incriminating, but all she could think of was that there were going to be more videos of her online.

She got off at Bathurst and trudged back to the pawnshop.

The OPEN sign was on, and Nita stepped in warily. Diana was sitting at the cash register, curled on a chair with her laptop in her lap.

She looked up when Nita came in. "Oh, hi."

"Hey."

"You okay?" Diana asked, frowning at the dried blood on Nita.

"Fine." Nita didn't want to deal with questions, so she redirected. "Any luck decrypting?"

"Not yet." She held up an empty tub of mint ice cream. "But I did order more ice cream for the store. We're out, and I swear Adair eats a pint a day."

Nita stared at the other girl and her tub of ice cream vacantly for a moment before saying, "Uh. Okay." Another short pause, because she couldn't think of anything else to say to that. "I'm going upstairs now."

Before Diana could respond, Nita was halfway up the stairs. She entered the empty bedroom and let out a breath, taking comfort in the familiar peeling walls and the leaky ceiling.

She flopped onto the bed and closed her eyes.

She tried to tell herself everything was going according to plan. She'd made a show for the black market. So what if Fabricio had hired other people? She'd kill them too. They'd just be more bricks in her reputation.

But she already felt tired, and the thought of making another plan and killing more people wasn't as appealing as it had been yesterday. It just seemed endless. How many times would she need to do this before it actually had a visible impact?

And next time, the victims probably wouldn't be smart enough to bite their own tongues off and kill themselves. Nita really didn't want to see the fallout of Kovit with a cheese grater.

She ran her hands over her face. She was supposed to be this badass the market would fear. How was she supposed to inspire terror if she freaked out every time Kovit picked up a cheese grater?

She sighed and closed her eyes for a few moments, her thoughts spiraling in circles.

The door cracked open, and Kovit came in. Nita sat up quickly, eyes scanning him for injuries. His eyes were tired, and some of the post-torture glow had faded from his skin. It made him look like a boy who hadn't slept in too long.

But he looked unhurt. Nita's shoulders loosened, and she let out a little sigh. "You're okay."

His eyes were exhausted, but his smile was all relief as he took her in. "I should be asking you that. You were the one chased with guns."

"I can heal bullet wounds. I'm fine."

"Were you shot?"

His eyes ran over her body, and she swallowed. "No. I'm fine."

He smiled, soft and relieved. "I'm glad."

Her heart flipped, and she looked away.

Kovit sank down on the other side of the bed. She yelped as the balance tipped and she rolled into his side.

"Miss me that much?" He laughed.

She sat up and rolled her eyes, then asked, "Did anything else happen after I left?"

"No." He frowned, and ran a hand through his hair. "Why? Should it have?"

Nita opened her mouth, then closed it. Where to even start?

"Tell me what you know about Tácunan Law," Nita said finally. The way Gold had said Fabricio's family's company made Nita worried. Like an order from them was as good as done. Like nothing anyone did could change the fate Tácunan Law decided.

"Not much." Kovit considered. "I just know it makes sure monsters don't get in trouble with the law. Offshore accounts. Legal shenanigans. Investigation coverups. The occasional witness silencing. But mostly money stuff. Money tells a lot of stories, and powerful people's money trails can destroy them. Tácunan Law is kind of like Switzerland, you know? No one wants to attack it, because the whole world keeps their money there and you'd make a lot of enemies. And no one wants to piss them off, because they can leak incriminating finances to the authorities."

They sounded like someone Nita didn't want to mess with.

Unfortunately, they messed with her first.

Fabricio was using his father's reputation to shield himself and kill Nita. If Nita could somehow shatter that reputation . . . No. Steal that reputation for herself . . .

Kovit sat down beside her. "Nita."

"Yes?"

"The woman who chased you." He folded his hands in his lap and looked down at them.

"What about her?"

"I know her." He swallowed and met her eyes. "She's part of the Family I worked for."

TWENTY

"SHIT." IT REALLY WAS the only response Nita could think of. "Did she see you?"

"I don't know." He ran his hands through his hair, fisting them before lowering them to his sides. "I don't know."

"Fuck." Nita closed her eyes. Everything she'd heard about this Family made her very sure she didn't want them knowing Kovit was here.

Kovit sucked in a breath. "They can't possibly know we're working together."

"No," Nita agreed. But if they found out Kovit was here, it would look damn convenient that they were both in the same city. "Tell me about Gold. What are we up against?"

"Marigold is the daughter of the head of the Family." He grimaced. "You remember the story about tricking a vampire into the sunlight just because she hated him? That was Gold. She's got a reputation."

Nita frowned. Not good.

"The Family has branches in multiple cities, so we only met last year. She was transferred to my branch to learn the ropes away from her father."

"Are you"—Nita chose her words carefully—"on good terms?"

Kovit shrugged. "Not really. She doesn't like me. But it's not personal, if that's what you're asking. She just dislikes zannies."

"Seems to be common." Nita's voice was dry.

Kovit rolled his eyes. "Very." He sighed. "She was friends with Matt. Before the Family decided to kill him."

"What did she think of that decision?"

"She was pretty angry. But not even she had the power to save Matt. Not after . . ." Kovit trailed off. "Well. Not after everything."

Nita raised her eyebrows.

"I'm not so much worried about Gold," Kovit admitted, deftly changing the direction of the conversation. "I'm more worried about her boss, the head of my chapter of the Family. Henry. If he finds out I'm alive . . ." He ran his hands through his hair. "He started phishing, you know, a few days after the market burned down. Casually emailing me to ask how I was. I nearly responded the first time before I realized if I answered he'd know I was alive. And that was why he was emailing. To figure out if I survived." He glanced at her. "Obviously I haven't answered any of his messages."

"Of course." Nita hesitated. "Were you close?"

Kovit stared at the ceiling. "Yeah. He's the man who recruited me for the Family. He got me settled in the States. He brought me food."

"He picked who you tortured."

"Yes." His eyes flicked to her and away. "He fed me. He took care of me. He was basically my guardian after my mother died."

Nita folded her hands on her lap. "I got the sense your relationship didn't end well."

"No." Kovit was quiet for a moment. "Henry's the one who ordered me to torture Matt. I said no. I'd never said no before, and he . . ." Kovit swallowed, and his lashes fluttered softly. "He was angry. He locked me in a room alone and told me if I didn't eat who he told me to, I didn't eat."

"Sounds like a nice guy." Nita snorted.

Kovit laughed, sharp and bitter. "He's used to getting his way. After a day, I told him I agreed, but when he led me to Matt, I helped him escape instead. Henry didn't take it well."

"Didn't take it well how?"

"He wanted me to be punished the same way anyone else who defied the Family was."

"Which was?"

"Me, of course." His smile was sharp and thin. "I dealt out all the punishments."

Of course. Nita frowned. "He wanted you to torture yourself?"

His gaze shuttered. "No. He wanted to torture me."

Nita stared.

"He knew all about my mother. What she'd done to me." Kovit's jaw tightened, and he blinked and looked away so she couldn't see his dark eyes.

Henry had been like an adoptive father to Kovit. And just like his previous parent, he'd wanted to torture Kovit. Nita could taste the stomach acid in her mouth from her fight.

Kovit cleared his throat, and his voice was steady. "Fortunately, the head of the Family disagreed. Gold's father. He sent me off to South America."

Nita nodded. She didn't know what to say.

"Henry used to be the torturer for the Family, until they decided they wanted the reputation boost of a zannie. Before I met him, I never knew regular humans could be as addicted to torture as a zannie." Kovit's voice was distant. "He supervised all my sessions growing up."

Kovit closed his eyes, and a dreamy smile crossed his face. "We had a lot of good times. He's so inventive. He used to call me an artist."

Nita's hands balled into fists. Something fearful and nauseous and unhappy slid along the back of her throat and scraped at the flesh, making her want to cough or gag or swallow.

She wanted to run away from Kovit.

She wanted to put a hand on his shoulder and hold him close.

She said, "I imagine that meant a lot to you as a kid. Being praised for something everyone else saw as monstrous."

"Of course it did. There's no child in this world that doesn't appreciate being praised for something they like doing."

Nita thought of her dissection table, her craving to take people apart. Some of her earliest memories were of her mother and father standing in an autopsy room, Nita on a stool so she could see the body. They'd take it apart, her father's gentle voice guiding and teaching, her mother's smile flashing approval when she'd done something well.

If she'd had a different life, would she still obsess over cutting people open?

She didn't know.

"You're better off without him." Nita's voice was soft.

Kovit's eyes snapped open, and he sat up immediately and grabbed her wrist. "Nita. Stop."

She stared at him, eyes wide. "Stop what?"

"Justifying me. Henry didn't make me who I am. My mother didn't make me who I am. *I* made me who I am." His eyes met hers with a fury. "I can see the justifications going through your brain. If Henry hadn't praised me, I wouldn't have done awful things. If Henry hadn't brought me people and enabled me, if Henry hadn't taken away consequence for crime . . . if if if.

"If everything were different, who would I be?"

Nita didn't deny it. A small, traitorous part of her had been imagining Kovit as a tragic figure with bad influences. And wondering.

"But the plain fact is, no matter how many *ifs* had changed, I'd still be me. Maybe not this me, here with you. But I'd always be a zannie, Nita. I *like* what I am. I *like* hurting people."

She yanked her hand from his, eyes narrowed. "Believe me, Kovit, I know. I was there when you tortured Mirella."

Sometimes, when it was quiet, she thought she could still hear Mirella screaming and Kovit laughing.

He blinked and looked away. "I'm sorry. I just don't want you to ever not see me. I know so many people see me as nothing more than a tool for pain. But the other side of the coin is when people make excuses for everything I do. They blame it on a tragic past. On what I am. As though *who* you are is defined by *what* you are."

His smile curved upward, soft and cruel. "You once told me I could get my food from hospital emergency rooms. Or maybe palliative care wards. You're right, I could. And it's a choice not to."

Kovit lay back down. "Every time someone thinks about me and imagines who I'd be in another life, they take away the choices I've made in this life. They make it seem like I was crammed into a life I didn't want." He closed his eyes. "They take away my power in my own life. Build me up in their minds into a person I'm not. How is that any different than the people who only see me as a tool or a monster?"

Nita blinked, slowly. "I suppose it's not. Just a different side of one-dimensional."

"Exactly." He favored her with a smile, a soft, genuine expression that was both sad and amused. "I am not a *good person*. But I am *a person*. I make my own choices."

Nita watched him. She thought about how long she'd wanted to leave her mother, how long she'd saved and dreamed of college. How perfect her chance for escape with Fabricio had been before she was sold to the market.

How she hadn't taken it. Escape hadn't even crossed her mind.

It was only now that she'd been torn away forcibly from her mother's influence that she was finally able to say no. To refuse her mother and choose her own path.

And she wondered whether Kovit really had been in control of his choices when he lived with Henry or if he clung to the illusion of control because there was so little he'd had power over.

She supposed the only way to know would be to see how he handled independence. Whether he stayed the course he'd been put on, or if he forged a different path.

The same would be true of Nita.

"Choices," Nita murmured to herself, "almost always involve regret."

Kovit closed his eyes. "Are you asking me if there's anything I regret?"

"I suppose I am."

He smiled softly. "Lots. Is there anyone in the world with no regrets?"

A smile crept across her face. "I doubt it."

He was silent for a time, before softly whispering, "I regret trusting Henry."

Nita waited for him to elaborate, picking at the stray threads on her jeans.

"I regret letting myself be blinded by him. I did love him. He saw me at my worst and accepted me anyway. I assumed that meant, in his own way, that he loved me too."

Kovit sighed. "He didn't. He loved the power I represented. I was a zannie, completely under his control. I was a tool, a very rare, dangerous tool, and he used me to show everyone who he was."

Kovit closed his eyes. "But unlike a tool, I had lines I wouldn't cross. I told him those lines in the beginning. I wouldn't hurt children. I wouldn't eat pain that was sexual. I wouldn't hurt my friends."

"But he didn't listen." Nita's voice was soft.

"I thought he had. He never broke them, never asked me

to. Until he brought Matt to me. And when I reminded him of them, he—" Kovit gave a sharp, short laugh. "You know what he said?"

Nita wasn't sure she wanted to know. "What?"

"'Monsters don't have friends.'" Kovit looked away. "He'd never called me monster before. Other people had—and it's absolutely true, I am one, I'm the first to admit it—but the implication, that I was just . . ."

Nita understood. "He never thought of you as a person."

"No. Just a tool to be praised when it did its job well and discarded when it broke."

Nita thought of her mother, who hadn't saved Nita from the market. Who only asked Nita to come home to do dissections, who shut down all of Nita's dreams.

"That's the kind of betrayal that's hard to forgive," she whispered.

"I'm not interested in forgiving. Or getting vengeance. I just want him to think I'm dead so I'll be left alone."

"He won't find out." Nita voice was soft and fierce, eyes locked on his as she promised, "And if he does, I won't let him take you away."

Kovit's eyebrows were downturned and his mouth soft and sad.

Nita shifted forward so she was inches from his face, her eyes locked on his. "We will never be prisoners again. And we will destroy anyone who tries."

Finally he nodded, his black eyes tracing her face as he whispered, "Never again."

TWENTY-ONE

THE TWO OF THEM lay together in comfortable silence for a while. Nita took the time to ease her various aches and pains until they were nothing.

Beside her, Kovit's shoulders relaxed slightly when she made all her minor pains vanish. She wasn't sure if it creeped her out that he'd been absorbing them all this time and tensing to avoid the shivers, or if she felt bad for him because he couldn't be near anyone without extremely tight control over his reactions.

She began strengthening her tendons and ligaments. Her newfound muscles and bones had served her well in the chase. But she could feel the strain on other things. So she densified and toughened and made her internal connections as close to indestructible as possible.

Kovit rose and stretched. "I'm going to wash the blood off."

"Blood?"

She turned to look at him and was surprised to find he was covered in dried blood. She'd managed to completely forget that their prisoner had vomited blood all over him.

She blinked. "Wow. Yeah. Go wash."

He slipped into the washroom, and soon the drumming of the shower filled the apartment.

The sound of running water calmed something inside her she didn't know was tense. She could imagine the water turning gray from dust and pink from dried blood, and strangely, that made her think of Mirella and her long pink hair and gray skin.

Nita didn't really know what she considered Mirella. They'd been prisoners together. They'd escaped together. When Nita had blown up the market, Mirella had slaughtered those who tried to escape. They were allies.

But Nita didn't know if they were friends. Nita had befriended Kovit, even though he'd tortured Mirella. And when she thought about that too hard, thought about the way Mirella would react if she ever learned that, something painful and guilty bit into her conscience.

But Nita wondered about Mirella. About what happened after they parted ways that final time on the river.

Hesitating, Nita pulled up her phone. Even though she knew there was probably nothing, she Googled Mirella anyway. She nearly dropped her phone when she saw the results.

She clicked the first article. *Amazon River being held hostage by dolphins.*

Pods of pink dolphins have been disrupting trade along the Amazon River, resulting in a total shutdown of trade routes and passenger shuttles.

Nita skipped down to a video. She put the phone on mute and turned the subtitles on.

There was Mirella. She wore a black eyepatch like a pirate, and her hair was a much brighter pink than Nita had ever seen it. It was tied back harshly, so her cheekbones seemed more prominent.

"We will not allow transit to continue along the Amazon River until the governments of Peru, Colombia, and Brazil agree to crack down on black market traders operating in their countries." The subtitles scrolled below in English and Spanish. "Far too many unnaturals are being exploited, and it's time for it to end."

Nita paused the video and stared at Mirella's determined face, her chin tilted high, her remaining eye vivid and clear and alive.

When Mirella had told Nita she wouldn't let the black market return, Nita had never imagined something so dramatic. But she had to hand it to Mirella, it was an effective strategy. Cutting off a major trade route? Getting international publicity?

Maybe she'd get people to listen.

Or maybe someone would get impatient and order men in helicopters with machine guns to kill all the dolphins in the Amazon River.

Nita pushed the thought from her head and put the phone back on the table, thinking about Mirella and how she'd used her power to hold something for ransom. How she'd taken things others needed to get something she needed.

So many ways to make people respect you. So many types of power. Which kind did Nita need to be left alone?

Kovit came out from the shower, hair dripping, and saw her expression. "Something up?"

Nita shook her head and cleared her thoughts. "No, nothing." Then she frowned. "Can you see if there's mouthwash in the bathroom?"

Kovit raised an eyebrow. "Mouthwash?"

Nita scowled. "My mouth tastes disgusting."

"Water?"

"Hasn't helped." Nita rolled her spit around in her mouth.

Kovit's eyebrows were still raised, waiting.

Nita sighed. "Gold caught me earlier and bound my hands. I spat stomach acid on her so she'd release me."

"You barfed on her?" A smile twitched at the corner of his mouth.

"No. Concentrated stomach acid isn't the same—"

Kovit's smile broadened into a full out grin. "You barfed on her."

Nita rolled her eyes. "Sure. Yes. Whatever."

Kovit laughed, hands over his stomach.

"I don't see why it's so funny," she said, but even as the words left her mouth, she couldn't help the smile curling her lips.

He just shook his head, still grinning.

His hair tumbled across his face and he brushed it out of his eyes with long fingers. They looked like they belonged on an artist.

She supposed he did play an instrument, though only he'd consider screams music.

She swallowed, wishing she could use mouthwash on her brain.

Her father had always told her that if she had bad thoughts and regretted them, they weren't really bad thoughts, they were just imagination getting away from her. She'd watched *Jurassic Park* at age eight, and told him the best part was when the lawyer got eaten and then felt bad. Which, in hindsight, was ridiculous, because it wasn't even real.

But even then, she'd been bloodthirsty.

Her father had said that everyone had bad thoughts and liked bad things, they just didn't like to admit it. It wasn't what you thought but what you did that mattered.

Nita's chest tightened at the thought of him, and her hands trembled.

A wave of grief crashed through her. She'd been so busy, so focused, she hadn't thought about her father since yesterday. It felt like a complete betrayal. Like by forgetting her grief she was forgetting him.

Fractured images of her father flitted through her mind before she seized on one. It was a summer day, and Nita couldn't have been more than six. He held her up and twirled her around and around until the world spun and his smile was the only constant. It looked slightly crooked because his left eyetooth was slanted, but it was big and warm and genuine. Her giggles clung to the air like bubbles.

"Nita, are you okay?" Kovit asked, leaning close.

Nita blinked, and wiped away the tears she hadn't noticed. She swallowed. There were no great heaving sobs this time, no seizure-like shaking. Her grief came quiet and small, tiptoeing in and gently trailing its fingers along her memories.

"It's nothing," she whispered.

"It's clearly not." Kovit's voice was gentle.

A small sound broke from her and she crawled over and curled up against him. He wrapped his arms around her and held her as the swell of grief washed over her like a tidal wave. He didn't know why she was crying, but he held her anyway, and Nita loved him for that.

Eventually, it passed, her sobs stilling into silence, until the only motion was her slow breathing, and her fingers clinging to the fabric of Kovit's shirt, pressing his body close to hers. The warmth of him helped a little. She didn't know why warmth helped, but it did.

Kovit touched her shoulder. "What's wrong?"

Nita swallowed, forcing back the snot collecting in her nose and the back of her throat, just waiting for her to start crying again.

"I'm fine." Her voice was hoarse.

"Really, Nita?" Kovit gestured to her tear-streaked face. "That's the line you're going with?"

She snorted.

"You wanna talk about it?"

"My father." She swallowed, the words catching in her throat. "I found out when I was in INHUP. He was murdered."

A hand, warm and gentle, linked through her own, and she looked up at Kovit. She was pressed against him, and looking up made their faces inches from each other. She could see the way his lashes curled softly, and that his eyes weren't black, just a very dark brown.

"I'm so sorry, Nita." His voice was soft, and she could feel the tickle of air against her skin. "Do they know who murdered him?"

She nodded. "You remember the vampire that came to see me in the market? The one with the zebra-striped hair?"

"Him?" Kovit frowned. "Why?"

"I don't know." Nita sighed. "I thought maybe he was working for Fabricio's dad? Getting vengeance for his son?"

Kovit shook his head. "That doesn't make sense. If he were working with Fabricio's dad, why would Reyes have refused to let him talk to you? I know Reyes worked with Tácunan, and you said Fabricio sold you to her. It doesn't make sense."

Nita opened her mouth, then closed it. He was right.

She frowned. "So, you think Zebra-stripes isn't connected to Tácunan? But the timing—"

"The timing is weird," Kovit agreed. "Why did your mother kidnap Fabricio?"

Nita shook her head. "I still don't know."

"Maybe they're connected. The same thing that made your mother lash out at Tácunan made Zebra-stripes go after your father."

"Those seem like very different consequences."

He shrugged. "We're missing information. We need to know how it started. It's like walking in on the middle of a movie—you're seeing Katniss bury a girl in flowers, and you're seeing an old man rubbing his beard gleefully, but without knowing what *The Hunger Games* is, or the premise of the movie, just seeing those two scenes side by side makes it seem like total nonsense."

Nita nodded slowly, eyes drying as her mind seized on something to think about, a problem to solve, a focus for her grief. "You're right. We need to figure out the rest of the story."

She let out a shaky breath.

His fingers, still linked through her own, squeezed her hand softly. "And someday we'll find Zebra-stripes and we'll slaughter him."

Nita's voice was hard. "Yes. We will."

"It won't make the pain go away. Not all of it. I know." He swallowed heavily, and Nita was sharply reminded that he'd lost his parents too. "But I promise you, it'll be all right." His thumb stroked her hand, and her skin tingled beneath his touch. "Maybe not today, maybe not tomorrow. But it *will* be all right eventually."

She closed her eyes and leaned her head on his shoulder, and didn't deny his lie. Because it was a lie. They both knew that. But she wanted to believe him, just for a little.

Kovit's fingers gently squeezed her hand, and she squeezed back.

Beneath them, the door to the pawnshop opened and slammed shut. Nita reached for a weapon, any weapon, out of sheer instinct before stopping herself.

A slamming pawnshop door did not a threat make.

Kovit flicked his switchblade out, and Nita felt a bit of relief. She wasn't the only one who went for a weapon at every loud noise.

Diana's voice rose for a moment, but her words were

indistinct. Another door slammed and the heavy sound of boots marching up the stairs echoed through the room.

The door to the apartment slammed open, and Adair stood there, different features on his face flickering in and out, like his illusions had glitches and he hadn't bothered to reset them. His nose became a literal bird beak before shifting back into something human, then flattening into two holes, like a snake. His skin rippled from white to black, smooth to scaled, ridges and spines appearing and disappearing like sheathed weapons.

He glared at them, and his shape stilled all at once, settling into the young man with black hair and swampy eyes Nita was familiar with.

"What the hell have you done?" he hissed.

TWENTY-TWO

NITA SWALLOWED and stared at Adair. His jaw was clenched, and even though his appearance had settled, Nita was far too aware that it was all an illusion of humanity, that there was something truly monstrous and very dangerous underneath.

"What did you do?" he repeated, words slow and quiet and far too calm.

Nita hesitated, eyes flicking to Kovit, but he just shrugged softly, knife still out. Finally, Nita said carefully, "What are you referring to?"

Diana rushed into the room behind Adair but stopped a step in, taking in the situation and quietly shifting just to the side of Adair. She cast worried looks at him, glanced at Nita and Kovit, and bit her lip.

Adair's eyes narrowed, and the floorboards creaked ominously as he took a step forward. "You told me you were only going to be here a few days. Lie low, get some cash, and get the hell out of here. That's what you said to me."

Nita hesitated, then said slowly, "Yes."

"You fucking liars," he hissed. "You just murdered four people in an apartment building on Eglinton. How the fuck is that lying low?"

Ah. That.

"Look, just because four people died, doesn't mean we did it." Nita shrugged. "It's not like there's any way to tie it to me, or to you."

He must have seen the online message boards where she'd posted as Scalpel. But that was all anonymous online, and while it might be clear in the industry what she'd done, there was nothing to tie any of that to Nita directly, and certainly not to Adair.

Adair took a step forward, and Kovit was beside Nita in a second, his switchblade low.

Adair ignored him. "There wouldn't be, if you hadn't been fucking filmed doing it."

Nita froze, her eyes widening. "What?"

She played over her memories of luring in the black market traders. There'd been no security cameras in the building, and she'd cut power before she'd entered, so the outside ones were off, if they'd ever been working in the first place. There were no traffic cameras on the street, no other security cameras pointing at the building entrance. Nothing like that. What could possibly have been filmed?

Adair glared. "Have you seen the news?"

Nita shook her head.

"Well, look at it." He crossed his arms. "I'll wait."

She hesitated a moment, not sure if he was serious or if it was some sort of sarcasm she didn't understand, then pulled out her phone and went to the news. The first thing she saw was a WANTED FOR QUESTIONING bulletin with Gold's face on it.

Below it was another WANTED poster with Nita's face.

Her fingers tightened on her phone, and her mind lurched forward, first sluggishly, then faster, trying to pick apart what this meant.

There was a police bulletin out on her. People would be looking for her. Not black market people, regular people. Normal people.

All the people in Toronto.

Six and a half million people.

Nita had millions of new enemies. She had no idea who would recognize her. No idea who would see her and think, *I should tweet about that girl* or *Aren't the police looking for her?*

Her fingers dug into the phone case, knuckles whitening from strain, and her throat was tight. She shouldn't feel this betrayed. She didn't know any of these people. They didn't know her. But perhaps it was because they didn't know her that they could so casually and ignorantly ruin her life.

She clenched her jaw. "Fuck."

Kovit leaned over her shoulder and looked at the bulletin and the wanted notice. His voice echoed Nita's. "Fuck."

"Fuck," mimicked Adair. "You got filmed running away from the scene chased by two armed people."

Nita breathed in and let it out. Slowly. She was wanted for questioning. That was all. "They have no evidence on me. I could have been an innocent bystander. Running away from people with guns is normal."

"Feel free to tell the police that after they question you." Adair's voice was frigid. "Tell me, did you lead them right here? Should I expect officers to come barging in to arrest you at any moment?"

Nita stiffened, but kept her voice calm. "If anyone saw me, the police would already be here."

"Excellent, then I imagine you want to stay here and never leave the room?" His voice had taken on a syrupy sweet tone. "Because this is all over the internet, and the minute someone sees you, they'll call the police. And I don't want police here."

"Why?" she mocked, trying to hide her own fear. "Have something to hide?"

"As a matter of fact, I do." He glared at them. "You. I don't want to be associated with your murder spree."

"It's hardly a spree."

"Four people are dead, Nita. We're in Canada. It's going to make the top ten list of most deadly attacks in Toronto's history!"

"I only did it to scare the black market dealers away from hunting me."

Adair's voice dropped. "You think you scared them? You think killing those people made you powerful? Made you a force to reckon with?"

"Of course it did."

"You're an idiot."

Nita blanched, then snapped, "Oh? Am I? Because I have dozens of people in the city trying to chop me up and now there's three less of them, so I did something right."

He snorted. "You think three people makes a difference?

The kind of people who are sending hunters after you, the kind of people who are so rich they can afford to murder teenagers and eat them on the off chance they gain some piece of your power—you really think those people care if you kill a few men?"

Nita blinked. She opened her mouth, but nothing came out.

"They don't care." Adair hissed. "Those lives mean nothing to them. They'll just hire more people. And if you kill those ones, they'll hire more. They have an infinite supply of disposable soldiers."

"No." Nita shook her head, even as his words crept into her soul. She grasped for the confidence she'd had before. "Eventually, if people keep dying, the soldiers will refuse. No one will be willing to try."

He rolled his eyes. "There will always be someone willing to try. Always someone desperate or dumb or determined enough."

Nita's lips thinned. "So you're saying I'll never not be in danger from them, no matter what I do."

"No." Dark hair fell in front of his eyes. "I'm saying your current course of action is stupid and pointless."

Nita clenched her jaw, telling herself she'd made the right choice. She'd made an impression. She'd shown she was powerful.

But a not-so-small part of her was terrified that Adair might be right. That this might all have been for nothing. That building her reputation this way was pointless.

That she'd murdered those men for nothing.

That the innocent woman Gold had shot had died for nothing.

"You're wrong," she scraped out, but she only said it because she didn't want him to be right.

He sneered and waved his hand at her phone. "I'm not. The police and the whole city are hunting you too. Tell me, was that part of your magnificent plan?"

She gritted her teeth. "You know it wasn't."

"And yet."

They stared at each other for a long moment, both breathing harshly. Beside her, Kovit flicked his switchblade open and closed, and on the other side of the room, Diana watched Adair with large, worried eyes.

Finally, Adair broke the silence. "Get out."

Nita swallowed. "What?"

"I want you out. I don't want police here, I don't want to deal with your newfound notoriety. Your list isn't worth it. Get out."

If Adair made them leave, there was nowhere to go. With Nita's face plastered all over Toronto, there was nowhere she could possibly go without being recognized.

She couldn't check in to a hotel, she couldn't sleep in a park. Nothing short of a bag over her head was going to hide enough of her face to allow her to walk around freely.

"You can't force us to leave." Nita tried to make her voice firm and hard, but it sounded small and weak, because this was his shop, and if he decided to kick them out, there wasn't much she could do to stop him. "We had a deal."

"And part of that deal was you not bringing your shit to this place." Adair's voice was icy.

"Adair, calm down." Diana stepped forward, her palms up. "They haven't brought anyone here yet. And you and I both know there's nothing in this shop that could incriminate you, despite all your stupid jokes about the basement."

His gaze turned to Diana. "Why the hell do you care if they stay?"

Diana sighed. "Because they need help, and if we turn them away, where will they go? If the police catch them, there's no telling what will happen."

"Diana, I know you don't trust the police." Adair's voice was calm. "And I know you like to help, but these are not good people, and you don't need to defend them."

Nita took a slow step forward, seizing her opportunity. She didn't know much about Diana, but she was smart enough to see that the hacker had some influence over Adair, and Nita planned to use as much of it as possible. "In my defense, I wasn't the one starting the gunfight. I was the one running."

"See?" Diana turned to Adair, eyes pleading. "Please, calm down. Let them stay. At least a day so they can get some cash and maybe a car to get out."

Adair locked eyes with Diana, and something Nita didn't quite understand passed between them. Finally, Adair clenched his jaw and said, "Fine. One day."

Then his gaze swung to Nita and Kovit. His eyes were intense and angry, the yellow in them beginning to swallow the green and the whites, making them seem alien even though his face looked perfectly human. "One more day, and I want you out. Steal a car and drive somewhere. I don't care. Just get the hell out."

He took one step away and then turned back, his eyes having lost all resemblance to humanity, slitted pupils and all yellow, no whites. "And if I so much as smell police or black market body hunters around my shop, I will hunt you down wherever you are, drown you, and eat you."

And he turned and left, slamming the door behind him.

TWENTY-THREE

IN THE SILENCE after Adair's departure, Kovit, Nita, and Diana all stared at the door.

The air hung heavy in the room, but the danger had passed, and Nita's shoulders slumped. Her hands shook a little, and she couldn't shake the feeling that she'd narrowly avoided having her face literally ripped off by Adair.

She thought of the teeth she sometimes glimpsed through his human disguise and shivered.

She should have anticipated that he'd figure out what she'd done. But she'd just blithely assumed he wouldn't care if she killed people. And she was pretty sure that was true—she just hadn't thought she'd ever get this much press. *That* he definitely cared about.

She closed her eyes, still trying to reconcile the idea that the police were after her. She was so screwed. She needed to get rid of that wanted notice. Somehow.

Kovit leaned forward, his breath soft against the nape of Nita's neck as he whispered, "I'm going to follow him and make sure he isn't going back on his word. I don't trust him. Pack our stuff in case we need to leave quickly."

Nita nodded, and Kovit slipped past Diana and out the door. He closed the door softly after himself, and his feet were almost silent on the creaky stairs.

Diana shifted from one foot to another. Her long dark brown hair had mostly come out of its ponytail, tumbling in messy strands around her face.

"Why did you help me?" Nita asked.

Did Diana have some other plan for Nita? She was a ghoul. Maybe she wanted to kill and eat Nita herself? Nita discarded that thought a moment later. She didn't think Diana was the type—but she'd been wrong about people before.

Diana shrugged. "I didn't think Adair should throw you out."

Nita's eyes narrowed. What was this girl's game?

"You don't mind I killed those hunters?" Nita asked, trying to feel her out.

Diana flinched. "I mind."

"Why? They were trying to kill me and sell my body parts online," Nita pressed.

"I don't like to see people get hurt."

"Strange company you keep, then."

"You know nothing about Adair," Diana snapped.

"Do you?" Nita leaned forward.

She was silent for a long moment. "I know enough."

"Do you trust him?"

She hesitated. "Yeah."

Nita tilted her head to the side. "Would you swim with him?"

"Hell, no!" Diana's eyes were huge.

"So you don't trust him."

"I trust him to an extent." Diana's mouth turned down. "And I trust his instincts. If he says killing dealers won't help you, I don't think it will."

Nita remained silent. As much as she mistrusted Adair, she had a terrible feeling that he was right. That everything she'd done was for absolutely nothing.

She let out a breath, shoulders slumping. She wouldn't know if it had made a difference immediately. Time would tell.

Diana was staring at Nita with pitying, almost judging eyes, and Nita bristled. Who was Diana to judge Nita's choices?

"Whether it makes a difference in the long term or not, you're not going to make me feel bad about the deaths of people who kill innocent unnaturals for money," Nita snapped, trying to project a confidence she didn't feel, just to get that look out of Diana's eye.

Technically, that was what Nita had spent her whole life doing. But Diana didn't need to know that.

Diana shifted, clearly uncomfortable. "I don't know. People are made of multitudes. I want to believe that even monsters have good sides."

Nita snorted. "That's why you get along with Adair."

She quirked a smile. "Maybe." She looked up at Nita and raised an eyebrow. "Or maybe he's not a monster."

Nita snorted. "Who was just telling me they wouldn't swim with him?"

Diana laughed, leaning back so her head was brushing the wall and her eyes were on the ceiling. "Fair point."

They were quiet for a moment before Diana said, "You shouldn't use that word. *Unnatural.*"

"Why?"

She shrugged. "It's demeaning. *Non-human. Unnatural.* They're all words that make us other. Make us different. Labels assigned to us."

"So?"

"So, we make our own labels."

Nita shrugged. She knew there were movements online, people who were trying to change the language, but it never really concerned her. Just because other people said unnatural like a slur didn't mean Nita had to stop using it. Why should she let other people change the way she referred to herself?

"You should use the word *legends* instead," Diana was saying, oblivious to Nita's meandering thoughts.

Nita groaned. "Is that what they're using now? Is there a more corny name in existence? It sounds like a video game."

Diana blushed, but her voice was firm. "I think it's a good name! Because we've always been here, like legends. And many of us are part of legends—"

"But legends aren't real."

"Some of them are."

Nita sighed, rubbing her temple. What about people like Nita, who couldn't really be connected to any one legend? Or Kovit, who wasn't actually sure whether or not zannies were connected to the Thai *krasue* legend? Whoever had picked this name really hadn't thought it through properly.

"You never answered my question." Nita shifted the conversation away before she could devote any more brain time to thinking of that awful name. "Why did you help me?"

"I guess I know what it's like."

"To get caught murdering black market dealers?"

"To be on the run." Diana's voice was cold. Then she sighed again and slumped against the faded lime green wall, her hand running through her hair and clenching in it.

Nita tilted her head. "What are you on the run from? Ghouls aren't on the Dangerous Unnaturals List." *Though they should be,* Nita thought, but didn't say aloud. "And ghoul body parts do absolutely nothing, so it's not like the black market has any interest in you."

Diana hesitated. "Several years ago, there was a news story about a kid who murdered a family of ghouls. Do you remember it?"

Nita did, actually. "The crematorium one? Ghouls stealing bodies from crematoriums, and some kid found out they'd stolen his father's body. Then he murdered them all with a machine gun?"

"Yeah." Diana wrapped her arms around her legs. "That one."

"It was a huge story, in the media for months." Nita shrugged. "I doubt anyone will forget it anytime soon."

Diana swallowed. "I know."

Then it clicked. Nita had been being dense. "You were part of that?"

Diana hesitated, then pulled up her sleeve. A shiny white scar, about the size of a coin, crossed her arm. She pulled up the bottom of her shirt, and there was a longer, wider scar on her stomach.

"That was my family. I was the only one who survived." Her voice cracked a little. "I was twelve."

Nita stared at the bullet scars a moment before sitting down beside Diana, sliding down the wall and landing with a creak and a thump on the wooden floor. "I wasn't aware there were any survivors."

"INHUP kept it a secret for my own safety. I wasn't even allowed to testify at the trial. They were scared the media would find out."

Nita understood. If the media found out Diana was alive, her life would never be her own again. She'd constantly have to worry about paparazzi, hate groups, murderers, the family of the deceased she'd eaten, and who knew who else.

Nita frowned. "I was pretty sure that happened in the States."

"It did. I'm from Seattle originally." Her hands shook a little, and she clasped them to her sides. "INHUP put me in protective custody, and I was moved to a foster home in Maryland. But . . ." Her hand rose unconsciously to her mouth guard. "They'd never had a ghoul before. The foster family, INHUP. They were trying to find legal ways to feed me. Sometimes there'd be an organ donor at the local hospital, and I'd get the parts that couldn't be transplanted into other people. But sometimes there was nothing. And everything was old, and not fresh. I was sick so often."

Her voice trembled slightly, and she turned to Nita. "My whole time there, there was this big public debate about whether ghouls should be added to the Dangerous Unnaturals List. I started getting nightmares."

Diana paused. "Well, I'd had nightmares since the shooting. I don't think I'll ever not have nightmares." She shivered.

"But these ones were different. In them, I would wake up one morning to find that INHUP made a law that ghouls were on the list now. My foster mother would be waiting with the boy who killed my family, and she'd tell me he'd been acquitted of all charges, because murdering my family wasn't a crime anymore. Then she'd shoot me."

Diana's voice had gone watery and soft, and she clenched her eyes tightly shut, but the tears still leaked at their corners.

Nita sat with her hands awkwardly in her lap for a moment, wondering if she ought to pat Diana's shoulder. But she didn't move.

Diana swallowed hard, and continued. "It was my biggest fear, that in the space of a minute the people taking care of me would hear the news and switch tactics and murder me."

Nita believed it. Not just that Diana was afraid, but that the people would very well do that. It had happened before. There was a small genocide every time a species was added to the list.

"I'd seen it before too," Diana continued, her voice soft. "How fast people change. I'd never really had trouble at my school. But when I was fourteen, there was this guy, the janitor. I didn't even know him. I guess his brother had died in combat, though. And the next day he came in and he started screaming at me and the only other brown kid in school like it was our fault. He kept saying we needed to go back to our own country. Stuff like that." Her jaw tightened, fists clenching at her sides. "My great-grandparents emigrated from Iran in the thirties. I don't speak Farsi. I've never even been out of North America. Where the hell would I go back to?"

She sighed, twisting a stray hair in her fingers. "The worst part was that everyone just . . . They just stood there and did nothing. I went home early that day and the school called my foster parents to tell them I was cutting class."

Nita blinked. "Wait, you got in trouble for it?"

She nodded. "Yeah." A sharp laugh. "Stupid, right? But I think that was the moment I realized how quickly people can turn. The janitor was awful, but I didn't really know him. It was all those people in the cafeteria who did nothing. The teachers. My friends. They all just stood there and let him scream at me."

Diana's voice went shaky. "If they were like that when they were fighting someone on the other side of the world who looked like me, what would happen if I was actually put on the list and considered a threat?"

Nothing good, of that Nita was sure.

Diana took a shaky breath. "So one day I ran away."

"And you ended up here?"

"Eventually."

Nita wondered what stories were contained in that "eventually." How a runaway American kid even crossed the border into Canada. How she met a murderous, manipulative kelpie.

"Why Canada?" Nita asked.

Diana shrugged. "I dunno. I guess I thought it would be better? Everything just seemed better in Canada."

"And is it?" Nita asked.

Diana considered. "I'm not sure that it's better or worse so much as . . . different. Canadians love to feel superior to Americans by talking about how much better things are here. But it's less that things are better and more that they don't have the same issues. Problems that run rampant in the US don't exist here. But at the same time, Canada has a whole lot of problems the States doesn't."

Diana sighed softly, resting her chin in her hand. "I think, more than anything, people like to feel superior to others. Canadians like to feel that they're better than Americans. Americans love to feel they're better than the whole world. And when people feel superior, it makes it harder for them to see the problems just beneath the surface. They don't want to believe them, to face them, because if they did, can they really claim to be superior anymore?"

Nita nodded slowly. She thought of her past self, feeling so superior, so much better a person for not being a killer like her mom. It didn't matter that she enabled her mother's work, helped her sell the bodies. The fact that Nita wasn't a killer made her a better person and let her excuse her own hypocrisy to herself.

"So none of the problems in the US exist here?"

"Oh, I didn't say that." Diana shrugged. "There's still racism here—anti-Muslim sentiment has been an issue lately. That was never limited to the US."

"No." Nita snorted, thinking about all the different places she'd lived. "It really isn't."

She thought about the old woman in the grocery store in Japan who assumed Nita wouldn't understand her, so instead of asking if she wanted chopsticks, hit Nita with them. She thought of how often people would come up to her on the street in Germany, either to speak to her in Turkish—which she didn't speak at all—or to gently tell her that the Turkish part of town was over there, and was she lost?

Everywhere she went, there were problems, even if they manifested differently.

"Do you like it here, though?" Nita asked.

Diana ran her hand through her hair and smiled faintly. "Yeah. Yeah, I do. I'm . . . I'm a lot happier here."

Nita raised her eyebrows. She wondered if it was because of or in spite of Adair. She thought it might be the first one. She didn't understand their relationship, but there was a relaxed familiarity, even when Diana was irritated, that made them seem close.

Diana shrugged. "Life here is a lot less complicated. Adair gives me food and promises he didn't kill anyone for it. And in exchange for not having to steal the bodies from morgues myself, I do all the computer things for him."

"You mean hacking."

"Yeah."

Nita blinked slowly. "You do realize he hides murders and you're probably eating someone else's victims."

Diana shook her head. "No, I'm not. He eats those. Kelpies only eat rotting bodies. They need to be under the water two, three weeks before a kelpie will touch it. But ghouls, we need our meat fresher than that. By the time someone calls him for a cleanup, he gets to a murder site, and gets the body to me, it's been out too long. Morgues and such refrigerate bodies—and if it was someone who died in a hospital, they go to the refrigerator really fast, so they last longer. That's what my family always ate." She swallowed. "I know Adair has people he pays to freeze bodies right after they die in the hospital."

Nita thought it was far more likely he went out and just

murdered people if Diana needed them that fresh, but she didn't say so. It would be cruel to shatter her delusions, and Diana had just prevented them from getting thrown out.

"Anyways." Diana wiped her eyes and got to her feet. "I don't know a lot about your situation, but I know you're wanted for sale on the black market, and I know sometimes we have to do shitty things to keep ourselves safe. I don't approve of murdering people, but I won't let Adair kick you out to be arrested or kidnapped or sold."

Nita rose too. Hesitantly, she said, "Thanks. I appreciate that."

Diana nodded. "Anytime." She smiled, cleared her throat, then looked away. "I should go back downstairs and keep trying to crack that encryption. Maybe it'll put Adair in a better mood."

Nita nodded. "Okay."

Diana gave her a tentative smile. "If you ever want to talk . . . I'm here."

"Thanks," Nita said, and didn't mention that she'd never be taking Diana up on that chat. Nita valued her secrets far too much to give them away so freely.

Diana nodded once and slipped out the door and down the stairs.

Nita sat back on the bed, and looked down at her phone, still glowing and open to the police wanted poster featuring her face.

She was going to have to do something about that.

TWENTY-FOUR

NITA WAS FINALLY ALONE, and she sank down on the bed for a moment, just to process. She closed her eyes, but the lights from the ceiling made the back of her eyelids pink. She opened them after a moment and pulled out her phone. She needed to know more about the wanted poster on her.

Nita scrolled through the information, but instead of finding more details about herself, she found three stories about girls who'd been murdered or kidnapped today.

They all looked like her.

Her stomach bubbled with nausea, and her hands shook as she tabbed through the stories. Everyone had a doppelgänger, or more than one. In a city as big and diverse as Toronto, there was bound to be a twin or two of Nita's.

There were. And they were disappearing.

According to the story, the wave of disappearances had started yesterday, shortly after Nita had come to Toronto. One girl was getting off the streetcar when her friends saw a dark sedan pull up and yank her in. One was a college girl who vanished from the bathroom of a coffee shop. And the last was only fourteen, stolen on her way to school.

The last two were taken after Nita had made her statement to the black market.

The hunters hadn't been discouraged at all. Adair was right.

They might not be able to track her by phone, but they had something better.

The internet.

The whole city was looking for Nita and Gold, tweeting, talking, texting. And the hunters were jumping onto the police search to mount their own.

She hadn't fixed anything. She'd made everything ten times worse.

She looked down at the pictures of the missing girls, wondering if they'd already been chopped up and dissected for the market, sold as pieces of Nita.

She should have expected this. Any high-end product on the market was bound to attract lower-quality forgeries.

But it still made her shake, to imagine these random girls, alive one day, dead the next because of a conflict in a world they didn't understand. She could almost hear their screams as the scalpel sank into their flesh, as their bodies were torn apart and put into glass jars.

Nita shivered at the thought of a scalpel, body tingling with a hunger, the cool metal in her hand as she pressed down on flesh. How long had it been since she dissected something?

She choked on her own disgust. Why did this happen every time? Why couldn't she think of bad things without wanting to do them herself?

She covered her face in her hands. She was so fucked up.

She wanted to dissect someone. She wanted to carve them up, to take them apart piece by piece and see how they worked. She didn't care who, she just wanted a body to fulfill her craving.

It would be even better if she could dissect something new. Something no one else had ever dissected before.

Like a kelpie.

Nita stilled. Then licked her lips. If Adair tried to hurt her, if he cut his losses and tried to sell her to the black market . . . Well, if there was a body, it would be a shame to waste it.

Her mouth curled up in a vicious smile.

Below, there was a small crash, and Diana's voice trickled up. "Damn chair! I know he's doing it on purpose."

Nita blinked, and the image of dissecting Adair vanished. Diana would never forgive her – not that Nita really cared what Diana wanted or thought. But it made him more human, and it was less easy to think about taking him apart knowing there was someone who counted on him.

Nita sighed. She didn't have time for these musings. She needed to get that wanted-for-questioning ad down.

She pulled the card from Quispe out of her pocket. Her phone number was printed on the back. Nita hesitated, looking down at her phone. She despised calling people on the phone. She didn't like talking and interacting in general, but she especially hated it on the phone. She much preferred texting. But this wasn't the kind of situation where she really wanted to wait around for Quispe to check her email.

So Nita punched in the numbers and waited.

The phone rang twice before Quispe picked up. "This is Special Agent Ximena Quispe."

Nita swallowed, and cleared her throat. "Hi, Agent Quispe, it's Nita."

"Nita!" Her voice rose slightly. "It's good to hear your voice."

"You too," Nita lied. "Um, are you still in Toronto?"

"No, I'm in New York at a conference right now."

"Oh." Then she hadn't seen the news. "Well, um, there was an issue here. A crazy black market hunter tried to kill me, and it was filmed, and now the police have my picture on a wanted-for-questioning poster."

Quispe was silent for a moment before she asked, "Are you okay?"

Nita blinked, and startled herself when she touched her face. Tears trickled from her eyes, and she wiped them away. It was such a simple thing to ask, but no one else ever asked. Her mother hadn't asked when she'd gotten out of the market. Diana hadn't asked.

Only Kovit had cared enough to ask.

And now Quispe.

Nita had tried so hard to be tough, to be confident, that she hadn't realized just how uncertain, how scared, how shaken she was by everything.

She'd been so sure the answer was killing the black market dealers. It had worked in Peru, it would work here too, right?

But everything had just gotten more and more messy, and nothing was going the way that it should. Her reputation hadn't been built with their deaths, the police were on her tail, Adair was going to kick them out or kill them, and Kovit's Family was in town, which could ruin everything if they found out he was here.

She choked back the tears and said, "No. I'm not okay."

Quispe's voice was firm. "I'm coming back to Toronto. We'll go to the police together and explain the situation. I'll try and get the wanted pictures taken down for now, but I don't know how much influence I can have on them. They'll need to speak with you."

Nita shook her head, then realized Quispe couldn't see it. "No. I'm not going in."

"Nita—"

"No. I'm not going to the police." Nita hesitated, the millions of reasons it was a bad idea running through her head, before settling on one Quispe would understand. "I've seen too much news. I'm scared of what they'd do to me."

Quispe understood. "You're in Canada, not the States. Canadians have a different attitude toward Latin America. There's fewer issues."

Nita *had* noticed that she hadn't received many strange looks on the street. Her memories of the States were fuzzy, but she remembered people noticing her distinctly Chilean features. They rarely *said* anything, but she could see the judgment in their eyes as they made assumptions about her. No one here except Bronte had given her a second glance. Yet. Maybe because Toronto was a lot more diverse than her Chicago suburb.

Though she was also with Kovit, and people might be too busy being distracted by their fear of him to notice her.

Quispe was still talking. "The police there use tasers more often than guns. There's less of a problem with police brutality too."

Nita noticed Quispe didn't say there was no problem. Just less of one. Somehow, that didn't comfort her.

"Please." Nita's voice was soft. "Can you just explain what happened so they can go after the shooter?"

Quispe sighed. "It's not going to be that simple."

Nita's jaw clenched.

"Look, I have some good news." Quispe's voice lightened. "I wasn't going to tell you until he'd arrived, but I think you could use the pick-me-up."

Nita swallowed. "He?"

"We were all so touched by your and Fabricio's sweet messages to each other that we decided to relocate him to Toronto for a bit so you two could reconnect. He requested that INHUP place him in the protection program and begged us to help him get as far away from everything that happened as possible. He has a new name and identity now, which means he can travel. While we set up the conditions of his protection program, we thought moving him to Toronto so you two could meet would be nice."

Nita's mouth went dry. "Fabricio's coming to Toronto?"

"Yes. We surprised him with the news this morning. He'll

be there tomorrow." Quispe's voice was a smile. "Why don't I come back to Toronto, and we'll talk to the police together. Then you can spend some time with Fabricio?"

Nita just stared blankly at the wall of her room before she smiled and lied, "Yes, of course, we'll do that."

She made some excuse, then hung up, still staring at the wall.

Fabricio was coming to Toronto. Her mind tried to process that information, failed, and tried again.

Nita's eyes narrowed.

He'd been using other people, staying safe behind a computer screen on the other side of the world, but now, with this, he was within shooting distance.

Nita's mouth curled up in a smile.

It was time to end this.

Murdering the dealers hadn't been the right move. Adair was right. Mass murder had worked in Death Market because it was isolated, and she eliminated everyone. That kind of strategy simply wasn't possible here. The whole world was involved, there was no way she could kill everyone.

Indiscriminate violence wasn't the answer. Nita was trying to dig out the heart of her enemies with an axe, and all it did was spread gore and make a mess. She needed to be a scalpel, neat and precise.

Adair's point was well taken. You never go for the pawns when you can go for the king. And who was more of a king in this game than Fabricio right now? He'd set this whole mess up, he was the one paying people to kill her.

She needed to end things with him, before he revealed her to INHUP and made everything worse.

Finally, a stroke of luck had come her way. Because the top of her murder list was coming right to her, gift-wrapped by INHUP.

Fabricio wouldn't leave Toronto alive.

TWENTY-FIVE

NITA TOOK A DEEP BREATH and rose from the bed, her mind already full of plans for dealing with Fabricio. She stretched, letting them swirl around before looking down at her phone.

There was one more thing she needed to check.

Her conversation with Kovit earlier had left her with questions about her father's death, and it was past time she started looking for answers.

Her hands were sweaty as she went online and found INHUP's Dangerous Unnaturals List.

She felt a strange hesitation when she clicked on the link. She didn't know why—it wasn't like there was any chance she'd be on the list, and Kovit would have known very quickly if he'd been found out.

The page opened with a list of the different dangerous unnaturals and how to recognize them. Kappa and their bald spots, vampires and their silvered hair. Zannies and their shivers.

At the bottom of the page was the link to the current

wanted list, where information about any confirmed but still free unnaturals was posted.

The list wasn't actually that long, only five faces. She supposed it was easy for INHUP to get rid of their most wanted monsters when they had the whole world hunting for them.

Nita looked at each face, eyes searching for Zebra-stripes. Quispe had confirmed that he was a vampire, which meant INHUP had confirmed it. Vampires were on the list. So it made sense, since Zebra-stripes was still alive, that he'd be on the public wanted list.

He wasn't.

Nita blinked when she got to the bottom and went back to the top of the page and looked through it again, but with the same result. Zebra-stripes hadn't been publicized as a monster and put on the kill list.

Nita clicked off her phone and frowned. Why? She'd never heard of someone not being put on the list.

Unless he was already dead?

Possible, but she doubted it.

Chewing her lip, she tucked her phone in her pocket. She was going to need a new plan to find information.

She headed toward the stairs, hoping Kovit was back. She wanted to discuss options with him.

She descended the stairs, but stopped when the bell on the front door jingled, announcing a customer. Did people still go to pawnshops? Nita had thought the whole thing was a money-laundering front and assumed they didn't actually sell anything.

Which, in hindsight, was silly. It had to at least look like it was a real business.

Nita didn't want to be seen by someone who might recognize her from the news, so she peered around the door to the shop to see who was there.

Diana was at the front counter with the laptop, silently working. Nita couldn't see if anyone else was in the store.

A footstep in the silence, then a voice. "Is Adair in?"

Nita blinked. She knew that voice.

Gold stepped into view. One side of her face and neck was covered in bandages. A sharp grin crossed Nita's face. Gold shouldn't have messed with Nita if she didn't want acid burns.

"He's just stepped out." Diana looked up from her laptop. "I can call his cell? He just went for a walk, so he's not far."

"Please."

Diana pulled out her cell phone and called. "Who shall I say is calling?"

"Gold."

Diana repeated the message and hung up. Nita crouched in the silence, hidden behind the door, and realized Kovit was checking on Adair. If Adair returned, so would Kovit.

Nita pulled out her phone and texted him. *Gold is in Adair's shop. DO NOT COME BACK.*

There was no response.

She resisted the urge to swear. He probably wasn't looking at his phone, but she didn't dare risk calling because she didn't want Gold to know anyone else was here.

The door jingled again, and Adair walked in with a half-eaten ice cream cone. Nita hadn't realized that when he said he needed to cool down, he literally meant he wanted to eat ice cream. But hey, to each their own.

"Gold. You cut your hair." Adair eyed her for a moment, then opened his mouth and put the entire ice cream cone in. He swallowed without chewing. His cheeks didn't puff out, his face didn't even change.

Gold, Nita, and Diana all flinched when he ate it. There was something decidedly wrong about seeing it. He shouldn't have been able to fit it in his mouth, and there was no evidence he had, except the swallow. It was the first time Nita had seen the flaws on the human part of his glamour—not the shifting, changing features, but the simple impossibility.

Beneath that fake human face was something with a very large mouth.

And teeth. Nita well remembered the teeth.

Gold cleared her throat and stepped forward, wiping the fear off her face and replacing it with practiced disdain. "Adair. I'm here for an exchange."

"And what do you have to offer?" Adair swept past her to join Diana behind the counter. Diana grabbed her laptop and slipped away, through the door Nita was hiding behind. They nearly collided, and Diana overbalanced, avoiding Nita and thumping onto her butt on the floor of the stairwell.

Nita peered around the corner, but neither Adair nor Gold seemed to have noticed. Diana rose and silently joined Nita in her eavesdropping.

"I have new information."

"You've already sold me everything I could ever possibly want to know about your Family's operations."

Gold ground her teeth. "You owe me, though. For the fuckup last time."

"I owe you nothing. I did exactly what I was paid for. It's not my fault that Henry tracked your phone and found out about it. That's on you and you alone."

She flinched, and her hard-planed face dissolved into grief for a moment before resettling into a cold mask. "I have new information."

"Oh?"

"About Fabricio Tácunan. Heard of him?"

A small smile flicked across Adair's face. "Some."

"I'll sell information on him."

"I'm not convinced you have any information on him I don't already know."

Gold frowned. "What do you mean?"

"You're planning to sell me his location, no? Or what will be his location tomorrow. I know that." Adair considered. "Or perhaps you're planning to sell me information about why he hired Henry and what he wants you to do, but I also already know that."

Nita blinked. How could Adair know that? Nita had only just found out that Fabricio was coming to Toronto and—

Oh.

The bedroom was bugged.

Of course it was.

Asshole.

Anything Nita knew, now Adair knew too. The whole shop was probably bugged, now that Nita was thinking about it. She should have been angry at the invasion of privacy, but she couldn't help but feel a grudging respect for him. It was clever. And that information was probably worth money to the right people, so he was getting extra from her and Kovit's stay.

It was a trick she thought she might use too someday, if she ever got the chance.

Gold hesitated. "I have other information. Things I haven't disclosed yet."

"Sure you do." Adair's smile was condescending. "And for these vague promises of information, what is it you actually want me to do?"

She met his eyes. "I want you to get the wanted posters from the police down."

Adair snorted. "Perhaps you should have thought of that before you went shooting up a building."

"I got a little carried away," Gold agreed easily.

"Trying to prove yourself after everything, hmm?"

She gritted her teeth. "None of your fucking business."

"Well, it is, because you're asking me to fix it." Adair shrugged and grinned. "But the answer is no."

"But—"

"No. What you want is close to impossible at the moment. I might be able to get you off—might—but it would require using up a lot of favors, making a lot of bribes, and owing people things. And given that, the price would have to be . . . Well, let's just say it's well out of your price range."

Gold clenched her fists. "What do you want from me?"

"Nothing." Adair's lips curled into a warped grin, showing a hint of too-white smile. "I've already taken everything you have."

Gold rocked backwards slightly, but her face stayed exactly the same. A trained poker face. It reminded Nita a little of Kovit. Whenever someone said something to hurt him, his face would do that same thing. Go into a perfect prepared mask. For Kovit, the mask was cruelty and derision. For Gold, the mask was icy calm with a hint of a sneer.

"Fine." Her voice was as frosty as her face. "I should have known better than to try and hire an *unnatural* anyway. You're all monsters."

Adair just raised an eyebrow and calmly said, "I never said I wouldn't do business with you in the future, but I would prefer you keep your prejudice under wrap. Rudeness will win you no friends."

She sneered. "Are you denying you're a monster?"

"Of course not." Adair's voice was mild. "But the same can't be said for every individual person of all four thousand and seventeen documented unnatural species you just derided."

Gold rolled her eyes. "Whatever."

Nita willed that to be the end, for Gold to just leave. She didn't want Kovit to come back and see her. If he'd received her text, he hadn't responded, and her heart raced in her chest, begging him to stay away.

Gold walked toward the door, but stopped when Adair called her name.

She turned back to him. "What?"

"A piece of advice." Adair gave her a mild smile. "No one likes to be wrong. So sometimes, when something proves us wrong, it just makes us more fervent in our belief of it. But it's okay to be wrong."

Gold stilled. "What are you talking about?"

Adair watched her for a long moment, and she fidgeted under his gaze. Finally, he looked away and shrugged. "Simply an observation."

She glared at him, her jaw tightening. "You don't understand anything."

Then she spun away, slamming the door behind her as she left. The frame rattled, and a ceramic statue of a ballerina tumbled off a nearby shelf from the force. It landed on the floor and cracked in half.

Nita expected Adair to be amused by the whole thing, but after she left, his face fell a little and he just seemed tired. His swampy eyes seemed to be looking somewhere else, and his mouth was pursed. He brushed a strand of black hair from his eyes, hiding his face for a moment.

Then he went over and picked up the broken statue. "She's going to pay for that next time. Four dollars plus tax."

TWENTY-SIX

KOVIT CAME IN less than a minute later, narrowly avoiding Gold.

Adair tossed the pieces of the statue in the trash, the solemn look gone, and his usual slightly arrogant smile back. He nodded to Kovit. "You just missed Gold."

"I know. Nita texted me." Kovit rubbed his temples. "I didn't know she was aware of this shop."

Adair hesitated a moment, then said carefully, "Matt introduced us a while back. He needed some assistance cleaning up an incident."

Nita winced. How many "incidents" had Matt had?

Kovit sighed and muttered, "Of course he did."

Adair turned away, and Kovit brushed past him. He opened the door to the stairwell and crashed into Nita, who fell backwards onto Diana, who tumbled to the ground.

All three of them shrieked, a tangle of limbs like a mutant octopus. Adair opened the door and burst into laughter at the sight, all signs of tiredness gone. He clutched his stomach as he doubled over laughing.

Nita, squished in between two people like a human sandwich, glared at Adair. She snapped her foot out and kicked his knee.

Adair yelped and toppled, but instead of toppling back into the other room like Nita planned, he fell on top of their pile and Nita grunted as the breath was crushed from her.

There was much swearing, death threats, and too many elbows as the four of them disentangled from each other and rose. Adair glared at them all when they were back on their feet. "Who kicked me?"

No one answered, they just turned in unison to glare at him. Diana stuck her tongue out and said, "You were being an ass about it."

"And this surprises you because?"

"It doesn't."

Nita rolled her eyes at the two of them, and hesitated. Gold had just come to Adair for his connections. Adair took pay in information. If there was something Nita wanted to know, Adair was a good person to ask.

If she could pay the price.

She turned to Adair. "Can I talk to you?"

He raised his eyebrows and smiled slightly. "Me?"

"Yeah."

He shrugged and gestured to the large dining room table in the center of the pawnshop.

Nita turned to Kovit. "I'll be upstairs in a minute."

He gave her a long, searching look, then nodded and climbed the stairs to their room. Diana looked at the two of them and sighed. "I guess I'll take the trash out."

Nita swallowed and made her way to the table as the others left the room. She sat down gingerly on one of the chairs, a hard, straight-backed Victorian thing that was ridiculously uncomfortable.

Adair sat across from her and leaned back in his seat, steepling his fingers and smiling slightly. "What can I help you with?"

Nita hesitated. "I want to know if you can find out about a vampire for me."

He tilted his head to one side, eyebrow arched. "Oh?"

"My father was murdered recently." A wry smile twisted her mouth. "Which I suppose you know, since you've been spying on me."

Adair gave a faux-innocent face as if to say, *Who, me?*

Nita rolled her eyes, and he sighed.

"It was the mention of knowing Fabricio's location, wasn't it?"

"Yes."

"Ah, bad move on my part." But he didn't sound angry, and his smile stayed firmly in place. "So, what about your father?

"I want to find his killer."

"And you think I can help?"

"Yes. It's a vampire. I figured you'd know who to ask to find out more."

Adair considered. "How do you know a vampire killed him?"

"INHUP showed me pictures of him."

"And you trust INHUP is telling you the truth?" An ironic twist of his mouth made clear what he thought of that.

Nita blinked. It hadn't occurred to her that they might be lying. But after a moment of consideration, she shook her head. "I don't think they're lying. The same vampire came to ask me questions when I was in the market."

Adair's eyes darkened. "What kind of questions?"

Nita waved it away. "Not important."

Adair snorted. "Do you think you can use that information to pay me for something later?"

Nita just shrugged. The truth was it was simple instinct now to protect her mother's secrets, to hide who and what her mother was. She'd been doing it so long it was second nature. Though now that she considered it, information on her mother was probably valuable.

But that didn't mean Nita was going to reveal it.

"So all you want is the name of the vampire?" he finally asked.

"Well, motive would be nice too, but I can find that out for myself when I catch him."

He raised an eyebrow. "Going to kill him and avenge your father?"

Nita's eyes narrowed. "Yes."

Adair considered her for a long moment. "You do realize if INHUP knows he's a vampire, he'll be posted online so people can hunt him down and kill him."

"I looked already. He's not on the wanted list."

That made Adair pay attention. He turned to her sharply, eyes narrowing. "Not there?"

"No."

"Has he died?"

“I doubt it. Agent Quispe would have told me.”

He tapped a finger on the table slowly. “Interesting. I’ve never heard of them not putting someone on the wanted list after they’ve been confirmed.”

Nita shrugged. “I thought maybe he was part of another case. Perhaps they’re tracking him, hoping he will lead them to someone else before they eliminate him?”

“Perhaps,” Adair acknowledged, but his eyes were narrowed in thought.

Hook, line, and sinker. Adair liked knowledge, and she’d given him a mystery to solve.

Adair considered her. “This will cost.”

Nita crossed her arms. “I think I’ve already generously paid you from the information you’ve gleaned from that bug in our room.”

“Hardly. I’ve barely gleaned anything from that, and this may be tricky information to find.”

“How so?”

He shrugged. “If you ask the wrong questions to the wrong people, sometimes the answers get locked away and the keys thrown in the ocean. It’s a delicate art.”

She snorted. “You’re a kelpie. Since when has a key being thrown in an ocean been an impediment for you?”

“It was a metaphor.”

“So was mine.”

He laughed then, and smiled. “Fair enough. But the information from the bug won’t be enough.”

“What do you want?”

He considered, swampy eyes flickering for a moment, so his

pupils almost seemed slitted. "I want to know about your family. About your father. About your mother. Vampire hit men don't get on INHUP's radar for killing regular folk. Normal mothers aren't kidnapping powerful men's children."

Nita blanched. "No."

He raised his eyebrows. "Then I suppose you won't be getting that information."

She swallowed heavily and looked away. "What, specifically, do you want to know?"

He laughed. "Trying to get out on a technicality?"

Nita rolled her eyes. "Well, I could tell you my mother doesn't like dacts and my father's favorite drink was ginger ale, but I doubt that's the information you're looking for."

He snorted. "All right. What does your mother do?"

Nita hesitated a long moment. Protecting her mother's secrets was so ingrained, so integral a part of her now she didn't know if she could reveal them.

But she needed answers. Her mother wouldn't give them to her, INHUP wouldn't give them to her. Maybe Adair could.

"She sells unnatural body parts on the internet."

"A black market dealer," he murmured softly to himself. "What's her username?"

Nita shook her head. "Get me answers, and I'll give you answers. That's all I'm saying until I have the name and location of my father's killer in my hands." She considered. "And a few other things."

She listed a few more things, inconsequential to someone like Adair, but important for Nita's plans.

Adair gave her a long, assessing look, his eyes flicking back and forth, swampy green to yellow. Then he smiled, slow and sure. “Deal.”

Nita didn’t like the way he said that, as though she’d given him far more than she intended.

Adair rose, and Nita followed suit. Their conversation was over, and Nita was left feeling deeply uneasy, like she’d made a terrible mistake.

TWENTY-SEVEN

NITA LEFT ADAIR on the main floor of the pawnshop and retreated upstairs. The staircase creaked ominously with every step she took, and she wiped her sweaty palms on her pants, trying to brush away the lingering nerves from the last few hours.

Kovit was lying on the bed when Nita pushed the door open. He rolled into a sitting position when she came in.

"Hey." His voice was soft.

She smiled at him, and a bit of the tension in her shoulders released, just being with him.

"What did you want to ask Adair?"

"I wanted to see if he could find anything about my father's killer."

Kovit frowned slightly, forehead creased in concern. "What price did he ask?"

She shook her head. "Don't worry about it."

He hesitated, then nodded and let it go. She sat down on the bed beside him, tired.

Kovit hesitated, and turned to her. "What happened with Gold?"

Nita shrugged. "Nothing. She came in looking for help, but couldn't pay Adair's price."

"You don't think she knew I was here, right?"

"No, she didn't say anything to indicate that."

He sighed, flopping back on the bed. "That was close, though. Too close." He ran a hand through his hair. "Thanks for warning me."

"Of course." She really didn't need Kovit's Family trying to poach him back. Or kill him. She frowned. "Maybe we should just kill Gold. To be on the safe side. If she knows about Adair's place, she might come back. And we have enough problems without risking her recognizing you."

Kovit gave her a look. "I'm not killing her."

Nita blinked, baffled. "Why not?"

"Because."

"Because why?"

"Because I don't want to," he snapped. "I'm not some murder machine you can just switch on whenever someone inconvenient pops by."

Nita flinched. "I didn't mean it like that. I just thought it's better safe than sorry. She's been hired by Fabricio to kill me, and she's been killing anyone in her way, including random bystanders. And you said you didn't get along—"

"If I murdered everyone I didn't get along with, the world would be pretty empty." He sighed. "Besides. We worked together. I don't necessarily like her, but I know her."

Ah. There was the real reason. Nita had seen it before, with

Kovit. With people he didn't know, it was like they weren't real, didn't exist to him. He could torture them and feel nothing. But the moment he put a name and a face and a life to them, he saw them as people. And once that distinction was made, there was no going back.

Nita sighed. "All right."

Kovit brushed the hair from his eyes. In the jungle, it had been so hot and there'd been so much sweat on people that when he'd brushed his hair back, it had stuck like pomade. But in the fresh spring air of Toronto, his hair just resumed its place in front of his eyes. He ran his hand through it, mussing it and tangling the strands together so it stayed out of his face.

"Need a haircut?" Nita asked with a small smile.

He gave a short laugh. "Probably."

His smile was tired, and for the first time, Nita noticed the dark circles like bruises forming under his eyes and the tightness around his mouth.

"Are you okay?"

"Hmm, why?"

"You just look . . ."

He looked away, and in that moment she knew. He was hungry. And not for pizza.

At first she was confused as to why he'd be hungry—four people had just died, and not all of them peacefully. But then she remembered his weird metaphor with trees and how much emphasis he'd put on duration. He needed an extended period of time eating pain, not a bite here and there before people died.

He just shook his head. "I'm fine."

She nodded slowly. "All right."

She would have to trust he would tell her if it was an issue. Or he would get food. Either way, she didn't want to bring up the idea of finding a new captive for him to torture.

She rubbed her temples. "Did you learn anything tailing Adair?"

He shook his head. "Nothing. He just went to the beach, bought six ice cream cones. No, I'm not joking," he clarified when he saw her face. "Six. Then he sat on the waterfront pier with his feet in the icy cold water eating them."

If Nita had ever needed more confirmation Adair wasn't even remotely human on a biological level, that was it. Ice cream in icy cold water? No, that was him trying to lower his body temperature significantly. Whatever he was, he wasn't a creature of the heat. It was spring now, but she wondered what he'd do in the summer. Toronto got hot.

"Did he do anything else?"

Kovit shrugged. "He put his earbuds in and listened to music."

No, not music.

The bug.

She'd only just found out Fabricio was coming to Toronto. Adair must have been eavesdropping with the bug then.

Nita looked around the room. If she were Adair, where would she hide a bug?

She checked the light fixtures first, unscrewing lightbulbs and examining the lamp.

Kovit leaned over her. "What are you doing?"

She bit her lip, then typed it out on her phone: *This room is bugged. Adair's been listening to us.*

Kovit's eyebrows rose, and then he started hunting too.

They scoured the room, and it was Kovit who eventually found the bug, underneath the wall socket cover. Nita yanked it out and crushed it beneath her shoe. It made a satisfying crack when it fell apart.

She let out a breath. "Ugh. I wonder how much intel he got from us."

Kovit rubbed his temples. "I don't think there was much. He probably knows why we're here and who we're running from, and I suppose he's learned a lot about Fabricio and some about my Family, but I don't think it's life threatening."

"All the same, I don't like him knowing who our enemies are. He's in this business for the money, and you can never trust people like that not to sell you out."

Kovit shook his head. "Nah, he's in this business for the dead bodies and the information. The money is just enough for living, but I don't think he cares too much about it."

Nita raised her eyebrows. "What do you mean?"

"Adair almost always takes payment in information over money when he can. Have you noticed? He's more concerned with staying abreast of what's happening in the world than he is about almost anything else."

"Why?"

Kovit shrugged. "Why not? Kelpies aren't on the Dangerous Unnaturals List, but they will be one day. Everyone knows it. Information gives Adair bargaining tools that money doesn't. Bribes can be refused, but blackmail is hard to ignore. I wouldn't put it past him to be selling things he finds out to INHUP in exchange for keeping his species off the list."

"That's . . . not a bad plan." Nita considered.

"He's sharp. And he knows that if people want to buy information from him, it's in their best interest to keep him alive. He's always trading in information. Sure, lots of people might want to kill him for his knowledge. But those same people use him to find things out. It's not exactly a safe position, but it's a powerful position if used right."

Nita tapped a finger on the bed frame. "So it is. Information can be quite useful." The idea of informational power swirled around in her head. "It's a little like Fabricio's father. He knows where everyone's money is, so he has the evidence to destroy them. It's the information that gives him power over people, and safety."

"Yeah, it's a similar concept." Kovit tilted his head. "Hard life to live, though. Hard line to walk."

"All lives are hard. But some leave you alive, and some leave you dead." Nita's voice was thoughtful.

Kovit rolled his eyes and plopped down on the bed. He pulled his phone out of his pocket. There was a suspicious smudge on it.

Nita raised her eyebrows. "Did you get ice cream?"

He laughed at her look. "It looked really good. And Adair had six cones. I wanted one."

Nita shoved his arm. "You didn't bring any back for me."

"It would have melted."

"Excuses, excuses."

He grinned and unlocked his phone. Then his eyebrows pulled together as he stared at his screen. "What . . ."

Nita frowned and looked over his shoulder.

"What is it?"

"It's an email." Kovit swallowed and looked up at Nita. "From Henry."

TWENTY-EIGHT

NITA'S HEART RATE SPIKED. An email from Henry.

"Did Gold see you?" Nita asked.

Kovit shook his head. "No, look at the time stamp. This was sent before Gold got to the store."

"Okay. That's good news at least." Nita tried to keep her tone optimistic. "Maybe it's another phishing email. You said he sent one before."

Kovit closed his eyes, as though drawing strength, then opened them and whispered, "I don't think I'll be that lucky this time."

Nita's heart sank, pulled down by oozing strands of dread. "What does it say?"

"He says . . ." Kovit swallowed, eyes flicking over the screen. His voice was small and cracked. "He says if I don't come back to him, he'll release my photo and evidence that I'm a zannie to the public."

Nita stared, horror widening her eyes and her heart popping like an overfull balloon.

No.

When Nita was seven, a woman in Los Angeles had been accused of being a zannie. The Dangerous Unnaturals List was in its infancy, and this was the first test of it. It had been in the media enough, and everyone knew there were no consequences to killing a zannie. So they went zannie hunting.

Problem was: the woman wasn't a zannie.

A jealous ex-boyfriend had posted the information online and Photoshopped the official INHUP notification on it. Then he'd spread it on every message board and forum he could find, and word spread, so fast no one remembered the source. The local news reported like it was fact, the city went into a furor, trying to find this zannie.

And when they found her, they slaughtered her.

Brutally.

Similar stories had cropped up of other people in other cities. After a while, people became more aware of the need to verify the facts with INHUP. But once things were verified, it was still an all-out massacre.

It was bad enough Nita needed to hide her face. Most people outside of the market wouldn't murder her on sight.

They would murder Kovit.

She could imagine the mob, a swarming mass of people, gunning down Kovit. In her mind's eye, Mirella led the crowd, followed by a sea of faceless victims she knew were littered through his past. Kovit's body would jerk when the bullets hit him, like a puppet whose strings had been cut. He'd fall to his knees, then down to the ground, the side of his face pressed into the pavement, blood trickling down the corner of his mouth. His bright eyes would go dim, his twisted, creepy smile slacken into emptiness.

No.

"Henry can claim anything he wants." Nita's voice was hard. "But it takes pretty damn good evidence for INHUP to convict someone as a zannie and put them on the watch list. And people are hyperaware of hoaxes these days."

Kovit's voice was thick. "He says he's attached a piece of the evidence he'd leak."

Nita's heart sank. Attached? If the evidence was electronic, it would be hard to destroy. And once it was online, there was no escape.

That was something Nita knew well.

Kovit clicked on the attached file, and Nita leaned over his shoulder.

A man, somewhere in his forties, was strapped to a table in the middle of a white room. The stainless steel table reminded Nita of her dissection room. There was even a tray of dissection tools on a cart nearby.

The difference was this man was very much alive.

He was gagged, and his terrified eyes swung toward the camera, then away, searching, begging. Nita's heart sped up, suspecting where this was going, but needing to see, to know, to confirm.

Kovit walked in.

He was young. Nita would have put him at ten or eleven. Before his growth spurt, his face still rounded with baby fat, eyes large and shining.

He smiled, wide and creepy, eyes laughing silently and his mouth curled into something almost inhuman.

His smile said, "I'm going to have fun. But you're not."

The video stopped, frozen with younger Kovit midstride. Nita blinked, thinking that was the end, until she saw Kovit's thumb on the Pause button at the bottom of the screen.

Kovit shook beside her, his eyes as wide and frightened as the man he'd tortured.

Nita reached over to press the Play button, but he caught her hand.

"Don't," he whispered.

She licked her lips. "We need to know if it—"

"It'll show what it needs to."

"You remember?"

"That one? Not really. But others. It will have evidence."

Nita licked her lips. "Maybe that you hurt him, but that you're a zannie?"

"Does it matter? I'm pretty sure they'd put a wanted ad out for a mafia torturer, even if I weren't a zannie."

True, that.

Kovit's voice was small. "If he outs me, I'll have to go back anyway. I'll need his help to hide and stay under the radar. I'd be doomed on my own."

It was smart. It was the kind of thing her mother would do.

Nita cleared her throat. "Why did you stop the video?"

"Isn't it obvious?" He turned to her, thick eyebrows pulled together. "I didn't want you to see."

Nita returned his gaze, unblinking. "Are you ashamed?"

"Not at all." A hint of a smile crept back into his face.

"I know what you are."

"I know." He looked away. "But there's a difference between knowing and *seeing*."

Nita swallowed, remembering Mirella's shrieks of agony echoing down the hallway, and Kovit's mad laughter as he did . . . things.

Things she didn't want to think about.

"If you see this," he whispered softly, "you'll run away. You'll leave and never look back."

She stared back at him, choking on her own breath.

He was right.

If she saw, she would run.

In all those stupid movies she'd watched as a kid, couples shared every dark secret, friends promised nothing hidden between them. They understood. They exposed each other, stripped each other bare, and loved even the ugly.

Nita was not those people.

If she saw this ugly, she would run. She would run far, and she would run fast, and she wouldn't look back.

She didn't want to know the darkest part of Kovit's soul. Didn't want to strip him of his secrets. His secrets were his to share or not. And sometimes people didn't need to know every part of each other's lives intimately.

Nita certainly didn't want to talk about her dissection fetish with him. He knew about it, but she would never ever ask him to watch her take someone apart. Not because she was ashamed, but because she knew there were parts of what she did that went beyond the normal and verged on the deeply disturbing.

She'd seen the way he looked at her when she'd cut off Reyes' thumb. The unease in his gaze, the crease between his brow.

But were they truly partners if they weren't completely open? It wasn't like he was lying to her. She understood what happened in that video without watching it.

She didn't know.

But she didn't want to lose him. And if she watched that video, she would.

Nita took her hand from the phone. "I understand. I won't watch it."

His shoulders slumped in relief, and he tipped his head up to the ceiling, as if thanking God. His voice was soft and scared. "I thought you were going to push."

Nita shook her head. "It's your past to share or hide. I respect you too much to push."

He nodded, lips pressed together tightly, eyes closed, and released a huge breath followed by a short laugh. Then he turned a tired grin on her.

She returned it, and rose. "We've had a long day. We'll make a plan tomorrow morning, after we've had some rest."

He saluted. "Aye-aye, Captain."

She rolled her eyes went to brush her teeth.

Nita dreamed of the market.

Mirella was screaming.

In the past, Nita had been trapped in the cage when Kovit tortured the other girl. But in her dream, the cage was still shattered from when she'd escaped. And Mirella's shrieks sounded like the skin of her throat had torn and each scream was made of blood. They gurgled.

Nita stood in front of the workroom door. Mirella and Kovit were behind it. If she opened it, she'd know everything. There'd be no going back.

She turned away from the door.

The scene changed, and suddenly Nita was in her apartment in Lima, in the dissection room. A cage was bolted to the floor, and Fabricio stared out at her, the side of his face bloody from where his ear had been ripped off.

"Why didn't you come?" he asked.

"You were right outside the door." Mirella chimed in.

Nita turned around, to where Mirella had spoken. The door to the workroom was open now, and the small girl lay on the metal dissection table, gray skin dripping with blood.

And standing over her was Nita's mother.

Who smiled.

Nita woke up with a start, body spasming as she jerked out of the bed, gasping for air. Her heart slammed in her chest, and her whole body shook.

Kovit rolled over in his sleep, his dark hair falling over his face. His expression was peaceful as he slept, lips turning up softly. He didn't look creepy at all, just human, like any other sleeping boy.

Nita swallowed, throat dry, and stumbled into the bathroom. She splashed cold water on her face.

She had spent her whole life looking away from her mother's crimes. *If I didn't see it, I couldn't have stopped it.* She'd ignored her mother, and by ignoring, she'd enabled who knew what kind of hideousness.

She'd refused to face any of the truths until she was forced. Until there was a boy chained in her room and her mother was standing over him hacking his ear off.

How was ignoring what Kovit did any different from with her mother? Wasn't she just enabling him by pretending not to see his crimes?

For the first time, she let herself consider: was she just replacing one monster with another?

TWENTY-NINE

NITA COULDN'T FALL BACK ASLEEP, and she didn't want to wake Kovit, so she crept downstairs. She wasn't sure what she was going to do in an empty pawnshop at night, but she knew she wasn't going back to sleep yet. She didn't want to have to lie down next to Kovit, hear his easy, peaceful breaths, untroubled by the things he'd done. She didn't want to feel the heat of his body creeping over in the space between them on the bed.

Right now, she couldn't be that close to him.

The light was still on when she went downstairs, and she opened the stairwell door and found Diana, cross-legged in one of the plush Victorian-style chairs, typing on her computer.

She looked up when Nita came in. "Oh, hey."

"Hey." Nita blinked at her. "It's the middle of the night. What are you still doing here?"

Diana sighed. She'd pulled her hair back into a ponytail and taken out her mouthpiece, so Nita got a glimpse of her real teeth. They were small and sharp, and reminded her of cat's teeth, but without the fangs. They didn't look particularly dangerous, because they were so small, but they also didn't look even the slightest bit human.

"I was working on decrypting the info from the phone you gave me." Diana looked up, saw Nita staring at her mouth, and quickly shoved her fake teeth back in. There was a click as they hooked around her molars and the real teeth were gone, covered by a retainer.

Nita pretended she hadn't noticed the teeth. "Any luck?"

She sighed. "No. Nothing."

Diana rose and cracked her back. She put her computer down and looked outside. "I hadn't realized how late it was. What time is it?"

Nita shrugged. "Around three, I think."

Diana groaned and ran a hand through her hair. "Well, there goes my sleep schedule."

Nita sat down on a dining chair across from her, careful not to knock over a hideous ceramic monkey in the process. "Did you have anything to wake up for tomorrow?"

"Not really. I'm doing some online courses in programming to get my diploma. Adair got me a new identity here, and I'm hoping I can have everything in place to go to college next year."

Nita felt a spike of envy. She wanted to go to college next year. Even this year. Any year, really.

It was nice in a strange way, though, hearing her own goals echoed back at herself. It made her warm a little to Diana.

"You and Adair seem close," Nita commented.

Diana looked away. "Who the hell knows with him. One minute he's getting me a fake ID, the next he's joking about murdering me in the basement."

"But he listens to you."

"Sometimes." She sighed and looked away, changing the subject. "What are your plans for tomorrow?"

Nita stretched. "I'm going to get rid of the person who sold me to the black market."

Diana shifted uncomfortably. "And by 'get rid of,' I assume you mean murder."

"Obviously."

"You know, Nita, murder doesn't solve every problem."

"But it will solve this one."

"Just like it solved your problems earlier today?" Diana's voice was hard. "That just got the police on your tail too."

True enough.

"This is different. Today was"—Nita swallowed, forcing herself to admit the words aloud, to acknowledge she was smart enough to know when she'd screwed up—"a mistake. I miscalculated."

Diana's eyebrows shot up.

"This is personal," Nita continued, before Diana could respond. "I saved his life, and he repaid me by selling mine." She crossed her arms. "He's already sold my location to the black market twice. If I don't get rid of him now, there's no telling what he'll do next."

Diana wrapped her arms around herself. She was silent for a long time, and her large eyes were lost in thought.

Finally, she brushed a stray hair from her face, and still not looking at Nita, she whispered, "You know, after I ran away from my foster family, I decided to kill my family's murderer."

Nita nodded. This seemed like a logical thing to do. Nita would have done the same in Diana's shoes.

Then she frowned. "Wasn't he in jail?"

"No. He was a minor when he committed the crime, and the courts were so divided on the whole ghouls-are-evil-and-eat-people issue, that he ended up with a really short sentence." Diana's smile was bitter. "I'm sure it didn't help that we were brown and he was white. He was out in a couple of years."

Nita scowled, wondering if her father's murderer had been human, he would have gotten a shorter sentence because her father was brown. The thought made her blood boil.

"That's a shit system," Nita finally said, the words pale and weak compared to her feelings.

"It is. I was unhappy with the ruling, to say the least." Diana sighed, folding and refolding her hands in her lap. "So I went after him myself. I was fifteen, homeless, and determined to make him pay."

Diana's eyes went distant, and her lips turned down. "It wasn't easy, tracking him down. It took a while. But I did it. He was living in Boston, working in a coffee shop, making lattes ten hours a day, and doing community college in the evening."

Diana swallowed. "I didn't want to get caught, so I set everything up with the utmost care. I followed him every day to learn his schedule and figure out when he was alone. I eavesdropped when he ordered food at restaurants to see if he had allergies. I wanted to kill him without a trace.

"But the more I followed him, the more I got to know him.

He did community service hours picking up garbage from the park, which I'm pretty sure was part of his parole. Sometimes he'd give directions to lost tourists when he saw them. He lived in a homeless shelter, but never got into fights."

She sighed. "I'd been watching him for nearly a month when one of those UEA members – you know, the hate group?"

"I know them."

The Unnatural Extermination Agenda. Fanatics who believed all unnaturals were evil and ought to be murdered. They were a huge group, often censored and arrested, but the more attention they got, the more they seemed to grow. There had been a *Post* article condemning them last month after they burned a family's house down to drive them out of town, and Nita swore that instead of making the UEA more hated, it had made them more popular.

This was why Nita hated people. They condemned things publicly then went and supported them in private. She didn't trust them. People said that there were more good people than bad, but Nita actually thought there were more bad people than good – because all the people quietly doing nothing ended up supporting the bad people anyway.

Like Nita supported her mother with her silence. And Kovit.

She squeezed her eyes shut. She couldn't think of this right now.

"Nita?"

"Sorry." Nita cleared her throat, trying to purge her thoughts from her head. "You were stalking your family's murderer. And the UEA came by?"

"Yeah. So, he was walking down the street, and a member of the UEA gave him one of their pamphlets. You know the ones telling people 'unnaturals are a conspiracy of the devil' or whatever?"

"Yep." She saw them all over the streets in some cities. Hate pamphlets littered across the sidewalks like evil paving stones.

Diana swallowed. "He took it."

Nita tilted her head to the side. "I mean, he did kill a family of ghouls. The UEA sounds up his alley."

Diana shook her head. "But he looked at it a block away, just stared at it for a long while." She paused for a fraction of a second. "Then he crumpled it up and threw it into the trash."

Diana let down her ponytail, so her hair swirled around her face. "I didn't know if he threw it out because it was part of his parole conditions or because it was a particularly crazy flyer. But my first thought wasn't any of that, it was *maybe he regrets it.*" She blinked rapidly, like she was trying to dust tears from her eyes. "Maybe he regrets what he's done."

Diana looked away, over the shadowy outlines of the pawnshop, into some place in the past. "And that's when I knew I couldn't kill him."

Nita shifted. "Why not?"

"Because I was making up excuses for him. I wanted him to realize he'd made a mistake. I wanted him to not be bad. And the minute I realized I was making excuses, I knew I could never kill him. I'd had a month, and I hadn't done it. It just wasn't in me. His death wouldn't bring back my family. And I didn't think he'd be killing anyone else—I'd seen enough to be reasonably sure of that."

Nita stared, and her voice was slightly incredulous. "You just let him go? Forgave him? After he murdered your whole family?"

Diana flinched. "No. Never. I won't ever forgive him. I just . . ." She trailed off, then sighed. "I just realized that hurting him wouldn't bring them back. Nothing would. Murdering him was only going to make me feel awful, and maybe get me arrested. He'd already taken away my past. Killing him might take away my future. I wasn't going to let him ruin the rest of my life too."

Nita sighed, finally seeing what Diana was trying to tell her. "Look, Diana, I appreciate the story. But we come from very different pasts. Fabricio is still actively trying to kill me."

"Because you keep trying to kill him?" Diana countered.

Nita opened her mouth, then closed it.

"Tell me, did he decide to kill you because you tried to kill him?"

Nita's eyes narrowed. "How do you know about that?"

"I didn't." She shrugged. "But I do now."

"You just . . . guessed?"

"Based on your character. I bet you'd tried to take vengeance and it hadn't worked." Diana's voice was soft. "And now he's after you because he thinks you're after him."

Diana might be right about that. Nita considered, and decided it didn't matter. "I still want him dead. He deserves to die for what he's done. Besides, if I don't kill him, he'll keep coming after me."

"You said you saved him. Do you really want to kill him?"

"Yes."

Diana pursed her mouth. "Murder isn't the answer."

"Some people in the world only understand violence. If I want to communicate with them, I need to speak their language."

"That's not—"

Nita sighed and rose. "Look. I get it. You want me to understand that murder is bad. That all of this mess is happening because I tried to kill someone and failed. But the thing is, murder *will* solve this. And it's a little late to be preaching morals at me. I'd say around a few hundred dead bodies too late to tell me murder is wrong."

And with that, Nita turned around and walked back upstairs, leaving Diana alone in the dark shop.

THIRTY

NITA WOKE UP when the morning sun spilled across her eyes and burned into her dreams. She cracked open her eyes, then immediately closed them. The light was too strong.

When she opened them again, she rolled over to the other side of the bed. She found Kovit sitting up, typing on his phone. He turned to her, and the morning light brushed his cheeks and dappled his skin with soft light. It spread through the gaps in his eyelashes so she could see each individual one, and softened the line of his jaw.

"What are you doing?" she asked sleepily.

He hesitated, then looked away. "Chatting."

"With?"

"Internet friends."

Nita blinked. She'd forgotten he had them. People he'd been friends with for years. People who had no idea what kind of person he was, but still cared for him.

She looked away. "What are you talking about?"

"Henry."

Nita's head jerked up. "What?"

Kovit swallowed. "Somehow Henry knows I'm alive. Only you, me, and this group knew I was alive. I know you wouldn't tell him. You didn't even know who Henry was before this."

Nita closed her eyes. "So you want to know—"

"If it's my friends." He shrugged. "I want to know if somehow one of them accidentally outed me, or Henry somehow hacked our chatroom."

She closed her eyes. "How can you possibly find that out?"

"By asking." Nita tilted her head to the side, and he elaborated. "They know I wasn't raised in great circumstances. I think they all think I had an abusive family. I guess it's close enough. Anyway, I said that I'd run away when I met up with Anna and the others in Detroit. But now I'm telling them he found me, and asking if anyone approached them or if anyone had anything suspicious happen to them lately."

"And?"

He shook his head. "No. If they gave me away by accident, they don't seem to know it."

She closed her eyes. "That was always unlikely."

"I know." He looked away. "But it was the best option."

Nita nodded. "I'm sorry."

He sighed softly. "I was stupid for not being more careful. I mean, Henry liked to micromanage everything else in my life, why not this too? He probably hacked the chatroom years ago and has been eavesdropping ever since."

Nita shivered. When Kovit had first mentioned online

friends, she wondered why she'd never considered that. But now she understood—somewhere inside, she knew her mother would've found out and ruined it.

No, friends were liabilities.

Kovit tucked his phone away. "Never mind. There are more important things to deal with."

Nita sighed. "You're right. It doesn't matter how Henry found out, I suppose. We have to handle it now."

He laughed, light and free. "Actually, I meant breakfast."

She stared at him. That was a joke, right?

He nodded to the table. "I ducked out to the Tim Hortons across the street."

It wasn't a joke?

Nita walked over to the table, and the moment she pried open the paper bags, her nose was assaulted with the smell of fresh bacon and eggs. Her stomach rumbled, and she dove in.

While she was eating, Kovit sat across from her and tapped his fingers on the table. "Though we really do need to deal with this."

"What exactly did the email from Henry say?" Nita asked through a bite of sandwich. "Did it give a timeline or anything for responding?"

Kovit blinked. "I didn't actually look. I think my mind sort of shut down partway through."

He pulled out his phone and checked the email. "He says if I don't respond within twenty-four hours, he'll release the video."

It had already been at least twelve since he sent it, probably more. Kovit would need to respond soon.

"Anything else?"

"It says he's in Toronto and wants me to join him. He'll buy me a plane ticket from wherever I am to come here."

Nita tapped her fingers on the desk. "We could ask him to get you a ticket from somewhere far away. Singapore or something. Buy some time."

Kovit shook his head. "Henry wouldn't believe it. Besides, why would I be in Singapore anyway?"

"I don't know. Maybe you're practicing your . . . whatever language they speak there."

"English."

"Oh."

Kovit sighed and leaned back. "Delaying things won't change anything."

"You're right." Nita's voice was firm. "We need to kill him."

"Kill him?" Kovit's voice was soft.

"Kill him," she confirmed.

He looked away. "Look, Nita . . ."

A stone sank in her stomach at his tone of voice. That meant nothing good. "Yes?"

"I don't think I can do that."

Right. He had his rules. She wished he were a little more flexible on them, given that his life was in danger. But fine, she could get around them.

"Okay." Her voice was cautious, each word walking a tightrope. "What if I kill him for you?"

He flinched and looked away. "No. I just . . ."

"You don't want him to die." Her voice was flat.

"I don't."

She stared at him. Her brain was encased in cement, and she was trying to crack it out so it could stretch over to whatever his line of thinking was. "He wanted to torture you. He wanted you dead. He's the reason you were sent to South America."

"Yes."

"And now he's trying to blackmail you into being his slave again."

"Yes."

Nita kept staring at him. "How can you not want to kill him?"

"He raised me." Kovit met her eyes, his gaze calm and implacable. "He may not have loved me, he may have thought of me as nothing more than a tool. But that doesn't mean I didn't care about him."

She sighed, suddenly tired. This was not the time for his morals to surface.

Nita gritted her teeth. "Kovit. Do you want to live?"

He stared at her. "Of course."

"Do you think you'll survive if he leaks that video?"

"No."

"Do you want to work for him again?"

He shivered softly, and Nita couldn't tell if it was anticipation or fear. He took a long time to respond, but when he spoke, his voice was firm. "No."

"All right. Then tell me—how are we going to deal with his blackmail?"

"I'll talk to him." Kovit tilted his chin up. His dark eyes were tight, and his face could have been a statue.

"All right," Nita said amicably. "Do you think that will work?"

He hesitated, then looked away. "Probably not." He let out a breath and met her eyes. "But I'm still going to try."

Nita bit down choice words of frustration. It would be so much easier to just kill Henry and get on with things. She didn't need this extra complication.

"Fine." Nita sighed. "If you can't talk him out of it, we kill him, though."

"Nita—"

"Is there another way to stop him aside from killing him?" she snapped.

"No." The words sounded like she'd scraped them from his throat with a butter knife.

"Then it's settled." She pursed her lips. "Now, we're going to need to deal with Fabricio first, since his plane is arriving shortly. I assume you have no problem with killing *him*?"

He smiled, slow and contented and full of anticipation. "None at all."

THIRTY-ONE

THE AIRPORT WAS BUSIER than Nita remembered, and she stuck close to Kovit as they walked through. There was only one direct Bogotá–Toronto flight, so it hadn't been too hard to figure out Fabricio's arrival time. It was the same flight Nita had taken. They could have chosen a flight with a layover, but Nita was pretty sure that INHUP would always use direct flights where possible.

Nita and Kovit walked along the passenger pickup and drop-off area, heading to the area where INHUP had waited for her before. Nita had been worried that they would stand out at the airport, her memories of North America tied strongly to her very white Chicago suburb, but this was Toronto, and she hadn't needed to worry. They blended in easily.

They rounded a bend and saw a section for airport vehicles. A black, nondescript van parked right at the end, one that looked exactly like the one that had picked Nita up, right down to the license plate in the front.

Found you.

They approached, and the same square-jawed driver that

had picked her up was drumming his fingers on the steering wheel. Nita frowned, ducking a bit behind Kovit, so she wasn't recognized.

Kovit turned to her. "You sure about this?"

"Of course. It'll be fine."

He looked doubtful, but he approached the van. Nita circled around behind another vehicle, out of view. Kovit rapped gently on the driver's window, and when it lowered, he asked, "Excuse me, I'm lost. Can you tell me where terminal three pickup is?"

Nita couldn't make out the words of the INHUP driver, but she slipped closer to the car, running low while Kovit kept the man occupied so that she was crouched in front of the grille. She ducked her face, keeping it down as she moved. When she did look up it was to check for security cameras.

The last thing she needed was yet more attention.

She couldn't see any pointing directly at them, though that wasn't a guarantee. And even if there were, they wouldn't be reviewed until well after she'd made her escape. Kovit, with his dark hair falling into his eyes and obscuring his features, would be unidentifiable.

Nita was a little more distinctive, since she was already known to INHUP. Which was why she'd tucked her hair under a baseball cap and brought fluid into her nose and cheeks so they swelled up, deforming her features. It was uncomfortable, and she was going to change it the moment they were out of the public eye, but it was good enough for now.

Kovit's eyes never even flicked to her, though she knew he'd seen her duck in front of the car. He backed up from the vehicle and started pointing. "So, I go that way, then into the building where that orange sign is? Or where the green sign is?"

The INHUP agent hesitated, then got out of the car to point for Kovit.

Perfect.

Nita slipped in behind him, shoved a needle in his neck, and pushed down on the plunger.

The man's eyes rolled up, but before he could finish falling, Kovit and Nita each grabbed an arm and casually looped them over their shoulders so it looked like the man was still standing. Nita popped the trunk, and they shoved the unconscious body inside.

Nita put the used needle back in the small metal case. The drugs and syringe were courtesy of Adair, items Nita had added to her deal with him. Nita didn't ask why he had a stash of ketamine in his shop already, or what he used it for. She didn't want to know.

She looked down at the unconscious man in the trunk and swallowed, her mind slipping back to when she'd been captured by Reyes. The feel of the needle in her shoulder, how fast the drug had covered her glutamine receptors.

She could still remember the sensation of her fingers scraping the floor and the all-encompassing fear, the desperate crawl to the bathroom to stall for time until her mother came. Only Nita hadn't made it more than a foot. And her mother had never come.

"Nita? You gonna close that?"

Nita blinked and looked to Kovit, eyes squinting in memory. "Hey, I never asked you."

He tilted his head. "What?"

"Were you there when Reyes drugged and kidnapped me in Lima?"

He shook his head. "I never got to leave the market. If I'd been in Lima, I'd've run."

Nita tried to pull up the memory again. Had it been Fabricio who injected her? She remembered a boy and a smile and Reyes' shoes. But nothing else.

Or had it just been some random lackey hired by Reyes?

Nita shook her head and closed the trunk. It didn't matter.

Kovit had taken the jacket and sunglasses from the unconscious man and now put them on and got in the driver's side of the car. "How do I look?"

Nita considered. "Fine, but definitely not like the guy who was here before."

"Is it the hair?" Kovit smoothed his tousled hair.

Nita snorted. "It's the skin. He was white as a Hollywood action star. And you're—"

"Not." He grinned. "I'm prettier, though."

"You are," Nita agreed, because it was true, especially after he'd eaten pain. Which, given the brittleness of his hair and the bags under his eyes, he should do soon. "But they're going to notice pretty fast you're not who you should be."

He shrugged. "You'll just have to be fast with the sedative."

Nita nodded and crawled in the back. After a moment, she reconsidered and got in the trunk with the unconscious man. Better angle.

Not a moment too soon. Because down the parking aisle, two familiar figures approached the car.

Fabricio walked carefully, his eyes nervous and flicking around, his mouth pinched. The angle of the sun cast his face in shadow, darkening the blue-gray of his eyes to a near black, and shot black and gold highlights through his dark brown hair.

Beside him was Quispe.

She turned to say something to Fabricio with a gentle smile. Her immaculate black suit was a sharp contrast to his floppy sweatpants and T-shirt.

Nita swallowed and uncapped her syringe, suddenly extremely glad they hadn't decided to take out the INHUP agents in a more permanent way, like Adair had suggested when Nita asked to buy his ketamine. She wouldn't have been able to go through with killing Quispe.

For the first time, she actually felt she understood Kovit's rules about not hurting people he knew. But it was still different. Nita *liked* Quispe. She knew Fabricio, and all she felt for him was a desperate desire to murder him.

Nita's heart jackhammered in her chest as the pair came closer and closer. Her sweaty fingers clutched the syringe, and she struggled to keep her breathing even.

Quispe opened the car door, and motioned Fabricio inside. He crawled in, pleather squealing in protest as he slid by. Quispe followed, with far less noise and far more poise.

She froze when she saw Kovit in the front.

"What—"

Nita drove a syringe into her neck, and the agent slumped onto the seat of the car, before her body weight pulled her down onto the floor of the back seat.

Fabricio freaked and went for the open door, but Nita slammed it closed and yelled, "Drive!"

The doors all locked automatically when the car started moving. Kovit pulled them away from the curb and into traffic.

Fabricio yanked on the handles repeatedly, then started smashing the windows, but nothing worked. He spun to Kovit, but Nita vaulted over the back seat out of the trunk and into the seat beside Fabricio. She kicked him in the face as she was in the air, and he yelped, falling backwards and cracking his head on the window.

"I wouldn't do anything to the driver if I were you." Nita's voice was calm as she settled into her seat beside Fabricio. She removed the swelling on her face and took off her hat. She slipped into Spanish without even thinking about it. "After all, we're driving, and we're about to get on the highway. People don't survive highway accidents very often."

Fabricio turned slowly to face her, his eyes huge. There was a small smudge of blood on the window where'd he hit his head. "Nita."

Nita smiled, sharp and predatory. "Hello again, Fabricio."

THIRTY-TWO

FABRICIO SWALLOWED and stared at her. Nita flicked out her scalpel—also courtesy of Adair, she'd never been happier to have a scalpel back in her possession—and gave Fabricio a smile. "I suggest you stay right where you are until we get where we're going."

He blinked watery eyes and gingerly touched the back of his head. "So you can kill me with less mess?"

Nita just smiled wider.

His eyes flicked to the front seat. "Who's your friend?"

"This is Kovit." Nita's finger gently traced the line of her scalpel, drawing blood and healing it. "You remember, I said that the market you sold me to had a zannie in its employ?"

Fabricio's face went gray, and his eyes flicked to Kovit. "You're joking."

Nita switched to English. "Kovit, he thinks I'm joking that you're a zannie."

"Well." Kovit took off his sunglasses and met Fabricio's eyes in the rearview mirror. "I'd be *delighted* to give him a demonstration, but I'm driving at the moment. When we stop"—a flash of teeth—"I'll make sure he won't doubt."

Nita opened her mouth to translate for Fabricio, but to her shock, he responded in English, lightly accented. "I'm fine without a demonstration, thanks. I'll take your word for it."

Nita swallowed the bitter taste in her mouth as she remembered how he'd faked not understanding English at all when he was her mother's captive. Just another of his many lies.

"It's no trouble. I do so love proving doubters wrong." Kovit gave Fabricio a warped smile, one of his patented grins that implied all the dark and cruel things Kovit wanted to do to his victims. Nita suppressed a shudder at the sight.

Fabricio swallowed and tore his eyes away from Kovit and back to Nita. "Nita, please, can we talk about this?"

"Talk about what? How you sent half the black market to kill me? How you hired a mafia family to gun me down in the streets?" Nita's voice was cold. "I think we're done talking."

"You poisoned me!" he cried. "You told me you'd stop at nothing until I was dead! I was trying to protect myself!"

"Like you were trying to protect yourself when you sold me out to Reyes?"

"Yes!" he yelled, then froze, eyes flicking back and forth and mouth turning down. "I mean, no."

Nita *tsk*ed. "It's a little late to be claiming innocence, Fabricio. Can't we dispose of this facade?"

He glared at her, then looked away. "Look, I made a mistake. I was scared and desperate and stupid, and I regret what I did."

"You only regret it because I got away and you got caught."

He winced. "That's not true."

"Save me your pity speech."

The car slowed, and Kovit angled it off the highway, down onto a small rural road. They bumped along, no other cars in sight. Fields stretched in front of them, occasionally blocked by a stand of trees. A row of quaint country houses sat just off the road, looking as pretty as if they'd been copied from a postcard. Just past them, a dilapidated farmhouse destroyed the picture.

Fabricio's eyes flicked over the scenery, then jerked back to Nita. "Where are you taking me?"

"Somewhere no one will find your body."

Kovit pulled into a small dirt road, down a winding lane to a small farmhouse that looked like it had seen better days. Much better days.

This was also courtesy of Adair—apparently it was one of his many safe houses. She'd initially assumed he disposed of bodies here, but then she remembered kelpies ate people, so any evidence of bodies was probably at the bottom of the lake after he'd finished eating.

They pulled up, and the car stopped with a crunch of gravel. Kovit killed the engine, plunging them all into sudden silence.

Nita leaned forward to menace Fabricio, but he twisted suddenly, foot coming up and snapping against her face. She flew back, and this time it was her head that smacked into the window.

He ripped out of the car, the doors having unlocked when

the car stopped, and pelted away, feet skidding on the gravel, breathing fast and panicked.

Kovit swore and scrambled for his seat belt.

Nita clutched her bruised face, cursing herself for not switching the child lock on. Her cheekbone ground unpleasantly and the back of her head hurt. She healed them as she opened the other door. She got out gingerly, stumbling as her vision wavered while she was healing one of the wounds, eyes peeled for Fabricio.

She didn't see him.

Kovit came around from the other side of the car and nodded toward the farmhouse.

He closed his eyes and licked his lips. "He went that way."

He shivered softly as Fabricio's pain trickled through him, those small micro pains that all humans had—a hangnail, a scrape, a bruise. No human had no pain. And Kovit was very good at detecting pain.

Fabricio couldn't escape from them.

Kovit pocketed the car keys as he walked toward the farmhouse. Nita fell in step beside him.

The farmhouse was small, and there was only one door. The faded red paint on the building had been worn down by the elements, but it still stood, albeit slightly crooked. The door, once painted in white, now flaking in gray, was ajar. Darkness swallowed whatever was on the other side.

Kovit nodded forward, and Nita took a tentative step, shoving the door open further. Silence. Darkness.

She reached a hand over for the light switch, and something smashed onto her fingers before she could push it.

Pain ricocheted up her arm, and she shrieked as her knuckles popped. She'd been densifying her bones, otherwise her whole hand would have shattered. As it was, cracks spread across her bones, spiderwebbing through them even as muscles burst and crushed blood vessels oozed into her skin.

Kovit gasped as her pain shot into him like a drug, his body jerking in a moment of ecstasy, and that was when Fabricio leapt outside, past Nita. He cracked a shovel over Kovit's head while he was distracted by the pain.

Kovit went down, and Nita screamed, launching herself at Fabricio, scalpel out.

He swung clumsily at her with the shovel, and she ducked, going under his guard and stabbing him with her scalpel. She caught him in the side, and he howled, blood seeping from the wound and staining his gray T-shirt.

He didn't drop the shovel, though, and swung again, a single, panicked motion. Nita dodged backwards, into the darkness of the farmhouse, and Fabricio's eyes widened a fraction before he reached forward and yanked the door shut.

Nita was plunged into darkness, and she swore, fingers scrabbling at the door handle, but there was a solid thunk as Fabricio wedged the shovel handle against it. The door didn't budge.

Swearing, Nita rammed her shoulders against it over and over until finally the wooden haft of the shovel snapped and she was free.

Kovit was groaning on the ground, rubbing his head, and Nita took a second to assess that he was okay. He was bleeding from the temple, and rubbing his head, but seemed otherwise fine. Relief made her shoulders sag for a second before she realized that Fabricio had taken the keys from Kovit and was heading for the car.

Nita swore and pelted after him.

Her feet crunched on the gravel as she ran, arms pumping, pushing adrenaline through her system. She sped up, faster and faster, her body a streak of tightly wound speed, like she was in a Terminator movie.

The trunk of the car was open, showing a still unconscious Quispe lying curled in the back. But the original driver, the INHUP agent, had stumbled out and was blearily looking around with an air of sleepy confusion. His eyes widened and he fumbled at his waist when he saw Nita streaking toward him, but thankfully she'd disarmed him earlier.

Fabricio shot past him, ignoring him completely, and leapt into the driver's seat. He didn't close any of the doors before starting the engine and slamming his foot down on the gas.

He sped down the gravel road and into the distance, one hand on the wheel, the other clutching his bloody side. He looked back once at Nita, his blue-gray eyes huge and terrified. Then he was gone.

THIRTY-THREE

"GODDAMMIT!" NITA'S VOICE ROSE, and she considered chasing Fabricio down, pumping her body until it could run with superhuman speed.

Then she remembered that Adair had said there was another vehicle in the farmhouse he used for disposing of bodies. They were supposed to transport Fabricio's body back to Adair using that vehicle and leave the INHUP car with the unconscious agents in a parking lot in Markham.

She spun around, racing back to the barn and snapping the light on. Inside was a beat-up white ice cream truck with little pictures of snow cones and Popsicles and smiling children painted all along the side.

Of course it was an ice cream truck. How else would you keep bodies at the right temperature?

Cursing Adair and his sense of humor, Nita hopped in. The keys were already in the ignition, and she slammed her foot on the gas. The engine roared, sputtered, and stalled. Swearing, Nita lifted her foot and shoved it back on the gas, but nothing happened.

She swore again and kicked the car. She looked down at the stick shift beside her, and stared at it, a horrified realization coming over her.

She had no idea how to drive.

No. Fucking. Clue.

She'd never been behind the wheel of a car before. The movies made it look easy, and Kovit had made it seem easy. But she didn't know what to do. There was a third pedal under the wheel, and she didn't know why it was there. There was gas, brake and . . . that thing.

That thing that was probably the key to getting the car to work.

Nita screamed and smashed the steering wheel with her fist before crumpling against it.

Fabricio was gone.

Even if she could drive, there was no way she'd catch him now.

She'd had him in her hands. He'd been right there. And she'd let him get away. Again.

First the poisoning, now this.

Why hadn't she just stabbed him while she was in the car? It would have been so easy. Yes, messier. Yes, more evidence. But that could've been dealt with. She could have tossed the car in a lake and left the INHUP agents lying on the ground in a parking lot, instead of in the car in the parking lot.

She should have stabbed him, ripped his heart out while they were driving down the highway.

Her hands shook against the wheel, and she felt the tears of frustration trickling down her cheeks.

Fuck.

Fuck.

Fuck.

Would he report her? He'd have to say something to INHUP to explain the kidnapping. But the same rules still applied—if he reported her, she'd report him, and it was clear he didn't want that.

No, she suspected now that he'd escaped from everything, he'd take his fake passport and the money from selling Nita, and buy a plane ticket to somewhere else.

Somewhere she couldn't get him.

But he could still get her.

She let out a breath. It was fine. She could figure out his new fake name. Then she could find what flight he got on. She wasn't sure how she'd do this yet, but she would. Fabricio wouldn't escape a third time.

Nita brushed her frizzing hair from her face, pocketed the car keys, and got out. Her feet scuffed the dirt and moldy hay on the farmhouse floor, sneakers kicking up sawdust and ancient horse poop, and she made her way outside to check on Kovit.

He'd seemed dazed but fine when she'd checked earlier, but his temple had been bleeding, so she should probably stitch that up while they made a new plan. A better plan.

Outside, the sun was too bright, and the long blades of grass in the field swayed softly in the breeze. There was silence.

Until it was broken by a scream.

Nita tensed, then ran forward, pelting down the gravel

path. She stopped abruptly, several paces from where the INHUP car had been. She'd forgotten about the INHUP driver, who'd gotten out of the car before Fabricio left.

The INHUP agent was on the ground now, arm twisted behind his back. Kovit crouched on top like a cat with a bird, whole body lithely arched and a smile twisting his mouth that was both playful and cruel. He yanked the arm tighter, until it popped with a crunch.

The agent screamed again, sharp and harsh, and began to sob, begging Kovit to stop.

"What the hell are you doing?" Nita's voice started normal but pitched high and shrieky by the end.

Kovit turned to her slowly. There was blood coating one side of his face, and his whole body shivered as he consumed the man's pain. "I thought it was fairly self-explanatory."

Nita opened her mouth, then closed it. She swallowed and said softly, "I thought we agreed not to kill the agents."

"We did." Kovit nodded agreeably. "But then this one woke up and saw both our faces."

Nita's stomach plunged. There was no way to make him unsee her face. And she didn't want either of them in the police station answering questions about why they'd kidnapped INHUP agents and Fabricio.

Kovit shrugged, and voiced the words Nita hadn't wanted to hear. "He has to die."

Nita bowed her head and swallowed. Her hands shook, and she told herself it was from all the adrenaline still coursing through her system after chasing Fabricio.

"Please, I won't say anything," the INHUP agent sobbed beneath Kovit.

Kovit casually reached around and grabbed the man's jaw, *tsk*ing. "That's enough from you. No one believes a word you say right now."

Then he casually jabbed his shoulder down into the agent's back, causing him to scream. And while his mouth was open, Kovit used his other hand to reach in and spear the man's tongue with his knife.

Nita jerked her head away before she could see what happened, but the shriek and the gurgling and the muffled "mahh tunhhh" the agent was screaming told the whole story.

Kovit hissed softly, and the shaking advanced up Nita's arm like a disease, spreading throughout her whole body.

Would you like me to pull out his tongue, Nita? Her mother's voice echoed in her memory, as clear as if she were here right now talking about mutilating Fabricio. *I have some pliers in the other room.*

"Nita?" Kovit's voice was sharp. "Look at me."

She took a shaky breath and turned her eyes to him.

His face was beautiful, each ripple of pain going through him making his skin glow with health, his hair shine a little more. He raised a bloody hand and slicked errant strands of dark hair off his face, the blood holding it back like pomade.

"This man has to die." His voice was quiet and sharp. "Tell me you understand that."

"I do." But her voice was too soft.

Kovit's mouth tightened. "This was *your* plan. You knew

the risks. I asked you, repeatedly, if you were sure you wanted to do this, if you understood the consequences if it went wrong, and you said yes every time."

She had. She just hadn't thought it would go wrong.

But that was stupid. Every plan she'd made here had gone wrong.

The INHUP agent screamed again with his gurgling tongueless voice, and something crunched like breaking a piece of celery.

The shrieking got louder. He began to beg, a soft, whimpering sound, pleading for his life but unable to articulate the words anymore.

Nita swallowed. "I . . . This is just . . . Let's just kill him and get it over with if we have to."

There was silence, then Kovit whispered, so softly she could barely hear him, "I'm hungry."

Nita's stomach tightened. She couldn't look at him. "Oh."

"He's going to die anyway." Kovit's voice grew stronger. "So I might as well get a meal out of him."

Nita swallowed and nodded, but she couldn't look at him.

Beneath Kovit, the man whimpered and renewed his struggles. Kovit snarled, and twisted the arm so the shattered bone ripped through skin and thrust itself into the air. The scream was enough to make Nita flinch.

Nita lay in her cell, powerless, listening to Mirella scream, the pressure from her voice tearing at her throat until her screams became gurgles of blood.

Nita wrenched her mind away from that. "I . . ."

Mirella screamed, high and harsh, the slightly mad sound of Kovit's laughter beneath it like a perverse symphony.

Nita reached up and clutched her head.

She could accept killing him. There was nothing to be done. He'd seen their faces. It hadn't been part of the plan, and Nita felt more than a little sick about it, but she couldn't see a way out of it now.

But torture hadn't been part of the plan.

Hypocrite. You asked Kovit to help you because of his skills, and now you're going to be squeamish when he uses them.

Something tight and painful pulsed in her chest.

The man on the ground wept, his body twisted and broken. Kovit vibrated from the constant stimuli, but his face was cold.

Nita closed her eyes, trying to drown out Mirella's screams. "I'm . . . I'm going to wait in the barn. Come get me when you're done."

She turned away before he could see her expression. She didn't know what it looked like, but she knew it wasn't something she wanted him to see.

She walked away quickly, as fast as she could without outright running.

"Nita, stop, wait." A sudden crunch, and the whimpering increased, followed by agonized howling. Nita stole a glance and wished she hadn't. The man's legs were a mangled mess. He wouldn't be running anywhere.

Nita closed her eyes and tried to burn the image from her brain.

Kovit approached and frowned. "Are you okay?"

"Fine." Nita looked away.

He hesitated, then in the softest voice whispered, "Are you afraid of me?"

Nita hesitated a moment too long, and his expression cracked and fell into something soft and real and painfully vulnerable before closing over in a dead poker face.

"No." Nita said, but it was too late.

He was silent for a long time. Then, "You don't like me eating."

"No," she admitted.

"You think it's evil."

"Of course. Not even you would deny that." She glared back at him, bristling, defensive, though she couldn't have actually explained why. She snapped, "Why are you pushing this? You stopped me from seeing that video because you knew this already!"

He ran a hand through his hair. "I'm sorry. You're right. I shouldn't have . . . I didn't want you to see that." His eyes flicked to the body still writhing on the ground. He swallowed heavily. "I'm just nervous. Eating makes me feel better."

"Like comfort food." Her voice was flat. "You're likening torturing people to eating ice cream when you feel shitty."

He bristled. "Don't tell me you wouldn't be crawling into that man's chest cavity and ripping his organs out if you were in my shoes." Nita flinched. "Fabricio got away and might report us. I'm meeting Henry in a few hours, and he might very well decide to punish me with death by INHUP. And I'm ravenous. Am I not allowed to enjoy a fucking last meal?"

But that was different. In Nita's eyes, his comfort food was more monstrous than the crime he was worrying about.

"I don't even get why this Henry thing is so hard," Nita snapped. "Why can't you just kill and torture *him*? He's actively trying to kill you or bring you back to the mafia. I can't think of a more deserving person for torture, except maybe Fabricio."

"I'm sorry I can't murder the person who raised me for ten years just for your convenience," he snarled, mouth twisting cruelly, voice dripping sarcasm.

"That's not—"

"No." His eyes were narrowed, and his voice suddenly went icy cold. Nita's eyes widened and she stepped back, instinct pulling her away. "You don't get to do that, Nita."

"Do what?"

"Judge me for not wanting to kill him. Judge *me*. You're uncomfortable that I ripped a stranger's tongue out. You, who blew up an entire market! Who lured strangers to a building to murder them! But you've got some sort of righteous rage that I won't murder the man who was like a father to me?"

"The people in the market were bad!"

"All of them? All the people? Even the prisoners?" His voice dipped low.

"That couldn't be helped." She swallowed. "I just . . . I have *some* morals."

"So do I." His eyes narrowed. "And they don't exist for your convenience," he spat. "They don't bend or change based on what you want or need at the time, Nita."

His eyes were black, and there was no light in the shadow

of the barn, masking his face in darkness. His voice was low and angry, and Nita's heart jackrabbited as he spoke. Sometimes she could see the monster inside him.

And sometimes he made her see the monster inside herself.

She swallowed and looked toward the INHUP agent, gasping on the ground a dozen feet away.

She looked at the man, with his wide, frightened eyes, face covered in blood, and she flashed back to another pair of frightened eyes. Fabricio, crouched in a cage, begging for help. This man had the same eyes.

She'd stood up to her mother and saved Fabricio. And he'd sold her.

If Nita saved this INHUP agent, if she followed that withered thing she called her conscience again, what would happen? He would thank her. And then he'd clap her in cuffs and send her to jail and Kovit to death.

Fool me once, shame on you, fool me twice, shame on me.

"Okay."

"Okay what?"

"I get it. I won't bring up the Henry thing again. Go eat." She swallowed. "I'm going to go to the barn. Come get me when you're finished."

His anger melted away, and he hesitated, like he hadn't expected to win this argument, and he wasn't sure he should have.

"Okay." His voice was soft. "I'll be with you soon."

She turned away and stumbled up to the barn. She slammed the door closed, but it didn't stop the screams from seeping through the wood and slinking into her mind like shadows.

Her body began to shake, and she crumpled to the ground, wrapping her arms around her knees.

And there, quietly, with the sound of an innocent man's screams in the background, being tortured because of her mistakes, she began to weep.

THIRTY-FOUR

THE SCREAMS STOPPED soon after, but Kovit didn't return. If she strained hard, she thought she could still hear gurgles and gasps. She wondered if Kovit had crushed the man's voice box so she wouldn't have to hear the screaming.

It was considerate, in a horrible kind of way.

She swallowed, her throat choking with phlegm from her tears and sniffling into her jeans. How had everything gotten so fucked up?

You teamed up with a zannie. How did you think this was going to end?

He'd made it very clear he had no rules about who he hurt as long as he didn't know them. He didn't care. Human suffering meant nothing to him.

She'd done it again, gotten lulled by the lighter side of him. Sometimes she could forget what he was, what he did. Until she was forced to remember.

She'd read once that people formed stronger bonds in wartime, and they did it faster. Shared trauma made people connect. She wondered if that was all she and Kovit were—a biological consequence of the constant tension they'd experienced together in the market.

How much of their friendship was just chemicals? Two people in a high-stress situation who clicked?

If that's all it was, did it make it any less real?

Her hand made invisible Y incisions in the air with her bloody scalpel.

She thought about the paused video last night, the promises of the monstrous things that would happen caught in a child's brilliant smile.

An image of the INHUP agent he was torturing outside flashed into her mind, bone sticking out through flesh, blood pooling around him, and Kovit's hungry, needy expression.

Stop. Stop thinking about it.

Her mind didn't obey.

And even though her imagination continued to supply her with awful images, her foot continued to tap on the ground, impatient for him to finish so they could get the hell out of here and kill Fabricio.

That scared her a little. The fact that even after this, even though she was terrified, crying in a barn trying to block out screams, she still imagined herself doing things with Kovit in the future. She still saw them as a team.

How fucked up was that?

"Nita?"

She turned around. Kovit pushed the door open and approached, worry lines creasing between his eyebrows. His hands were black with dried blood, and the blood in his hair had dried and kept it out of his face like hair gel. It blended into his natural hair color so it was completely invisible.

Nita cleared her throat. "That was fast."

He hesitated. "We have things to do, places to be."

He looked away as he spoke, but she didn't press him for the real reason he'd cut his meal short. She didn't want to hear the words. That he'd died too soon. That blood loss from ripping his tongue out had caused him to go into shock and feel less pain.

That if Nita hadn't been there, he could have drawn it out much longer, that she was stifling him.

Nita looked up at him. She felt like she'd known him for ages, the darkness of his eyes more familiar to her than her own.

Maybe that just meant she should look in a mirror more often.

Sometimes she thought there was nothing left of her soul to burn away, that everything was long gone. And sometimes she wondered if she wasn't more normal than she wanted to admit.

She'd told herself she'd face the darkness in herself, in her mother, in others. She wouldn't turn away and pretend it wasn't there. But she'd been doing just that since she met up with Kovit again. She'd been willfully ignoring the parts of him that didn't suit her and taking advantage of the parts that did.

Kovit was not all evil. But the fact was that the evil was there. And it wasn't going away.

She didn't like knowing what he did. She didn't like seeing

that man's eyes bulge in pain, didn't like hearing Mirella's screams echoing through her memory. But when she didn't see it, she didn't care.

She really had just replaced her mother with another monster.

"Nita?" Kovit's voice was soft. "Are you okay?"

She blinked and focused on him. He stood a few steps away, hands loose at his sides, and his eyes were dark with concern. Her heart gave a little flip for an entirely different reason.

She was so messed up.

She massaged her temples. "It's fine. I'm just on edge."

He put his hand on her shoulder.

She flinched.

He jerked his hand back and lowered it. His face went from shock to sadness, then a moment of deep, pitiful guilt before smoothing over into a poker face.

"I'm sorry." Nita reached to take his bloody hand, but he moved away.

"I get it." He gave her a tight smile, but he didn't look her in the eye.

She opened her mouth, wanting to tell him she didn't know why she'd flinched, she knew he wouldn't hurt her. She wanted to explain that whenever he touched her, her heart raced and she wanted to lean into it, but at the same time, she could still hear the screams of his victims rattling around in her skull. And the two emotions swirled around each other, tangling and intertwining until she didn't know what was happening.

Could you simultaneously be horrified by someone and still desperately want them to stay close?

But she closed her mouth. Because she didn't know how to put it into words.

Nita let out a breath. She had a job to do. She would sort this out later.

They stood there a moment, and she had the worst feeling, like she should say something more, like she'd walked away in the middle of a fight.

The silence stretched between them longer and longer, like an unraveling thread, and Nita was scared if she spoke it would snap, but if she didn't it would all come apart.

But she didn't say anything. She didn't know how.

"Let's go see Henry," she said instead.

THIRTY-FIVE

THEY DIDN'T SPEAK on the drive back into town. Kovit had loaded the body into the ice cream truck after they'd called Adair. It was in the freezer, keeping fresh for Diana.

Nita wondered if Adair would tell the ghoul where her meal came from, and decided if he did, he'd lie about it.

They'd parked the ice cream truck on a side street, where Adair was coming to collect it. Nobody wanted the truck left alone while Nita and Kovit saw Henry.

Not that Nita would be seeing him. But she'd be watching.

In her hoodie pocket, the INHUP agent's gun weighed heavy. Their security.

Henry had agreed to meet Kovit at a Starbucks. It was a busy one on Queen Street—familiar territory. Nita had met her mother in this street. She recognized the Venezuelan restaurant they'd gone to as they walked by.

She wondered what her mother was doing now.

Nita imagined her, sitting with a bowl of popcorn, watching the news and following the black market discussion boards, silently laughing as Nita got herself in more and more trouble. Nita could almost see her black and red fingernails clicking against her phone, typing a message reminding Nita that if she just came home, all her problems would be solved, and her mother would make sure the black market regretted targeting her.

Nita swallowed the thick, viscous fear of defying her mother, and pressed shaking hands against her side. A hunt like this was just the kind of thing her mother would have loved to participate in.

"We're too early." Kovit considered the Starbucks where he was supposed to meet Henry. "Why don't we get lunch in the meantime?"

"All right."

They made their way across the street to a sports bar. The interior was dimly lit, making it seem like night. There was only one other customer, drinking at the bar. In the corner, a flat-screen TV mounted on the wall played one of Lyte's live concerts. She was an aur, a type of bioluminescent unnatural, and when the lights went off and the music started, she used her ability to cast spiral shadows through carefully designed holes cut in her clothes. People said her concerts were works of art.

The bar smelled like grease and fries, which reminded her of Vietnam. Her mother had hated the taste of lemongrass and ginger, which were in practically every dish there. So she'd made her own truly terrible burgers. Nita had to fake liking them, but whenever her mother went out, she'd grind the burger meat up, soak it in chili oil and spices—lemongrass and ginger included—so she couldn't taste what her mother had done to it, then eat it on rice noodles or in pho.

Nita and Kovit took a booth to the side. Nita tentatively ordered a burger, hoping that it would be better than her mother's.

The silence stretched awkwardly between them, and finally Kovit cleared his throat. "When it's time to meet Henry, you should stay here. We don't want him seeing you."

"I'll be in disguise." Nita kept her eyes on the table. She still couldn't look at him. "Shall I show you?"

He swallowed and nodded, hands pressed tight to his sides.

Nita closed her eyes. First, she did her hair. She removed the keratin in it so it fell straight, and changed the melanin levels. It melted from medium brown with a faint orangish tint into a soft gray with hints of white.

Next Nita targeted the skin cells on her face, and deepened the wrinkles on her skin until she looked old, aged well beyond her years. Her eyes peered out from heavy folds of skin, and her mouth was pulled down by deep-set wrinkles.

She'd considered just making her face swollen like she had at the airport, but she was worried that a swollen face would gather more attention, not less.

The thing about disguises was people could see through them. Her mother used flashy distraction, colored hair and lipstick and nails, to make people remember the wrong things.

But if they were looking for her, they'd see her.

If people were looking for Nita—a seventeen-year-old

unnatural—and they saw an old woman, they weren't going to look twice.

Kovit stared. "Wow."

Nita cracked a smile. "How do I look?"

She rose and got out the booth to spin around for emphasis.

He blinked and tilted his head. "Like a very sporty grandma."

Nita snorted. "I'm sure there are grandmas who wear hoodies."

"Undoubtedly." His voice was solemn, but the corner of his mouth twitched. Then he frowned. "Couldn't you just look like this all the time? The black market would never recognize you."

"I haven't actually changed my features, just loosened skin and taken the color from my hair." Nita sighed. "I don't want to look seventy for the rest of my life."

Kovit gave her a small smile. "I bet you'd never get carded. You could pick up alcohol for all your friends."

Nita laughed. "You mean like you? Aren't you already legal?"

"Here I am. Eight more months in the US."

Nita rolled her eyes as the waiter returned with their burgers. He did a double take when he saw Nita, then shook his head, shrugged, and left.

Both of them dove into their food like they hadn't eaten all day. Which they hadn't, now that she thought about it.

The burgers were definitely better than her mother's. Too

salty, though, but she'd been finding everything in Canada too salty after living in Peru. The Coke tasted different too, sweeter, and not in a good way.

She couldn't help touching her face as she ate. She'd never tried messing with her age before. She'd always been scared it would be irreversible. What she'd done now, that was temporary. She could slough the skin cells off, and it would be fine. It was no more than a mask. But really changing her age, the deep, internal stuff, that she'd never tried.

As she ate, she wondered if it was as simple as surface stuff. Healing issues as they appeared. Healing her cells so they stayed young.

Her mother had looked the same for Nita's whole life, even as her father grew gray at the temples and the lines around his mouth deepened.

Her mother was permanently about thirty.

Nita had always figured it was an illusion, much like what she'd just done.

But she wondered—with a body that could self-heal, and the ability to appear young . . . How old *was* her mother?

It was a slightly disturbing thought, because Nita wasn't really sure.

They slowly finished their food, still awkwardly not looking at each other. Kovit was polishing off the last of his fries when he froze, staring at something beyond Nita's head.

Nita stiffened, and slowly turned around. There was no one there.

"Excuse me!" Kovit called to the waiter. "Can you turn the volume up on the news?"

The waiter shrugged and obliged.

Nita blinked, and opened her mouth to ask Kovit what was happening, but he held up a hand and stared intently at the TV screen.

Nita looked up at it. The caption below said TEEN MURDERED BY UNICORN IN MONTREAL. The screen showed a school photo of a smiling white girl with long blond hair.

"Miss Lyon was found at four in the afternoon by a man walking his dog. Her eyes were open, and missing their irises, which prompted the man to call INHUP immediately."

The eyes were the window to the soul, as the saying went, and anyone who lost their soul was missing their irises. It was the signature of a unicorn attack.

Someone onscreen was now talking about unicorns. They looked like human men, and could steal a soul with a simple kiss, or in some cases, even a touch. They could only steal unstable souls, though, souls that weren't comfortable in their bodies. Most children and teens, and many younger adults, had unstable souls, which was where the virgin association started. But the truth was, lots of people who weren't virgins or who were older also had unstable souls. Instability of the soul had less to do with age or virginity and more to do with mental stability and being settled in one's body.

The horse concept, explained the man on the television, was because in the past, unicorns would lure people away to eat their souls. However, if the soul was too established in the body, they needed to destabilize it before they could eat. So they would "mount" the youth and pierce them with their "horn." Raping the victim usually caused sufficient trauma to destabilize the soul so that the unicorn could eat it.

Nita made a face and looked to Kovit. "Is there a reason we're watching this? Unicorns are creepy."

His mouth tightened, and his eyes stayed on the screen. "Zannies are creepy too."

"I never said they weren't," Nita agreed pleasantly. "Is this a friend of yours or something?"

"I don't know any unicorns." His mouth twisted in distaste for a moment. "That's a lie. I met one once. It tried to eat me. I was unimpressed."

Nita snorted. "I met one too, when I was a kid. It also tried to eat me."

Her mother had whisked her away and killed the unicorn. Nita's chest tightened at the memory. It would be easier if her mother were all evil, then Nita could hate her. But she wasn't, she was kind too.

Like Kovit.

Nita turned her eyes back to him, just in time to see him visibly stiffen, eyes widen as he stared at the screen.

"And now we're back to Agent Vidthuvitsai, the INHUP agent in charge of the investigation here in Montreal. Agent Vidthuvitsai, tell us, are there any suspects currently?"

Onscreen, a small brown woman with long black hair smiled a PR smile at the reporter. "I'm sorry, at this time, we can't disclose details of the investigations."

The woman had thick dark eyebrows and a slight hook to her nose. Mid-twenties, pretty, but there was something older in the set of her mouth and the tilt of her head. Her eyes were dark and thoughtful, and somehow deeply sad.

Nita frowned and turned back to Kovit. His fingers were clenched tightly around his napkin, and his eyes were glued to the screen.

The same dark eyes as the woman on the screen.

Nita's eyes widened, and she whipped back to the screen, but the news had shifted onto something else.

Kovit slumped in his seat, swallowing.

"Was that . . . ?"

"My sister," he whispered, horror slowly overtaking his features. "My sister's an INHUP agent."

THIRTY-SIX

NITA STARED AT HIM.

Kovit rarely talked about his sister. But Nita remembered the few anecdotes he'd told her. How she'd hid him from INHUP when they came in to kill his mother. How she hadn't cared that he was a zannie and had saved him. They'd seemed close.

When Kovit had left Nita in Brazil, he'd told her he wanted to find his sister and meet her again. He hadn't talked about it much since, but judging by the rawness of his expression, she was just as important to him as she had been before.

"She's not far from here," Nita whispered. "If you wanted to meet her. Montreal is only an hour by plane. Less than a day by train."

He opened his mouth, then closed it. Finally, he said quietly, "I know."

She hesitated. "Do you want to go?"

"We have to deal with Henry. And Fabricio."

"I know, but after?"

He shrugged, looking away.

Nita frowned. "You said you wanted to see her. She's so close. Why wouldn't you go?"

He was quiet for a long time. The dried blood in his hair had cracked a little, and a few strands fell in front of his face.

"What if she regrets saving me?" he whispered.

Nita reached over to put her hand on his, but hesitated. She hadn't realized how accustomed she'd become to casually touching him in the past few days. She lowered her hand, worried he'd move away again. "What if she doesn't?"

He smiled, just a slight curl of his lips. "There's a part of me that hopes that. That imagines finding her and having a tearful reunion." His smile twisted, warping into something self-deprecating. "But I wonder if it isn't better to keep the memory as is. Remember her as the person who saved my life, who loved me unconditionally, rather than face the reality that she and I are now very different people. Whatever relationship we could build now would likely be complicated and painful for both of us. And not end well."

Nita couldn't deny the truth of that. She didn't know what she'd do in his situation. Cling to a memory, or bring the memory back to the present and risk tarnishing it forever?

She understood his reluctance—especially given how poorly his meeting with his internet friends had gone.

"Just because she's in INHUP doesn't mean she doesn't still love you," Nita whispered.

Kovit snorted. "Well, I suppose she could be corrupt."

"Maybe she's there to try and change the Dangerous Unnaturals List and remove zannies from it."

He rolled his eyes. "And that's why she's hunting unicorns."

Nita admitted, it did seem a bit far-fetched. "Unicorns are on the list too. It could be a steppingstone job."

He sighed and shook his head. He was silent for a moment before murmuring, "I can't believe she joined INHUP."

"Canadian INHUP at that."

He shook his head. "I don't think she joined in Canada. But all the recruits are trained at the central headquarters in France. And they all have to do a term in a foreign country before they become certified and go to their full-time jobs. It's pretty common for them to be shuffled all over."

Nita raised an eyebrow. "You know a lot about INHUP."

"Know thine enemy." He shrugged, then his face darkened. "If she's working on a unicorn death, she's probably positioned here in the Toronto headquarters."

"I wonder if she knew the man you murdered," Nita mused, then froze, realizing what she'd just said.

Kovit stilled, shoulders tightening. His lips pressed together, and he turned to glare at her. "That *we* murdered, Nita. I may have killed him, but it was *your* plan."

"That we murdered." She swallowed, then leaned forward. "I didn't mean it. I wasn't trying to—"

"You weren't trying to remind me of how much I disgust you? How mad you still are about that?" Kovit's voice was cold.

"You don't disgust me."

"I saw your face, Nita, when that INHUP agent had to die. I know what you think of me." His jaw was tight. "Just the monster you need for a job until it's too much monster to handle."

"That's not . . ." But it kinda was, and she couldn't finish her sentence.

He shook his head and got up. "It doesn't matter. You're right. She might have known him. How do you suppose that would go? Sister, it's me, your evil brother! We haven't seen each other in a decade. Also, I just tortured and murdered your colleague. Aren't you happy to see me?"

Nita flinched from the sarcasm in his voice. There was something deeply cruel in the way he said it, and her heart began to ricochet with fear.

Nita swallowed. "You just don't tell her that part."

"Sure. Because lying is a great plan. It definitely won't backfire when she realizes what I've been doing for the past decade." His mouth twisted. "And of course, she'll get to see it all in gruesome detail if Henry sends INHUP those videos."

Nita opened her mouth, then closed it. She didn't know what to say. Because he was right. And there was nothing she could say to change that.

Kovit turned away from her, a single, sharp motion. "It's time to go see Henry."

Nita looked at him a long moment before following. He didn't look back as he headed for the door, as if he didn't even care if she came along or not.

She'd just screwed this conversation up in a monumental fashion, and she had a terrible premonition that it would come back to bite her.

THIRTY-SEVEN

THEY LEFT THE SPORTS BAR and crossed the street, heading for the Starbucks. And Henry.

The sun was still high, and people flowed down the street in chattering streams, some laughing, some talking on their cell phones. A small child sat on the curb and cried while an adult, presumably her mother, told her to get up in an increasingly loud voice.

It felt so *normal.* The people here were unaware of the monsters walking among them. Nita wondered what they'd think if they realized the person from the shooting in the news was walking by. Or a zannie who had tortured and murdered an INHUP agent.

They'd probably run screaming.

But no one noticed the two monsters crossing the street. No one ever did.

Kovit turned to her just before they reached the block with the Starbucks on it, and looked down to where her gun was hidden. "Nita—"

"Don't worry, I won't do anything unless you give the signal to shoot."

He swallowed heavily. "All right."

He turned away sharply and kept walking. Nita followed, her fingers running over the gun hidden in her hoodie, the metal warm from proximity to her body.

They entered the Starbucks separately. Kovit took the corner seat near the window, and Nita took a table across and down from his. It had a nice clear shot of whoever sat in the second seat. It was far enough away a normal human couldn't eavesdrop. Heck, the Starbucks was so loud, a normal human wouldn't have been able to eavesdrop from the table next to them.

Nita was not a normal human.

She enhanced her hearing and focused it. She planned to catch every word of their conversation.

When a man finally approached the table, Nita almost ignored him, until she saw the expression on Kovit's face.

Henry.

He was white, with gray hair and deep lines around his mouth and eyes. His skin had the ruddy tan of someone who was outside a lot, but despite his age, something about it looked tough, like a rhinoceros.

Kovit's eyes were dark and wide, his mouth slightly open. He swallowed. "Henry."

Nita's jaw clenched, and she stilled herself before she could grind her teeth off. Henry had made everything so much more complicated.

"Kovit!" Henry grinned. "Always a pleasure."

Kovit's face was still, and it was strange. In any other context, he'd have pulled out a creepy smile, twisted and warped, and whispered in a voice full of dark promises, *Oh, the pleasure is all* mine.

But he didn't. He just gestured for Henry to take a seat.

"I thought you were dead." Henry raised his eyebrows and sat. A slight smile quirked his lips. There was something deeply creepy about his smiles, and it took Nita a moment to realize they strongly resembled Kovit's. It was like seeing his expression on someone else's face.

Kovit shifted away from Henry. "I don't suppose you'd consider continuing to think I'm dead?"

Henry burst into laughter. He crossed his arms and looked at Kovit from under heavy brows. "Now, how could I do that to my favorite protégé? I've missed you, Kovit. I've been grieving."

Henry didn't look terribly grief-stricken, and Nita's fingers tensed around the handle of her hidden gun. The metal was warm and slick.

"How did you find out I was alive?" Kovit's voice was soft.

Henry smiled and touched his nose. "Ah, a great magician never reveals his secrets."

Nita sighed, heart hurting for her friend. Kovit was right, Henry was definitely monitoring his online conversations somehow.

Henry eyed Kovit. "You didn't ask me for a plane ticket."

"I was already in Toronto."

"Doing?"

“Probably the same thing you are.” Kovit sounded calm, but his shoulders were tight, and his hands tensed and released compulsively.

“Hunting.” Henry smiled, slow and thin and full of malicious promise. “Wonderful, let’s do it together.”

“Let’s not.”

Henry mock-scowled. “Kovit, why are you being so distant? We’re Family.”

“We were.” His eyes tightened. “Until you threw me under the bus to save face and sent me to South America to rot in the jungle.”

“That’s not fair, Kovit.” Henry sighed deeply. “You disobeyed a direct order and helped an enemy of the Family escape. I couldn’t just let you go with no consequences.”

Kovit’s eyes narrowed. “You told me you wanted to kill me and I was lucky to be alive.”

“I was very angry!” A flash of teeth, probably meant to be a smile, but it looked more like he was going to bite Kovit. “You know how I dislike it when people misbehave.”

Kovit’s fingers curled into his jeans. “Of course.”

Henry sighed, and ran his hand through his hair. Another gesture that Nita had seen echoed in Kovit. “I didn’t come here to fight. This isn’t going at all how I planned.” He sighed again. “I’m sorry about our argument. But one little spat shouldn’t take away a decade together.” Henry put his hand on Kovit’s shoulder in a way that seemed fatherly. “Kovit, Kovit. I promise nothing like what happened before will happen again. If you say no, I won’t push.”

Kovit stared at him with dark eyes. "A bit late for that."

Henry put his other hand on Kovit's opposite shoulder and faced him. "It's never too late. We may be Family, but I really do think of you as family. I raised you, Kovit. You're like my son. Sure we have spats, but have I ever been anything but supportive of you? Haven't I fought for you, haven't I shielded you from the ignorant fools who were afraid of you?"

Guilt coiled in Nita's stomach. *Are you afraid of me?* he'd asked her.

She remembered the way his face cracked and the hurt in his eyes when he realized she was.

"Yes." Kovit's voice was small.

"Is there anyone in the world who knows you as well as I?"

Kovit looked away, eyes drifting toward Nita before jerking back to Henry.

"Come home, Kovit." Henry's voice was gentle. "I'll sort it out. Life without you has been wretchedly dull."

Kovit didn't respond, but his eyes were on the ground. Dried flecks of blood fell from his hair like dandruff and clung to the shoulders of his shirt.

"Your room is still exactly as you left it. I haven't touched it." Henry leaned forward.

Kovit's voice was soft, and he swallowed. "I'm not . . . I came here to ask you to leave me alone. I just . . . I want to be on my own for a while."

Henry sighed. "You know I can't do that, Kovit. Gold is here, with me. You know she'll report all this to her father. I either come back with you or I come back with your body."

Kovit's voice was slow and dangerous. "And if Gold weren't an issue?"

A smile twitched the corner of Henry's lips. "Much as I would enjoy being free of the watchdog, I suspect it would be a death sentence for me too. And I don't trust her enough to try bribing her."

"Ah." Kovit looked away and was silent for a moment. Then, "Why threaten me with the videos?" He looked down at his hands. "You know if you leak those videos, no zannie will ever come within a hundred miles of working for the Family. No vampire either. You may also lose human contractors, hit men, bruisers. Most people won't want to work for an organization that leaks its members' secrets instead of dealing with them in-house. It's a terrible career move. I can't imagine the rest of the Family will approve." Kovit met Henry's eyes. "So why?"

Henry's face stilled as he studied Kovit. Finally, a slow smile slunk across his face, and he reached over, as though to cup Kovit's cheek, but his hand stopped partway, hovering just shy of Kovit's face. "Don't you understand? I don't care about any of them. I care about *you*."

Kovit blinked and leaned away from the hand. "What?"

"I don't want another zannie. I want the one I raised." Henry paused, his eyes on Kovit's, before leaning back and shrugging. "And the head of the Family is behind me. You know too much. He's approved any and all measures I choose to take to deal with the security risk."

"My information isn't worth so much that you'll risk alienating future employees."

"The head of the Family might be under a different impression." Henry winked. "But I don't need new employees. You're worth ten of them, anyway."

Kovit looked away. "Is that so?"

"Of course it's so." Henry shifted closer. "Kovit, you're the best of the best. And I don't mean at torture. I mean at everything. I've spoken to other zannies since you left. I even hired one for a time."

Kovit snorted. "How did that go?"

"Awful." Henry's voice was short and cold. "There was nothing remotely resembling humanity in her."

"Isn't that what you wanted?"

"No." Henry pursed his lips. "It was difficult to interact with her. It's the impulse control. You know, I thought I wanted someone completely amoral. But the problem was that she didn't understand or care about the value of life, and so she didn't understand the consequences of taking it. She didn't care, so she couldn't understand why others did.

"You could tell her not to hurt certain people, but it was more like a guideline than a rule. When she was hungry, she wasn't patient. She wouldn't wait for me to bring her someone we needed punished. She just picked the first person she saw on the street."

"I imagine that's gone well?" Kovit's smile was thin and sharp.

Henry's gaze was flat. "She nearly had the entire city on the hunt for us. She kidnapped a fucking three-year-old from a park and . . . Well, afterward she just ditched the body in a construction site. Do you know how angry people get about tortured and mutilated children?"

"No—people don't like to see children hurt?" Kovit's voice dripped sarcasm, his mouth twisting into something cruel. "I never would have guessed."

Henry snorted. "I had to kill her and hand the body over to INHUP. Nothing would have slaked the mob's thirst short of death."

Kovit's eyes were cold. "I see. Another zannie you've given to INHUP. Quite friendly with them, aren't you?"

"Don't mock." Henry's eyes narrowed. "I'm trying to apologize, Kovit."

Kovit blinked, then frowned. "Oh? That's not what it sounded like to me."

Henry pursed his lips. "I was dismissive of your rules. I never understood their purpose. When you refused to torture Matt, I was furious." He scowled. "But having seen what happens with someone that has no compunctions, I've found that I rather appreciated a zannie with some morals, no matter how withered."

Kovit stared, then bowed his head, hair falling into his eyes.

Henry leaned forward. "I miss you. I miss the fun we had. No one will ever accept you the way I do." He put his hand on Kovit's shoulder. "Come home."

Kovit looked up and met Henry's eyes.

And Nita knew.

He wasn't going to give the signal to shoot Henry.

It didn't matter if Henry didn't budge or wasn't going to

take back his threat. Even if Kovit couldn't talk him down, he wasn't going to let him die. Henry's hold on him was too strong.

Watching the two of them, the way Kovit stared at Henry, mouth opening and closing, searching for an answer, a new, slick fear coiled in the pit of her stomach.

What if Kovit went back?

The idea of being alone didn't bother her. Nita could and would handle herself if she needed to. But the thought of losing Kovit, of having him turn away from her because she couldn't handle him and he wanted someone who could, made her sick.

Nita's eyes narrowed and her fingers clenched tighter on the gun.

No. She wouldn't let Henry con him back. Kovit would go back only to end up dead for misbehaving again. Hell, it might even be a trap to quietly lure him somewhere to kill him.

Kovit still hadn't answered Henry. He was looking at the floor.

Henry gently squeezed Kovit's shoulder. "Please, Kovit, come home. I'm man enough to acknowledge I made a mistake. It won't happen again."

Kovit didn't shake off the hand still resting on his shoulder, and Nita's fingers trembled. He was thinking about it.

"Come home," Henry whispered again, leaning close.

Kovit closed his eyes softly and bowed his head, strands of hair falling in his face. He didn't look at Nita at all, didn't acknowledge her presence in the slightest.

Then he looked up, met Henry's eyes, and said, "Okay. I'll come home."

THIRTY-EIGHT

No.

Nita stared across the room, mouth open slightly.

Henry clapped Kovit on the shoulder. "Excellent!" He rose from his seat and pulled Kovit to his feet. "I have so much to show you. I've been experimenting with boric acid, you're going to love it."

Nita had to stop this. She couldn't let him be conned back. Her fingers tightened on the gun, and she pulled it halfway out.

Then she stopped.

She couldn't do it. She couldn't kill Henry.

Oh, physically she could. She could pull her gun out and unleash chaos in the Starbucks. Shattered glass and blood in lattes.

But Kovit would never forgive her.

Hadn't he said that Henry was like his adoptive father? Kovit couldn't kill him, and he couldn't let him die. Kovit would never forgive her if she murdered someone he cared about. Even if it was for his own good.

But he wouldn't see it that way. He'd see it as her trying to control his life. If she killed Henry against Kovit's wishes, she had no more respect for his rules and boundaries than Henry did.

Her fingers loosened on her gun. There was nothing she could do.

Henry tugged Kovit away. Kovit's head was bowed, hair falling in his face, and his shoulders slumped. He looked back, just once, and met Nita's eyes. His were sad, dark, and heavy lashed, and his gaze skittered away from her.

He looked down, and Nita's phone buzzed.

I'm sorry, read the message. *It's for the best.*

Then he was gone.

The door clanked shut after him, and Nita rose and took a step forward, as though to chase him, before she stopped.

He didn't look back.

She slowly sank to her knees, the tears in the corners of her eyes finally coalescing and slipping down her cheeks as his figure vanished down the street.

Customers streamed in and out of the door, and baristas screamed out orders. It was all a buzz of noise of movement. Nita stared through it vacantly, after the vanished silhouette of a broken monster.

She swallowed, trying to understand why he'd done it. Why he'd let Henry con him back. Kovit had always been so adamant about his desire to leave, to get away, as long as she'd known him. He had so much he wanted to do out here in the real world.

Her heart sank as understanding bloomed. He'd done it all. And it had left him worse off.

He'd wanted to meet his internet friends, only to find out that in person he couldn't handle being around them. He'd wanted to find his sister, only to realize that she was an INHUP agent, he'd probably tortured and murdered her friend, and she'd surely arrest him if they ever met.

And Nita, who was supposed to be on his side, couldn't hide her terror of him.

Guilt swirled in her stomach, making her nauseous. Because she knew the role she'd played in this.

But at the same time, a small part of her wondered if this was such a bad thing. No matter how much Nita wanted to, she wasn't able to ignore the monster in him—no, that was wrong. She was able to, but she didn't want to.

Maybe it was better that they part ways.

Why had they started working together in the first place? In Peru, it had been desperation. They needed each other to survive. Nita would have worked with the devil himself to escape. Sometimes she thought she had.

But here? In Toronto?

She could work with anyone or no one. She wasn't trapped or isolated. Neither was he. Why had they teamed up again?

Nita gazed vacantly at a coffee tumbler covered in stylized trees as her mind stumbled for answers. University students with backpacks swarmed from a subway station into the line, gasping for coffee, and she watched them for a few minutes, her eyes lingering on the textbooks peeking out from holes in their bags.

She wished she were them. She wished she could live that life, that she could go to school like them and study unnatural biology. Become an expert in her field. Go to conferences. Live her life the way she wanted, without the black market looming over her, waiting for an opportunity to capture her and take her apart. Make her just another face on a missing persons poster like the three she'd seen earlier today.

How had she managed to screw it up so terribly?

She'd spent the morning murdering an INHUP agent and trying to pretend that his screams didn't bother her, and now here she was pathetically wishing the monster who'd tortured him hadn't left her?

She remembered when Kovit had shown up, fresh from the disastrous meeting with his internet friends. She felt like she understood why he'd come to her. He was alone for the first time in his life, and he was lost. His "normal" friends weren't accepting, but he didn't want to go back to the mafia. She was the only other option he knew.

And Nita? Wasn't she just the same? She was alone for the first time, and rather than running off and proving to her mother and the world that she wasn't bothered by being alone, that she could take care of herself, she'd gone and clung to the person who appeared and offered help.

They were using each other to stopgap their own isolation and figure out their messed-up, broken lives.

It was pathetic.

Nita clenched her teeth, even as the yawning, gaping hole inside her expanded.

She didn't need Kovit. She could kill Fabricio perfectly well all by herself.

She continued to tell herself that, even as small tears trickled down her face like scars.

THIRTY-NINE

NITA MADE HER WAY back to Adair's place on the subway. She sat silent and stiff, trying to pretend that Kovit's departure didn't affect her. She didn't need him. She wasn't even sure she wanted him.

She needed to focus on the important things: finding a way to catch and kill Fabricio. She also needed a more reliable source of money than a dead man's credit card, which was probably flagged, and some still unconverted cryptocurrency, because Adair was going to kick her out eventually.

But her mind wouldn't focus, ideas skittering around and dying before they even fully formed.

The pawnshop was closed when she got back, but Adair was lounging behind the counter, texting on his phone. He looked up when she returned and raised his eyebrows.

"You look wretched."

"Thanks." She sighed, rubbing her temples. She needed to stop thinking about Kovit and focus on her other problems. "Have you found anything out about the vampire?"

"Yes and no."

"What does that mean?"

"It means that I don't have a name." His smile flickered, needle-sharp teeth showing for an instant. "But I did find something else."

Nita let curiosity pull her forward. "What?"

"Your father's murder case has been classified by INHUP. Only the highest level can access information on it."

Nita frowned. "Why would they classify it?"

"Because there's something sensitive in there. Something important, or connected to something important." Adair shrugged. "It could be your father, his killer, the motive, even the place where it happened. Without having access to the file, there's no way to know." His eyes were alight. "It's very intriguing."

What in the world about her father's murder could be classified? Had they found out what he did? No, if that were the case, Quispe would have had some very different questions for Nita when she went to INHUP. Likely, it was related to his killer, who mysteriously wasn't publicized on the list.

"Can you get access to the file?" Nita asked.

"I don't have that kind of pull. We'd need to be talking to the director of INHUP for that."

Nita sighed. Stalled again. Nothing was going right.

"I believe you owe me a username now."

"Why? You didn't get anything. I don't have anything but more questions."

He considered her for a long moment and then nodded, just once. "I'll keep looking."

She gave him a ghost of a smile. "Thanks."

They were both quiet, the silence only broken by the soft clink as Adair brushed past an old tea set and the faint hum of a fan somewhere in the building.

Finally, Adair asked, "Where's Kovit?"

Nita swallowed, hating the sudden pain that bloomed in her chest. "He went back to the Family."

Adair's eyebrows rose. "Oh?"

Nita looked away. "They were blackmailing him. He didn't have a choice."

"There's always a choice. It's just that sometimes one choice is worse than another," Adair murmured. He looked at her with narrowed eyes that flickered between swamp green and yellow. "But I'm surprised he left you."

Nita shrugged, but didn't respond.

"Trouble in paradise?" A thin, crafty smile curled Adair's features. "Perhaps having to do with the body I got earlier today. It had clearly been . . . appreciated."

Nita flinched.

"Ah." Adair leaned forward over the counter. "I thought so. Don't like Kovit's more extreme tendencies, do you?"

"I don't think many people do."

"No, I imagine not." Adair put his chin in his hand. "And yet he still chooses that, despite how it isolates him."

"He can't choose to not eat."

"But he could choose how."

Nita bowed her head. She'd thought that many times before too. "I know."

Adair tapped a finger on his counter. "Have you ever

thought about how Kovit would behave if zannies weren't on the Dangerous Unnaturals List?"

Nita blinked. "Not really."

"How do you think his behavior would change?"

"I have no idea."

Kovit's whole life had been shaped by that list. His mother had been killed for it, he'd run away to the mafia to hide from it. Kovit wouldn't be Kovit without it.

"You know what I think?" Adair steepled his fingers. "I think Kovit wouldn't ever have hurt anyone if that list didn't exist."

Nita frowned. "He's a zannie. It's literally his biological imperative to hurt people."

"It's also my biological imperative to drown people and eat them, but here you are, not underwater or eaten." Adair rolled his eyes. "And it's a human biological imperative to reproduce, but you sure don't look pregnant to me."

"Of course not!" Nita nearly gagged in revulsion, but she saw his point.

"The thing I've always noticed about Kovit is that he's a bit of a fatalist." Adair continued. "See, there's no point in trying when there's no chance of success. Why try to be a good person when you'll be shot on sight anyway? Why try not to hurt people you don't know when they'd kill you if the places were reversed?"

She'd never really thought about it that way. Kovit had lived with a sword at his throat his whole life, and no matter what he did, good or bad, that would never change.

"Kovit's been prejudged." Adair's voice was soft. "He's been found evil. And if you tell someone they're bad long enough, they'll believe it. Especially children."

Nita frowned, remembering her earlier conversation with Kovit. "You're trying to excuse Kovit's actions by his upbringing?"

Adair considered her. He seemed to reach some sort of decision, and he came out from behind the counter and gestured to the dining table. "Sit."

Nita sat, nearly knocking over a headless Greek statue in the process.

"Tell me, Nita." Adair sat across from her, his pale skin almost glowing in the semidarkness. "Who benefits from the Dangerous Unnaturals List?"

Nita blinked. "People. Humans. Everyone who doesn't die because a unicorn is on the hunt for a soul or a kappa is hungry for some organ juices. The list saves lives. That's why it exists."

"And people like Kovit?"

Nita was silent. Adair had made that point already.

"Let me ask you something." Adair's voice was low and soft. "Would you want a zannie as your doctor?"

"No!" Nita jerked away. "Of course not!"

"Why not?"

"They'd be more likely to make the pain worse for their own pleasure than heal it."

"Is that so?" Adair smiled. "But they can sense your pain. They know exactly where and how it hurts. They've felt thousands of pains and have a vast swath of data to compare it to. Do you think their diagnosis would be better?"

Nita hesitated, then nodded. "Maybe."

"And their blood is one of the strongest painkillers in the world. The black market is full of people with chronic pain paying through the nose for a jar of zannie blood to make into cream for their pains." Adair raised an eyebrow. "So a doctor who could immediately diagnose your pain and fix it. I don't know, sounds pretty ideal to me."

Nita considered. She'd never thought about it that way before. Now that she was thinking about it, zannies would probably make excellent doctors.

If they chose.

"But they wouldn't." Nita blinked up at Adair. "Zannies like to make their own pain. They'd hurt their patients."

"So you're saying the entire species is born psychopathic? Not a single one would consider getting their pain from the hospital without hurting someone?"

Put that way, it seemed far-fetched.

Nita's eyes narrowed. "What are you really trying to say?"

Adair leaned back. "I'll rephrase my earlier question: Who *profits* from the Dangerous Unnaturals List?"

Nita's stomach began to flutter as things began to click together.

Her mother profited.

The people buying body parts, killing the creatures on the list.

The crazy dictators who sheltered zannies and used them as torturers.

"The black market," Nita finally answered, the words heavy on her tongue.

Adair's smile was sharp and thin. "Exactly."

Nita swallowed, and her fingers clenched into fists by her sides.

"Have you ever noticed," Adair whispered, "that every creature on the list is also profitable? Unicorn bone is used as a drug. Zannie blood is used for pain relief, and zannies themselves are popular pet torturers for dictators. Kappa organs are a powerful poison. Vampire bodies can extend your life by decades."

Nita's voice trembled slightly. "Lots of other creatures' bodies have properties."

"But other dangerous ones?" Adair shook his head. "Ghouls eat people, but they're not on the list. Their corpses also do absolutely *nothing*."

Nita shook her head, but she was already mentally listing other creatures she knew that were particularly dangerous. The ones whose bodies couldn't earn money weren't on the list.

None of them.

Except . . .

"Kelpies." Nita met Adair's eyes. "Kelpie bodies would make a lot of money on the black market. No one's ever dissected a kelpie. They're unknown. People would pay for that."

Adair's smile tightened, and his eyes were hard. "I know. Why do you think I trade in information? Cash alone would never be enough to keep my species off the list. I make my bribes in knowledge."

Nita stared at him, and swallowed. "You're serious."

"I'm always serious."

She raised an eyebrow. "Those basement jokes . . ."

"How do you know they're jokes?" He grinned.

Nita rolled her eyes, but her mind was still whirling, trying to process all the significance of what she'd been told.

"Why?" she whispered.

"Why what?"

"Why is it like this?"

"Ahhhh." Adair's smile turned crafty. "That is a good question, isn't it?"

"And you know the answer."

"I do." He laced his fingers together. "But I'm not willing to give it up for free."

Nita narrowed her eyes. "What do you want?"

"I want you to find out why the heir to the Tácunan fortune, the doted-upon son of Alberto Tácunan, Fabricio, is running to INHUP and selling out people who save him for petty cash." Adair leaned forward. "And why the hell he hasn't gone back to his father's mansion in Argentina."

Nita's mouth thinned. "I'm going to kill Fabricio."

"I'm sure." Adair leaned back and examined his nails, which were turning sharp and black at the end, the tips of claws. Then there was a soft ripple and they were human again. "Just get me some answers first. It might be nothing." He turned to her. "But I smell a mystery, and answers to mysteries keep me alive."

He rose and grinned at her. "So before you eviscerate him, I want you to make him sing. If you want to know more about the list, that's my price."

Nita jerked her head once. "Fine. I'll get you your answers."

Adair clapped his hands together. "Excellent."

Nita was rising to thank him for the information, when the door to the pawnshop smashed open.

Both of them spun to face the door, Nita already pulling the gun from her hoodie and Adair's hand reaching for his phone.

"Don't move! Toronto police!"

FORTY

NITA FROZE. Two uniformed officers stood in the door. Neither had their guns drawn, but she could see them at their hips, opposite the tasers.

Beside her, Adair's face was still, ruthlessly covered by his glamour, but when his gaze flicked to hers, it was enraged.

Do not bring the police to my shop.

Oops.

Adair raised his hands, palms outward, and the smile he turned on the intruders was the epitome of politeness. "Is there something I can help you with, Officers?"

The one in the lead, a tall black man, said, "Don't worry, sir. You've done nothing wrong. It's your customer we'd like to talk to. Ma'am, I'm going to have to ask you to come with us."

Nita swallowed, heart jackrabbiting in her chest. She thought of all the news stories she'd seen, people reaching for phones or looking the wrong way at the police officers and ending up shot. That was in the States, she told herself. Quispe said Canada was better.

Nita clung to that, and the fact that one of the officers was black. Maybe it was better.

You can heal bullets, Nita. Let them try and shoot you.

But just because she could heal bullet wounds didn't mean she wanted to get shot. And just because they might not shoot her didn't mean they wouldn't lock her away for the rest of her life if they knew her crimes.

"May I ask what I've done?" Nita was careful to keep her voice calm and polite.

"You're wanted for questioning regarding an incident yesterday."

Nita hesitated. "Oh. I am?"

"It's been all over the news." The officer gave her a look of mild disbelief. "A woman getting off the streetcar recognized you from the bulletin and called you in."

Of course. Nita had been careless, forgetting her disguise. She'd been so preoccupied with Kovit leaving she hadn't even thought about it.

"I had no idea. I don't watch the news," she finally said.

The officer's smile was tight. He didn't believe her. Nita didn't blame him, it wasn't a particularly great lie. "All right. But I'm still going to have to ask you to come with us."

Nita's mind scrambled, trying to find a way out of this, but she couldn't come up with anything short of overpowering the police officers and running away. They'd probably shoot her in the back as she ran. Unless she killed them.

The image of the screaming INHUP agent flicked into her mind for a moment, blood running down his face like tears as Kovit hissed in pleasure.

She swallowed. She couldn't handle more innocent deaths today.

She slipped the gun behind her back into a large wooden bowl and hoped no one saw.

"Okay," she said, stepping forward, hands in front of her, palms out. "Lead the way."

The officers led her out of the building, and Adair gave her a murderous look as she passed. She tried to look apologetic, but he clearly didn't appreciate it.

The police had parked their car on the curb, and Nita was led into the back seat. She sat down on the squishy pleather seat and folded her hands in her lap. She wasn't cuffed, which was a good thing, but she was also very clearly still a prisoner.

Fuck.

The car drove off, and Nita pulled out her cell phone.

"We're going to have to ask you to leave that for now." The officer in the front gave her a sympathetic smile. "Until we get this sorted."

Nita hesitated. "I need to call my m—aunt."

"Your aunt?"

"I'm a minor. I don't think I'm allowed to say or do anything without her there."

The cop hesitated, then said, "We'll call her at the station, okay?"

Nita slipped her phone back in her pocket and nodded.

She couldn't believe she'd been arrested. All her life, she'd been so careful, her parents drilling into her the importance of staying safe. Because if they caught you, if they put you in prison, then you were a sitting duck, trapped and waiting for your enemies to murder you.

Or eat you, as would happen in Nita's case. She knew it wouldn't be long before word of what she was got around and she was torn apart and consumed.

She shivered at the thought, imagining the way her limbs would protest as they were ripped from her body, flesh stretching and shredding and clinging, blood spattering the floors and the walls, inmates desperate for immortality licking at the blood, gnawing on her bones.

No. That wouldn't happen. She was being detained, she wasn't arrested or in prison yet.

She leaned her head against the glass window. She would call her mother at the station. If anyone could get Nita out of this, her mother could. And oh, how her mother would gloat about it. Her mother would delight that Nita had finally cracked and admitted she needed her. She'd smile, sharkish and cruel.

Nita wished she could call her father instead.

Her heart tightened, and she squeezed her eyes shut. Not now. She couldn't afford to have a breakdown now, the cops wouldn't understand that it wasn't fear of them, that it was grief. She couldn't look weak.

But she also couldn't stop imagining how her father would have handled this. How he'd come in, slow and quiet, voice soft and heavy as he gently explained the misunderstanding and brought Nita home. How he'd smile at her when they left the station and ask if she wanted ice cream.

Nita stifled a sob and dug her fingers into the pleather seats. She missed him so much.

Her father had been the only truly good person in her life. Yes, he had been complicit in her mother's business killing unnaturals and selling their body parts online. But he had a soul.

She wasn't sure she could say the same thing about her mother.

When she'd been a child, he was the one who did things with her. They went to carnivals, he told her fairy tales before bed, he picked out her birthday presents and held her when she cried.

Nita let her mind drift back as the car continued through the heavy Toronto traffic. On her eighth birthday, it had blizzarded. The snow was so dense it was impossible to go out. They'd planned to go to a movie and have ice cream. Instead, they were housebound, just the two of them. But her father, undeterred, had taken liquid nitrogen from the garage and made ice cream with it. The two of them had geeked out over science, then taken their ice cream and watched Disney movies on repeat.

When Nita had asked her mother why they had liquid nitrogen in the garage, her mother said she used it to assassinate people, as it was odorless and tasteless. If Nita wasn't a good girl, her mother would release the gas in her room while she was sleeping and she'd never know what killed her.

Later, her father told her that her mother had just been messing with her. It was actually there to cryopreserve blood, sperm, and other more delicate bodily fluids from dissections. He told her if her mother wanted to kill her, she'd use a more direct, less expensive method.

Nita was surprised at how comforted she'd been by those words. Her father hadn't said, *Your mother would never do that,* because even at that age, Nita wouldn't have believed it. Instead he'd told her she didn't have to worry about invisible gases as the method. It had saved Nita years of paranoid nights lying awake wondering if she was inhaling gas at that moment.

Her father had always understood. He'd always known exactly what to say to make everything better. Nita always took his advice seriously.

Until he'd told her not to free Fabricio.

And look how that had turned out.

Her heart clenched with regret for not listening to his final request, and she forced herself to wipe her watery eyes. She wondered if the grief would ever subside, or if she'd always be like this, caught in a spiral of pain whenever she was reminded of him.

She felt awful as soon as she thought it. She was supposed to feel bad he died. But she didn't want it to hurt like this. She wanted to be able to think about him without feeling like her body was breaking from the inside out.

The police car lurched to a stop, and one of the officers opened the door. "We're here."

Nita let out a breath. Her father wouldn't want her to be caught up in grief now. He'd want her to keep a cool head and get out of this situation.

So when Nita exited the car, all trace of pain was gone from her face and she held her head high. "Lead on."

The station was new, all shiny glass and steel. It looked like a modern art sculptor had been trying to design a building that said *we're watching you, but you can watch us too*, because everything was glass and mirrors and giant black security cameras like warts. The artist had failed, because all the building did was say *we had a really weird architect, please don't look, this is embarrassing.*

Nita was led into a small room, white walls all around and a big security camera on the front. A metal table sat with four fold-out chairs, two on each side.

The officer who'd caught her at the store gave her some paperwork and left. A different cop, wearing a button-up white shirt and slacks, came in. He frowned, then asked, "Can we see some ID?"

"I don't have any."

He looked baffled.

Nita shrugged. "I'm seventeen, what do I need ID for? I don't drive, I can't drink."

"Do you have a school ID?"

"I'm homeschooled."

The cop rubbed his forehead. "You mentioned an aunt."

"Yes. Can I call her now?"

The officer nodded and handed her a phone.

Nita took it before remembering she had no idea what her mother's new cell phone number was. And she couldn't email. Damn it.

Her mom was an expert at getting out of arrests, and she had Nita's ID. Nita needed her.

She chewed her lip. There was only one place that would have her mother's cell number.

INHUP.

Well, Quispe *had* offered to go to the police with Nita. Hopefully the whole getting drugged and left in the back seat of a car hadn't changed that. It wasn't like Quispe knew Nita was responsible. Hopefully.

Nita pulled out Quispe's card from her pocket and dialed.

It rang a few times, and Nita uneasily wondered if Quispe was still unconscious in the back seat of the car they'd stolen. Or if Fabricio had killed her and dumped her body somewhere after realizing she was in the back of his getaway vehicle.

Quispe finally picked up. "Hello?"

"Agent Quispe!" Nita's voice pitched a little too high in relief. "I'm at the police station, and they want to question me, and I need you here to help explain things. I also forgot my aunt's new cell phone number. Can you call her please?"

Quispe let out a heavy breath. "Okay, okay. Hand me over to the officer there."

Nita dutifully handed the phone over and crossed her arms while the two of them talked. Or rather, while Quispe talked and the officer frowned deeper and deeper. He ran a hand over his short fuzz of brown hair and nodded along at something.

Finally, the officer said, "All right, we'll see you soon," and hung up.

He looked at Nita, a slight frown on his face. "So, Nita, is it?"

"Yes."

"I'm Detective Malcolm Levesque. Agent Quispe is on her way, as is your aunt." He sat down across from her. "Why don't we get started?"

Nita crossed her arms and set her mouth. "I'm not saying anything until they arrive."

"Look, kid—"

Nita turned her head away from him, lips pressed together.

He tried a few more times before sighing and giving up.

Nita closed her eyes and ticked off the minutes until Quispe arrived. Between her and Nita's mother, surely they could sort something out?

She tapped her foot on the ground, fast, matching the nervous rhythm of her heartbeat.

Finally the door opened and Quispe entered.

Her usually pristine suit was a little rumpled, and her eyes had dark circles under them. Clearly, being drugged and shoved in the back seat of a car hadn't suited her well.

Nita had a terrifying moment where she wondered if Fabricio had told Quispe everything, but then the agent gave Nita a tired smile and sat down beside her. Nita nearly sagged in relief. Fabricio must *really* want to keep his identity a secret.

Detective Levesque sat across from them and told Nita, "Agent Quispe has apprised me of your situation. We only have a few questions for you."

Nita hesitated. In the back of her mind, her father's voice told her to stay silent, to say absolutely nothing. But she didn't think she'd ever leave if she said nothing. And she *was* the victim here. Or at least, mostly.

"All right," she said, after a pause.

Detective Levesque steepled his fingers and leaned forward. "So, can you tell me what happened yesterday at the apartment near Yonge and Eglinton?"

"My aunt was busy." Nita swallowed, mind searching. "I went shopping. Then a crazy lady started chasing me down the street with a gun."

"Had you ever seen this woman before?"

"No."

"Do you have any idea who she is?"

"No clue."

Detective Levesque tapped his pen on his notepad. "So, you say you were wandering shopping, but we have footage of you fleeing an apartment building, with this woman in pursuit. Why were you in the apartment building?"

"I got lost." Nita blinked. "I was trying to find someone to ask directions, and figured the apartment lobby would have a security guard."

"Why would the apartment lobby have a security guard?"

Nita frowned. "All my apartments have had security guards in the lobby."

Levesque didn't look convinced, but Quispe interrupted. "It's common in Latin America."

It was common in many parts of Asia too. It was Canada that was weird in Nita's opinion.

"That's right, Quispe mentioned you'd been living in Peru. How long did you live there?"

"A bit. How is this relevant?"

Levesque shrugged. "Well, it's a country where INHUP has no power—"

"And?" Nita didn't like where he was going.

"Just musing." He switched topics, but he didn't look like he'd let it go. "Did you hear or see anything suspicious before the woman started chasing you?"

"No."

Detective Levesque sighed and twirled his pen in one hand. Then he took out some papers from his folder. "Do you know what the darknet is?"

Nita hesitated. "It's where bad people buy illegal things on the internet."

"Yes, including unnatural body parts." Levesque looked to Quispe. "I've been informed it's also where a video of you was leaked by your former captor."

Nita's lips thinned. "So I've heard."

Levesque pushed the papers forward. They were printouts of a black market product: Nita's location.

There, under the top-rated review, was Nita's threat.

You hunt me and I hunt you, in Peru or Canada. I will burn you down.

"Do you see the top one, from username Scalpel?"

"I see it." Nita's voice was steady, and she pressed her hands against the cold table so no one would see them shake.

"The time stamp makes it clear the killer is the poster." Levesque sucked his teeth. "While one body, found in the hall, appears to be a building inspector in the wrong place at the wrong time, we have identified the three bodies found together as known associates of a black market group based in Buffalo."

Nita's jaw clenched tighter. This was bad, very bad. "Is that so?"

"It looks to me like some hunters after you were lured to that location and killed."

Nita kept her gaze steady on him. "I can't say I feel sorry for them. They were trying to kill me."

Levesque's eyes narrowed. "That's very true. You have a lot of motive to want them dead."

Nita raised an eyebrow, playing it cool as a cucumber even as inside she screamed. "Are you insinuating I murdered these men?"

He tapped the paper. "This Scalpel person claims to be you. They claim to have blown up Mercado de la Muerte in Peru and killed these people here in Toronto."

Nita's fingers curled into fists. "You're blaming me based on some anonymous internet user's comments? That could be anyone."

"So you're not Scalpel?"

"Of course not." Nita swallowed and turned to Quispe. "You can't just sit here and let him accuse me."

Quispe pursed her lips. "He has a good argument. We spoke before we came in here."

"You don't believe I did it, though, right?"

Quispe sighed. "I don't know, Nita. I was drugged and kidnapped this morning when someone tried to kidnap Fabricio. Outside of INHUP, only you knew he was coming today."

Nita's fists were tight balls in her lap. They had nothing, this was all speculation.

But was speculation enough? What if she had been caught on camera? At the airport? A traffic camera?

Sweat slid down her back and pooled under her arms. Her breathing came too fast.

Too late, she realized she'd been silent too long. What would an innocent person say here?

"Are you okay?" she asked Agent Quispe, trying to muster concern. She didn't wholly succeed. "Is Fabricio okay?"

"We're both fine, but the driver is missing." Quispe's eyes were hard on Nita's. "And Fabricio has decided he doesn't trust INHUP's protection anymore and has left us."

"Oh." So, Fabricio had stayed long enough to make sure Quispe woke up before telling her he was leaving. It made sense – he didn't want to be classified as a missing person and have INHUP hunting for him.

Nita cleared her throat. "And neither of you saw your attackers?"

"No." This clearly pained Quispe. "We didn't. We're combing through security footage now."

"I'm curious what we'll find on the tapes." Levesque's eyes slid to Nita. "Or who we'll find."

Nita swallowed. "You don't really think I had anything to do with *that*? You can't blame me for every bad thing that happens in Toronto!"

Detective Levesque smiled. "No one's blaming you, Nita. We're just having a discussion."

Discussion. Yeah, right.

Nita's eyes flicked between the two of them, panic rising. She felt trapped, like a caged animal. They knew everything. She thought she'd been so clever, and now she was sitting here, the consequences of her actions staring her in the face. They were going to arrest her and take her to prison.

The walls seemed to pulse around her, closing in. She was in a cage, just like the market, and they wanted to put her in another cage forever. Nita would never get out of jail given her crimes. Even if she survived the experience, which she doubted.

Sweat dripped down Nita's forehead, and the silence dragged.

Then Quispe asked, "Is there something you want to tell us, Nita?"

Nita's breath came in short, sharp gasps, and she looked up at the camera that was recording everything.

How could she get out of this?

Then the door opened, and Nita's mother stood there. Her hair down, red streaking through the black like it was dripping blood.

"Hello, everyone. What did I miss?"

FORTY-ONE

NITA HAD NEVER BEEN so grateful to see anyone in her life as she was to see her mother right then.

Detective Levesque rose. "You can't . . . How did you . . . ?"

Nita's mother waltzed into the interrogation room like she owned it. Her boot heels clicked on the floor with each slow, deliberate step, and her wide shark smile was hypnotic. She smiled at Levesque like she was Adair, with his terrifying mouth, just waiting to swallow the detective whole.

"I just told the officers out front I was here to see my niece, and they led me here."

She sauntered over to Nita and stood behind her. Her mother wrapped her arms around Nita from behind, and reached for the papers Detective Levesque had been showing her.

"What's all this?" She raised an eyebrow, taking in the papers and Nita's rigid stance.

Detective Levesque frowned. "We were discussing Nita's involvement in certain events in Toronto."

Her mother's fingers curled possessively on Nita's shoulder. "Such as?"

"The shooting that occurred yesterday. Nita was filmed fleeing the scene, chased by an armed woman."

"Yes. What about it?"

"We were just establishing what kind of relationship Nita had with the murder victims."

Nita's mother gave him a skeptical look, and her voice went flat. "So let me get this straight. Nita was running away from a woman wielding a gun. A woman who you know was *at the crime scene*. And we're sitting here talking about if Nita was involved?"

Detective Levesque straightened, heat coming into his face. "It's not that simple." He slid the printout of the darknet chat over to her mother. "Someone online is claiming responsibility."

Her mother picked up the paper and looked at it, then gave the detective a withering glare. "This seems to be an online site selling my niece's phone GPS location."

Levesque looked uneasy. "Well, yes. But if you look at the top comment—"

"The anonymous comment, that could have been posted by anyone. For example, another dealer on the black market trying to scare off the competition so he could catch Nita himself."

Levesque blinked. "That's one possibility."

Her mother put the paper down slowly and slid it back to Levesque. "So you're saying you saw that my niece was kidnapped, sold on the black market, and attacked when she got out, and you thought to yourself, *I wonder if she's been the villain this whole time*?"

Levesque scrambled and then repeated, "It's not that simple. And she's never given a satisfactory explanation why she's the only survivor of Death Market's destruction—"

"Fire." Nita interjected. "One of the generators blew, and it set off a chain reaction. If I couldn't heal my burn wounds, I'd be as dead as everyone else."

His mouth opened and closed, but he remained silent.

Her mother's voice was icy. "Was there more?"

Levesque turned to Quispe, who'd been silent for the duration of Nita's mother's visit, just watching and listening.

"You were kidnapped with INHUP's other charge at the airport," Levesque said. "Only Nita and INHUP knew where you'd be and when."

"That's correct," Quispe agreed, but her voice wasn't accusatory. Just a statement.

"Oh?" Nita's mother snorted. "I see. Were you trying to pin that on my niece too?" She leaned forward and glared at both of them. "Because you know what it looks like to me? It looks like INHUP isn't a safe place to be. We get out of INHUP, and within hours, my niece's cell phone GPS location is on sale. You try to transport another person, and you're ambushed and kidnapped when you arrive. It sounds less like my niece is the problem and more like your organization is riddled with corruption."

Nita felt a surge of smugness. No one could argue with her mother. It was impossible. All the traits that scared Nita, the tangible threat of her presence, the way she could manipulate a conversation, everything that made Nita want to run, made her hate her life—seeing them used in her defense was incredibly satisfying.

In any other circumstance, Nita would have laughed at her mother's manipulation strategy. Using known corruption in INHUP to hide that it was Nita and Fabricio responsible for it all. There was a strange sort of irony in using INHUP against itself.

Detective Levesque glared. "How dare you insinuate that INHUP is—"

Quispe laid a gentle hand on his arm, and he stopped.

Then she sighed softly. "I think that's enough."

"But they—"

"I said that's enough." Quispe's voice was soft. But her face had gone a little gray, and her mouth was pressed into a tight line.

Nita's mother pounced. "You already suspected this was a possibility, didn't you?"

Quispe's expression smoothed into a poker face. "I'm not at liberty to say."

"You just did." Her mother leaned back and shrugged. "It would have been remiss of you not to consider the possibility, especially given how large the Toronto and Bogotá offices are. You can't account for the quality of every person in both of them." Her mother snorted. "Especially considering your other option is that a seventeen-year-old unnatural trafficking victim somehow sold herself on the black market, killed some dealers, and tried to kidnap someone she'd met days ago."

Levesque was beet red, and he looked to Quispe.

Quispe's eyes fell on Nita, and they seemed infinitely sad. Like she was taking everything that had happened as a personal failure on her part.

"I won't say your theory lacks merit," Quispe finally said. "And if someone in INHUP is responsible for this, I *will* find them, and I *will* make them face justice."

Quispe's face was hard and determined. Nita believed that Quispe would find the corruption. Not that there was any this time, given it was actually Nita's fault. But there was enough corruption in INHUP that Quispe would find some.

Nita wondered how easy it would be to tear it all down.

The way Quispe looked now, she'd either destroy it or die trying. Nita hoped it was the former and not the latter.

"Thank you." Nita's mother said, her face solemn. "That means a lot to us."

Quispe nodded. "I apologize for all this hassle. I'm glad we clarified things."

Nita's mother stroked Nita's hair and shook her head in fake sadness. "I hope you find the people responsible."

Quispe turned to Nita. "I promise you, Nita. I won't let this happen again."

You can't promise that, Nita wanted to say. Quispe didn't know about Fabricio or Gold or Henry or any of the other things that meant this could very well happen again. But Nita didn't want to spurn the agent, the passion in her eyes. There were very few people in the world who genuinely wanted to help Nita, and she thought Quispe was one of them.

So she whispered, "Thank you. I appreciate everything you've tried to do for me."

Quispe leaned forward and gently squeezed Nita's hand. "Be safe until I find out what's going on, okay?"

Nita nodded, throat a little tight.

Her mother put her hand on Nita's shoulder, pressing just a little too hard. A warning. Her mother didn't like how familiar Quispe was getting. "Come on, Nita. We're done here."

Nita rose slowly, and nodded at Quispe and Levesque. "I hope that wanted picture of me on the news will come down?"

"Of course." Levesque frowned. "We wanted you for questioning. You've been questioned."

Nita nodded and didn't respond, just followed as her mother directed her from the room.

Nita's mother gave them all a cheery wave. "Have a nice day."

She pulled Nita down the hall. No one followed.

FORTY-TWO

NITA TOOK A DEEP BREATH of fresh air when she exited the police station. It smelled a little muggy and full of grass and spring things. Also car exhaust. But mostly, freshness and freedom. Nita swallowed, her body shaking a little at the sheer relief at being out of that room. It reminded her too much of her cage in Death Market.

Her mother took her wrist. "Come on, let's get a little distance."

Nita nodded and followed.

They wove down the street, between groups of pedestrians and up another road. A park loomed ahead, with large, budding trees sweeping over small benches with nameplates. Nita and her mother walked up the hill and into the park, weaving down densely covered paths and into a private glen. A bench dedicated to someone who died twenty years ago perched in one corner, and a picnic table in another.

Nita collapsed onto the picnic table with a sigh. She let herself breathe. She was out. She was free. They couldn't catch her, they had nothing on her.

Her mother sat down across from her. "You okay?"

Nita nodded. She didn't think her mother had asked her that before. Ever. She wondered if it was a trap of some kind. "Yeah, I'm okay. It's just been a long day."

"So I've heard. Kidnapping an INHUP agent this morning, were you?"

Nita sighed and rubbed her temples. "Yeah."

Her mother laughed, full and free, and gave Nita an admiring smile. "I'd expect nothing less of my daughter."

A small flash of pride swelled in Nita before she pushed it down. It was a trick. A manipulation. Besides, she didn't want to be the kind of person her mother admired. Did she?

Her chest tightened. She kind of did. Even if that meant being the kind of person who kidnapped INHUP agents and murdered black market dealers in cold blood. That praise meant a lot.

"Thanks," Nita said, trying to change the subject, "for getting me out of there."

"I did nothing." Her mother's hair caught the light as she tilted her head toward Nita. "You could have walked out of there anytime. They had nothing on you. You just needed to get up and leave. They couldn't have stopped you."

Nita looked away. "They got in my head."

"I do recall your father and I tried to warn you about that."

Nita's throat tightened at the mention of her father. She missed him.

"That's what they do." Her mother waved it away. "They almost never have evidence for something. They make an art of manipulating confessions out of people, whether the person did it or not."

Nita raised her eyebrows. "I did do it."

Her mother laughed. "Oh, I know." Her smile fell slightly. "But the mental tricks work just as well on the innocent. You know how many people confess to crimes they didn't commit?"

Nita stared at her mother for a long moment, at the tightness of her mouth and the way her eyes stared into the distance. Nita had read the news as much as anyone else, and she knew there were lots of places with high populations of innocent people in prison. But there was something in the way her mother said it that made Nita think she wasn't talking about statistics in the paper.

"No." Nita's voice was soft.

Her mother snorted, the sudden sadness gone as if it had never been. "Never trust that the police have your best interests in mind."

Nita nodded. She'd been raised to be afraid of the police, because her family were criminals. She'd always known her mother's fear was more than just that, but she'd assumed her mother had been raised somewhere dangerous, where money talked louder than crimes, skin color made you guilty by default, or being an unnatural was a death sentence. Not that Nita had any idea where her mother came from – she had dozens of passports with different names from different countries. Nita didn't even know her mother's real name.

But for the first time, Nita felt like she understood something else about her mother's hatred. She could see that, buried somewhere in her life, her mother had a story, and the police were its villains.

"Okay." Nita met her mother's eyes, wishing she could press for details, but knowing there was no point. She'd never answer. "I understand."

A brief smile crossed her mother's face. "Good girl."

She reached over and ruffled the top of Nita's head, like she was petting a dog. Nita wriggled away.

Her mother leaned her chin on her hands. "Well, I'd say you've proven yourself the past few days. Murdering your enemies was a lovely touch, and that notice on the black market as Scalpel has certainly started some conversations." Her mother grinned. "I also took the liberty of starting a discussion pointing out flaws in the video of you healing, so maybe in time we can get it discredited."

Nita blinked. "Thanks."

"Of course."

Nita swallowed, eyes searching her mother's. "You're not mad at me?"

Her mother raised her eyebrows. "For what?"

"For leaving, causing a mess, and needing you to rescue me from the police—"

Her mother took Nita's face in her hands. "Nita, I've never been prouder of you."

Nita's throat choked up. Words wouldn't come out.

"You've done so well on your own. For years, I've been so scared something would happen. That a careless movement would expose you to the world and they'd descend on you." Her mother sighed. "I might have been a bit overprotective, but I love you, and I was scared for you. You were always so squeamish, never wanting to see people die. And those dacts! You couldn't even stand animals dying, I was sure the market would eat you alive."

Her hands fell from Nita's face, and her eyes shone. "Now look at you. I never needed to worry. When the going got tough, you got tougher!"

Her mother slapped her on the shoulder, and Nita jerked forward from the force. "What?"

"You've done amazing!" Her mother's eyes were soft. "I see now that you never needed me to be that clingy and protective. It must have been stifling, I'm not surprised you were resentful."

"I wasn't—"

Her mother snorted. "You were. I didn't realize how much until you left me the other day."

Nita swallowed. "I'm sorry about that."

"Nonsense. You needed to prove yourself. I get it." Her mother looked up at the sky, at something far away. "I think all teenagers go through that phase."

Nita bowed her head. "I guess."

Suddenly Nita's hand was warm, and she looked up to see her mother's hand covering it. "Just remember home is waiting for you if you want to come back. Your dissection table is ready."

Nita opened her mouth, but no words came out. She'd been so wrong about her mother, always assuming the worst, always shying away from her controlling influence. Always doubting, looking for any excuse to vilify her.

"Thanks." Nita choked, the words barely coming from her tight throat.

Her mother smiled. "Of course. I'm your mother. I love you. Anything you want, just ask."

Nita nearly asked her if she could come home now. She could have someone else deal with the market, someone else keep her safe. Nita could curl up in her bed and sleep, dissect to her heart's content. It would be so easy. So simple.

There wasn't anything holding her back. She'd proven she could work on her own. She'd murdered her enemies. There was only Fabricio left, and he was probably long gone. Her mother could help her track him down.

It wasn't like anyone in the outside world was waiting. Kovit was gone.

Nita's eyes watered at that memory. She hadn't even begun to examine the snarled, tangled mess of emotions around that.

Nita let out a deep breath.

"I have a question." Nita's voice shook a little.

"What?"

She raised her eyes and met her mother's gaze. "What do you know about Dad's murder and the vampire?"

Her mother's face immediately shuttered. "Nita—"

Nita sighed. "That's what I thought."

"It's complicated."

"Then explain."

Her mother shook her head.

Nita nodded and rose from her bench. "Thanks, Mom. For getting me out of the station. For being here for me." She brushed a leaf from her pants. "I'll keep in touch. Visit. But I still have things to do."

Going home was the easy choice. And the easy choice was almost never the right one, in Nita's experience. The easy choice was hiding, letting other people make decisions for her.

Nita didn't want that.

As much as her mother said she cared, as much as her words meant to Nita, her mother was still the same person. The person who had started some sort of turf war with Fabricio's father, who wouldn't reveal what she knew about her father's killer. The person who'd terrorized Nita for so many years, who haunted her nightmares. Kind words didn't erase facts.

Besides, Nita had things to do.

Fabricio was still on the loose, and she wanted to handle him herself. It wasn't that she needed to prove herself to her mother. She just didn't want her mother fixing it. Nita wanted to handle him her own way.

After she'd handled Fabricio, she would deal with Zebra-stripes. Her father's murderer wouldn't escape justice, no matter what Nita had to do.

And when all of the blood she needed to spill was spilt, when her vengeance was complete and her enemies were ashes, she wanted to live.

She wanted to build her own life. A life where she went to school. A life where she knew more people than just her mother. A life where, if Kovit came back, she could see him without fear he'd be murdered when her mom came home. Because her mother could never ever know about Kovit.

Her mother squeezed her hand. "I'm always here if you need me."

Nita nodded, still unable to say anything. Her eyes burned with tears, and she didn't know why.

Finally, she whispered, "I love you, Mom."

Her mother rose and embraced her. "I love you too, Nita."

Nita sank into the warmth of the embrace for a long moment before she finally pulled away with a shaky breath. She nodded at her mother, lost for words, then quietly turned and walked away.

FORTY-THREE

NITA TOOK THE STREETCAR back to Adair's place. About halfway, she realized she'd forgotten to get her passport from her mother, and she swore viciously at herself. But there was no helping it now. She would have to email her mom and set up a time to pick it up later.

She turned her mind to more immediate concerns: Fabricio. Adair's words played over in her head, and she wondered: Why had Fabricio sold her out?

Vengeance? Then why not go after her mother?

Money? But as Adair said, he was the heir to a very rich, very powerful man.

Fabricio had said he wanted a new life, to disappear into INHUP's protective program. At the time, she'd assumed it was a lie, meant to explain away his connection to his father, to make him seem like a good guy.

But again—why jeopardize everything with INHUP to sell Nita? INHUP would have taken care of him. He didn't need money to gain their protection. Nita in a cage actually hurt his chances, if she ever got out, or if INHUP confiscated his phone.

So why?

Her mind circled around, and it stalled again for a moment on the Argentinian-Chilean hostilities. But she let it go quickly. If he'd done it out of hate, surely she'd have seen other signs of it. He would have made annoying barbs about Chileans like her father used to about Argentinians whenever the soccer games were on.

No, whatever reason Fabricio had for betraying her, it was something much more complicated and dangerous than that.

She remembered that moment in the car with Fabricio, where she'd said she'd do anything to survive, and he said he would too. He'd confessed to selling her then, but he'd also confessed to being desperate.

But again, the question was: Why?

Maybe Adair was right and she should ask Fabricio some questions before she murdered him and dumped his body in the Don River.

She got off at her usual stop and stepped into the cool night air. The light was fading, and darkness had begun to sweep through the city like a gentle cloak. Streetlights popped on, casting a too-orange glow on everything. The gray sidewalks faded until they looked like long strings of giant polished pebbles and the road was a great river of darkness between them.

She took a deep breath, and she could still hear her mother telling Nita she was proud. Words she never thought she'd hear.

For the first time, she really felt like she could do this. She could survive on her own, she could eliminate Fabricio, make her reputation so powerful she was untouchable, go to school and become the researcher she'd always dreamed of being.

She didn't need INHUP. She didn't need her mother.

She didn't need Kovit.

Her steps slowed, and she let out a breath. Kovit.

She'd thought that the ache of his absence would go away, that she would remember he was a monster, that he'd made her sit in a barn crying while he tortured an INHUP agent. That she'd feel better, more stable, without him there.

But the pain still clung, squishy and sharp, stinging like a jellyfish and slowly poisoning her bloodstream.

She looked up at Adair's shop and wondered if Kovit had come back. If he'd ever come back.

And she realized, no matter what, she didn't want this to be the end.

She didn't want him to go. Monster or not. He was her best friend. She trusted him more than anyone else in the world.

She wondered when being able to trust someone had become more important than whether they were a monster or not.

She took out her phone, but she couldn't think of the words to text him, so she put it away again. Tomorrow. If he hadn't come back by tomorrow, she'd text him. She didn't know what she'd say yet, but she'd find a way to fix this.

She sighed, the cool night air misting her breath in front of her.

She unlocked the shop with Adair's key. The lights were off, and neither Adair nor Diana were anywhere to be found. That was fine. Adair was probably pissed at the moment because of the whole police-in-his-shop thing he'd specifically told her not to let happen.

She wove through the messy shop, trying not to knock over anything. A purple glass chicken stared vacantly at her, and she shuddered and walked past. Old-times people had terrible taste.

She clopped up the stairwell and fumbled for the key to the apartment door. She opened it and flicked on the light.

Henry sat on the bed, fingers steepled.

"Welcome back."

FORTY-FOUR

No sooner had Henry spoken than Nita felt the cool press of a steel barrel on the back of her neck. She turned her head and caught a glimpse of short blond hair, white bandages, and an ear full of studs. Gold. Beside her, the other man who'd chased Nita also had his gun trained on her.

Henry sat on the bed, legs crossed, a faint smile on his face. A gun hung loosely in his hand.

Nita was sure if she resisted, the gun would be in motion faster than she could react. Three against one. Nita didn't even have the gun in her hoodie pocket anymore.

The gun barrel pressed against her neck, forcing Nita forward. Gold closed the door behind her, trapping the four of them in the small room.

Henry shifted on the pastel sheets, his eyes cool and assessing, his smile creeping wider. "So nice of you to return."

Nita opened her mouth but he spoke before she could respond. "Don't bother screaming. When I met Adair earlier today, he told me he had this whole shop soundproofed years ago. He seems pleasant enough. Not too happy about the police swarming his shop looking for you." Henry flashed her a smile. "Can't say I blame him."

Adair. That scheming, traitorous kelpie.

Nita ground her teeth. If she survived this, she was going to make him pay.

The gun vanished from the back of Nita's head, but before she could move, hands grabbed her wrists with professional speed and zip-tied them. Tightly. Tight enough to cut off the blood circulation to her hands almost entirely.

Nita swallowed, wondering if it was cruelty or strategy. Nita would need to waste resources ensuring the cells didn't decay without blood, and it would be more difficult to break out of them with restricted blood flow.

More difficult. But not impossible.

She shifted her hands, testing the zip ties, but before she could make a determination, Gold dragged her over to the chair by the table, gun back at her head.

Nita bit her lip. Even if she could break out of the zip ties, she'd just be shot in the head.

Henry smiled at Nita. "I don't believe we've been formally introduced. I'm Henry."

Nita wondered how far she could spit stomach acid. "Nita."

Henry laughed. "Hello, Nita. As you may have heard, your friend Fabricio contracted me to kill you."

"I know."

"Of course you do. You're dumb enough to make an enemy of the most powerful company in the world, but at least you know who they hired to kill you." He leaned back, shaking his head. "I have to say, I don't know what Kovit sees in you."

Nita swallowed. Had Kovit betrayed her too?

Henry nodded to Gold and Nita felt hands roughly pulling at her pocket. Her cell phone came out, and Gold pressed it to Nita's finger, unlocking it, before tossing it to Henry.

"Now, what shall I say to get him to come running?" Henry's smile was cruel. "Ah, I know."

He typed something into her phone, then tossed it on the bed. "Let's see where his loyalties really lie, shall we?"

"Who's Kovit?"

Henry rolled his eyes. "Please. Aside from the fact that I just messaged him on your phone, it was painfully obvious you two were working together."

Nita shook her head, but didn't say anything.

"Think about it. Kovit never asked me for a ticket to Toronto—which meant he was already here. Everyone from the black market coming to Toronto right now is here to hunt you." Henry tapped his nose. "But I know Kovit. Kovit isn't a hunter. He's never been a hunter.

"To be a successful hunter, you need to get inside your prey's head. You need to get to know them, their lives and routines. To catalog their friends and enemies. To understand them enough to predict where they'll go and what they'll do in a situation." Henry smiled, slow and creepy, a poor echo of Kovit. "It's very intimate."

Nita understood immediately. Kovit wouldn't harm people he saw as people. The minute he humanized them, he couldn't hurt them. Hunting someone required learning about them, and learning about them would humanize them, thus defeating the purpose of the hunt. Anonymity was a key to everything about Kovit. He could never harm people. But the shapeless, nameless, voiceless things who went into his torture chamber weren't people.

Just like the ones who ended up on her dissection table.

"I knew right away that Kovit wasn't hunting," Henry continued. "But he came all the way to Toronto from the jungle, so it had to be related to you. I don't believe in coincidences."

Nita didn't either.

"Then I realized, Nita, that you *knew* Kovit. That Reyes had been your captor and Kovit had been working with her."

Nita's stomach roiled. She knew where this was going. It was all so logical. Anyone who knew Kovit could have sussed this out.

"There were only two possibilities. Friends or enemies. Kovit isn't big on vengeance – it's too personal, you see, killing someone you know. He can't kill people he hates just like he can't kill people he loves."

Henry spread his arms and shrugged. "So, it was fairly easy to figure out."

Nita clenched her teeth. She'd been a fool.

No. Wait.

Nita's eyes narrowed. "And you figured that out all on your own? I doubt it. You're not that smart."

He raised an eyebrow, and a muscle twitched in his mouth.

Nita sneered. "You know what I think? I think you had no idea we were connected until Fabricio came running to tell you I was working with a zannie."

Because he would have. Nita was a fool not to have thought of it earlier. She knew Fabricio was in contact with Henry.

Obviously he'd warn Henry about Kovit. And Henry would put two and two together.

Henry's lips curled, and Nita knew she was right.

She laughed. "Aww, did I spoil things? You wanted to look like a genius who was so great at profiling Kovit's personality, hmm? You're pathetic."

He smiled, wide and vicious. "Call me as many names as you want. It won't change what's going to happen today."

He nodded to Gold, and the pressure from the gun barrel disappeared from the back of Nita's neck. Gold came around in front of Nita and took a series of pictures of Nita in the chair. Nita glared, and Gold looked to Henry.

"Good." Henry took out his own phone. "Let's see how much we can sell her for."

How was she back in this situation? Sure, this time her captor didn't want to eat her—just sell her to someone who did. This was going to be her life. Always captured, no matter how hard she tried to protect herself. Always sold for someone else's desires. Always trapped like a rat in a cage.

Nita clenched her jaw and leaned forward, zip ties slicing her skin so deeply it bled. She was not some ignorant, weak child. She'd escaped before, she'd escape again.

She had to do it before Kovit came. Otherwise he was walking right into the lion's den. She didn't know why Henry was setting a trap for Kovit when he'd already won Kovit back, and she didn't want to find out.

Nita's eyes found Henry as she began to calculate trajectories. She might be able to get out of the zip ties—*might*—even if it meant dislocating her thumbs and shedding some skin and muscle to fit through. But in the time she took to do that, Henry would have shot her.

Nita didn't want to be shot again.

Her eyes flicked to Gold and the other man, both with weapons. Could she use one of them as a shield and then shoot Henry?

"Ah, I've already got a response." Henry grinned and leaned forward, the bed creaking with the movement. "You're going to make me a lot of money."

Nita's eyes narrowed.

She lunged forward, hooking the chair with her foot as she did and toppling it sideways into the man beside Gold. He fell with a crash, and Nita sprang through the air.

Something smashed on the back of her head.

Her cheek pressed into the wooden floorboards. She didn't even remember falling. She blinked, trying to focus, but the world tilted and swirled. Or maybe she did.

Concussion.

She blearily tried to repair the damage, but she couldn't hold her thoughts together long enough to issue orders to her body.

"Well, now you've gone and killed her, Gold."

"She's not dead."

Nita needed to focus. Needed to. Before her brain began swelling too much.

She closed her eyes, but that made her sleepy, so she opened them again.

Focus.

Words swirled around above her. Someone grabbed her

arms and roughly yanked her up and into the chair. They zip-tied her already bound arms to the chair. And her ankles.

Nita lay limp, not resisting. Her mind was too fuzzy.

Head wounds. Bad.

Focus.

She clenched her teeth. *Lower the swelling. Lower it. That will help clear the fuzziness.*

She wasn't sure how long she sat there, drifting in and out, before she managed to beat back the fuzziness enough that the world stopped spinning and she could actually start fixing herself.

It was dark outside, and the moon hung like a flashlight beam on top of the world.

For the first time, she hoped whatever text Henry sent, whatever plea he'd made as Nita, that Kovit ignored it. That he didn't return to her. Nothing good would happen if he came.

As if summoned by her thoughts, there was a click as the door unlocked.

Kovit walked into the room.

FORTY-FIVE

KOVIT STOPPED in the doorway and stared. The skin around his eyes was faintly red as though he'd been rubbing at them, but his hair was glossy like a shampoo commercial, and his skin was smooth and almost seemed to glow.

He'd eaten recently.

If ever there was a time for comfort food, she supposed now was it.

Nita forced herself not to think about it. Now was not the time.

"Hello, Kovit." Henry's voice was warm, and he smiled, but it didn't reach his eyes. "We've all been waiting for you."

Kovit's head slowly turned away from Nita and over to Henry.

"Henry." Kovit took a step forward, but Gold and her partner both raised their guns. Kovit stopped and lowered his hands to his side. "What are you doing here?"

"Meeting Nita, of course," Henry said, eyes never leaving Kovit. "I think it's always important to introduce the girl you bring home to your parents."

Kovit's voice was scraping and harsh. "You're not my parent."

"Oh my." Henry touched his heart as though wounded, but kept smiling. "I'll forgive you for that. Under the circumstances." He ran his hands over the sheets of the bed. "I had no idea you had it in you, Kovit. You've never showed any interest in the fairer sex – or any sex, really."

Nita's face heated up at his implications, but she remained silent. He was just trying to get a rise out of her, and she wasn't going to let him succeed.

Kovit's face didn't change at all. It was like his expression was frozen, like Henry had caught him in the middle of reading a book he wasn't enjoying.

"But, Kovit." Henry turned faux-sad eyes on him. "I thought better of you. Consorting with merchandise! You know that never ends well."

Kovit ground his teeth. "Neither does sending people who displease you to the middle of the jungle."

"Oh, don't be bitter! I apologized for that." Henry spread his arms magnanimously. "I acknowledge my mistake. I never should have sent you away. You forgave me and came home."

Kovit didn't respond, face shadowed.

"But you didn't really come home." Henry's voice was sad. "You were keeping secrets. You knew how important the commission from Tácunan Law was to us, and you didn't disclose where Nita was. You never really came back, not really, not if your loyalties were torn this way."

Still Kovit remained silent.

Henry shook his head. "I know it's been hard, Kovit, but I think it's important we leave the past behind."

Kovit's voice was soft. "Important for who?"

"For you, of course!" Henry laughed. "You'll see. I'm doing you a favor."

Kovit pursed his lips. "A favor."

"Exactly." Henry smiled, wide and bright.

Kovit stared at Henry, eyes black, before his gaze swept to Nita. A sense of déjà vu swept over her. She remembered a similar situation with Boulder demanding Kovit be his pet monster, earn him prestige.

She found it ironic that it always came down to this. Everyone wanted Kovit as their pet and Nita as their prisoner. Neither of them was anything more than the sum of the reputation they could give others.

"What are you doing to Nita?" Kovit asked.

"Oh, don't worry about that. I learned my lesson with Matt, you won't have to touch her." Henry waved a hand. "I'm going to kill her, send a picture of her body to the Tácunan brat, and sell the body." He sighed. "I'm sure I could sell her for more alive, but Fabricio has been insistent that she has to be dead, and I can't risk offending his father. So she'll be dead soon enough."

Kovit's voice was flat and cold. "I will never work for you if you harm Nita. Or sell her."

Henry raised an eyebrow. "Don't tell me you've grown a conscience or something? You're not going on some angsty teen emo self-hate spiral, are you?"

"Of course not." Kovit snorted with such derisiveness that

Henry relaxed. Then Kovit smiled, wide and creepy, promising a darkness only he and Henry knew. "But I won't bend on this. Hurt Nita, and I'll never work for you."

Henry's smile fell. "Kovit—"

"No." His eyes were fierce, and Nita felt the fluttering in her chest grow stronger until she thought butterflies might choke her.

It took a special kind of brave to say that, with the threat of INHUP hanging over him like the sword of Damocles. He was always doing this. Putting friends first. Henry or Nita, Matt or his internet friends. Nita always put herself first, her quest for her own safety over everything. Over her relationship with Kovit, over the lives of people in her way.

"Kovit, Kovit." Henry rose from the bed. "Please, enough with all these emotions. I know you get attached to people easily, but this has gotten out of hand. I admit, I made a mistake with Matt. Six years of friendship can't be wiped out so easily. But this? You can't have known her for more than a month! If that!"

"She's my friend." Kovit's voice was calm, composed.

Henry threw his arms into the air. "Why couldn't you just be satisfied with your internet ones?"

Kovit's eyes narrowed. Suspicion confirmed. "You knew?"

"Of course I knew. You really think I was going to let you online without supervision?"

"So what, you spent hours scrolling through a bunch of tweens talking about a video game?" Kovit frowned. "I find that hard to believe."

Henry brushed him aside. "Of course not. I don't have time

for that. The head of the Family and I found a much better solution."

And his eyes turned to Gold.

Gold stiffened, and her fingers tightened on her gun. She worried at the piercing in her lip.

Kovit turned to her, uncomprehending. "Gold? What does Gold have to do with this?"

Henry laughed. His shoulders were back, posture radiating arrogance. "You still haven't figured it out?"

Kovit was frowning, but Nita's mind had already skipped several steps ahead.

"You're one of the people in the chat group." Nita's voice was soft.

Kovit's eyes widened, and his mouth fell open. He turned to Gold with a soft, horribly vulnerable expression.

"I didn't know." Gold couldn't meet his eyes. "I didn't know it was you. I was just told to keep an eye on one of the younger members of the Family." She shuddered, and when her eyes came up, they were full of rage. "I never knew I was supposed to be keeping an eye on a *zannie*." She practically spat the word.

"You . . ." Kovit's voice was soft and hurt. "When I logged back in, you turned me in?"

"That she did!" Henry laughed. "And my, was I surprised to hear about it. It took me days to even believe it."

When Kovit and Nita had met up days ago, it had already been far too late. Henry already knew. Kovit was already doomed. He'd unwittingly dug his own grave.

Kovit closed his eyes, and she could see him coming to the same conclusion.

He took a deep breath and turned to Gold. "Who are you? In the chatroom, who are you?"

"May." Her gun shook in her hand. "I'm May."

Hadn't Kovit said he was closest to May?

Kovit was shaking all over. "And it was all lies? Everything?"

"Are you kidding me?" Gold's face twisted in a snarl. "*You're* asking *me* that? You pretended to be human, you pretended you were a real person with real feelings and emotions!" Her voice caught, choked. "I thought you were my friend."

Kovit's voice was sad. "We were friends."

"Don't lie to me!" Gold snarled, but it looked like she was close to tears. "Zannies don't have friends. You're monsters, all of you. You can't feel anything except joy at hurting others."

Kovit jerked his head away, as if he couldn't bear to look at Gold for one more moment.

Nita closed her eyes, heart breaking for Kovit. She'd seen how much his friends meant to him. To be betrayed that way, to not even be thought of as a real person, was the worst kind of crime.

"Oh, Kovit, don't be so hard on her." Henry smiled. "You know she thought Matt had risen from the dead when she first saw you back online. She'd thought it was Matt all this time."

Kovit stared at Henry, face slowly breaking apart, one muscle at a time. "Matt is dead?"

Gold's face crumpled, and Henry snorted. "We caught Matt. A week or so after you were sent away. In Toronto, actually! He'd tried to cross the border, he'd enlisted some local to try and get him new papers."

Nita's mind flitted back to the conversation Adair and

Gold had in the shop, and more and more pieces began to slide together. That was how Gold and Adair had met—trying to smuggle Matt out. And failing. Adair had known Matt was dead from the start. He just had kept that information from Kovit. Probably waiting for the right price.

Nita replayed more of the conversation with her new knowledge and wondered if he'd also known about Gold and Kovit and the chatroom. What other secrets had he kept to himself?

"Of course," Henry continued, "whoever tried to get him his new identity hadn't realized we'd tagged him with a tracker."

"No." Kovit was shaking all over. "No. What did you do to Matt?"

Henry smiled softly. "Well, let's just say I put your old tools to good use."

Nita leaned away from the scene, horrified. There was something obscene about a human talking about torture in such a casual way. She hadn't realized she'd been desensitized to Kovit, but she had. He ate the pain. He needed the pain. He didn't need to get the pain the way he did, but in a twisted way, she could understand him.

This was different. Henry's clear obsession with torture was wrong on so many levels.

Kovit fell to his knees on the ground and clutched at the ugly green rug. "No. No, please, you didn't . . ."

"He's quite dead now, not to worry." Henry smiled, smooth and clean and predatory as he leaned in to the wounded and battered Kovit for the killing blow. "And I thought, as punishment for hiding from the family and hiding the lovely Nita here from us, I could do the same things to one of your little internet friends."

Kovit's head snapped up and Gold gasped.

Henry waved dismissively at Gold. "Obviously not you."

"You . . ." Kovit couldn't seem to finish his sentence.

Henry leaned over him, a peregrine falcon over a kestrel, one predator dominating another. "You've been very bad, Kovit, keeping Nita a secret. And going to her in the night, when you thought we were all asleep. No, this is exactly the kind of behavior that led to the whole mess with Matt."

Henry smiled. "So how about every time you screw up, I murder one of your friends?"

Kovit just kept shaking his head, as if by continuing to deny what was happening, it would make Henry stop talking, his words lose their meaning.

"I'll make sure it takes a while too." Henry leaned forward. "I know how much you appreciate pain."

Kovit closed his eyes. "I'd rather have INHUP catch me and just die."

"I'll still kill them." Henry rose and twirled a pen from the sideboard in his hand. "Even if you're dead."

Kovit stared at him for a long time, the only sound in the room his harsh breathing. Finally, he asked, "Didn't you tell me earlier you liked my morals? That it was better having a zannie with lines they wouldn't cross?"

"Oh, I do! It's much better." Henry nodded for emphasis. "So much easier to control them. It's hard to control people who aren't attached to anything." He shrugged. "I mean, obviously, I'd much rather you didn't have any of those weird rules about friends and attachments. They're so inconvenient, always getting in the way. But if I can't get rid of them, I'll use them."

Guilt sank deep into Nita's bones at Henry's words. Kovit had accused her of trying to control him too, to make his morals fit her needs.

She closed her eyes as understanding fell over her. She always knew trying to change someone was a fool's errand. People who fell for bad boys hoping to reform them were idiots.

No one fell for Kovit hoping to reform him. He was too evil for those people to want, and too good for the people in the market.

What would it be like, everyone despising you for being a monster, but also wanting you to be more of a monster? Wanting you more ruthless on one thing, less on another. They wanted to mold him into the person most convenient for them at the time. And that was impossible.

No one is perfect. No one is exactly who you want them to be. There is something in every person, even your closest friend, that you don't like.

Kovit was loyal.

Kovit tortured random people.

Kovit went above and beyond to help his friends.

Nita had befriended him for his good side, and hated herself for caring for a monster. But when it came time for the true acts of monstrosity—luring strangers into buildings to kill them, demanding that Kovit murder the man who raised him—it was Nita, not Kovit, who pushed for it.

Her throat closed. The monster in the room right now wasn't Kovit. It was everyone else. Including Nita.

"Henry," Kovit whispered, rising shakily to his feet. His legs trembled slightly, but he stood tall. His eyes were focused and glazed at the same time, like he was intent on something far in the distance only he could see.

"Yes?" Henry looked bored.

Kovit was mere inches from him. "Are you afraid of me?"

Henry laughed. "Hardly. You never hurt people you know. I've been safe for years."

"Yes." Kovit agreed, voice distant. "I never hurt people I know." Then he met Henry's eyes, and his voice was a promise. "This won't hurt."

He reached out and snapped Henry's neck in a single swift motion.

FORTY-SIX

NITA DIDN'T WAIT. Before Henry's body was on the ground, she head butted the person closest to her. His gun tumbled to the ground.

She ripped her ankles free from her zip ties, and leapt at him before he could pick his weapon up, dragging the chair still attached to her wrists with her. She slammed sideways into him, bashing his skull into the wall. It shattered like a fragile egg, spraying her with blood.

Just like Kovit had killed Reyes.

You can dissect it later too.

A bright, crazy grin crossed her face. She could. She could move the body somewhere else, somewhere private, take a scalpel, let it sink into its flesh . . .

She shivered, body rippling like Kovit on pain for a moment. Then she pushed it down.

Not now.

There was still another enemy.

Gold was staring at Kovit and Henry, her eyes wide. Her gun was raised, but she just stared. "You killed him."

Kovit turned to her with that same glazed and focused look in his eyes. Then he moved, darting forward and twisting the gun out of her grip and pinning her to a wall.

Gold shrieked. "Let me go!"

"Why?" he snarled. "Because you pretended to be my friend for years?"

"I didn't pretend! You pretended!"

"Liar!" Kovit pressed forward, and Gold's shoulder popped with a squelch and she shrieked, high and harsh.

Nita wrestled with her wrist zip ties but quickly gave up, popping her thumbs out and shedding the flesh from her wrists so they were nothing but bone. She yanked her hands free, then reattached the skin.

She stepped forward and put her hand, gory with her own blood, on his shoulder. "Kovit, stop."

"Why?" His eyes turned to her, dark and dangerous and utterly shattered. "You don't like the sound of her screams? Or is it just any screams you didn't cause yourself?"

"That's not—"

"You stand there and judge me, but you've killed more people in the last week than I've killed in my life!"

Nita flinched.

Gold tried to kick Kovit's leg out, but he twisted his leg around hers, eliciting another horrible pop as her knee dislocated and her body slumped, only supported by the pressure of Kovit's hand on her throat, pinning her to the wall.

"You're nothing but a monster, no matter what you tell yourself." Gold choked, gasping in pain and tears soaking into the bandages on the side of her face. "A real person could never do this to someone they thought of as a friend."

Nita swallowed. "She's not wrong, Kovit. You don't hurt your friends. Remember? It's a rule."

"What rules?" His voice was bitter, and tearstains carved paths down his cheeks. "I've broken my rules. I just murdered Henry. What does any of it matter anymore?"

He was crying full out now, sticky wet tears coating his face, chest heaving in sobs as he twisted Gold so she screamed and his whole body shivered in pleasure.

Nita grabbed his arm and ripped him away from Gold, who crumpled to the ground. She spun Kovit to face her. "Kovit, look at me."

He couldn't, and Nita grabbed his cheeks and forced him to look her in the eyes.

"You're hurting," she whispered. "I get that. And if you need pain, if you need comfort food, I promise you, I can give myself more pain than any other human in the world if that will make you feel better."

Sudden, naked hunger spread across his face, and his fingers curled at his side.

Nita swallowed the rising terror inside and plowed ahead, voice thick. "But I want to know that you'll be able to look me in the eye afterward." She leaned closer. "I will do anything for you, Kovit, but you have to promise me it won't break us."

And just like that, the hunger was gone, and Nita forced herself not to let out the sigh of relief that he hadn't called her bluff.

He looked away, and her hands fell from his face. "I wouldn't. Be able to look you in the eye, I mean."

"I thought so." Nita took a deep breath.

On the other side of the room, Gold crawled to the door and into the stairwell, whimpering. Kovit continued shivering like he had goose bumps from her pain, but he ignored her as she dragged herself away.

Nita leaned close. "No matter how broken you think you are, Kovit, you still care about your friends. Hurting Gold will just make you feel awful."

He swallowed and looked at the floor.

He turned away from Nita abruptly, and slowly walked back to Henry. Each step looked like it took a monumental effort, and when he finally reached his old mentor, he stood there, staring silently at the body for a solid minute.

Finally, his hand reached out and brushed a gray strand of hair from Henry's eye. His fingers trailed along the skin before reaching the eyelids and gently closing them.

Nita took a step toward Kovit, reaching a hand out, not knowing what to say, only knowing she needed to stay near him.

He didn't look at her, hands still lingering on the corpse. He blinked wet lashes. The light caught on his tears so they sparkled against his cheeks.

"I tried so hard," he whispered. "To let myself enjoy who and what I was, to let myself revel in the pain while still keeping myself sane. I drew lines, I made small sand castle walls to keep out the darkness, to make sure I never became like other zannies I'd met. Like the woman Henry hired."

He blinked up at her. "But it never mattered. Henry didn't want that kind of person. Gold was lying the whole time. Matt is dead. And you . . ." Tears matted his lashes together. "You can't stand me. You freak whenever even a hint of what I am surfaces. You can only stand to be near me by ignoring the parts of me you don't like."

His head dipped, and his hair fell across his eyes, masking his tears. "I suppose Henry won. He always wins. I've broken my own rules. I've become exactly what Henry wanted me to be."

"No." Nita took a step forward. "That's not true."

His gaze snapped to hers. "Don't tell me you're not happy that he's dead. That this is over, that he's out of the way."

Nita's mind scrambled for the right words, because she couldn't be silent this time. If she didn't manage to tell him how she felt, if she didn't manage to say it right, she knew she'd lose him forever.

"I wouldn't lie to you like that. I *am* happy it's over. I was scared. For me. For you." She took another step forward, voice slightly choked. "But I'm not happy about how it ended. I never wanted you to break your rules. I never wanted to cause you pain."

"You're the one who wanted me to lure him somewhere so we could murder him."

"Yes." She let out a breath, and finally confessed, "I was wrong to ask that of you. And wrong to blame you for not being able to go through with it. I'm sorry."

His eyes met hers, dark and wet, and Nita wondered if anyone had ever apologized to him before.

"I made a dumb mistake. I've never . . . I mean, I haven't really had many friends before." Nita looked away. "It's hard for me to understand sometimes. That you're your own person, with your own desires and wants that don't always match mine. And that's okay. I may not be comfortable with some of your choices. I may be scared by them." She swallowed. "More than scared. I won't lie: the screams . . . they bother me sometimes.

"But I can't pick and choose what aspects of a person I want and make a new person for myself. That's not how it works."

She met his eyes again, then reached out and cupped his face in her palms. "You've picked the path you want. And I will always respect that. It's your path to walk, not mine to criticize." She laughed. "Look at me. I dissect people. I burned a market full of people alive. I murdered a bunch of strangers in cold blood. I've no place passing judgment."

His skin was warm beneath her fingers, his tears damp. "I'm your friend, Kovit. And I will always support you, whatever you want to be." Her voice shook a little. "I can't promise I won't make mistakes again. I can't promise I won't freak out when you do something that scares me. I'm not perfect. But I can promise I'll always try, and I'll always be on your side."

He stared at her, eyes wide. "Nita—"

She pressed a finger to his lips. "One more thing. For what it's worth—I don't think you broke your rules here. Henry betrayed you. He wasn't your friend anymore. He wasn't even really the man you thought you knew at all."

Nita lowered her finger down to his chin as she continued. "You had to make a choice, and one of us was going to die. He'd tortured and murdered your best friend, and threatened to do worse. If ever there was a reason to bend a rule, that would be it.

"Forgive yourself, Kovit." She kept her eyes on his. "It's human to care about the wrong people. Forgive yourself for making a mistake and being cornered into a desperate choice."

Her finger trailed down his chin, and her whole body shivered at the feeling. She trembled, aware of how close they were, how warm he was, how her heart fluttered as he gazed into her eyes.

He blinked, eyelashes still damp. "Thank you." He looked toward the open door, where Gold was presumably still crawling down the stairwell, and his body shuddered softly as another wave of her pain passed through him. "And thank you for stopping me before I really did break myself."

"Always." She leaned forward and pressed her forehead against his. "I won't let you break."

He breathed in deeply, leaning against her. Their noses were almost touching, and her heart beat faster and faster, and before she realized what she was doing, she leaned forward that last bit.

And she kissed him.

His lips were soft beneath hers. His body tensed for a moment, when she first pressed against him, but then it released, and his mouth parted slightly. His arms wrapped around her back in a hug, and her thumbs stroked the tears from his cheeks.

Swallowing, she pulled away. Her mouth felt cold without his against it.

His eyes were dark and huge. She turned her head away, clearing her throat.

His hand brushed her side and came up to her chin, tilting her face to his. His eyes flicked back and forth, as though searching for an answer in her eyes or her blush or her tingling mouth.

Then he pressed his forehead against hers and breathed her name. "Nita."

Her whole body was hot, and the areas pressed against him burned. Her breathing was sharp, and her throat was so choked with butterflies she couldn't make a sound.

He shivered softly as pain from the next room slid through his body. Then, still trembling from Gold's pain, he leaned forward and kissed Nita.

Something inside her relaxed at that, at the knowledge that this weird, amorphous thing in her wasn't one-sided, that he wanted her the way she wanted him.

And even though she was sure everyone in the world would think they were so wrong, right there, at that moment, with his mouth against hers and her body humming with electricity, everything felt just right.

FORTY-SEVEN

NITA WASN'T SURE how long after the kiss ended they stood there, foreheads pressed together, noses touching, eyes closed. But eventually she pulled away and took a step back.

She cleared her throat, and looked down at Henry's dead body. The first time she and Kovit had killed someone, Nita had felt like a monster for laughing over the dead body a few minutes later. How times had changed.

Kovit seemed a little out of breath, his lips swollen. His tears were gone, but his eyes still shone.

Nita cleared her throat. "We should, ah, get Gold."

Kovit blinked. "Right." He cleared his throat and took a step away from Nita. "Yes. Let's."

They found her halfway down the stairwell, her body twisted from the effort of getting down the stairs. She was weeping softly, tears coating her cheeks and pain carved in every line of her face. Kovit thrummed with her pain.

Gold gasped when she saw them and opened her mouth to scream again, even though there was no one to hear her.

Kovit knelt beside her. "It's okay. You don't need to be afraid. I won't hurt you."

"Of course you will. It's your nature," she spat, curling in on herself like a wounded animal.

He sighed, soft and sad. "Whether you believe me or not, May, it's the truth. I won't hurt you."

Gold hesitated. Nita wondered if she understood the significance that Kovit was choosing to name her, to specifically give her the label of friend in his mind.

Gold narrowed her eyes as she examined Kovit. "You called me May."

"Would you prefer Gold?" he asked, kneeling over her and examining her knee. Nita knelt beside him, her fingers running expertly over the skin. Just dislocated.

Gold swallowed and shook her head. "Gold will follow in her father's footsteps and run the Family by any means necessary. May is a nonexistent girl who has internet friends and cried when Matt died."

"May, then." Kovit's voice was decisive. "All right, May, we're going to pop your joints back together. It's going to hurt a lot for a moment and then it will feel a lot better."

She hesitated, eyes flicking to him, fear lurking in their depths.

"I'll pop them in." Nita moved around to get a better angle. "Kovit's just going to hold you still."

She looked like she was going to reject the offer, but then she nodded, mouth firming into a tight line.

Before she could say anything, Nita grabbed her knee and snapped it back in.

Gold gasped, but didn't scream. Beside her, Kovit jerked, a small moan escaping his lips.

"Better?" Nita asked, examining her handiwork.

Gold nodded tightly. "Much."

They did the same thing with the shoulder, and Gold groaned softly as Kovit shivered in pleasure, his whole body shuddering like he'd been dunked in cold water.

Gold leaned against the wall of the hallway, her fingers trailing gently over her tender knee and shoulder.

"You probably shouldn't walk on that leg or use that arm for a bit," Nita told her.

She nodded. "I know."

They were all silent for a long moment.

Finally Gold spoke. Her voice was soft and curious and slightly suspicious. "Why didn't you come back to Henry right after you got out of the market?"

He shrugged, and looked away. "I didn't really enjoy being his pet monster."

"But you're so good at it." Her voice was mocking. "I thought you'd be chomping at the bit to go back to your torture chamber."

"I guess you don't know me that well, then," he snapped.

"I think I know more than enough." Her mouth was tight, and there was undisguised hatred in her eyes. "You're evil."

"Look at the pot calling the kettle black."

"There's something called scale. Shoplifting isn't the same as robbing the Federal Reserve. What I do is nothing compared to what you do."

Kovit clenched his jaw, and it was like a switch flicked off, and he met Gold's eyes with a ferocity that seemed to burn him up from the inside out. "Enough is enough. I'm sick of you using me as an excuse to feel better about yourself as a human."

"I'm not—"

"You are. You're so terribly convinced that zannies, that all unnaturals, that we're all nothing but monsters. That you're so superior. That you're just a better person. Well, guess what, you're not."

"How dare you? You're not even a *person*."

"You know that's not true, May. Seven years in a chatroom together, half of the time spent on private chats between us. You know perfectly well I'm as human as you. You just don't want to face that fact because it means that if I'm not biologically, fundamentally worse than you, you have to ask questions about yourself and how bad a person you are."

"I know I'm not as bad a person as you." Her voice was high and sharp and angry.

He smiled at her expression, and it wasn't a nice smile. "Let me tell you something, Gold. Anything I've done, you're just as culpable of. Why? Because you knew what was happening. And you never tried to stop it. You had so many options. Talking to me. Your father. The police. INHUP."

He leaned forward. "So don't try and tell me you're better than me, when all you've done is express tacit agreement for the Family and their choices with your inaction. Your silence is deafening."

Gold stared at him, and for a moment her face was a perfect mask of shock before it morphed into rage.

"Fuck you," she snarled. "How fucking dare you."

"No, May. How fucking dare *you*. We were *friends*. We were allies. And you turned on me the second you found out I wasn't human. And don't tell me it was because I was 'evil'. You were a spy, you *knew* I was in the Family, and you were still my friend. You only changed your tune when you found out I wasn't 'human' the way you thought I was."

Gold was quiet for a long moment, and something inside her seemed to shift, her back straightening and her eyes hardening. Finally she said, voice soft and cold, "I won't apologize for my assumptions. I didn't think zannies were capable of the kind of emotion and personality I knew your online presence had."

"Had you even met a zannie before?" Kovit's voice was as smooth and slippery as butter.

"Yes. I had. You." She glared at him. "And you, the you I saw in the Family events, the you that people whispered about in the hallways, were a very different person than the boy in the chat."

Kovit's face hardened.

"And you can't blame me for being afraid of that boy and thinking he was a monster. I'm trying to reconcile two very different people, and you can't claim to be this misunderstood tragic hero, because I fucking know what you did for the Family, and I've seen the videos Henry was blackmailing you with."

Kovit didn't react except for a slight tightening of his shoulders. "Fine. So you don't like me now that you know who I am."

"I don't know you, though." Gold's anger melted away, and grief took its place, her mouth turning down and lips pressing together like she was holding her emotions in. She looked at Kovit like she was looking at the dead body of her best friend. "Not really. I know who you pretended to be for the Family. I know who you pretended to be on the chatroom. But you? I don't know who you are."

Kovit was silent.

Gold wrapped her arms around her knees, sadness whispering through her voice. "I don't know you at all, Kovit. Just the masks you've worn."

Kovit let out a long breath. His hair fell across his eyes, and Nita wasn't sure she wanted to see what expression they held right now. Because Gold, whether she knew it or not, had called all of his online friendships fake. She'd isolated him even more.

"I understand." Kovit's voice was dead.

Gold tried to straighten and cursed.

Nita let out a long breath. They'd dallied enough here. "Kovit, take Gold and go to wherever Henry's staying. Message me the location, and I'll see you there later."

"Wait." Gold's eyes widened. "You can't leave me with him. What if he hurts me?"

"I won't hurt you." Kovit's voice was frosty.

"My shoulder and knee tell a different story," Gold snapped, turning back to Nita.

"May." He turned to glare at her. "I get that you don't like me. But just pretend you're with Kevin from the chat."

Nita laughed. "Your online name is Kevin?"

He shrugged. "I wanted something close to my name that sounded American-y. I don't know. It was stupid, I wanted to blend in. And it wasn't like they could see me over the internet."

Nita frowned, imagining a small desperate child wanting nothing more than to fit in. To belong.

She thought of Adair's comment—that if Kovit hadn't been hunted by INHUP, he never would have become who he was. And she thought about all the things he probably did to try and belong in the Family. She wondered if perhaps Adair was right.

Not that it would change anything.

Nita turned to Gold. "Look, he's not going to hurt you. You're going to be fine. I need you guys to go ahead while I deal with the bodies."

Kovit's face shadowed as he looked up the stairwell toward the room where Henry's body lay. Nita reached over, grabbed his chin, and turned him to face her.

"*I* will deal with the bodies." Her voice was firm. "*You* will go and find Henry's computer and get rid of all trace of those incriminating videos he was emailing you."

Kovit swallowed. "Adair can deal with the bodies—"

"Adair," Nita hissed, "is going to be one of the bodies soon."

Kovit's eyes widened.

Nita leaned forward. "No one sells me out and doesn't pay for it."

Kovit swallowed. "Do you need—"

"Backup?" Nita shook her head. "Oh no, I can deal with Adair all on my own."

Adair was going to learn that Nita didn't need to dissect a kelpie to know their weaknesses.

Kovit hesitated, then nodded. "What will you do with the bodies?"

Nita raised her eyebrows. "Do you really want to know?"

Kovit looked away. "No."

Nita's smile was tight as she turned away.

"Nita?"

"Yeah?"

"Don't . . . I mean . . . Henry's body . . ."

Nita sighed. "I'll get rid of it. Respectfully."

"But you won't do anything . . . unnecessary to it." His eyes couldn't hold hers.

"No. I won't dissect his body. I promise."

She didn't say anything about the other one.

He gave her a soft smile. "Thanks."

"Always."

He knelt beside Gold, hauled her up by her good arm, and acted like a crutch so she could walk. She was tense and tight, and Nita couldn't tell if the thought of being touched by Kovit made her skin crawl or she was in a lot of pain. Kovit wasn't reacting, but he had a lot of practice controlling himself.

Kovit smiled at Nita, a soft, sad expression that reminded her that while they'd had their moment, he'd still broken something inside, and it ate away at his soul. She had the most horrible feeling that he'd taken a step toward the darkness, and he could never take that step back.

It was a feeling she knew well.

Then he was gone, hauling Gold along with him. Nita forced herself to turn away from them and return to a room with two dead bodies.

Nita let out a breath as the shop door slammed behind them. The world seemed emptier without him there.

Sighing, she opened the apartment door and examined the scene in front of her. The only sign of violence was the bloodstain on the wall. And obviously, the bodies.

Nita nodded. She could do this.

First, she would set up a trap for when Adair returned.

And while she waited . . . well. She had a scalpel. She had a body. And she had all the time in the world.

FORTY-EIGHT

NITA TOOK HER TIME with her dissection.

It was hard to slow herself down, to not punch a hole in the body's chest and start ripping out organs. But she didn't. She was controlled, contained.

She sliced the skin of the chest in a Y incision, and used her enhanced muscles to crack the rib cage with brute force. Greedy fingers reached in, and her eyes shone with a desperate hunger.

When Adair came in and interrupted her, Nita was nearly done.

The door opened, and Nita rose from the floor, her arms up to her elbows covered in blood from where she'd ripped the man's organs out of his chest and lined them up alongside him like she was preparing to embalm an Egyptian mummy.

Adair stopped in the doorway. His black hair was mussed, and his skin pale, stretched tight by the frown across his face, which melted into shock as he took in the room. His eyes flicked between Nita, crouched over one gory body, and Henry's body, still lying on the bed where it had fallen.

In that second of staring at each other, the tub of hot water Nita had perched on top of the cabinet beside the door slowly tipped over, tugged by a string attaching the basin to the open door.

Scalding hot water poured over Adair.

He gasped as the water hit him, and steam rose where the water made contact with his cold skin.

He began to melt.

Kelpies were designed for cold. Adair needed to regulate his body temperature—that was why the shop was so cold, why he ate ice cream, why kelpies only ever lived in northern climates. Which meant he was very susceptible to sudden climate changes.

Put a reptile in icy water, and its body would shut down. Cold-blooded, they called them.

Put Adair in hot water, and well . . . the idiom didn't come from nowhere.

The melting started with his head. His face flickered a few times before becoming completely translucent and shimmery, like he was wearing a liquid mirror. The hot water melted it off his skin, dripping down and off his face like some sort of mucus. And Nita finally saw Adair for what he really was.

A monster.

Black scales rippled across his skin, almost crocodilian. His head was a little too long, and more than half of it was filled with a giant mouth, large enough Nita could probably stick her whole head in, if not for the teeth. Razor-sharp teeth, each one as long as a finger, but half as thin. Hundreds of them, each overlapping, creating layers of jagged, vicious teeth.

His eyes covered the rest of his face, yellow and slitted, like a dragon. His nose was flat and almost invisible, and he had no ears or hair, just smooth black scales and a ridged, bumpy spine starting just between his eyes, going up over his head and down along his back.

Adair cried out as the water burned off his illusion, his still-human-looking hands coming up to cover his face and hide it from view.

Nita grabbed the desk chair and smashed it over his head while he was still stunned, and he went down across the ground.

She'd lit everything she could in the room before he arrived, lights, candles, anything that generated heat, until it felt like a sauna. Bad for the dead bodies, but worse for Adair.

She took another tub of hot water and poured it over him as he lay on the floor, and this time, he screamed, his cries of pain rising into the air and mingling with the smoke from all the candles and steam from the boiling water. He choked, as though trying to beg her to stop, but the words couldn't come out from between the cage of his jagged teeth.

His body started to melt too, his clothes first, and Nita was disconcerted to realize even those were fake, built from the same mucus-y substance that created the human illusion of the rest of him. The scalded mucus pooled on the floor around him, sloughed from his skin and leaving his body bare.

Since he was crouched on the floor, it was hard for Nita to

get a sense of the shape of his body, but he did have two arms and two legs, though there was a lot of webbing between them. His body was thick, and his arms set closer to the main part of the body than on a human. Probably an adaption for the cold.

"Stop!" he screamed as Nita hefted another bucket of boiling water.

"Stop?" Nita hissed, and poured the water on him while he screamed. "You fucking sold me out!"

Adair's voice trembled with rage, and his words were distorted by his teeth. "Oh, did trouble find you at my store? My store, where you said you definitely wouldn't bring problems? I recall you saying you just wanted to hide out—then you got on the news for murdering people. Didn't you promise me no police? And look who I got raided by."

Nita gritted her teeth. "So, this was vengeance?"

Adair coughed and tried to lift himself from the floor, but failed. "I don't do vengeance, Nita. It's stupid and pointless, and if you fuck it up, it just makes more problems."

Nita flinched, feeling the truth of that in her encounters with Fabricio.

"I'm a businessman, Nita. I do what I do to stay alive. I helped you, even when it wasn't in my best interests. You put me in danger, over and over. You were going to keep doing it, you didn't *learn*," he gasped, voice hoarse, and a sticky film covered his yellow eyes. "So I took action."

"I gave you INHUP agent names as payment." Nita's voice was tight. "This wasn't about danger, you just knew I'd run out of names."

Adair curled on the floor, chest heaving. On his neck, gills fluttered softly. Nita would love to dissect him and see how his body was adapted to breathe with both gills and through his mouth.

"Those names of corrupt INHUP members? At least half are dead, and the other half I knew." He choked softly. "I knew from the start it was unlikely you would give me anything useful."

Nita frowned. "Then why did you let me stay?"

He snorted, nostril holes flaring, spines on his neck rattling, and Nita had a sudden image of him as a dragon. A weak, small, wingless dragon. "I felt sorry for you."

Nita flinched.

"You're lying," she said, more because she wanted him to be than because she believed he was. The idea that he had helped her out of pity hurt too much. "You're just trying to manipulate me into not killing you."

"Are you going to kill me?"

Nita wrinkled her nose as his black scales began to flake and a strange green ooze coated the floor. He wriggled toward her, and Nita leapt back, pulling out Henry's gun. Adair froze, his scales shining.

They stayed that way for a moment, Nita with her gun at the ready, Adair on the floor, watching her with reptilian eyes. Nita's gaze kept being drawn to his teeth, massive and long and viciously sharp.

Downstairs, the door of the pawnshop slammed, and Nita jerked.

She waved the gun barrel at Adair. "Who's coming?"

Footsteps barreled up the stairs.

Adair sighed. "The only other person who has a key to the shop. Who I texted after I got the – presumably fake – call that the shop was flooding from a hole in the roof."

The door smashed open, and Diana stood there. Her long hair was down, and her shirt inside out. She stared at the scene in front of her, taking in Nita, the gun, and the monster on the floor.

"Adair?" she asked, hesitantly stepping toward the kelpie.

He curled away from her, trying to hide his face, like he didn't want her to see him that way. "Yes."

Her mouth set in a firm line, and she turned to Nita. "Put the gun down."

Nita's hand tightened on the handle. "He betrayed me. I nearly died."

Diana moved forward slowly and stood between them. "I said, put the gun down, Nita. If you want to kill Adair, you'll have to go through me."

Nita swallowed, chest tight. "He's a monster. Why are you protecting him?"

"Why did I protect you when he wanted to throw you out?" Diana asked. "Because it was the right thing to do." Her jaw clenched. "And you're far more of a monster than he is."

Nita raised an eyebrow and looked at Adair. "Have you seen him?"

"I judge by actions, not appearance." Her voice was cold.

Nita didn't respond.

"Here's what's going to happen," Diana said, voice steady. "You're going to lower that gun. I'm going to shove Adair under a cold shower until he's not a toothy fish anymore. He's going to thank me and not" – she glanced over her shoulder – "make any stupid jokes about murdering me in the basement lake, because I'll beat him up." She turned her gaze back to Nita. "And you're going to leave."

Nita looked at Adair. He'd sold her out, but he'd also helped her. He'd let her stay, given her information, even when there was nothing in it for him. And he was right. She'd been a pretty awful guest.

Nita lowered the gun, anger melting away as quickly as Adair's fake skin had under heat, leaving only emptiness behind.

"All right." She met Adair's slitted eyes. "We're even now. I don't want to hear of you coming after me."

Adair glared at her, eyes yellow but still recognizably his. "Believe me, Nita, I don't care a whit about you. I told you – I don't do vengeance. Ever. It makes you stupid, and it exposes you to threats you don't need."

Nita looked away. She hated it when he was right.

His voice was soft. "And most of the time, you're going after people for the wrong reason, or without knowing the whole story."

Nita put her gun away and glared. "I didn't forget what you said about Fabricio's motives, if that's what you're trying to say."

He just looked at her, completely and fully inhuman, and said, "No, that's just what you decided to hear."

Diana pursed her lips. "Enough. Go, Nita."

She turned her back on Nita and grabbed Adair's arms and hauled them over her shoulders, so that terrible toothy, throat ripping mouth was right next to her face. Diana didn't seem to notice how close her cheek was to those teeth, or perhaps she just didn't care.

She began dragging Adair with difficulty to the washroom and cold water. He stumbled, leaning heavily against her, gasping for air, until they were in the washroom. The sound of the shower running drowned out his whimpers.

Nita swallowed, unmoving as the bathroom door closed behind them. She could still hear Diana's voice, faint and soothing, through the wood.

Finally, Nita turned away sharply and left the room, closing the apartment door softly behind her.

FORTY-NINE

KOVIT HAD TEXTED HER the location of Henry's apartment, so Nita took the subway north. She washed her hands in the washroom of the pawnshop before she left and picked out an old jacket to cover the blood stains on her shirt. It looked like something Queen Victoria might have worn and she got more looks than if she actually was riding the subway covered in blood.

While she sat on the train, she flipped through the conversations in Henry's phone, looking for something specific.

There.

Fabricio.

Henry had texted him when he caught Nita, and Fabricio had responded. *She looks pretty alive. I said contact me when she's dead. Is she dead yet?*

Soon.

That was over an hour ago. There was no response. Henry had been talking to Nita and Kovit. Then he'd died.

The phone buzzed as another message from Fabricio came

in. *I found your online sale, and she looks pretty alive there too. Our deal is off if she's not dead.*

Nita tapped her finger on the side of the phone and finally responded, *She's dead now. Do you need to see the body to confirm?*

She got off the subway at Yonge and Eglinton, the same stop that she'd gotten off when she'd murdered those black market dealers. It turned out Henry was staying a ten-minute walk away from there. Nita went into a tall chrome building, taking the elevator to the third floor. She checked her phone to see if Fabricio had responded. He had.

Yes, I want to confirm she's dead. Do you have the body?

A wicked smile crossed Nita's face. Fabricio was still in the city. He hadn't fled. He should have run while he had the chance.

I do. You know where I'm staying?

Of course. I'll be there in an hour.

See you soon.

Nita clicked off the phone as the elevator dinged on her floor.

Her eyes searched the long beige hallway until they lit upon the sign: HEAVY HITTING RECORDING STUDIOS.

She walked over to the fire-engine-red door and knocked.

The door opened quickly, and she was facing Kovit.

He blinked and looked away. There were shadows in his eyes she didn't think he'd ever escape, and there was a softness to his movements. A slowness. Like a piece of well-oiled machinery slowly winding down before it stopped for good.

Nita swallowed. She didn't like that idea.

She stepped into the studio and closed the door behind her. They were in a reception room with black couches and a small black coffee table. Magazines were stacked all over the end tables, and two heavy doors led to what Nita assumed were the recording rooms.

Of course Henry would rent a music studio while he was here. Given what she knew of him, he would want a place to indulge in his sick tastes without other people interrupting. So, soundproofing.

Nita turned her mind away from that thought. "Where's Gold?"

"In music room A. She said she wanted to sleep, but I think she just wanted to be away from me for a bit."

Nita resisted the urge to flinch. There was something deeply fatalistic in the way he spoke. She'd brought Kovit back from the brink, but he still stood near the edge, and she didn't know how to lead him away from it.

"Is she okay?" Nita asked.

He held up his arm, which had a long cut on it. "I used some of my blood to numb her pain, and we picked up some slings and crutches at the drugstore."

"That's good," Nita said.

They stood there for a long moment, neither speaking. Nita desperately wanted to fill the silence, because it was strangely awkward. She didn't know where she stood anymore.

"Is Adair dead?" Kovit finally asked.

Nita slumped. "No."

He raised an eyebrow. "He got away?"

Nita couldn't meet his eyes. "I let him go."

There was a long silence before Kovit whispered softly, "I'm glad."

Her head jerked up. "Pardon?"

"I'm glad you let him go." Kovit met her eyes. "I've lost enough today."

"He betrayed us."

"Well, that's Adair." Kovit shrugged. "We knew going in that he might. I don't feel like blaming him for something we both suspected he'd do."

"So you just wanted to let him get away with it?"

"Yeah." Kovit brushed a hair from his face. "I did."

Nita was silent for a long time. Finally she asked, "Why didn't you tell me you felt that way?"

Kovit shrugged and turned his face away, his messy hair tumbling over his eyes. "I don't know. I didn't think it mattered."

"Why wouldn't it matter?"

Kovit snorted. "Nita, when you want to do something, you do it. You never listen to my cautions."

"You've never told me not to do something," she protested.

"I've been telling you since we met. I asked if you were sure about luring those black market traders to their death, about kidnapping Fabricio—"

"You asked if I was sure, you didn't tell me not to do it."

He looked away. "It's your decision."

Nita closed her eyes, replaying all the times he'd asked her to think something over twice. All the times he'd hesitated.

Nita had never really had much interaction outside her

mother. And when her mother didn't want to do something, she was extremely clear, and Nita crawled in a corner and obeyed.

Kovit wasn't her mother. They weren't playing power games with each other. They'd been trying to be partners, and Nita simply hadn't thought about what that would mean in terms of objecting to things.

She looked down. "I'm sorry. I didn't realize you were uncomfortable with so much. All this time."

He shook his head. "I should have spoken up more. I should have been more blunt. I've never had a relationship like this, and I didn't really know how to tell you to stop without making you angry. And I didn't want to lose you."

Nita's throat tightened. "I don't want to lose you either."

He hesitated, then stepped a little closer, and Nita swallowed, feeling the heat of his body next to hers. But he didn't touch her, didn't move.

He took a deep breath. "I'm sorry about the INHUP agent. I knew you didn't want me to hurt him, I know you don't like to . . . You don't like that. I was angry and hurting, and I felt like you were ignoring my warnings and just using me like Henry did, and I wanted to hurt you like you hurt me."

Nita tried to get the memory of the man's screams out of her mind. "I'm sorry too. It was my stupid plan that went wrong. You never wanted any part of it, and I didn't see that."

He nodded once, tightly, and sat down on the couch. Nita hesitated, then sat beside him. He shifted so that their legs were touching, and she didn't move away.

He let out a long breath. "Where do we go from here?"

Nita picked at the fabric of her jeggings. "I'd like you to stay with me. If you feel comfortable. I'm still in a bit of a mess with the black market hunters trying to kill me, but I've got a new plan. A better one." She swallowed. "One that doesn't involve murder or blowing up anything."

Kovit's smile was soft and disbelieving. "Somehow I doubt that."

Nita snorted. "Okay, less murder." She licked her lips. "And after this is all settled, I want to go to college. Maybe you could join me?"

He blinked, slowly. "I don't know what I'd do in a college."

Nita shrugged. "It might be fun to find out."

He considered, his eyes off in some distant place. "Maybe."

"And we could find your sister?"

"I don't know," he whispered. "I don't know if I want that yet."

"Is there anything you'd really like to do?"

He considered. "I want . . . I want to go back to Thailand one day."

"That sounds nice." She was relieved there was something he could think of. "I'd like to visit too."

He smiled slightly. "I'd like that."

Nita's heart clenched so hard it hurt, and her hands trembled where they were folded in her lap. "I think if we stay together, we should make some new rules."

He tilted his head to one side, a question.

"I have rules to not break me." Nita's voice was soft. "You have rules to not break you. But I think we need rules to keep from breaking us."

Kovit regarded her with dark eyes. "What kind of rules?"

"I talk through my plans with you, and if you veto them, we think of new ones. Bizarre as this feels to say, I think you have a better moral compass than me. Even if you ignore it a lot."

A soft smile flitted across his face. "That's not something I ever expected to hear."

Nita snorted. "It's not something I ever expected to say, either."

Kovit was quiet a moment, before he said, "I won't torture people where you can hear, unless you ask me to. And I'll try not to hurt people that would bother you. I know the INHUP agent bothered you. And the dolphin girl. So I'll try and find more natural sources of pain, and keep my . . . habits to people you can brush aside more easily."

Nita swallowed, throat choking up. "I'd appreciate that. It would mean a lot to me."

Kovit nodded, then looked to the floor. Nita looked down at her own folded hands, not sure what she was supposed to do now. The silence stretched, not in a broken way, but in a way like they were both waiting for the other to do something.

Nita raised a hand and leaned toward him, heart pounding, but there was a sudden click and a rattle at the door.

Nita shot to her feet, and raised her gun. Kovit flicked his switchblade out, body already sliding away from hers and into the ready position. The door swung open.

Fabricio walked in.

FIFTY

FABRICIO STOPPED in the doorway and looked between Nita and Kovit. His blue eyes were huge, and the blood drained from his face, making it look gray, almost like Mirella's skin.

He spun around and ran.

Nita raised her gun, but with the hall door open, the room wasn't soundproof and she might get them in trouble. She lowered it and darted after him.

Her feet slid on the polished floor as she barreled down the hallway after Fabricio, who was stalled at the elevator, desperately pushing the button.

Swearing, he tore himself away from the elevator banks, eyes skimming the hallway, probably for stairwells.

Nita slammed into him, and both of them went tumbling to the ground. She smacked her elbow on the floor, pain shooting up her arm and spiraling through her bones.

Fabricio opened his mouth to scream, and Nita clapped her hand over it. He bit her.

Snarling, Nita grabbed him by his hair and smashed his head into the ground.

Fabricio gasped, his nose broken at an odd angle, blood dripping down his face.

Kovit was there a moment later, body shivering with their pain. He helped Nita haul Fabricio to his feet and drag him back into their soundproofed recording studio.

Fabricio tried to scream as they dragged him, and Kovit jabbed his throat with two fingers, sending Fabricio into a gasping, coughing fit. He only regained his voice when they had already dragged him into the second recording studio and started duct-taping him to a chair. Finally, he began to scream.

"This place is soundproofed, you know," Nita told him.

"Let him scream." Kovit ripped off another piece of duct tape. "I like screams. They usually mean something fun will happen soon."

Nita paused and stared at Kovit, wondering if he'd actually been trained like Pavlov's dogs to love the sound of screams or if he was just saying that to terrify Fabricio. There was no way to tell from the creepy smile that crossed his face or the hungry look in his eyes.

Fabricio swallowed and stared at them both, the blood running down his face from his nose. "Please, Nita."

"Don't you dare 'please, Nita,' me. You hired Henry to kill me."

"You poisoned me! And kidnapped me!"

Nita's eyes were cold. "I'm not listening to your excuses again, Fabricio." Nita waved her hand at Kovit. "You've met my friend here, the zannie I met in the market. I'm going to ask you some questions. If you don't answer, Kovit will make you answer."

Fabricio's eyes turned to Kovit, dread lurking in their depths. "You're going to do that anyway, aren't you?"

"No. If you answer all my questions, Kovit won't hurt you."

Fabricio looked at her, his eyes flat and dead. "I don't believe you."

"Well, you can answer my questions and take a chance on whether you'll get hurt after." Nita shrugged. "Or you can just get hurt."

Fabricio's head fell, and he stared at the floor. "What do you want to know?"

Nita considered, then started with a softball. "Your father's name?"

"Alberto Tácunan."

"And he runs Tácunan Law."

"Yes."

Nita licked her lips. "Do you know the law firm well?"

"I dunno what you mean by that. Are you talking about the legal stuff? Because that's all over my head."

"No. The layout of the building."

Fabricio blinked, and a frown crossed his features. "Yes."

"Do you know how to get into the building?"

"Obviously." He blinked. "Oh, do you mean, could I get someone else in?" He considered. "Maybe?"

"And do you know where all the files are stored on the clients there?"

He nodded slowly. "It's electronic. The computers in the

offices are all on a closed network, so any terminal would do, but you'd need the right password to access certain details."

"I assume people like your father can access everything."

"Yes."

Nita's eyes narrowed. "Do you know your father's password?"

Fabricio's body slumped. "You won't believe me if I say no, will you?"

"Probably not."

"Look, you can't break in there."

Nita crossed her arms. "Why not?"

"It's . . ." Fabricio struggled for a moment. "It's just a bad idea. You'll die."

"That's my business."

"The building is a labyrinth. You'd need me to guide you and key in all the security codes."

"Then I suppose you'd have to come with us."

"Then it's my business too."

Nita leaned forward. "Fabricio. You have a choice right now. You can do what I want, and live a while longer. Or Kovit here can slowly torture and murder you. Which will you pick?"

Fabricio's body trembled, and his eyes flicked to Kovit, then quickly away. "Why do you want this information?"

"Because it's protection." Adair had given her the idea, with all his talk of using information to bribe himself off the Dangerous Unnaturals List. It made her think of how untouchable Tácunan was, how powerful he was.

Nita had been going about building her reputation all the wrong way. She wanted people to fear her, to not want to risk attacking her for fear of the consequences. But she'd tried to do it with violence—and no one on the market feared violence. They were too accustomed to it, too desensitized to it.

Violence was a tool, an important one. But it wasn't going to make her feared.

If she really wanted to keep the powerful people away from her and protect herself, she needed something far more frightening. She needed their secrets.

She needed the information contained in Tácunan Law.

Fabricio was staring at the floor, his blood dripping silently onto the beige carpet from his chin. He finally whispered, "Okay. I'll help you."

"You mean you'll play along until you have a chance to escape, and then you'll run for the hills." Nita pulled out her phone. "Don't worry—I prepared for that."

All her time in Toronto, Nita hadn't been thinking enough moves ahead. Nita didn't play chess, but she imagined it was like a chess game—she couldn't act based on the immediate result. She needed to think of how her opponent would respond, and how she'd respond to that and so on, imagining as far as possible into the game. She needed to be thinking dozens of moves ahead, to try and predict what ripples each of her actions would cause other people to do.

She could never imagine all the ripples, because she didn't know all her enemies. The whole market was after her, nebulous and unknown, and she wasn't sure what any group was doing at any given time. But she could guess, and she could plan based on the people she knew were after her.

She was going to start with Fabricio.

"You see," Nita continued, "I've been taking screenshots and compiling information against you." Nita showed him the folder on her phone, pictures of his conversations with Henry, his demands to kill Nita. "I've been recording this conversation too. I'll blur my own voice, but you've confessed to plenty. If you try and run off, I'll just release all that info."

"You leak me to INHUP, I leak you." His voice was cold.

"Oh, I never said I'd leak it to INHUP." She smiled. "I'll leak it to the black market. I'm sure a lot of people will be interested in you. And your knowledge." She winked. "I can't be the only one thinking how easy it would be to rob Tácunan Law using you."

He paled. "You wouldn't."

"Why not?"

"Because . . . Because that was what happened to you! Would you really do that to another person?"

"To you?" Nita leaned forward, her voice lowering into a hiss. "Fabricio, there is no torment in the world I wouldn't inflict on you."

He stared at her, eyes wide and frightened, breathing short and sharp.

"So, you'll help me break into your father's offices and steal the information. Won't you?"

He nodded, eyes never leaving her. "Yes."

Nita clapped her hands together. "Excellent."

Fabricio swallowed. "Will you let me go now?"

"Oh, no. I still have more questions."

He slumped.

Nita licked her lips. “Does your family have a vampire on the payroll?”

Fabricio considered. “Not directly, no. But there are vampire clients. I suppose it’s possible my father could ask them to do things for him.”

Nita scratched off a piece of dried blood from her chin as she thought. “Do you know what these vampires look like?”

“No. I’ve never met a vampire.”

It hadn’t been much of a hope. The more she thought about it, the more sure she was that Zebra-stripes wasn’t directly connected to Fabricio’s father. It didn’t make sense. If they were working together, why would Reyes have turned him away at the market?

No. Nita suspected that Zebra-stripes was another faction somewhere in this mess, and something that had happened around the time of Fabricio’s kidnapping—perhaps the reason for Fabricio’s kidnapping?—had led Zebra-stripes to her father.

Nita crossed her arms and asked him the last question, the one Adair had told her she should focus on. “Fabricio?”

“Yes?”

“Why didn’t you go home after I set you free?”

He froze. “Personal reasons.”

“Tell me.”

“No.” His voice was soft.

Nita raised an eyebrow. “Kovit is still here, ready and eager to torture you.”

He glared at her. “I’ll never help you get to my father’s files if you let that monster hurt me.”

Nita shrugged. "Sure you will. It's that or death. I'll ask Kovit not to do anything too permanent."

Fabricio stared at her, his blue-gray eyes wide. "You're a monster."

Nita leaned forward, so she was nose to nose with Fabricio. "I became what I had to become to get out of the market *you* sold me to."

Fabricio flinched and looked away.

"So tell me, Fabricio. What are you running from? What's so bad back home that you felt the need to sell off the person who saved you and go into hiding?"

Fabricio's eyes squeezed shut and small tears leaked out. He shook his head. "I can't tell you."

"Can't and won't are different things." Nita shook her head slowly. "And since your mouth seems to work, and your brain seems to work, I think you should be saying 'I won't tell you.'"

He bowed his head and began to cry. "I'm sorry for what I did to you. I'm sorry I couldn't find another way to get the money I needed to run away."

Nita sighed. "You didn't need the money. You were going to INHUP."

"I couldn't stay there. It wasn't safe. I knew I only had a short window before I was recognized."

"By someone in INHUP?"

He nodded tightly. "They'd sell me the way they sold you."

Nita stilled. "Pardon?"

He swallowed. "Like how they sold your location online."

Nita's mind raced. "I thought that was you."

Fabricio frowned, confused. "Why would I sell your phone

GPS and hire Henry? They'd just get in each other's way. I only hired Henry. Besides" – he shrugged – "how would I have even got access to your phone to bug it, anyway?"

He couldn't have. INHUP had sold her location online. How had Nita not seen it before? She'd been so focused on Fabricio, so laser set on him, that she'd ignored the fact that INHUP had always been the only one who could have planted the bug.

She gritted her teeth and thought of Quispe starting what Nita had assumed would be a fruitless hunt. How foolish she'd been – even Quispe had realized it had to be her own organization.

Nita had more enemies to hunt down and eliminate.

She let out a breath. Later. She'd deal with INHUP later.

"So, Fabricio." She raised an eyebrow. "If INHUP is so corrupt, why did you even go there in the first place?"

"I just needed a doctor from INHUP and a place to hide out while I had my own fake documents made." His eyes beseeched her. "I knew I couldn't use any fake documents they gave me – too easily compromised. I needed money to escape, and selling you was the only thing I could think of for fast cash." He swallowed. "I really thought your mother would kill the dealers. If it makes any difference. I never thought they'd actually succeed."

Nita's face was hard as stone. "If my mother had been there, it might've made a difference. But she wasn't."

Fabricio wept. "I'm sorry."

"Then tell me what you're running from."

He shook his head. "No."

Nita thought about Diana, and how she couldn't get her vengeance because she kept thinking about what was going on in the head of the boy who killed her family.

She thought about Adair and how he refused to get revenge because it caused more problems. About how Nita had let him go, had chosen to let him survive betraying her.

She thought about how poisoning Fabricio out of vengeance had started a chain reaction that had led to more chaos and death than she'd ever wanted.

And she thought about how she'd decided that her one rule would be not to hurt people simply for the pleasure of it.

"Kovit?"

He looked up at her over Fabricio's head, his eyes a question. "Yes?"

Nita met Fabricio's huge blue-gray eyes, the tears falling from his cheeks and redampening the drying blood on his face, coloring his tears pink.

Nita pocketed her gun and handed Kovit her scalpel.

"Make him scream," she hissed.

Then she turned and left the room.

FIFTY-ONE

NITA CLOSED THE DOOR behind her, just in time to hear the opening chords of Fabricio's screams before they cut off.

She leaned her back against the door and breathed out. She thought about what was happening on the other side of the doorway. She didn't weep. She didn't shake. She didn't feel much of anything, except a slow, steady calm. People said vengeance was something you'd regret, that it would make you feel ugly inside, that the guilt would eat you up.

But Nita had felt far worse when Kovit was torturing that INHUP man she didn't know. Now she just felt . . . victorious.

She didn't care why Fabricio had betrayed her. She didn't care about whatever sob story he came up with. He'd sold her out so he could survive, and she wasn't going to forgive and forget.

She would still use him, though.

She walked away and marveled that she was the exact opposite of Kovit in many ways. He couldn't hurt people he knew—only people he didn't. She struggled hurting strangers, but could easily consign her enemies to eternal pain.

She wondered which one of them was more fucked up.

She left Kovit and Fabricio behind and went back into the main reception room, then across to the other recording studio. She opened the door.

The room was filled with hard suitcases, and two cots had been set up, blankets mussed. Gold sprawled on one of them, staring at the ceiling. She looked up when Nita entered.

"Hey," she whispered.

"Aren't you supposed to be sleeping?" Nita asked.

Gold snorted and rolled her eyes. "Yeah. This is me sleeping."

"Different definition of it than I have."

She shrugged. "Even if I did want to sleep, it's not like I could. Kovit took my phone, and I don't know how I'm supposed to sleep without an hour of scrolling aimlessly through social media first."

Nita snort-laughed. "I guess you'll have to figure that out."

Because there was no way she was getting that phone back. Gold was too much of a wildcard. Kovit had been right to take her phone. Better to make sure she couldn't call INHUP or anyone else in the Family.

Though what they were going to do with Gold after this, Nita had no idea. And she was far too tired to think about it right now.

Nita sighed to herself and looked around at the room, full of half-open suitcases and piles of dirty laundry. "All of this is—"

"Our stuff. Mine and Daniel's." There was a slight pause as both of them remembered Nita cracking open his skull. Though Gold didn't know about the dissection that came after. "Henry had a private room he rented with a bed next door, but Daniel and I had to sleep here."

Nita frowned. "So Henry's stuff isn't here."

"No." Gold sat up with effort. "What are you looking for?"

"His laptop. I want to find out where all that blackmail against Kovit is and destroy it."

Gold frowned. "Henry has everything backed up in the cloud. You'll need to get all his stuff there too."

Nita rubbed her temples. "I suppose no one knows his password?"

"No."

"Well, it's not like he can get to it anymore." She crossed her arms. "So I suppose we can just leave it there to gather dust."

"The internet doesn't gather dust."

"You know what I mean."

Gold shrugged, then winced. She rubbed her shoulder. "You might be able to access some of it from his phone?"

Nita pulled out the phone. It had a four digit passcode lock, but it was obvious from repeated screen smudging which numbers went in. Nita tried several combinations until she found the one that unlocked the phone.

She changed the passcode to something easy for her to remember, in case she needed to open the phone again. She opened his cloud account and scrolled through the files until she found one labeled *Kovit.*

It was absolutely full of videos.

Nita shivered, too scared to click on any of them. She knew enough.

She looked up at the permissions, to see if she could delete the whole whack of them, and froze.

In the permissions was another person's name.

Nita swore. Then calmed herself. So there was someone else with the files. Okay. Fine. One person wasn't the end of the world. She could find a way to delete their files.

"Gold, who is Nathan Rand?"

"The Family lawyer." Gold frowned. "Why?"

"The files on Kovit have been shared with him."

Gold stilled. "Oh."

"What?"

She hesitated. "Check Henry's emails. You need to see if he put a failsafe in."

"A failsafe?"

"Henry is—*was*—careful. Anytime he blackmailed someone or did something, you know, that would make someone want to kill him, he'd send the files to Nathan and get him to release all the blackmail if anything went wrong."

Fuck.

Nita went to the inbox and scrolled through.

There. Yesterday. Henry emailed Nathan and told him to leak all the photos and videos of Kovit.

To INHUP.

After Kovit came back to him. *After* Kovit agreed to work for Henry in exchange for not having those files leaked.

Henry had lied.

She skimmed the message, eyes snagging on one line: *This time, we'll make sure he has nowhere else to go.*

Nita stopped reading.

Kovit's name, picture, and identity had been disclosed to INHUP. They knew he was a zannie. His face would be going up on all of the most wanted lists, news shows, everything they could think of until he was found and killed.

She checked it again, following the chain of mail. This Nathan person had emailed Henry INHUP's response.

Thank you for making us aware of one Kovit Sangwaraporn (alias; real name unknown). We're looking into the evidence you've given us. If the evidence proves that he is indeed a zannie, his name and photo will go up on the public listing of dangerous unnaturals in one week, and a global manhunt will begin.

Rest assured, INHUP will eliminate this monster.

Nita looked back toward the room where Kovit was making Fabricio scream. Her plans began to fall apart, crumbling in the absence of Kovit's presence, and through it all, the image played over and over in her head of Kovit's body, riddled with bullets, falling to the ground, lost forever. Of mobs celebrating his death, of his beautiful eyes darkening into silence.

Nita clenched her fist around the phone.

She wouldn't let that happen.

No one had survived being put on the Dangerous Unnaturals List bulletin. But no one had ever escaped from Death Market, and Nita had destroyed it. She'd blown up her enemies, murdered those who sought to kill her. She'd kidnapped INHUP agents.

Nita would do whatever it took to get Kovit off that list before it became official.

She wouldn't fail him.

ACKNOWLEDGMENTS

This book was a nightmare to write.

It was my first book under contract, my editor changed right before I started writing it, my debut was coming out, and there was a major family tragedy. To say I wasn't in a great place mentally while writing is the understatement of the year.

The first time I wrote the book, it was *alllll* wrong. The plot was wrong, the character arcs were wrong, everything was just . . . bad. And I didn't know how to fix it. So I sent the book to my amazing friends J. S. Dewes and Kim Smejkal, and they were honest with me—there were some great things in the book, but it was really, really broken.

So I took a deep breath, moped, took long dramatic walks in the brisk winter air, and I rewrote the book. New plot. New characters. The only thing I kept was half of one character arc and the first few chapters. The rest went into the trash bin folder, and I rewrote the book, basically from scratch.

So, a million thanks to J. S. Dewes and Kim Smejkal, because without them, it would have been a much harder journey.

Thanks also to my other beta readers, who provided incredibly valuable feedback on that rewrite—Aurora Nibley, Stacey Trombley, Xiran Jay, Erin Luken, Yamile Méndez, Rania, Natasha, you're all rock stars, and I'm super grateful for all your feedback.

I also need to express a million thanks to my agent, Suzie Townsend, and her assistant, Cassandra Baim. My debut year was a bumpy ride, and I'm so, so grateful to them both for helping fix problems, explain things, smooth things over, and just generally being amazing.

Thanks to my editor, Nicole Sclama, and the entire crew at HMH Teen, especially Leila for all my publicity stuff, Tara Sonin for being a bubble of wonderful energy and getting things done, Tara Shanahan, Veronica, Emma, and everyone else involved in the HMH Teen fall 2018 tour for making an author dream of mine come true. I love you all, and I'm so grateful to everyone. Also thanks to the team at Raincoast Books, especially Federica, for all my Canadian publicity. You guys are awesome.

I wanted to thank everyone who kept me sane on my rollercoaster debut year and while I wrote this book. The Electric Eighteen group, for being a font of knowledge and support. Elly Blake, Sara Holland, Rebecca Sky for your wonderful blurbs, your advice, and your kindness. Rachel Lynn Solomon and Lianne Oelke for doing events with me and making launch WAY less terrifying. All the Pacific Northwest writers who came to my book launches to support me! You're all wonderful. And all my friends and family who came to the launch, you're all the best.

I also need to thank Julia Ember and Laura Lam for the industry perspective and wisdom I so desperately needed in my debut year, and for putting up with all my anxious shit while I bumbled around Edinburgh. I also want to thank the lovely people I met in the Edinburgh writing meet ups and the operator for my tour of the Scottish Highlands for all his kelpie stories.

Thanks also to the book bloggers, bookstagrammers, librarians, bookstore employees, and other people who recommended and talked about *Not Even Bones* and *Only Ashes Remain*. All of you make this dream possible.

Finally, thanks to everyone who kept me sane in some way on this journey. In no particular order, special thanks to Julia Ember, Xiran Jay, Judy Lin, and Kim Smejkal.

Last, a million thanks as always to my family, who's so supportive. To my grandparents and aunt and uncle and cousins who flew out for my debut launch, to my parents for buying and giving away copies of my book and for always being encouraging about a very unstable career choice.

And thank you to all of you, my readers, for supporting me. I hope you enjoy this book!